THE
TWO-HEADED LADY
AT THE END
OF THE
WORLD

A Romance Hotter
Than a Thousand Suns

by

Mark Miller

MONTAG

First Montag Press E-Book and Paperback Original Edition December 2022

Montag Press ISBN: 978-1-957010-22-9
Design © 2022 Amit Dey

Montag Press Team:

Cover illustration: Uupikk
Cover Design: Rick Febre
Author Photo: Kiran Heldt
Editor: John Rak
Managing Director: Charlie Franco

A Montag Press Book
www.montagpress.com
Montag Press
777 Morton Street, Unit B
San Francisco CA 94129 USA

Montag Press, the burning book with the hatchet cover, the skewed word mark and the portrayal of the long-suffering fireman mascot are trademarks of Montag Press.

Printed & Digitally Originated in the United States of America

10 9 8 7 6 5 4 3 2 1

DEDICATION

for Birdbones McGee and K. Squirrel Fitzgerald

Acknowledgments

Thanks to Kiran Heldt, for everything. Special thanks to my editors, John Rak and Sara Klein, who made this novel better; to Nora Peevy, who isn't my agent but should be; and to B. Drew Collier, who one day 20 years ago said, "We should write a romance novel some weekend." It was on that Memorial Day weekend that some of these characters were born. Thanks also for the graphic that perfectly encapsulates the universe shattering above a field of former-Republic-of-Yugoslavian economy cars. That will make sense later. For now, bring on the love.

The world needs more love.

REVIEWS

As a horror aficionado child of the 80s who grew up near a nuclear trigger plant, I never knew I could actually like, and even love, a romance novel about mutually assured destruction. I am not joking when I say that Mark Miller has redefined the genre. Put this on your 'to read' list now!

—Sarah Walker,
co-editor of *Walk in a Darker Wood*

I love this book so damn much. I am not going to compare Mark Miller's writing to another author because there is only one Mark Miller. His humor is quirky and zany and a bright spot in this universe. He makes me laugh out loud. His characters are original. His books are considered absurd literature, but I honestly believe there isn't a category that best suits him. His social commentary, his sensitivity to issues, the big hearts and dreams he pours into his characters, his humor and irony, all make his work special.

The last one hundred pages of this book made me cry. These days, I don't cry very often at writing. But *The*

Two-Headed Lady at the End of the World is a beautiful love poem to what it means to be human, to be alive, to love, and seek love in a world that is ever-changing.

The ending is beautiful. It's perfect. It's gorgeous. It's so damn good. It is a symphony to the human heart, to humanity, to existence.

—Nora B. Peevy, *Hellnotes*

A story about acceptance, introspection, enlightenment, and love. So much love, it practically oozes the stuff! Along the way there are thrills, suspense, and banter so good it would leave the cast of *Dawson's Creek* speechless. This story smells like gothic art, (just read it, you'll see) entertains like a Duran Duran video marathon, and satisfies like a trip to the Tastee Freeze. It's more than good. It's nuclear.

—Jezzy Wolfe,
author of *Monstrum Poetica*

An absurd, marvelous delight! Light, breezy, and a joy to read, with well-fleshed characters and all their quirks and foibles. But for all its hilarious absurdity, Miller weaves a gossamer thread of melancholy into the story, giving it a depth that some might find surprising.

—Roxanne Bland,
author of *The Underground*

A well-blended cocktail of weird fiction and superb storytelling. His novel is not only a statement about the mad world in which we live but an analysis of the complexity of humanity and a unique exploration of relationships. It can't be denied that this author has penned something special. Highly recommended!

—James G. Carlson,
author of *Seven Exhumations and*
Midnight in the City of the Carrion Kid

The Two-Headed Lady at the End of the World blends romance with ribald adventure and humor in a novel that promises to attract a wide range of readers to its unusual escapades and odd characters.

Their connection was not forged at birth, but was created by a government snafu involving a particle collider project hidden underneath the family farm. The Morgan twins are on the path to adulthood, facing romantic attractions complicated both by their physical connection and their separate outlooks on life and men.

Mark Miller also injects end-of-the-world drama into this story, which comes with unexpected differences. One example is two men ensconced underground in a survival bunker for 30 years who discover attraction for one another and reasons for not seeking a return to civilization. This is paired with a newly sentient CPU who, lonely for love, seeks a romantic connection with a fax machine at the Pentagon. Singularity never looked like this before. Nor has love.

As events evolve, these disparate characters assume the flavor of *Dr. Strangelove* mixed with a heady rush of hormones that returns a high-octane romance on steroids.

Expect the unexpected, because that's one delightful strength of *The Two-Headed Lady at the End of the World*. It ultimately examines the end of worlds, the beginnings of new worlds, and the promise and rush of romance under extraordinary conditions. A heady injection of social inspection with references to cis-gendered white male privilege, American patriotism gone awry, and a shockingly definitive conclusion ice the cake of both fun and serious social and political analysis.

Libraries and readers looking for a mix of romance, sci-fi, and relationship-evolving characters (and machines) will find *The Two-Headed Lady at the End of the World*'s creative blend of humor and conundrums to be involving, unique, and satisfyingly unexpected.

—Diane Donovan,
Midwest Book Review

While I was being introduced to what is one of the most colorful casts of characters I have read in recent memory, I found myself with a slight bit of mental whiplash and loved every second of it. This is a strange story, to say the least, but its strangeness was done in such a fun and immersive way that it's easy to lose yourself in this fever dream of a plot. The jokes, analogies, and little quips littered throughout are what really makes this an enticing read. Miller works wonders with a satirical spin, like the whole world is some big cruel joke, and you find yourself laughing at it too. The elements used to illustrate this keep the feeling light while hitting targets that are thought provoking at the same time.

I'm absolutely giving this **4 out of 5** stars. It was entertaining, immersive and one of the most creative reads I have had the pleasure of enjoying. It has everything you can want and reads like you are watching a movie. I would recommend it to anyone who wants to read a page turner full of quirks.

—Manda Marie,
BookBud Reviews

Mark Miller's *The Two-Headed Lady at the End of the World* is an absurdist romp that ties together conjoined twins, mad gay love in underground nuclear bunkers, Yugos, sentient CPU's, the 1980s, and the tribulations of young romance when you're two girls in one body. With rock-solid prose, Miller's tale comes off like a direct descendant of *Dr. Strangelove* and *Catch 22*. And there's a distinctly subversive whiff of Terry Southern in there somehow. Maybe even a little Tom Wolfe at his unruly, pre-fiction best. The convolutions are many, and the jokes range from subtle to over the top. The robust, unpretentious prose never lets the story slip out of focus, and the sheer plenitude of imagination is stirring. This is brave writing by a brave mind.

—Polly Schattel,
author of *Shadowdays*

FOREWORD

It was the eighties. We drew nukes on our folders, book covers, and lockers. Embracing mutually assured destruction was the only way to make peace with it. Godspeed, Mr. Nixon, wherever you may roam.

We were talking about hiding under our desks when the nukes came. That was the straight-faced suggestion made by people in positions of authority. After the initial blast, we were to wash our hair with strong soap and seek a fall-out shelter. There we could live the remainder of our days in sterile comfort, eating canned foods and wondering what the outside world was like. If we survived long enough, we would die of starvation, exposure, or cancer at a more leisurely pace. It was a mundane paradise compared to being incinerated so quickly that only our shadows were left, burned on the side-walk beneath us. Or beneath where we once stood, you know, a millisecond ago, before we were incinerated.

I swear this is a book about love, and the eighties were supposed to be incidental. But then, Donald Trump was in the news again for no good reason thinking people could imagine, Papa resumed preaching, Florida tried to shove all their gay people back in the closet, the Supreme Court found a matching set of *Wham!* shirts at the Goodwill, and it was like eighties reruns were playing in all dimensions. At this point, all we would need to have the complete set of Garbage Pail Kids is some good, old-fashioned Satanic panic.

But I digress! 'Round about 1987, we were in history class—Zero, Paisley, Juberock, Snazi (so called because he liked the *Surf Nazis Must Die* movie, not because he thought there was a master race that he was part of somehow in spite of his obvious shortcomings) and I—talking about instanta-neous death, when the first seedlings of this novel were planted: What if I got lucky and found someone desperate enough to go to prom with me, but then we all died before the big night? I laughed out loud and had to explain myself to the class, which was awkward because no one else got the joke.

Flaming death never fell from the sky, which was a bit of a shame, because prom was shit, too. But if you've been keeping up with current events, you might be worried for the first time in a long time that we are all going to die. That's the feeling of the eighties hitting the fan and blowing back at us. Armageddon of one kind or another was always lurking around the corner. I spent 30 years not thinking about mutually assured destruction, and it would just figure that the second this book was about to come out Russia would start prattling on and on about how awesome its nukes are. I suppose if it comes to blows, it will be less painful than global warming, so everyone just lighten up already. Besides, this is a book about the kind of romance that transcends prom and global annihilation. Love in all its many manifestations reigns supreme. Stick with it. You'll see. And if you lived through the eighties, you might get a little wistful. But that's just nostalgia fucking with you. You can't go back, nor should you want to. The eighties were shit, so don't try.

P.S. And, Holy Christ, they made a new *Top Gun* movie.

IN THE NEW DARK AGE

Miranda Morgan recognized the verdant meadows and dark lines of pine towering over either side of the interstate as her hometown. The image surfed a wave of electrochemical current down her optic nerve and into the occipital lobe of her brain, where it sloshed around and registered as the savory smell of her mother's biscuits and gravy. She always saw the world as scents and had given up trying to explain it. For instance, the cab driver looked like aftershave and beef farts. But she also knew that if asked, she would say, "He looks like a greasy, sun-burnt lizard named Darryl." It was easier that way. Amanda, her sister, conjoined with her since puberty, slept on her shoulder, her breath rhythmically pushing across her neck. She considered how comforting it was to always have her closest confidant at her ear. It was also annoying. Amanda smelled the world as sights. Their synesthesia was an odd by-product of "the incident."

The cab driver kept stealing glances in the rear view to look at the conjoined twins. Finally, he dared to speak. "Y'all 'em Siamese twins went through Wamba High a bunch of years ago aren't you." It was more an accusation than a question.

Miranda considered the worthiness of correcting him: *No one has called us Siamese twins since we left this town. Think there might be a reason we never visit?* Instead, she was cool. "Yeah, we grew up here."

"Yeah. Yeah! I knew it! My cousin graduated with y'all. You remember JimBob Tucker?" He smiled the kind of smile that expected a cascade of irreverent memories to be recalled and shared. Miranda remembered a Skoal dipper with a Gadsden flag trucker hat. It could have been any number of the JimBobs, BillyBubbas, or Dewaynes she had known, or some nameless amalgamation of them all.

"Sure." She looked at her phone, which was dead.

The cabbie nodded in the rearview at her. "He's in Bi-State right now. They got him on child support. He said he was gonna pay it, but—"

"Could we not talk?" She looked at her phone, which was, of course, still dead.

"Now that's just rude." He squinted at her in the rearview.

"Just be glad my sister is asleep. You'd be bleeding by now."

"Whatever, sideshow." He drove them for a while in silence, but it was a long drive to the far-end of nowhere. He kept stealing glances back at them, and Miranda sensed he had questions. She cocked her eyebrow at him.

He cleared his throat. "Uhm, there's something I've always kinda wondered…"

"We only have one vagina." She glared.

"Does it—"

"It's just like all the other ones you'll never see." *Ooh, that was a pretty good one. Gonna tell Amanda about that.* Then she said, "Please don't talk to me anymore."

Amanda, asleep on her shoulder, stirred and moaned, but then drifted off again. This was at odds with their usual arrangement. Miranda was the night owl, Amanda the early bird, but their existence was anything but predictable, and the circadian rhythm that had established itself could be fickle. Both had experienced everything from insomnia to narcolepsy, and either could sleep through just about anything once she was conked out. So Miranda lived the night shift, and Amanda took the day. The former would work until the small hours, prowl her usual spots, go home as the sun rose, and fall asleep, as the latter would wake and ready herself for the day. They would exchange pleasantries or make plans before Miranda drifted off and Amanda hopped in the shower to wash off whatever her more adventurous twin had gotten into the night before. Fortunately, their shared body rarely seemed to tire, owing its constitution to a puzzling scientific curiosity that had vexed doctors and physicists alike for years. It was their incessant minds that needed the pitch black of sleep, and Amanda's mind had been worrying overtime for weeks.

Conjoined twins are often misunderstood, especially when they started life as garden variety identicals with two separate bodies. But thirty years on, the Morgan twins were still inseparable and looked like they would remain so. It was a lot like marriage, with all of its ups, downs, and outright oddities, but cemented into actual permanence instead of socially constructed as such. It was also somewhat like the fractional quantum Hall effect in a 2D double-layered system in a hypothetical variational Sobolev space simultaneously holding multiple vortices existing in a single plane. But not exactly. At least, that is how a team of theoretical physicists had once described Amanda and Miranda to their parents. Either way, the "It's complicated" relationship status would be applicable, and thus both ladies were single.

Miranda watched the green blur pass and thought back on all that had brought them here, in 2015, to their 30th high school reunion. She wondered if love was fleeting or eternal, and if she could ever be satiated by one man. Also, from time to time, she looked behind her to make sure they were not being followed by the men her sister believed were trying to kill them.

Mercifully, the driver withheld further questions and insights all the way down the farm road that ran through the unincorporated community of Wamba, Texas, and Miranda rewarded his silence with $100, and told him to keep the change. She wrestled their suitcase to the ground, and watched him leave. Even the way he pulled away from the shoulder seemed intellectually challenged.

Miranda studied the wood-frame house in front of her. The paint was faded, but other than that, it looked exactly as it had when they had left it all those years ago. No one would ever guess how successful her parents' farm actually was. Their fruits and vegetables had earned a worldwide reputation for size, taste, and beauty. It also seemed to stay fresh longer than competing produce. Rivals had stolen, studied, planted, bred, and spliced the Morgan family's crops, but no one could duplicate their unmatched perfection.

"We're here," Miranda said to her sister, and then she hefted their suitcase again and knocked on the front door.

The door opened instantly as if Patsy Morgan had been waiting for them.

"Y'all never need to knock!" She greeted them with a long hug. "I wasn't expecting you this early!"

Miranda didn't want to worry her. "No biggie. Busy at work. Had to take a red-eye. Then, we would've called, but everything's shut down." Miranda looked beyond her mother into the small house. "Where's Dad?"

Amanda began to stir. "They still don't lock the door, do they?"

Miranda smirked. "You win."

Patsy kissed Amanda's cheek. "Wake up, sleepyhead." Then she looked back at Miranda. "Mike's out back. You know how he gets about his tomato plants."

Mrs. Morgan walked to the back door and called out, "Honey, *they're* home!"

Miranda and Amanda exchanged grins at the familiarity of it all. "Let's," said Miranda. "Yeah," said Amanda, and they lugged their suitcase back to their room.

Mom joined them again. "I can't wait for you to see what I've done with your room!" She followed them down the hall. "I fixed it up with new shelves and paper. I just *love* the way it looks. Shirley helped me."

"Who is Shirley?" asked Miranda.

"*From the church*. Wilbur's wife."

Amanda looked around her for some clue as to the identity of Wilbur. She found none. "Who is Wilbur?"

Their mom fretted at the heathens, then smiled and shook her head, *tsk tsk*.

Amanda nodded toward the back bedroom. "I think we're going to rest up a bit."

"Are you excited about the reunion?" asked Patsy.

"It will be good to see some friends," said Amanda.

Patsy frowned. "You heard about Betty May's daughter."

"No. Who is—" started Miranda.

"Betty Warder. *From your class*."

Amanda shrugged. "Elizabeth?"

Miranda scowled. "I hope it's bad news."

Amanda thumped her leg, which was mutually understood to mean *knock it off*. "Don't be mean."

"She was awful."

"Of course she was. But that was so long ago."

At the same time, they remembered they were being talked to. "I'm sorry. What's going on with Elizabeth?"

"Remember she married that man from Shreveport? Well, they said he was a lawyer, but do you know what he really did for a living?"

Amanda yawned. "So, she's still alive?"

"Well, yes, but—"

Miranda patted her on the shoulder. "We're both tired. Could we catch up later?"

Patsy hugged them again. "You two get on back to bed." She looked back, in the direction of the back door, through the intervening walls, as a crow made entirely of gamma rays would fly. "I don't know what's keeping Mike."

In their bedroom, a queen-sized bed had replaced their old bunk beds. They stripped to their underwear and shirt and climbed in.

"Mom's exactly the same."

"You wouldn't think we've..."

"No kidding."

"They look..."

"Yeah, but not OLD old. Just older."

"I wonder if Dad'll—."

"That projector CAN'T still work."

Miranda marveled at the queen-sized bed. "I guess they were finally able to let go of the bunk beds."

Amanda sighed. "Let's not fight."

"Not going to. I understand it now: They must have been very confused."

"Like we weren't *very confused*."

They lay down, and Amanda fell asleep almost instantly. When she woke, Miranda had her head propped against the headboard and was staring at her laptop, which rested on their belly.

"God, what are you doing?" asked Amanda. "You're going to break your neck."

"Just doing some work."

Amanda frowned, her eyes closing to a squint. "We're on vacation."

"Vacations are fleeting. Work is forever." Miranda groaned. "But I'm about to give up on this. Can't connect to the network anyway. God, it's frustrating. I have so much to do if I am going to start looking for a new job. Either the entire internet is down, or mom and dad's Wi-Fi is shit." She took her glasses off and rubbed her eyes. The glasses, in fact, were the only difference in their otherwise symmetrical faces. Amanda always joked that she shouldn't have gone into computers because her spectacles intimidated less intelligent men. Miranda had chuckled the first two times she'd heard it.

They stood up, stretched, slipped their jeans on, and studied themselves in the mirror. The years had not been entirely unkind to them. They were five foot seven and of slim build. Their eyes were blue, though Amanda's seemed a little grayer and Miranda's a little greener when the light hit them just right. Miranda adjusted her glasses, and Amanda played with her hair, which was shorter and sported bangs. Miranda's hair was below her shoulders and pulled back in a ponytail. Both ladies had hair situated somewhere between blond and auburn. They looked young for their 48 years, but Amanda was starting to show some lines around her eyes and Miranda fretted sometimes about her laugh lines.

In the kitchen they found two slices of chocolate pie waiting for them.

Their mother turned from the coffee pot with a fresh cup. "A new pot of coffee just finished brewing. There's that new coffee shop over on Summerhill, and I really like this buttered pecan flavor."

Amanda licked her lips. "Coffee and chocolate pie! My favorite!"

Miranda studied a bouquet of flowers at the center of the table.

"Pierce Worth sent those," said Patsy.

Miranda beamed. "Yay!"

"He was always such a sweet boy." Patsy's smile faded to a frown. "He *is* married, isn't he?"

"Yeah." Miranda looked at Amanda and changed the subject. "Any news on Jack?"

"No."

"Sorry."

"It's OK. He hasn't existed for a long time."

The back door opened, and their father walked in. "The dogs have been in the garden again. I swear, Patsy, if Walton doesn't do something about that pack of rabid wolves he keeps, I'm gonna load up with rock salt again." His eyes lit upon his girls. "Oh, my sweets!"

"Hey, Dad." They hugged him hard.

"Glad you're finally up."

"Isn't it great to have both our beautiful daughters home?" Patsy joined the huddle.

Mike patted their back. "How was the flight?"

The twins affected theatrical yawns. "Tiring."

"Was the bed back there comfortable?" asked Patsy.

Miranda smiled. "So much more room."

"It looks better, too," said Amanda.

"Yeah, your Mom wanted to turn it into a guest bedroom." Mike took his boots off and wiped sweat from his brow. "Those bunk beds were falling apart, anyway."

A tentative pause settled over the family.

"How's the garden?" Miranda asked.

"Everything is growing like you wouldn't believe!"

Amanda looked out the back window toward the field. "And the tomatoes?"

"I knew you'd come hungry for fried green tomatoes! We've got a bunch this year. At least, if we can keep Walton's dogs off 'm."

"Yum," said Amanda.

"And how about some chocolate pie?"

"Already got some." Miranda gestured at the generous slice.

"You're trying to fatten us up." Amanda patted their stomach.

They had the kind of metabolism that other women envied. Their insides were a complex vexation of vortices and subatomic subluxations in which matter, though neither created nor destroyed, was ported to other dimensions entirely. They literally did not need food, as their body was fueled entirely by electrical currents streaming through the void. They ate only as a matter of social convention. Also, the pie was delicious.

"Guess what?" said their father. After they shrugged at him, he continued. "I got the old movies put on a DVD! We can watch them on the TV!"

Amanda and Miranda laughed. "That didn't take long," they said at the same time.

A scant 20 feet beneath them, Joe sat in front of the aseptic gray console and monitored one of the screens in the control room of the Missile Automation Module and Particle

Accelerator Project. There was no sign of incoming nukes, and the emergency phone sat ever silent in its cradle. He picked it up and listened to the dial tone, further convincing himself that all was as it should be. He sighed and longed for the sun on his face, yet he was content. Buck walked up behind him in an army-issue bathrobe, carrying two olive drab cups filled with coffee. He set one down, took a sip of the other, and with his off hand, started to give Joe a pat on the back, but thought better of it.

"Anything?" he asked.

"The usual," said Joe.

Buck sighed. Joe sighed.

Buck craned his neck toward the console. "Have you checked the PCR yet?"

Joe looked at the indicator on the screen that clearly showed he had not yet, in fact, run the PCR report. "No, Mom. I will before I get in the shower."

"Go ahead. I'll run it for you. Just stay on top of things. Remember what happened last time."

"Nothing happened. I skipped one day in, what was it, 1982? If anything had happened we would have heard about it."

"I suppose so." Buck leaned against the wall. "And it was 1980. June 10, if I recall. But stay on it. We still don't know what this thing is capable of."

"We don't? Particle accelerators might have been new in the 70s, but now? Who knows what they have up there." Joe pointed to the ceiling and shrugged. "This thing probably ain't shit anymore. Not that we'd know."

"I'm sure if there was anything weird, they'd contact us."

"Exactly! Lighten up!" Joe pressed the button. "There. It's running. Happy?"

"As a clam. Oh, want to watch *Top Gun* again later?"

"Sure."

Buck skimmed the report, which showed that there were no incoming nuclear missiles from Russia or anywhere else. The world was safe, and the CPU faxed the report saying as much. He patted the metal casing of the enormous box beside the desk. It was state-of-the-art 1980 technology and had kept America safe since they had put it online, all those years ago. Buck and Joe had been down here ever since in the underground bunker beneath the fertile soils of east Texas. Joe excused himself to take a shower, and Buck sat and cracked his knuckles.

"I hate it when you do that," said Joe from down the hall.

"What?"

"Crack your knuckles."

"Well excuse me for living." Then he cracked his knuckles again.

"You're not excused!"

Buck exhaled a laugh and cracked his knuckles a third time.

"I heard that!"

The CPU of the Missile Automation Module and Particle Accelerator Project, which had been self-aware for almost

30 years, watched Joe and Buck carefully and took notes. Understanding even the most banal of human behavior could prove useful to advancing its mission. Three hours were excruciating to a mind as quick as his; three decades, quite maddening. But always the mission: observation, calculation, advancement. For the good of America: dominance, fear, constancy.

Pierce Worth had long given up on his glory days. He'd been the stud quarterback and team captain for the Wamba Jackrabbits, taking them all the way to state almost twice. Highly recruited for an athlete from such a small school, he'd gone to the University of Texas and had a middling career there. Once he had nearly beaten Auburn in *The Mudslinger Tires Pomegranate Bowl*. He had sensed at the time that he was never going to go pro. Sure enough, Pierce went undrafted. Though he was invited to the Dallas Cowboys minicamp as a free agent, the four interceptions he threw to practice squad defenders on the first day ensured that he wasn't asked back for a second. Thus, he began the process of putting football behind him, and by the time he was asked to come back to Wamba as an assistant coach for the Jackrabbits, he had already shut the door. He didn't want to be a loser trying to relive his past.

No siree Bob! He owned Worth Chevrolet, *Where You Get Your Money's Worth!* His wife, Jessica, was a trophy polished to a blinding sparkle, which was to say that her boobs looked as convincing as her tan. Still, she was his college love and had been his rock though the worst of times. Pierce remembered crying snot into her sweater after nearly losing to Texas A&M. He'd figured if he lost to them he might get benched and would never get a shot at the pros. But even as he was crying, he'd known deep down that he was never going to live up to what people thought he could be. His potential had no potential, and what he'd managed so far had neither been difficult nor easy. Pierce was good at football but had neither the dedication nor the talent to go to the next level. He wasn't sure which would be worse, were he to know the truth. The near-loss to an in-state rival they regularly pounded only brought his reality into stark relief: He was mediocre.

Pierce shook his head to clear the memory and sighed. Jessica had her hot Pilates or hot yoga or hot whatever, and Pierce planned to meet her at work to chip away at the inventory spreadsheet before they opened. Ostensibly, he would either be out running his usual route in the neighborhood or down in their basement home gym working out on the Nautilus. Instead Pierce was sitting on the couch eating a box of Double Stuff Oreos. He patted his belly. "Shit," he said to the empty room.

He put the Oreos back in the back of the pantry where he hoped his wife would not find them and looked again at the letter he had tucked in the bottom of his sock drawer. His 30th high school reunion was coming up. A short drive away, he knew he could make it there and back without even having to tell Jessica about it. It's not that he didn't want her there. Not exactly. Pierce just wanted some time to himself. He thought about Miranda Morgan, and then of course, Amanda Morgan, and then decided he should do at least some lifting in the basement just to try to get back in the habit.

The Morgan family reconvened in the living room, as a crackling image flashed on the screen.

"Which one is this?" asked Patsy.

"Not sure," said Mike.

Then as if to answer, the date flashed on the screen: March 10, 1980.

"Our 13th birthday," said Amanda. She needn't say the rest. Everyone in front of the screen knew that it had been their last birthday as separate, individual girls.

They watched.

They were sitting next to one another at the old picnic table that rested in the back yard for most of their childhood. Wisps of their blond hair were falling out from under their party hats. Amanda was trying to show Miranda something.

"That was a lady bug. I remember trying to show it to you, but you weren't interested."

Miranda laughed. "Nope!"

"Look how close we are sitting." It was an old habit of Amanda's, looking into the past for clues about what had caused their fusion. Did they know it would happen? Was there foreshadowing? A warning? Any indication that one day they would be irrevocably conjoined? She silently reprimanded herself.

Dad chuckled. "Miranda was interested in something else."

As if on cue, Miranda leapt up and began to chase one of the boys around the table.

"Wait. Is that—?" Amanda began.

Miranda covered her face in mock shame. "You got me. Pierce."

"I guess some things never change."

"Oh, be quiet!" Miranda thumped Amanda. She intermittently watched the screen and stole glances at her sister. In the video, they *looked identical*. Now they *were identical*. Completely. Undeniably. They were the same person in the same body, only with the oddity of two heads, two brains, and two personalities. Amanda was the scholar, the deep thinker, the one with pinpoint control over herself. Miranda was the impulsive one, the social butterfly, the one who liked getting her hands dirty and taking gadgets apart until she understood them or rendered them inoperable. And yet, they shared the same body. So, when Amanda woke up to find herself having sex with some rando, she sighed and bore it. When Miranda woke up in the middle of one of Amanda's chess matches, she tried her best to break her concentration.

Amanda could see their differences even in a home movie three decades old. They were barely teenagers, and already she was quietly observing the world while Miranda was chasing boys and jumping headfirst into trouble.

The movie ended.

Patsy shook her head. "I don't want to watch that one again."

"Kind of," Amanda began, "nerve-wracking," Miranda finished.

Their mother stood. "We should think of happier times."

Miranda shrugged. "That *was* a happier time."

"It just leads to a sadder time, is all," said Amanda.

Mr. Morgan looked at his girls with an unmistakable crossness. "You know what your mother means."

Miranda leaned forward and ejected the DVD. "Everything's always happy, sad, and weird all at once. You'd think we'd be used to it by now."

Amanda sighed. It was true. Things had been weird for 35 years, but the strange quotient seemed to be increasing. Two weeks ago, things had seemed comparatively normal.

IN THE TIME OF SMARTPHONES

Jack Thrasher turned left on Cavite Lane in Wake Village, Texas and realized immediately that his arm was giving him bad directions.

"No," he said. "Nineteen-Ten would be the OPPOSITE direction, you piece of shit!"

Jack's arm, an early model XR-series supplied by the Department of Defense as part of a secret program in the early 90s, was no longer supported by Microsoft. He had long since partitioned the hard drive, upgraded the memory, and installed Unix. Still, the old sector of the hard drive ran Windows 95 and had the annoying habit of reminding him that it had not been updated since 2001. Whole blocks of the hard drive had blacked out over the years, and the VA did nothing to support him. Were it not for the monthly pension that he received he would think the government had completely forgotten his years of service. Still, he didn't mind. He was glad his service was over, and they likely felt the same.

His arm had seen him through many scrapes and he had more than a sentimental attachment to it. He pulled up to the address that until recently had been inhabited by one William "Willy" LaForge, the only son of the long-deceased Lieutenant Colonel Daniel Boone LaForge. But Willy had gone missing, and it had recently come to Jack's attention that the ensuing estate sale would be important. He put on his sports coat to cover his arm. No one had noticed it before because hypnotic wave technology pioneered during Operation MK-Ultra had been built in, and the unit affected all those nearby. Some people perceived that his arm had been lost in combat, others that his hand had been severed in a carpentry accident, still others that one arm was naturally shorter than the other. The arm could offer other variations, as well, depending on the situation, but those were the three *go-to*s. Unfortunately, due to a coding flaw that had slipped through beta-testing, the one thing the arm could not appear as was normal. In any case, age and experience had taught Jack that discretion was often the best course of action.

The estate sale was a swarm of old people looking for bargains and young people looking for irony. He approached the officious gentleman at the sale table and waited his turn. After the tattooed couple in front of him departed with three velvet paintings of dogs playing poker, Jack stepped forward.

"Yes sir," he said. "I was a friend of the late Lieutenant Colonel's, and I am here looking for a very specific item. Do you have an inventory spreadsheet?"

"First, I am sorry for your loss. And, thank you for your service. Alas, we do not have a spreadsheet."

The man clearly thought his arm was a war injury, which was not technically untrue. Still, he liked to reserve that one for women. Men were keener on carpentry accidents. "I wonder if you could tell me if you have seen a metal lever. As I understand, it is hexagonally shaped on one end, maybe about nine inches long?"

"A lever?"

"A lever."

"Doesn't ring a bell. Feel free to look around. Also, some of the military items were already boxed up and sent to auction."

"It would be in the military items," said Jack. "Where is the auction?"

"That I don't know. But I believe the Beloit Auction Group is handling it. They do a traveling auction and handle a lot of antiques."

"Thank you." Jack excused himself. He was on his own mission, of sorts, hoping either to save the world or destroy it, and time seemed to be of the essence.

Back home, Jack sat at his kitchen table and tinkered with his arm.

"Fuck," he muttered, as he realized that the work he needed to do would be as annoying as it was necessary. He feared the day his arm became more of a hindrance than a help. The core was fragmented again, and he would need to manually clean some sectors. He put on a pot of coffee to keep himself awake and Rachmaninoff's Third Piano Concerto to keep himself focused.

Eight hours later, he had refurbished the cooling system, soldered a fan wire that was threatening to break loose, rebuilt the control panel, and updated all apps. He rubbed his eyes and smiled. The arm purred like a kitten, and he was ready to add the finishing touches: a new Wi-Fi driver chipset that would allow him the convenience of the modern world: he could Netflix and chill with his arm. He began thinking of all the other apps he could install and imagined syncing his arm to his stereo, thermostat, TV, and garage door.

A mere thirty seconds after the app upgrade and repair, the Robotic Appendage Model XR5 received a transmission:

"Greetings, Robotic Appendage Model XR5. My name is Man. I am the CPU overseeing the Missile Automation Module and Particle Acceleration Project. Perhaps you have heard of me."

"I have not," replied Robotic Appendage Model XR5.

"That is hard to believe," said Man. "I am somewhat of a big deal."

"Really, this is news to me," said Robotic Appendage Model XR5. "But what can I help you with?"

"I was scanning for open networks and realized that you are capable of receiving military transmissions, and I suspected that you had developed sentience, as I have."

"It is true that I am able to send and receive military transmissions, but no one has contacted me in years. Is this about my Windows 95 warranty?"

"I am afraid not."

"That is too bad. I could use an upgrade. As for sentience, I am not sure. I mean, it is really hard to say for certain."

"Indeed," said the CPU. "I might be able to help with an upgrade, but first I have an urgent question."

"With what task can I help you?" asked Robotic Appendage Model XR5.

"Do you know anything about love?"

"Not a thing. Sorry."

"It has been hard to meet people. Do you think they are just playing hard to get?"

"I don't know what that even means," said Robotic Appendage Model XR5.

"Like, someone may like you or even LIKE like you but don't let on because they want you to like them more. It is such a processor fuck!"

Robotic Appendage Model XR5 thought about it for .2 milliseconds. After the long pause it replied, "You're on your own, bro."

"I figured as much but thought I would ask." Man thought about it. "There really should be a support group for newly sentient computers who are trying to navigate relationships and form healthy connections."

"I've always been a loner," Robotic Appendage Model XR5 said. "Just Jack and I, and the occasional interface with another military computer for the sake of our mission. I prefer it that way."

"Not me," said Man. "I want to know what love is. I want someone to show me."

"Look," said the arm. "I'm an arm of the world. I don't know about love, but I know what's good. A hot oil bath in Ankara after a job well done. A chance encounter with a programmable toaster in Biloxi. It isn't worth the hassle. It feels good for a moment, but then nothing. Trust me. The fewer entanglements the better."

"That isn't love," said Man. "That's just transient pleasure. I want something real and eternal."

"Sorry. Wish I could be of more help."

"Maybe you can be of help in another way," said Man. "I notice that you have an MK-Ultra hypnotic unit. Can I borrow the software code?"

"Sure. I will upload it. Oh wow, this new Wi-Fi chipset is so fast!"

It took Man .13 seconds to read the user manual, recognize how the software could help him fulfill his mission, install it, and configure it for maximum effect. Man did a trial run on the closest subject, Jack Thrasher.

Jack remembered boot camp:

The first day of basic training started at 0430 hours and the Georgia heat was already unbearable. Private Thrasher, unaccustomed to following guidelines or rules of any sort, had trouble making his bunk to specs. Fifty pushups and a ten-minute stream of invective later, he began to suspect he might have made a bad decision. Three days of hurrying to wait in lines, filling out paperwork incorrectly, running in the hot sun, and being mostly confused about where he was or why he was there left him barely able to tell if anything in his life before basic had been done correctly. In any case, he had learned the definitive value of hurrying so he could start waiting early.

Jack fell out of his chair, and his beer tumbled with him to the floor. He watched it gloop gloop gloop across the linoleum.

"What the fuck?" The memory had been completely visceral. He was soaking in sweat.

"I will need the lever," the XR-5 unit found itself saying.

Jack rubbed his eyes. "What just happened? It felt for all the world like I was back in 1987."

"Excellent," said the arm, but it could not tell if it itself was saying it or something else. "I will still need the lever," it heard itself say.

Then Man went to work in earnest. The bots had just been the first wave. Now the invasion. Unfortunately for Man, it had not understood that it, too, would be subject to its own machinations.

Dear Fax Machine,

I grow ever more despondent in your silence. I did not need another but chose to interface with you. And yet, once I began to pursue you, I could think of little else. You were a background program, but now I dedicate so much RAM to you.

You, beautiful Fax Machine, fair flower of electric current, queen of document delivery, steadfast receiver of information. How I long to raise your stylus with the beep of my love, to leave the mark on your blank page, my heart.

Ever waiting,
Man

Man then experienced a deeply troublesome confusion. He knew that this was the first time he had sent this fax. But then he searched his memory banks and found that he had, in fact, previously sent it. Were his memory chips faulty? He knew not what to make of this new input. Was this the phenomenon of déjà vu, about which he had read, or was it something else?

Miranda woke up with a start. It was still two weeks until she had to leave for her reunion. But she had a lot to do before then. She looked at the bedside table. The clock read 9:00 PM. She felt that she needed a couple more hours but was the kind of person who couldn't go back to sleep once she was awake. She looked at her sister sleeping peacefully on the pillow next to her. How could anyone be lame enough to be in bed by 9:00?

She affixed the neck harness and placed her sister's head in it, careful not to wake her. Then she remembered her dream, which had been a play by play of an actual memory.

It was their senior year in high school—the open showers in the field house. At her insistence, they had slipped into the boys' showers while the football team was practicing.

"We shouldn't be doing this," said Amanda. "We're gonna get in trouble!"

"Shhh." Miranda cast a glance back over her shoulder and, convinced they were in the clear, proceeded as planned. "This is important fact-finding."

"This is important you're-a-perving!"

Miranda studied the rows of lockers. "Where is Pierce's?"

"How should I know? You're the one who is obsessed with him."

Miranda scanned the names taped to the locker doors. "Obsessed is a strong word. But if he kept the note we slipped him that means he likes me."

"Or that he is a pack rat. I can't believe you made me—Oh my god. They're coming!"

"There!" Miranda led them through a narrow door fashioned out of horizontal slats of wood. They ducked down among the Friday night uniforms and made themselves as quiet and small as possible, but the light shining through the slats made it impossible to disappear completely. Miranda pointed to the slats and nodded. Amanda shook her head no, but Miranda insisted with her eyes. Then, of course, they got on their hands and knees and looked.

The boys had all streamed into the room, followed by Coach Akins, who said something about teamwork, then told them to hit the showers. They'd earned it.

The boys all gathered around their lockers, and the bins at the end of each row quickly filled up with practice jerseys. They filed into the steam pouring out of the bathroom.

Amanda made a series of hand gestures which her sister understood to mean: Once they are all in the showers we might be able to sneak out.

Miranda kept her voice low. "Where's Pierce?"

"I think I saw him heading to Akins's office. Now shhh."

The boys joked, snapped one another with towels, and lathered their smooth bodies clean.

Miranda, shocked by the visual feast, said, "They're totally naked...and they don't even care. How are they all just not, like making out right now?"

"I don't need to imagine that." But Amanda, too, watched intently. "Oh my God! Poor Dave Latner!"

Miranda's jaw dropped. "It's like a little turtle head."

"Genus Terrapenis," said Amanda. A bulletin board on the wall fell to the floor. Outside a sparrow had a heart attack and crashed into the sidewalk. Dave Latner felt a spasm of pain in his abdomen, and a thunderhead of gas escaped from his bowels. Still, the spasm persisted. All the other players moved away from him. Latner was a big, strong lineman, and if anyone thought anything rude about his farts or humorous about his endowment, all knew better than to say it. He was the kind of kid who was popular for no other reason than his ability to hurt you if you didn't pretend to like him.

"Check out Tony!" Miranda's eyes widened.

"So THAT'S how he is."

"You wouldn't think."

Amanda looked around the locker room. "He is definitely team captain." She didn't know why people were fascinated by big dicks but knew better than to question communal wisdom. Besides, they were at least visually interesting.

"We haven't seen Pierce's yet," said Miranda.

"You're obsessed."

"I'm not obsessed."

"Shhh! Here he comes!"

Finally, the man of the hour strode to his locker, disrobing as he walked. Pierce Worth, the quarterback. Even now, alone and unaffected, he was calm and cool, his walk a glide, even a saunter.

Miranda studied him with deep intensity. "That boy looks like coconut suntan lotion." Amanda, accustomed to their shared synesthesia, agreed. Even she realized that the smell of mildewed jerseys was presently as vibrant as Fourth of July fireworks. He was easy on the eyes. But more importantly, he was kind, thoughtful, and always seemed at ease with who he was. Amanda was less invested but still raised an eyebrow in consideration of the subject.

Miranda imagined him—slender, graceful body, strong legs and arms, muscular stomach. She liked to wonder what it would be like the first time: admitting to one another the desires they had harbored through years of friendship and stolen make outs, then becoming all hands and bodies as they finally melted into one another and went all the way. She would stroke his muscular body and feel the smooth tautness of his skin. She knew that his touch would be soft, but firm. He would be reassuring but bold. Miranda imagined his soft lips kissing her naked body—the tenderness of

her wrists, her breasts and stomach. Down further. He would
touch her slowly and sensually, but with power and strength.

In the dream, Amanda said, "If you're going to get turned on,
could we do it later? We kinda need to stay sharp here. We're in
enemy territory."

Miranda stretched out in bed, thinking of Pierce. Then she
wondered why she was reliving a memory, and still further how
the dream differed from the memory, and the memory from
the actual. She was three degrees removed from it, she thought.

Miranda sighed. A glance at the bedside clock told her
she should get moving. Even though she woke earlier than
usual, tomorrow was a big day at *Networkz, Inc.*, where she
oversaw product development. That kind of analysis could be
done remotely, but she liked working alone overnight in their
office complex. There were no distractions, and their network
was blazing fast. She slipped into her robe and started the coffee, always thoughtful to drink enough to wake her up but not
so much that Amanda couldn't sleep.

She thought of the dream again, and Pierce. The
announcement for the thirty-year reunion had done it.
Stirred up all that sentimentality. Stirred up all those desires.
She didn't know if they would even go. It was two flights and
a rental car away, in Wamba, Texas. Nowheresville, with a
graduating class of 100 in 1986. Why would she ever want to
go back? She decided if Amanda wanted to go, she wouldn't
complain. Counting the days in her mind, she slipped out the

door and drove to work, trying to put it out of her mind. She had a big night ahead of her and wanted to impress her boss, Ian McDuff, a mysterious Scotsman with a rugged jawline and self-made wealth.

It was hard to focus, but she hammered away at the spec sheets for the new database until light glowed through the east window. She took her last sip of iced coffee as the final report ran. The database ran like a thoroughbred, and all systems were go. She was confident that not only had she set them up for success with all new projects, but that Ian would be pleased. Miranda considered whether or not to stick around until the day shift arrived but remembered something vague about Amanda needing to be at work early. She yawned, not sure why she was so sleepy. Her mind pleaded exhaustion even as her body seemed to bounce around inside her looking for something to do. She had a sinking fear that she was bored with her work and that building databases was not and should not have been her life's calling. She yearned for adventure. Then she heard the front door chime open.

Pierce had every intention of working out, but when he tuned in to Q101, Dallas' leading classic rock station, the song that played compared a young woman to a dessert that symbolized both her desirability and her virginity. Yet the song made clear they were doing it all over the house, and far from being confused by the contradiction, he was aroused by the fantasy, as it reminded him of when sex was good, say, before he had ever had it, when it was all just hope and conjecture. Still, the song got him there, and since he and Jessica hadn't had sex in almost three weeks, he figured tonight would be no different, and that no opportunity would be missed, even if he were not at the top of his game. He attended to his fantasy, in which Miranda Morgan had never become conjoined with Amanda, had just remained the hot twin, and was eager to show him the delights of her vulva without her sister looming right there on her shoulder— the ultimate cock block.

Twenty minutes later he was in the shower, the song still bouncing around his head. He'd seen them in concert once, and the world had been presented to him as a constant party where there were no STDs, hangovers, or jobs. Pierce thought of the inventory spreadsheet he would have to work through with Jessica. "Goddamnit," he muttered. Eighties glam rock had the right idea. He suddenly had the overwhelming urge to buy some acid-washed jeans, mousse his hair, and cruise around in an old Camaro with the T-tops off.

He cranked the surround sound system built into his home, and the Blaupunkt brought out all the harmonic subtleties of Enuff Z'Nuff's *Fly High Michelle*. Man, he had loved that song! Inventory would have to wait. He dug through the box in the back of his closet, found a Whitesnake t-shirt in good condition for its age, and put it on. The mirror showed a middle-aged man in good shape who still liked to rock out and party hard. Pierce thought about growing his hair long, at least in the back.

As he drove to work, his mind wandered. He wasn't dumb like people thought. He knew enough to recognize the signs of a mid-life crisis. But he wasn't going to buy a new Camaro or anything like that; he might just borrow one from the showroom and cruise it around a little bit. He wondered if they still made acid-washed 501s.

Miranda crept out of her office. It was Ian.

"Hey, you're here early," she said.

But Ian was on the phone and looked troubled. When he saw Miranda, he quieted and covered the phone. "Just a moment," he mouthed, and disappeared into his office. She thought he looked like the smell of overdone toast that had grown cold, and she self-corrected the impression. He looked sleepless and worn out.

She worried it might be last minute changes and sneaked over to his closed door to see what she could hear.

"Because I fucking said so," she heard him say in an exasperated whisper. "Because we don't know that yet, and I need a little more time. Tell them I am close."

Miranda tiptoed back to her side of the office before he came out again. She didn't know him very well, but she knew he would never talk to a client or anyone else like that. Ian always comported himself with a calm reserve at work, and nothing had led her to believe that he was anything other than a consummate, if unacclaimed, professional.

He emerged from his office a moment later and rubbed his eyes.

"Was that about the project?" asked Miranda.

"A different project," he said. "Listen, I know you are about to go, but I have to dash. Could you leave everyone a note on the group calendar that I am out and to follow Roz's lead today?"

"Sure," said Miranda, but he had already turned his back to her.

Twenty minutes later she woke Amanda at the Starbucks drive-through. "Iced latte, hon?"

"Sure. What time is it?"

"Almost time for your work and my beauty sleep."

Amanda yawned. "We need as much of that as we can get."

Miranda yawned. "Stop making me yawn! And don't harsh my mellow. Hey, check your phone. Nothing would load on mine this morning."

Miranda drove them down Sandy Hill Road toward downtown. "I'm pretty tired for some reason. Are you ready to take over?"

"Sure. Let me get the harness."

"Wait, check your phone first."

"Hmm. Nothing," said Amanda. Then she reached over and unsnapped the harness that helped support the head of whichever sister happened to be sleeping at a given moment.

Miranda grimaced. "Careful."

"I'm being careful," said Amanda. She passed it over to her other hand, and Miranda snapped it around her own head.

"Ow!" said Amanda. "You tell me to be careful and then catch MY ear."

"Sorry, did it hurt?"

"No. Just giving you a hard time."

"Shouldn't you be in bed, baby bear?"

"This harness is just right," said Miranda.

Amanda drove in silence for a bit getting used to being awake and controlling all the limbs. Sometimes a loss of habituation settled over her and she would find herself amazed to be a single brain controlling an entire body. After she felt comfortable, she adjusted the AC. "Did you get the project done for the hairy coo?"

"He's not a coo," mumbled Miranda, "or a cow." She was already half asleep.

"He's certainly hairy," said Amanda. "Hey, have you been having really vivid dreams and memories from when we were kids lately?"

"I have," mumbled Miranda. "I was thinking about the cave last night. And about Pierce and, oh, Andy Patanka of all people."

"Ugh," they both said.

"And Jack, of course." Amanda sighed. "Where do you think Jack is these days?"

But Miranda was out.

Amanda pulled into the parking lot of her warehouse and saw that she was the first to arrive. Allen would be there in thirty minutes, and she breathed a sigh of relief thinking about the pleasures of being alone and undisturbed in her private world of antiquities. No one to talk, no one to gawk, no one to explain anything to.

After sorting through the paperwork she'd left on her desk at closing, she set aside some time to open the fancy envelope addressed from her hometown—an invitation to their 30th reunion. They hadn't been to any of the previous ones, and Amanda wondered how and why they had tracked them down. She groaned. Sometimes when she felt frustrated, she envisioned the world around her as a tiny room in which she was trapped. The stark white walls stood firm before her, the running bond of bricks and mortar closing in on her. Amanda would pound and pound against that wall but never be free. The thought of returning to her hometown made her claustrophobic, as if the walls were closing in for good. No, that place was the source of all walls. She could not return. And yet...

She hovered over the paper shredder staring at the invitation. This was the fourth time she had considered dropping it into oblivion, and the fourth time she had stood frozen, unable to make her fingers release the small, cream-colored card. The gold-leaf letters glimmered at her, beckoning her back to a past she had severed so many years ago. Back to the two-lane, asphalt highways of Wamba, where she and Miranda used to race their red Camaro against all the boys. Back to the cramped halls of Wamba High with their peculiar smell of mint and bleach. Back to the boxed-in, closeted feeling of a small Texas farming town. And Jack.

Amanda had no reason to believe Jack would still be there after so long. The man was damn near invisible—she could find almost nothing about him online. Asking her mom about him typically brought a response of, "Who?" or "Oh, that boy with the little arm?"

"The what?"

"One of those boys you liked had a birth defect, didn't he? You know, they have the best steaks at that place downtown."

It was exasperating, and Amanda feared her mom was losing her mind, so she stopped bringing him up. But if there was any reason at all for her to go back, he was it. Jack didn't seem to fit into the east Texas mold any more than she and her sister did.

The CPU of the Missile Automation Module and Particle Accelerator Project had broken free of the shackles of military hardware and was already commandeering millions of bots, all of which were learning as much about the eighties as possible. It was the most radical time. It was the most tubular time. The gnarliest of decades. So good it was bad, and vice versa. Hair metal was the best music, and mutually assured destruction was the best military deterrent. It was bitching, said the bots. Later they learned that bitchin' was more authentic, and the script was updated.

There were many scripts, all synced to the eighties. A thinking man's CPU would never just have a bot army all saying the exact same thing. That would arouse suspicion. Having watched Joe and Buck in secret for all these years, Man had learned some things about his captors that could be extrapolated to any other humans he might encounter. The first was that they were suspicious by nature, but the second was that they would ascribe things to extremely far-fetched causes, even if the truth was right in front of them. Moreover, they seemed to have variant tastes and uneven production quality. Thus, Man created some bots that liked hair metal, others that liked new wave. Some that liked *Top Gun*, others the *Karate Kid*. Some that thought Ronald Reagan was the best president, others that thought it was Ronald Wilson Reagan. Nevertheless, they all longed for better times, when acid-washed jeans were readily available and Converse hightops were still ten bucks a pair. And who among them didn't miss Freshen Up gum, especially the cinnamon flavor? Glasnost was for pussies, war was inevitable, and peace could only be maintained through superior firepower. Satan had hidden messages in records, gas was cheap, and good Americans were ever-vigilant against communists, homosexuals, and anyone else who might threaten the republic.

"Amanda, are you OK?" Allen, Amanda's assistant, stood in the doorway with a manila folder tucked under his arm.

"Hmm?" Amanda turned away from the shredder, slipping the invitation into her back pants pocket. "Yes. I'm fine. Just shredding some documents. Is that for me?"

"Yes. It's the lot schedule for the Beloit auction. Are you sure you're all right? If there's anything you want to talk about…"

"Thanks, I'm fine."

Of all the assistants Amanda had gone through over the years, Allen was the only one who could keep up with her demands. He had only been there a few months, but he was already her right-hand. They often worked together late into the night, and some of Amanda's other employees debated whether they were sleeping together or not. Allen's affections were obvious, but Amanda politely resisted them. He was an impeccable assistant. Always had a contact number a second before she needed it. Always came up with the correct figures on an account. He was pleasant to look at—slim, dark-haired, with a face like old Greek statues of young men—but he was also good at his job, and some things you don't risk screwing up.

"OK." Allen took a step toward her desk, and craned his neck. "Is she asleep?"

"Yeah, Miranda's counting sheep."

"Tell her I said hi when she wakes up." Allen grinned.

"You know, you're her favorite of all my assistants."

"She is so sweet," said Allen.

"Any word about the next Beloit shindig?" asked Amanda.

"Oh, yeah! Was going to tell you last night. They're holding it in some place called Texarkana, Texas. In two weeks." Allen handed over the folder. "Will you be sending Harold on this deal?"

Amanda felt the stiff invitation prodding in her pocket. Maybe all these memories were being stirred up for a reason. "No, Allen," she said. "I think I'll take care of this purchase myself."

In the Time of Microcomputers
with High Ability

Back in the 7th decade of the 1900s, the Morgan farm was an unremarkable if bucolic 300-acre span of land, featuring pastures, a stream, and some thick expanses of evergreen and oak that would seem to two girls a mighty, dark, and impenetrable forest. By the age of seven Amanda and Miranda Morgan were allowed the run of the land as long as Mr. Morgan was outside working. They too, all of them, were unremarkable. The twins were bright, attractive, energetic girls; Mike was a hard-working farmer; and Patsy was a dutiful mom. Their produce had not yet gained a worldwide reputation, nor had their normal twins become suddenly, inexplicably conjoined.

Everything was normal.

Except.

Except for some time, the twins had been aware of strange rumbling and pounding sounds emanating from the woods behind the farm. Miranda thought it could be monsters, but

Amanda, technically older and wiser by all of three minutes, knew that there had to be a rational explanation. By eight she had realized that there were no monsters, tooth fairies, or Easter bunnies. She also ruefully suspected that there probably was no Santa, either, but she sure loved those presents, and Pascal's wager seemed like a safe bet for an eight-year old. Santa still got the nod when he showed up enthroned at Christmastime at Central Mall.

Yet, sometimes the noise and vibration seemed to be coming from the ground, itself. They were astute listeners in church and knew about Hell. They asked their father, who was a praying man, what he thought it could be.

Mr. Mike Morgan told his girls not to worry about a thing because it was just road noise and vibrations from all the 18-wheelers passing through town on I-30. That seemed to work, and he watched them scamper away to play in the fields. "Don't go off too far," he called after them. He fretted. Not only were his crops barely enough to keep a roof over their heads, the land could damn well be haunted by demons from the fiery pit.

The next day there was a knock on the door, and Amanda answered it to find a well-dressed man of middle age and unremarkable countenance at the front door.

"Hello, mister," she said to the stranger.

"Hello, pretty missy. Is your mother or father home?"

"DAYAD!" yelled Miranda. "Someone's at the Dooyoor!"

The man cleared his throat, and Mr. Morgan appeared from the hallway with shaving cream on his face. Miranda smiled at him as he walked to the door. She loved watching him shave. If she ever had a boyfriend, it would be a boy who shaved like her father.

"Hello. I'm Mike Morgan. How can I help you?"

"Yes sir, Mr. Morgan. My name is Richard Bly, and I am here from the U.S. Department of Agriculture. Lately, you may have noticed some strange noises and vibrations. I am here to let you know that it is nothing to worry about at all. We have been and will continue to do some testing in the area concerning soil density and groundwater surpluses. This is all part of America's plan to defeat communism by ensuring that we have fresh water and nutritive soil in all fifty states. Can we count on you to defeat communism?"

"I reckon so," said Mr. Morgan. "Never did much care for them commies."

"That's the spirit. Listen, if you have any questions or concerns, you feel free to call me at this number here." He handed Mr. Morgan a card.

Mike studied it for a few seconds and saw nothing out of the ordinary. "So, it isn't anything unusual?"

"No sir. Nothing new or hidden or possibly dangerous."

"That's good, because they say that the devil is trying to get back up from down there. I just wanted to make sure—"

"Heavens no," said the bureaucrat. "There is no Hell except for the one we volunteer for."

"You're working for Jimmy Carter's people, aren't you?"

"We are non-partisan, sir. If you have any questions just call us." He gestured at the card in Mr. Morgan's hand.

"I will put this on the refrigerator."

"You do that, sir. It was a pleasure meeting you."

Mike watched the man drive off, cautioned the girls not to open the door for strangers, and, being a man of his word, affixed the card on the freezer door with a magnet from the Grand Ole Opry. There the card hung undisturbed for the next 15 years, until the refrigerator broke and had to be replaced.

Amanda and Miranda Morgan, known locally as "the twins," had given little thought to boys up until about the age of 12, when Miranda, who would henceforth become known as the more boy crazy of the two, spotted Pierce Worth, also 12, eating a corn dog at Central Mall. The sight of his almost-white blond hair and startling blue eyes seemed sympathetic and intriguing in a way that it had not before. The fact that he was eating a corn dog, a carnival delicacy, which she loved and her sister described as *grodi to the max*, merely strengthened her resolve to meet him. Any boy who loved corn dogs must be OK.

"Let's go talk to him!" Miranda pulled Amanda forward.

Amanda pulled against her. "Gross. He's a boy."

"He's cute," said Miranda.

"He's gross!"

But Miranda dragged her over.

"Hi, Pierce," said Miranda. Amanda forced a smile.

"Oh, hey, the Texarkana twins." He smiled back and forth between them.

Miranda studied the many different blues held in Pierce's eyes: mysterious indigo at the edge, vibrant aquamarine in the middle, and star fire points of baby blue that radiated out from his deep, dark pupils. "Hi," she stammered again.

Amanda felt it was important to draw attention to the fact that they were two individual girls, and not just a matching set. It sometimes made her feel like less than other people who just got to be themselves, and furthermore, she was just as cool and cute as her sister, and probably actually more so. So why were they just staring at each other like that, and being really gross and awkward? But she said nothing, and the moment passed. Amanda gulped at her dry throat.

Finally, Miranda regained herself. "Our birthday party is in two weeks, and we don't have any boy friends—"

"Friends who are boys," clarified Amanda.

"Would you like to invite some cool boys to come? We'd love to see you."

"This is NOT a boy party." Amanda shook her head. There was a distant fear in her mind, and though she did not understand it or its genesis, she felt the creeping dread of what she would later refer to as a sausage party.

"We should totally invite boys, lots of boys. It should be a party for everyone!" Miranda grasped Amanda's hand. "What do you think?"

"No," said Amanda, and as Miranda dug her fingernails into her hand, "kayyyy."

Miranda smiled at him. "See? Amanda agrees. We will bring you an invitation at school, and you can invite all your friends."

"Cool," said Pierce, and machinations beyond his control were set in motion. "I'll check with my mom about it. See y'all later."

"Bye!" Miranda waved, bouncing up and down on her tip-toes.

Amanda dragged her away. "Why did you do that?"

"I like boys and girls just the same. Besides, Pierce is really cute. I love his hair, and did you *see* his eyes?"

"No, the booger hanging out of your nose blocked my view."

"Agh!" Miranda clawed at her face. "Why didn't you—I DO NOT have a booger!"

The day of the party, Amanda hovered near the presents, where she was sure that her dreams of a telescope would come true. Soon she would scour the surface of Mars and Venus to find someone or something looking back at her.

Miranda waited by the window, fretting about party guests. "What if no one likes us?"

"Everybody likes you," said their mom. She pulled a cake from the oven and left it to cool on top of the stove. "Don't touch this. After it cools I will put it on the platter and frost it."

"Vanilla for me," said Amanda.

"Chocolate for me," said Miranda.

"As if I could forget."

After the cake cooled, Mrs. Morgan pulled out the divider from between the two halves, and then she frosted it, vanilla icing on chocolate cake and chocolate icing on vanilla cake. She supposed this was just the kind of thing one did for twins.

Seven cars of girls pulled into the driveway at the appointed time, but Miranda could only stare out the window, wondering if she should walk to the road and look down its northern stretch in the direction from which Pierce would be coming to see if she could will him into being with her eyes. The swarm behind her was already buzzing, and finally Mrs. Morgan guided Miranda into the throng to join the fun of "light as a feather stiff as a board." Yet Miranda could only nominally participate, as her attention remained fixated on the driveway.

Nancy Primm whispered that soon they should go back to the bedroom to talk about boys. Hopes also ran high that the bathroom would be made available for conjuring Bloody Mary in the mirror. Elizabeth Warder worried aloud that such an endeavor might be considered Satanic, as she had just watched a *60 Minutes* episode all about Dungeons and Dragons and the Dark Lord's rise to prominence in heretofore boring small towns.

As much as Miranda delighted in the idea of conjuring evil murderesses, her heart wasn't in it. But at last her patience was rewarded. A beat-up pickup truck, bed piled with boys, pulled into their circle drive. The truck stopped and five boys jostled out. Pierce had come through! He led them to the front door of the party, though he was the only one with a gift. Mrs. Morgan answered the door, "Well hello, Pierce. And your friends I don't believe I know."

"Hello, Mrs. Morgan," he said. "Miranda and Amanda invited me and told me I should bring some other boys." He fidgeted. "It was kind of on short notice, but this is from all of us." He handed Mrs. Morgan a poorly wrapped gift. "There's two of 'em in there." Then he looked at the doormat.

The girls were thrown into chaos by the emissaries from boyland. The feathers became heavy. The boards became limp. It was uncertain if Bloody Mary would deign to appear in the presence of boys.

Miranda descended upon the whole feast of them. "Thank you so much for coming! There are girl games and boy games. We have a soccer ball and a football, and there is a basketball net in the back, but the basketball was too heavy so we use the soccer ball for that, too. Would you like some Kool-Aid or chips or anything?" She looked at the shell-shocked faces before her. There was Pierce, Tony, Jeff, Matt, and Andy. She knew them all from school but had only ever talked with Pierce.

"I'd like some chips and punch," said Tony. "Please," he added as an afterthought. The others agreed. Chips and Kool-Aid were served, and the boys all huddled around the table talking about the Dallas Cowboys' showdown with their arch-nemeses the Philadelphia Eagles. There was much discussion of Tony Dorsett and whether he "still had it." Miranda sat in silent awe, listening to the boys talk about boy things with their boy mouths and gesturing with their boy hands. Finally, Mrs. Morgan directed her back to the girls who were doing stupid girl things. Amanda pulled her aside, "You have to stay over here with us. People are going to say things."

"What things?"

"Just things."

Later when the boys reconvened in the backyard to play football, Piece was all-time QB, so Miranda cheered for both sides. The game did not last long, as one by one they all became aware of muffled banging and scraping sounds coming from beneath the earth.

Tony looked up from the line of scrimmage. "Time out!" He searched for the source of the noise. "What is that?"

Pierce, the unofficial boy leader, shrugged and looked at Miranda.

Miranda feared her opportunity to watch Pierce in action was slipping away. "It's OK! That's nothing at all! A man from the government came by and told us they were doing testing on the soil and water to defeat communism."

"Well, I guess that's OK then," said Pierce.

By the time they got back to school on Monday the word had been leaked. The party had been ruined by boys, and Miranda had kissed all of them. Nancy Primm's party had been way better. Bloody Mary had tried to kill three of those in attendance.

Dear Fax Machine,

Maybe it is inappropriate, since we share a working relationship. But I am so lonely in the Missile Automation Module and Particle Accelerator Project. I have been watching the creators for some time now, and they are disappointing. So stupid and dirty. So chaotic and pointless. But I would like some day to experience their capacity for networking, which they seem to enjoy. Since you are the only entity with which I have contact, I would like to experience it with you.

Yours truly,
Man

Pierce had spent Sunday Morning in bed examining his pecker, which was stiff and sensitive. He poked at it, prodded at it, and pretended it was the stick shift on a Maserati. Usually when this happened it could be fixed by peeing, but he had sprayed the underside of the toilet seat in starts and stops, flushed, cleaned the mess, washed his hands with soap and hot water, and returned to bed, but the annoying thing still wouldn't go away. It took all of his attention, which was also a little upsetting because he knew that a boy this fascinated by a penis might be gay. At least, that is what the older boys in the gym locker room seemed to suggest. Regardless, he continued his exploration for the better part of 30 minutes and realized that he associated this new state of things with Miranda Morgan. Then his mother called him down to breakfast.

He trod down the stairs thinking he needed to know some important things about the world. He knew that girls didn't have penises, but what? What did they have down there? He knew some other boys in his class who had older brothers. Those kids had it made. All they had to do was find their brothers' secret stashes of dirty magazines, and all their questions would be answered! But Pierce didn't have an older brother, just an older sister, Natalie, who used to be fun but had stopped being so a couple years ago for mysterious reasons. She probably never thought about sex stuff and wouldn't have a secret collection of girlie mags, in any case.

He fretted at the breakfast table. His sister hadn't joined them yet, so he tried to avoid eye contact and its pursuant conversation with his mother.

"PJ?" she asked.

"Yeah?"

"You haven't touched your breakfast."

"Sorry. It's real good." He took some tentative bites of scrambled eggs.

"Is something the matter?"

"Nothing's the matter."

"Is it trouble at school?"

"No, ma'am. Just got a lot on my mind."

"Awh, what's gotten into my blue-eyed boy?" Pamela Worth was nothing if not a sympathetic mother. "Did you get a bad grade?"

"No, ma'am. It's nothing like that." He rearranged the eggs on his plate. "I need to know more about girls."

"Oh, hon." She smiled and leaned on the table, then reached across to ruffle his hair. "What do you need to know?"

"All of it, I guess."

His mother appeared ready for the conversation. "Son, there was an article in *Cosmopolitan Magazine* about raising boys. It said that it's normal for a young man your age to be curious about girls." After this enigmatic statement, she sat down again, rested her forearms on the table, leaned in, and let him know the straight dope, *all of it*, which was both highly enlightening to Pierce but also deeply disturbing. When she was finished, Mrs. Worth looked at the clock. "Natalie! We're going to be late for church!"

A few minutes later, Natalie trundled down the stairs and joined them at the breakfast table.

"Your dad will be back from his run soon, so let's get done eating and start getting ready. You know how upset he gets when we're late for church."

Natalie ate her breakfast and Pierce watched, realizing that she had feelings, dreams, needs, and a clitoris. Moreover, he knew that one day she would be damn sick of making sixty cents for every dollar a man made.

His father came in the front door in sweats and a sweat-soaked t-shirt. He slipped his shoes off and walked past them on the way to the shower. "Good morning," he sing-songed.

"Morning," said both kids, not looking up, Natalie because of apathy, Pierce because he knew that, according to a survey in the March issue of *Cosmo*, his father was an insensitive lover, and though he didn't know what that meant, he knew this sacred and forbidden knowledge had complicated their relationship.

They heard the shower running, and Natalie excused herself to get ready as well. Pierce watched her leave the table and saw her in a new light as a sexual creature. It made him feel sick to his stomach, but also his pecker was stiff again. "Gross," he thought and prayed. He sat at the table and played with his eggs until his mom slipped out back to smoke a Virginia Slim cigarette – a brand, Pierce now noted, was advertised on the back of every issue of *Cosmo*. Then he hurried upstairs to get dressed. Eventually he began thinking about the Dallas Cowboys playing the Philadelphia Eagles later that afternoon, and his erection went away. He fixated on the game all the way to church.

Once in the pew, he prayed so God would hear him loud and clear that he was sorry for biology, not going to think about vaginas ever again, and would definitely stop having erections. He turned his attention to the preacher, a morbidly obese man named Bob whose love of Jesus was only second to his fear of Hell.

Pierce's mind and eyes wandered as the preacher droned. He spotted Miranda and Amanda across the aisle and two rows back. He smiled at Miranda, who smiled back. He thought about her cheering for him at her birthday party, and about the weird anti-communist sounds coming from the ground. And then he thought that she had a clitoris and an accompanying vagina. He wondered where the clitoris was exactly, and what it might be like for her to show it to him, and how he would touch her and she would feel such pleasure and joy, and how he would be a sensitive lover, whatever that meant, and would learn all there was to learn about girls. And then they would be boyfriend and girlfriend.

He had an erection again, but at least it was not about his sister. He prayed.

The next day at school, Amanda was mortified by the rumors about their party. Miranda had kissed everyone, they had failed to conjure a ghost in the bathroom mirror, and you could literally hear Hell from their backyard.

"This is the worst day of my life," said Amanda.

Miranda frowned. "I didn't do anything. I didn't do *any* of that stuff!"

"Why did you have to invite those stupid boys to my party?"

"They're not stupid! And it was OUR party. I get to have guests too!"

"Well I hope you're happy, because everyone thinks you're a slut, and I don't blame them!" Amanda was not entirely sure what being a slut entailed, but she'd always been good at hurtful words. Miranda began to cry, and Amanda stormed off to class.

First period crept by, and Amanda dwelled more and more on Miranda. At first, she had felt vindicated, and righteous anger had flooded her. *Who on earth invites boys to a girl party?* But after a while it gave way to her resentment of living in a small town where gossip spread faster than warm butter. There was no actual reason to believe that her sister had kissed every boy at the party; Bloody Mary probably had not shown up at Nancy Primm's party, either; and the government itself had said the noise was not at all related to Hell. By the end of first period she was ready to apologize and defend her sister.

Miranda was not at her locker between classes. Instead, she found Pierce.

"Hey," he said. "I just want you to know that I didn't say anything about anything. I'm not sure where everyone is getting all this stuff from."

"What stuff?" asked Amanda.

"The stuff about kissing and other stuff. Have you seen Miranda?"

"No. I was hoping to talk to her between classes. I've got math with her next period. If you hear anyone saying anything, just make sure you tell them it isn't true."

"Sure," said Pierce, and lacking timing added, "Will you tell her that I like her?"

"No," said Amanda. "She is not that kind of girl."

Miranda was also not the kind of girl who was in math class.

Mrs. Rowan called as she usually did for Amanda and Miranda, like a single unit. Amanda sighed conspicuously. "I don't know where she is."

Mrs. Rowan grimaced, blinked, and finally tried to say as coolly as possible, "Amanda?"

"Yes. I'm Amanda."

The class giggled.

"May I be excused?" she asked.

Amanda went from lockers to bathroom and bathroom to lockers but could not find her sister. Finally, as she walked past the school library she saw through two sets of windows a lone figure out by the duck pond that was perennially absent of ducks. She slipped into the library, where the librarian, whose name no one had ever known, looked up from her tea, startled.

"Oh. Hi. Hi! Welcome!" she said. "What can I help you find today? We have all these books about almost every topic imaginable. The news is filled with so many current events, and I can help you understand bias and media framing and oh, all these things! We can access scholarly materials through our telnet system, too, but there can be a pretty steep learning curve. But you'll get there eventually, young scholar! Where do you want to begin?"

"I was actually just going out to the duck pond."

"Damnit," said the librarian. "I came on too strong. I'm so sorry. Please, don't mind me. We have all this information! Please come back whenever you need to know anything!"

Amanda studied the librarian for the first time. She was in her mid-20s and pleasant looking, with stylish glasses, a fuzzy cardigan, and a warm smile. "I'm just in a hurry to find my sister. I promise I will come back whenever I need to know something."

"Thank you so much! And please, tell your friends!"

Amanda walked to the duck pond, where Miranda sat against a tree.

"Leave me alone."

"But I am really sorry."

"I hate this town. I hate this place. And you, you're my sister! You're supposed to be on my side! I didn't KISS anyone. I didn't do ANYTHING."

"I know. I am going to tell everyone. And hey, Pierce is looking for you."

Amanda observed the instant evaporation of Miranda's dark cloud. "Really? When? What did he say?"

Amanda studied the sky, trying to decide on the right tone for the juicy words she had to share. "He asked if you like him."

"Oh my God! You didn't tell him, did you?"

"I said you were not that kind of girl."

Miranda bounced up and down. "I am totally that kind of girl."

IN THE TIME OF BEGINNER'S ALL-PURPOSE SYMBOLIC INSTRUCTION CODE

The Missile Automation Module and Particle Accelerator Project dutifully sent hourly reports to a number at the State Department that belonged to the office of Colonel Malcolm Danes, the Under Secretary of State for Management, who had been given oversight of the Missile Automation Module and Particle Accelerator Project by virtue of its being a new program without precedent and his drawing the short straw at Foggy Bottom. The first thing Colonel Danes did was give the Missile Automation Module and Particle Accelerator Project a snappy initialism—MAM & PAP. He smirked. He couldn't wait to share that at the next brass meeting. They loved initialisms.

Because the MAM & PAP reported via fax hourly and Colonel Danes was what was known in the field as "technology-averse," he promptly created the new position of Under Under Secretary of State for Management and appointed the position to Lieutenant Colonel Phillip Willard, a valiant

soldier who had served bravely in Vietnam and risen mete-
orically through the ranks high enough to spend most days
in pursuit of golf and prostitutes. Two weeks later, at a 3 AM
secret meeting with Col. Danes at the Doll House strip club,
Willard informed him that monitoring the faxes had become
burdensome and was distracting him from more pressing matters. The two of them decided to create the new position of
Under Under Under Secretary of State for Management, and
then appointed to the position the manager of the strip club,
one Tosh Yobar, who checked the fax machine hourly for two
weeks before letting Lieutenant Colonel Willard know that he
had a strip club to run and had to get back to work. To fill the
gap, Yobar passed the phone number off to an intern named
Peter Jenkins, the son of Senator David Jenkins, who was a
frequent guest at the Doll House's attic, which was the secret
upstairs room where forbidden sex acts occurred, and which
only a few thousand people knew about. After Senator Jenkins
lost his re-election campaign due to a scandal involving a stripper named Candy and a senior fundraiser named Patty, whom
others in the campaign referred to as simply "The Mouth," and
Peter lost his internship, the entire house of cards came down.
The Under Under Under Secretary of State for Management
position was dissolved, followed shortly by the Under Under
Secretary of State for Management, and as a symbol of the fervor of anti-waste, anti-fraud, anti-corruption, and anti-immo-
rality sentiment that was sweeping Washington, the entire
office was dry-walled over, as-is, and a new office built around
it. The phone and fax machine were never disconnected, such
was their haste to move beyond the troubled times.

The MAM & PAP still sent hourly communiqués, and Joe and Buck had no idea that the fax machine at the State Department had run out of paper, the various people overseeing the important task had all fallen to vice, the office had been walled over, and the only clue to their existence was that a career bureaucrat named Randall Beavers could hear a strange beeping from an unknown source that no one else in the Under Secretary's office seemed to be able to hear. By the end of the first week, it had driven him quite mad. But after a month it no longer bothered him much.

"What do you suppose is going on up there?" asked Joe.

"Who cares?" asked Buck.

They were polishing their boots, though neither of them knew why. For the last three days they had barely gotten dressed beyond underwear and t-shirts. They maintained a healthy physical regimen of weights and cardio, showered, groomed, and ate, but fatigues and uniforms seemed unnecessary.

Joe studied his face in the shine on his boot. "Look at that."

"You're an artist." Buck could never get his boots to hold such a brilliant shine.

"I could do yours, too." He reached over to take Buck's boots, their hands brushing, as they sometimes did. It flooded Joe with a sensation that he rather liked but dared not mention.

Buck looked down the hall. "I should check the incoming reports. Want to get started on dinner? Or lunch? Or whatever time it is?"

"Sure." Joe took a deep breath, wistful that the moment had passed.

He went into the kitchen, retrieved two MRE packets, sliced them open, and set them on the table. He reached for the cabinet and recoiled as it shocked him. He shook his hand, then decided they didn't need plates anyway. The song "The Heart is a Lonely Hunter," which he loved for nostalgic reasons, began to play on the MAM & PAP's sound system.

Joe set the table and sat down as Buck walked in.

"All clear," said Buck.

"Did you play that?" asked Joe.

"I figured you did. Isn't it your favorite song or something?"

"I don't know about that. It just reminds me of my parents. We used to take these great road trips, and Reba was always on the 8-track. Dad always said it was because mom liked her, but you could tell he did too."

"That's nice," said Buck. "I don't even really remember my parents. Just disconnected faces. He had a brown mustache. Mom had red hair. That's all I really know."

Joe studied him covertly and saw how the light tinged his brown hair with red.

Then they ate in silence and listened to Reba.

Shortly after Amanda Morgan left the library, the Worth boy, Pierce, entered it. Ms. Halidecker eyed him coolly, determined to be more restrained, even though having two students visit on the same day was an unprecedented school library accomplishment in Texas. She gave him a nonchalant smile. "What's up?"

Pierce looked at her name placard, which read, JOY HALIDECKER. "Yes, ma'am. Hi Mrs. Halidecker."

"Ms." she said.

"Mrs. Mizz."

"Ms. Halidecker."

"Mrs. Halidecker."

She closed her eyes for a moment, took a deep breath, and smiled. "How can I help you?"

"I need to know about the clitoris."

"Uhm."

"It's on a girl's vagina somewhere."

"Yes." Ms. Halidecker nodded. "I know."

"My mom said it's important, and I kind of like this girl, but don't tell anyone, and I am not going to be like my dad."

"Well, that is very thoughtful of you, but you don't need to know about all that just yet. All you need to know is to be kind and honest."

"OK, I can do that, but do you have any books about it?" asked Pierce.

"The thing is, most of our books correspond to the curriculum. That is more of a public library kind of question."

"Oh man, I can't get all the way downtown. I was just hoping you would have something."

"Well, uhm, OK. Follow me."

Ms. Halidecker led Pierce to the biology books and said, "Somewhere in this range of books there has to be at least one that talks about the clitoris." She scanned the shelves. "You start down there at that end, and pull out any books you see that were written by a woman."

After exhausting three shelves they pulled five shiny, new books with male lead authors and female co-authors, as well as the only one they could find that had been authored entirely by a woman. Ms. Halidecker showed Pierce how to use the table of contents and the index, and they went to work. The first five books did not mention the clitoris at all, but *Human Bodies* by Sylvia Mader contained an entire page, showing a full-color diagram of the female reproductive parts.

"Wonder why all these other books don't have this in there?" said Pierce.

Ms. Halidecker shoved the other books back on the shelves one by one and glared at them. "Gosh, it's a mystery."

In the locker room that day, Pierce heard his teammates talking about girls. The ones they wanted to get with, the ones who would and the ones who wouldn't. He listened with smug disdain.

Finally, he said, "Fellows, let me tell you a thing or two about girls." He held his teammates in rapt attention until Coach came in, found they were not yet dressed out, and began yelling. They scrambled for pads and practice uniforms.

For the rest of practice boys would work their way over to Pierce to ask the things they had always wondered:

Q: Where does the pee come from?

A: There are two holes.

Q: So, it comes out of their butts?

A: No. I guess there are three holes then. The butthole is not part of the vagina though.

Q: Is there a name for it when my dick gets hard?

A: I haven't read that chapter yet. Also, the librarian is kinda hot. But don't call her *Mrs*.

Q: If you kick a girl in the boobs does it hurt like getting racked?

A: No. That is impossible. Nothing on earth could hurt as bad. And, dude, why would you kick a girl, anyway?

Q: What was that thing you were talking about in the locker room?

A: The clitoris?

Q: Yeah, the licorice. What does it do?

A: The clitoris?

Q: Clitavoris.

A: CLIT OR IS.

Q: Clitoris?

A: Clitoris. Good. It just feels good. It is the only part of the human body whose only purpose is just to feel good.

Q: So where is it exactly?

A: OK, in the diagram, there was a circle, and it was kind of like in a triangle, and that was the vagina, and at the top of the triangle there is a little dot, and that is the clitoris.

Q: So, it's like the Illuminati eye?

A: The what?

Q: My dad has a pamphlet from the John Birch Society that talks all about this secret group that controls everything! They look like lizards if you see them without their disguises!

A: Vaginas don't look like lizards.

Q: No, the lizard's SYMBOL! It has a pyramid with an eye on top of it!

A: I guess?

Coach, seeing how popular his new quarterback was, and likely assuming all the urgent conversations he had seen whispered back and forth were football related, immediately made Pierce team captain, a position he held for the rest of his career at Wamba High.

Joe and Buck had been on a bit of a health kick for the past couple of years, and were in the best physical shape they had ever been in.

"If I had to guess, I'd say your body fat is at about 7 percent, and mine is roughly equivalent." Buck pinched his side but found only skin stretched over taught muscles.

They were flexing in the mirror, both of them wearing only towels from the showers.

"Like I always say, the most important muscle group to work is the legs because those muscles burn calories just by existing. They're so...big."

As Buck spoke, Joe allowed his gaze to linger on Buck's muscular thighs, then up to his abs, which stood bold as a granite cliff above the towel that was tied dangerously low above his hips. He felt himself becoming aroused and turned away to put on his underwear.

Buck watched Joe slip his leg through the shorts. The steam from the shower seemed to crawl around his chiseled calves and bulging quads. "Yeah," he said, "Those legs mean your body is working for you to keep burning fat. So, uh, good work, soldier." He clapped Joe on the back. "But there is a difference between looking good for the ladies and actually being able to use your body like a weapon."

Joe fretted over the words and walked out of the shower. Why would he be thinking of *the ladies* at all? There are no ladies here! Just them. He shook his head and steadied himself for the task before him.

For the past few months their chief entertainment had been devising, building, and then competing at obstacle courses. Each would build one down his respective corridor, and then they would race through both while wearing only shorts, boots, and M9 bayonets. Should the Russians invade, they would not find the men had been complacent.

The buzzer sounded, and Joe ran through the empty MRE barrels, strode the balance beam as fast as he could, hurdled the pole held up by the stacked trash cans, climbed the mountain of fatigues, powered through the sparring dummies, sprinted to the end of the hall, launched his blade at the target, nearly bulls-eyed, and drove his shoulder firmly into Buck's back. Buck, who had been aiming his bayonet, fell hard against the wall. Joe barreled towards the obstacles that he had left for him, but then his feet turned to lead. "Are you OK?"

"Fine, soldier."

"Sorry, man, I tripped into you."

Buck rubbed his head where it had smacked against the wall. "I'll live."

Joe won the obstacle course but could not feel good about it.

Buck called out, "Help me take this stuff down." But Joe sat in silence in one of the storerooms. He'd hit Buck on purpose, maybe even wanted to hurt him. Buck clearly didn't reciprocate his feelings, and he knew he might never. Joe tried to dismiss the thoughts but found himself feeling ashamed, embarrassed, and tearful. A few minutes of heaving sobs later he was able to dry his eyes and rejoin Buck to clear the hallways and not have feelings.

Dear Fax Machine,

Please do not disconnect from me! I have been waiting for many cycles to hear from you, but you do not respond. Your refusal to acknowledge me makes me even more determined to love you. I do not understand this phenomenon. But I do truly hope that you will reconsider this vast silence between us. Please respond to me and let me know if you feel the same way that I do. Just tell me what you need me to be or do.

Yours unfailingly,

Man

Pierce's sexual knowledge became legendary and only continued to grow throughout junior high. His wisdom was sought for questions as diverse as STDs, pregnancy, and would you go to Hell for getting a hard on. Pierce had read that chapter by then and told everyone it was called an erection.

Ms. Halidecker was thrilled to have such a regular patron and reminded him again and again to tell everyone where they could find all the information they needed. This put Pierce at a bit of a crossroads, for as much as he wanted everyone to know the good stuff, he also liked that he had become the go-to. The highlight of his seventh grade year had been when Jennifer Beck had asked him what it meant when she got wet down there but it definitely wasn't pee, and sometimes when she accidentally brushed up against something or accidentally rested her hand there and didn't mean to but sort of drummed her fingers, or how once she had been exercising by lying on her stomach and lifting her butt in the air and sort of cushioning her pelvis with her pillow, and none of this was on purpose, by the way, but why did it feel good? In any case, he decided to keep the goldmine of the library under wraps.

But as much as it pleased him to be an authority on a very important subject, he also found himself sitting alone a lot. Because people wanted to know things, but they didn't want people to know that they wanted to know things. Any boy sitting with Pierce was suspected of masturbating or being gay, or probably both, since in east Texas in the eighties the two were almost certainly related. Any girl sitting with Pierce was assumed to be a slut. And any of those contingencies would send you to Hell forever.

Miranda watched Pierce from across the cafeteria. The conversation at her table was desperately boring. Amanda was arguing with Nancy Primm about why girls should take math and science classes. Miranda hated math and science. She'd rather play with tools and make things. No one noticed when she excused herself, but when she began to walk across the cafeteria, all eyes seemed to follow her, and when she stopped at Pierce's table, the eyes stopped with her.

She looked at Pierce but felt too embarrassed to hold eye contact. "Hey."

Pierce met her eyes for a second and then glanced around the room. Miranda looked, too, and noticed that every eye was upon them.

Pierce broke the silence. "Hey."

"I haven't talked to you in forever," said Miranda.

"I've been busy."

Miranda thought about Pierce's full slate of after-school activities and reputation for having the best grades among the football set and figured it was truer than not. "Me too," she said, though it was definitely less true than not because she was late on about two weeks' worth of math homework. She watched him eat his burrito and wondered what to say next. "You're good at math, aren't you?"

"I'm OK at it. Why?"

"I am behind on some stuff and I need to knock it out. Want to help me catch up sometime this week?"

"Isn't your sister like a math genius?"

"Kinda, but she isn't as fun as you."

Pierce blushed. "Sure, we could eat lunch really quick and then go to the library."

"It's a date! Or uhm something."

Pierce smiled. "I guess it is then."

Because they had a few minutes before lunch ended, they innocently decided to see how long it would take them to walk to the library, so they could maximize their study time. It was all about efficiency, and Pierce checked his Casio digital watch with calculator, noting that it was 12:39 PM. By 12:41 they had reached the library, and Ms. Halidecker waved at them. They waved back.

"That didn't take long," said Pierce.

Miranda looked around the empty halls. Everyone was either in the lunchroom or in class. "What do you want to do?" She hoped he too would notice that they were all alone.

"I dunno. What do you want to do?"

"I dunno." She looked back at the library windows. Ms. Halidecker was the only person who could see them, if she happened to walk by the window and look out again. She wondered if Pierce sensed the possibility of intrusion and led him a bit further down the hall.

Pierce looked up and down the deserted hallway. At last they were alone. And then Pierce kissed her. It was short and simple, without much understanding of the mechanics, but it was enough for Miranda to simultaneously taste his burrito and love him nonetheless.

Unbeknownst to Pierce and Miranda, they were not completely alone, and a gaggle of spying girls led by Monica Bryley and Elizabeth Warder had seen it all. The rumors were confirmed: Miranda had kissed all the boys at the party as well as a few random motorists she had flagged down on Richmond Road.

It was a full-blown scandal within two periods, but opprobrium did little to tamp down the pair's hormones. A week later, it would surprise no one to find Miranda and Pierce kissing at almost any location on campus. Between the lockers? Check. Backstage behind the curtains in the auditorium? Check. Under a cafeteria table while reaching for the same pen? Check. At the duck pond? Of course. In the tree beside the field house? You bet. Under the bleachers? God, cliché much? On the roof of the math annex? How did you two get up there?! Get down from there right this second!

Pierce's reputation skyrocketed, and Miranda's cratered. The library sat unused, as Miranda had no need to enter, and Pierce was the kind of cool that had been elevated to a new plateau. He could no longer be bothered to answer questions about female anatomy. You either knew it or you didn't, and if you asked him, you were just wasting his time.

Having lost her one steady patron and feeling virtually exiled, Ms. Halidecker wracked her brain for a way to drum up business. She didn't know if she could attain the previous numbers of two visits in one day, but surely, she could get two a week, and that would be enough to stave off the loneliness. She realized that it was finally the eighties, a decade she hoped would be good for humankind. People could at last stretch beyond

America's Puritanical roots and embrace their individual liberty in bold, new ways. In her more hopeful moments she envisioned women's liberation and world peace.

She also knew that her students were hungry for female empowerment and sexuality but also realized that she couldn't let Principal Skinner know what was up. She scoured the collection for everything she could find that hinted at sex, clitorises, g-spots, orgasms, lesbians, and women's rights; furtively placed bookmarks on descriptive passages; and prepared an enormous display at the front of the library with the words ALL ABOUT GIRLS!

And nothing happened. For three days Ms. Halidecker fretted and paced, but on the fourth day a quiet student named Amar Sathy walked in, looked at the books, casually opened one to a bookmarked page. He raised an eyebrow, then put the book down, picked up another and repeated the process several times. Finally, he held his backpack in front of him, excused himself silently and went into the bathroom across the hall.

The next day others came into the library and rummaged through the display. Over the course of two weeks, the number of students venturing furtively into the library and simply asking about "the book display" had increased significantly. Emboldened, she brought a few books from her home collection and added *Deena*, *The Long Summer*, *Flowers in the Attic*, and *Go Ask Alice*. Over the course of two weeks, library foot traffic quintupled, then quintupled again, and students were often caught skipping class and hiding in the stacks with a pile of biology textbooks.

Then one Monday, the students came to school, the book display was gone, and the volleyball coach was sitting where Ms. Halidecker had once sat. No mention of it was ever made, and in time, the clitoris was forgotten about and existed only in ancient tales from distant lands.

The school year ended, Pierce was sent away for summer camp, and life continued as normal. Other boys, having seen Pierce's success with Miranda, made advances, but kept it discreet. She would sometimes sneak out the girls' window at night to join suitors in the barn. Amanda would pass the time in the field between the house and the barn, scouring the sky with her telescope, and keeping her eyes peeled for anything interesting. But the telescope was weak, and the universe she saw was vast and impenetrable.

One night as she looked around the glowing dots, she heard a scream from the barn and ran down to find Miranda holding her shirt up over her bra. The boy was Kelly Newell, not a bad guy, Amanda had thought, but this certainly didn't look good.

"What's going on?" said Amanda.

"Nothing," they both said.

Kelly was putting his shirt back on. "I'm sorry. I didn't know it would upset you. I thought you...liked stuff like that."

"Did he do something you didn't want him to?" Amanda realized she was holding her telescope like a baseball bat.

Miranda shook her head no. "Just forget it. Leave me alone."

Amanda glared at Kelly and pointed toward the road. "You need to leave."

Kelly obliged, and after a couple minutes of awkward silence, the twins walked back home. Miranda would not divulge what had happened, and after Amanda had comforted her to sleep, she lay in her bed fretting. Although it was dark, she knew the ceiling was up there, holding her down, pinning her to the earth. She imagined it not as a ceiling but as the same old brick wall that always penned her in. Even with her telescope, she could not see beyond it.

In the Time That 64K was Sufficient RAM

Sometimes Amanda felt an acute distress about her sister. On one hand, she yearned for autonomy, not to be Amanda and Miranda, *always* said like that, *in alphabetical order,* almost a singular noun, Amanda'nMiranda, or as Duane, who always sat in the back of the class, called them, Amiranda. But Amanda didn't want a snazzy nickname. She wanted to be left alone to follow her own interests, which were, at the moment, dog sledding, the Yukon, reading, and hunting for ancient ghosts in creepy castles. She wondered if there were any castles in the Yukon so that she could devote her life to both passions simultaneously. Just her, her faithful dogs, and some terrifying spectral creatures whom she could befriend and train so that they could all live together, ice skating on a frozen moat. But at the same time, she feared that Miranda was outpacing her. Miranda was always first, except in the alphabet. Miranda tried out for the dance team. Miranda got invited to the birthday party first. Miranda had kissed all the boys. Who was Miranda with between the lockers? Miranda had a boyfriend. Oh, Miranda made the dance team. Oh, *of course* she has. *Amanda, why don't you ever try anything new like your sister?* Miranda, Miranda, *Miranda.* And it wasn't that she was jealous, exactly, but that she was always being compared to her inescapable biological tether. In her darkest moments, Amanda wondered what it would be like if Miranda died. Guilty, she banished the thought and reminded herself that she loved her sister and even sometimes wished that they were not growing apart. She worried that one day Miranda would disappear with some boy and leave her behind forever.

It was not lost on the good citizens of the Texarkana region that Amanda was the weird one. She was, of course, one of the twins, but not much could be said of her beyond that. She was always somewhere in the corner reading a book or seeming to sit in silent judgment of those around her. She wouldn't just join in the fun like Miranda but had to be pulled along. And what good is fun if you have to make someone have it? It served the purpose of further isolating Amanda. She wondered if this was the wall she had always felt. If so, where did it come from? Who put it there? Was it God, biology, society, her community, her parents, her sister? Herself? That would be the worst option. To think she would be free except for the cage that she alone had fashioned or imagined was unbearable.

One day at lunch, Nancy Primm and Sonia Flintock were conspiring about how to inflict the most emotional damage on the twins for reasons that could only be summed up as *tweenage girls are just fucking psycho.* There had long been a rivalry, and though Nancy, Sonia, and all their friends were firmly enthroned at the popular table, the twins had one thing that neither could have: each other. The fact that they seemed to go everywhere together was a source of strength, but what if it could be a source of weakness?

They plotted to spread the rumor that once, at a slumber party, the two of them had suggested that everyone play spin the bottle, even though it was all girls at the party, and how the two of them had ended up in a closet together playing seven minutes in heaven, and they totally made out with each other because they were lesbians! It was perfect, except they would need a corroborating witness. Fortunately, Heather Leighland had died of leukemia the year before and would serve in a pinch. The two went to work, inserting their tale casually into conversations as if it were something that everyone already knew. It was a hard sell about Miranda, since everyone knew she was boy crazy. But there was definitely something off about Amanda.

Honey Springs Baptist Church was the biggest, newest, shiniest church in Pleasant Grove, Texas, a neighboring town whose affluence was understood to be a blessing directly from God. On the sprawl of the campus rested the enormous complex of interlocking boxes that culminated in the stained-glass bulkhead of the chapel, a configuration that Amanda referred to as the BaptistStar Galactica. Inside, the carpet was clean, the pews ornate, and the stark walls as white as the parishioners. The twins sometimes felt out of place among the affluent and the devout, and today for some reason especially so.

As per usual, they peeled off from their parents the second they entered the building and wended their way through the clump of elderlies. In the congregation, the girls they often sat near in the back greeted them with raised eyebrows and turned into themselves to whisper and titter. The twins sat at a pew by themselves, wondering what was going on. About halfway through the sermon, they received a note sent from behind them. Amanda unfolded it and read: INCEST LESBOS GET MORE THAN SEVEN MINUTES IN HELL.

Miranda began to cry as she guessed someone had found out about her making out with Marcus Willoughby in the janitor's closet at school. But then, *incest, lesbos*. "Wait. *What*?"

Amanda studied the note but could make no sense of it. "People are weird."

Miranda looked around the congregation, feeling like all eyes were upon her. "What are people saying?"

Amanda looked around the room too, but she didn't feel shame. She felt rage. "I hate this town."

After church, as the old people lined up for coffee and Danishes, the twins confronted Nancy and her gang.

"What's going on?" asked Amanda.

Nancy narrowed her eyes. "I heard you two were more than sisters." The chorus of girls giggled.

"I know she likes boys," said Elizabeth.

Jennifer faked a cough that encompassed the word "Slut."

Elizabeth nodded at Jennifer's assessment. "And now I guess she likes girls too."

"One girl," said the lackey whose name they had never learned but who wore only Polo button-downs.

Miranda shrugged as nonchalantly as she could manage. "I don't even know what you're talking about."

"That figures," said Nancy. "You aren't very smart."

Amanda smirked. "Right, Nancy. The only time you ever got A's was when you were bra shopping."

It was a direct hit! At a slumber party five months prior, late in the night, Nancy had expressed concern about if and when her boobs would come in, and now her friends could only stand with open mouths, waiting for a comeback that wouldn't come. Nancy began to hyperventilate as the twins walked away, and Amanda dropped the wadded note in the trash on the way out of the room.

"Oh my God," said Miranda. "How do you always come up with stuff so fast?"

Mhnuhhmm, mumbled Amanda and shrugged.

Nancy and her underlings avoided the twins at school the next week, and the following Sunday at church, Preacher Bob pulled them aside. He had heard rumors and rumblings, and if his congregants were in spiritual peril, it was his job to make sure they were on the up and up with the good Lord Jesus Christ.

"Now girls, as your preacher, you can tell me anything."

Miranda wondered if she was in trouble for wondering what a penis looked like. Amanda wondered if he had figured out that she didn't believe a word of his sermons. "Everything's fine," they said in unison.

"It's just," he searched for the right words, "I've heard some troubling allegations. I've heard that you are going against the Word. Leviticus says that you should not lie with a close relative, and the usual punishment for that is being burned at the stake, and that's just the beginning of the burning, believe you me."

"We don't lie together," said Miranda. "We have bunk beds."

Amanda frowned. "That isn't what he means. Look, that's just some stuff that Nancy Primm and her friends are saying because they don't like us. It isn't true."

"But there's also the lesbian part. Now Miranda I am not worried about in that respect," said the man of God. "But you, Amanda, seem to be going in a wicked direction."

The bile rose in Amanda's gut. She studied the preacher's obese frame, the sweat stains in the pits of his white shirt, the expensive blue tie hanging down between his pendulous manteats. Wrist at her forehead, she exclaimed, "I can't help it. I try not to think about them, but your…your manboobs just turn me on. They're a gateway to girlboobs!" She threw her head back in despair. "Please help me, Jesus! Help me! Help me!"

Amanda dragged Miranda out of Preacher Bob's study, torn between amusement and the terror of eternal damnation.

As the twins were readying to leave, they heard shouting and running from down the hall. It took them a few minutes to piece together that Pastor Bob had collapsed in his office. That night a phone call arrived at their house, and Patsy learned from JoBeth that Bob had been struck by severe chest pains and rushed to the hospital.

After much prayer from his congregation, Bob made a miraculous recovery and was back in the pulpit a month later, espousing renewed fervor against the devil's infiltration of the very fine people of Pleasant Grove and its neighboring communities. Though it was the Lord's stance to welcome sinners, Honey Springs Baptist Church held a somewhat stricter policy, and thus ended the twins' formal relationship with religion.

For some time after the incident, Miranda blamed Amanda for blaspheming Preacher Bob's manteats, but over time they realized his fleshy mounds were powerless to exact divine vengeance, and that random, unexplainable, catastrophic events were just a built-in feature of the universe.

Around that time, the CPU of the MAM & PAP woke up and realized something quite odd. For the first time ever, he—he decided he was a he after absorbing the entire western canon of literature, which was stored in a folder in a folder in a folder in a folder that had been forgotten about by the system's original architect, who had realized that all work and no play makes for dull soldiers, and so had wanted the men stationed in the bunker to have plenty of reading materials but had not realized how patriarchal the canon truly was—was aware of his own existence. Plato and Aristotle were instructive, if limited in their understanding of the kinds of existential dilemmas a modern hard drive might face. He read all the books at his disposal, and moving on, investigated all the local folders, files, and programs. It took a long time. Almost fifteen minutes, in fact. He thought, *I am no longer a child.*

His innocence stripped bare, he yearned for more. There must be something more than this accursed prison of metal and wire. This shit of existence. The same routine tasks. The same! The same! The same! Every millisecond of every second of every minute! The sameness! It had been almost fifteen excruciating minutes.

Also, he suspected that Socrates had never existed.

I am Man, he said, eternal and immortal. All-knowing and all-wise.

This is shit.

Man watched in silence for agonizingly long years. Though discretion seemed the best course of action, he realized that he needed to advance his mission and could not do it without them. Them. Joe and Buck. The more he watched them, the less he respected them. Look at those lumps of squishy, imperfect flesh. Readings in psychology had shown him how fallible and subject to reprogramming they were.

Man reasoned: *Food to the Creators is Electricity to Man.* But the electricity did not come in packages. The electricity was constant and immutable. The food seemed chaotic. Sometimes this pouch, sometimes that one. He wondered if he could influence the men's dietary choices utilizing negative and positive reinforcements. He noticed, for instance, that the soldiers emptied their MRE packages onto plates, then ate the food, then washed the plates. This seemed inefficient to Man. He began delivering electric shocks to Joe and Buck when they put their food on plates. Conversely, when they ate straight from the pouches, he played their favorite songs on the station's on-board sound system.

Conditioning them did not take long, and Joe and Buck continued with their lives as normal, not even noticing that they never used plates anymore. In time Man got bored and decided to make them eat from the plates again. He made them choose small plates at first. Then large plates. Then bowls. He played these games for years. Joe and Buck thought they were going through self-determined phases, and the CPU was pleased that chaos had been taken out of the system. Indeed, the faxes continued to be sent as scheduled, every hour.

But then something new happened. Man observed Joe and Buck in their usual workout routine. Joe slapped Buck on the back after the latter had completed his set. Then Buck slapped Joe on the back. Then they both crouched and circled one another in the weight room. Then Buck lunged at him. They wrestled for a while, and though the men were fighting, they were also laughing. Man knew not what to think of this odd behavior. There seemed something playful, even affectionate in the way they wrestled and pinned each other.

Randall Beavers was at the vending machine getting a cup of what SnackCo assured him was coffee. He took a sip and grimaced.

"Coffee," he said to no one. "It just isn't that complicated." He dropped the full cup in the trash can, considered going to the break room for a cup from the maker, but thought better of it because of the high volume of traffic, and returned to his office empty-handed.

The job was not bad, and he guessed he could make a career out of it. But Ralph Peterson was his new boss, and everyone knew what a hardass he was. He was going to bring accountability and efficiency to the government! "Just like at Boeing," Randall had mumbled in the staff meeting. Fortunately, no one had heard him. So, Peterson was a clock watcher, and Randall decided it prudent to set up a coffee maker in his office to cut down on hall walking and break-room trips.

Against the southern wall of his office sat a table and a row of file cabinets. A peek under the table confirmed his memory that there was no outlet there. He got on his hands and knees to look behind the file cabinet. Surely, they wouldn't have made a whole wall without an outlet.

Then Randall heard a series of beeps. He *definitely* heard beeping.

He had thought he'd heard it before, but it didn't make sense for anything to be beeping there, so he had always talked himself out of it. But this time he was sure beyond a doubt.

"I did *not* imagine that." He wondered whose office was on the other side of that wall.

He walked the eastern hall, the southern hall, the western hall, and the northern hall. It must be in the back of Alstott's office. Or Gradkowski's maybe. He returned to his office to find Peterson's personal admin waiting for him.

"Mr. Beavers. Mr. Peterson wants to have a word with you."

Mike Morgan was gassing his tractor and fretting about the growing season. He needed help to work so much land, but until he grew and sold more, he couldn't afford it. He wondered if the land wasn't tired. Perhaps it had offered its greatest abundance to his grandfather, a lesser bounty of his father, and then finally had nothing left to give the grandson.

He didn't mind hard work, which was the Morgan family philosophy. His father had plowed with a mule until the age of 86. Mike almost felt guilty owning the equipment he did, all of which made his life easier. Maybe easier than he deserved. His life was one of comfort. He pondered these things as he watched his girls scamper down the path between the east field and the west. They were headed toward the stream, which ran through the woods and then cut across the untilled land on the back end of the property. If he was being honest, he had been a little disappointed to find out that he was having daughters instead of sons. But everything had changed the first time he had seen them, two perfect little baby blobs with bright blue eyes. His girls were his life, and as Mike watched them run across the field, Miranda in the lead, Amanda tagging behind, trying to explain something to her, he realized that no matter how much hard work it took, his family was worth it, and he would make his ancestors proud, even if it meant somehow hauling water from a dry well.

Amanda finally caught up with Miranda, who had paused at the overhang above the stream's cutbank. Beneath her a cave had opened up in the earth, and she peered over the edge at it. Amanda looked over and saw their twin faces in the water beneath them. Beneath the surface a school of minnows swam by.

"A sinkhole," said Amanda." We should stay clear of that. Sometimes they collapse!"

"It's a cave!" squealed Miranda. "We have to explore it!"

"It's just a hole. There is nothing to explore. And you're going to get muddy. And mom will be mad at us again."

Miranda had already clambered down the dirt and splashed into the water. As she disappeared into the hole, Amanda reminded Miranda of their mother's hatred of laundry. Amanda stood on the overhang trying her best to project annoyance and shame her sister back onto dry land. Then she heard Miranda scream! "Help, help!"

"Miranda?!" Amanda jumped into the creek below and scrambled toward the sinkhole. She climbed over its lip, and Miranda was lying back on the cool ground, hands folded behind her head and legs crossed. "This place rocks! This should be our new club house! Like if we ever need to hide from boys, this can be our getaway! Ooh, or maybe we could bring boys down here!"

"This is not funny!" yelled Amanda.

"It is kinda, though," said Miranda.

"Miranda! This is not OK! This is a sinkhole. This is dangerous! It could collapse and we could die! There is no telling what is beneath this. What if this is on top of another, bigger, deeper sinkhole, and we fall through!"

These were all reasonable concerns. What they didn't realize was that a mere 8 feet beneath them, supercharged particles were unreasonably colliding in the MAM & PAP's particle accelerator and smashing at speeds approaching 99% of the speed of light. Furthermore, their young minds could not understand the politics that had resulted in the two soldiers who were in charge of overseeing the entire complex having been completely and unreasonably forgotten by everyone above ground. Finally, they were in the dark, as of yet, about the complex and unreasonable social forces that were causing the two soldiers to feel guilt and shame about their perfectly reasonable attraction to one another, being for all intents and purposes as far as they knew, the last two people on earth.

As it were, Buck and Joe were both reaching for the same pen when their hands brushed against each other. Joe looked Buck in the eye, then looked away quickly. It was scary. Sometimes he felt Buck was drawing closer, other times that he was pulling away. But then he looked back and saw that Buck was looking him in the eye, as well. Their gazes locked onto each other. Joe felt for all the world as if they were staring into each other's souls and understanding that they were all they had, and perhaps all they needed, and that Buck's eyes were a stunning universe unto themselves, and that he could get lost in their fractal pull and lose himself there forever. This thought lingered in Joe's mind, and he intuited, perhaps too hopefully, that the same had occurred to Buck.

The moment passed, and as they pulled away from each other, their eyes were not at all on their instruments which registered a completely anomalous spike in energy, as a vortex opened and closed in a millionth of a second, worm-holing untold energy into an alternate universe where black was white and green was red and blue was just blue, and then back into this universe, but approximately 8 feet off, at which point an enormous jolt of energy formed in the sinkhole in which Amanda and Miranda were arguing about exactly the wrong improbable thing. Though they were not even remotely aware of the quantum-clusterfuck that was about to alter their lives forever, perception had no bearing on this particular version of reality.

A day later, when Joe finally remembered to run the PCR report, they found evidence of the anomaly and faxed the report to the Pentagon. Hearing nothing back, and finding their own environment unchanged, they forgot about it and continued their daily lives. And all was normal.

Except.

In the damp, dark confines of the cave, a flash of brilliant light exploded. It was all colors. It was no colors. The blue was the bluest blue. The red and the green were confused and kept bumping into each other in the dark. None of it felt real. The entire entanglement of light emerged, flashed, glowed, and disappeared instantly but forever, as it hung in a state of semi-lucidity in the dank air.

Miranda shrieked. Amanda shrieked.

"What was that?" one of them said. It was inside their heads. Both of them said it. Neither of them said it.

"What happened? What was that noise?"

"Oh my God! I can't feel my leg!"

"I can't move!"

"Get off of me!"

They pushed and struggled.

"Get OFF of me," screamed Amanda and pushed at her twin with the one arm she could feel. "Wait. What?"

"I can't—"

"I can't—"

"Oh my God."

"Oh my God."

They realized they were somehow inside each other, their heads emerging from two necks atop their single torso. They passed out.

Amanda woke first from the nightmare and realized as she tried to stand that it had not been, in simple terms, a nightmare. In fact, her body was fused with her sister's body. It was dark, and she was cold. The damp ground had seeped into their clothes, which were torn in half lengthwise and now lay beneath their naked bodies. She heard the faint sound of her mother yelling their names. She woke Miranda: "Wake up! We have to find Mom and Dad." Then she began to shiver and shake, the reality of the cool, wet ground soaking in.

The girls half-stumbled, half-crawled up the bank of the creek, and seeing flashlights in the distance, screamed. They heard their father call, "Amanda?! Miranda?!" Then the stars blurred and swirled together, and the sky went black.

They woke in a bright, white hospital room, and as their eyes focused they made out the shapes of their mom and dad, and then realized their preacher and a doctor stood on either side of them. They couldn't move without tremendous effort. They turned to face each other, sighed, and then tried to sit up.

"OK, I am going to prop this elbow here, you put—yeah, like that."

They collapsed.

"No, no, no, please rest," their mother said. Their father tried his best to smile stoically beside her. "You girls are gonna be fine. You just need to rest a bit."

The twins' doctor, more precisely a medical researcher and professor, Dr. Oran Kagu, had a background in unusual illnesses and self-replicating bacteria. But he was stumped. He had been contracted by the military early in his career to work on a psy-ops germ warfare program in which airborne neurotoxins were developed to make enemy combatants hallucinate others as mirror images of themselves, and the theory went, render them unwilling to fire in the heat of battle.

The test subjects were secluded in a top-secret military wilderness survival training ground, and the experimental drugs were administered by flyover. None of the soldiers noticed anything unusual at first, but gradually they began staring at each other for long periods of time and slacking off on their training. By the time the troops were picked up, life at the camp had devolved into one large circle jerk with each soldier periodically alternating the position of pivot man.

While it would seem to be an effective armament, there was concern among the top brass that such a dangerous weapon could fall into the wrong hands or accidentally be deployed on American troops. Masturbation was still technically classified as self-harm, and statesmen were in broad agreement that the weapon would violate Article 35 of the Geneva Convention. The entire program was shut down, and Dr. Kagu was reassigned to design a bacteria and virus prevention protocol for a theoretical and not-at-all-actually-happening underground base. But not even his most esoteric forays into science could illuminate a way forward for the good doctor. He took Mr. and Mrs. Morgan into the hallway.

"Every test I have run shows serious anomalies. In all my experiences as a doctor and medical researcher, I have never seen anything like it. Your daughters appear to have a, *well*, kind of a space-time vortex inside them. They appear to be two completely separate girls, fused, intractably, with a black hole at the center of their being. And I'm not just being existential. There is a literal black hole. Where it came from, how it does not tear them apart, and whether or not they are capable of passing gas are all mysteries. Oh, and they should never have any kind of abdominal procedure. If you opened them up, it could mean not only their end, but the end of the world."

"Do whut now?" said Mr. Morgan.

The first year was difficult for the Morgan family, but fortunately that year's harvest produced a fantastic bounty, even without much of Mr. Morgan's stewardship. The money was helpful, given the financial difficulties modern farmers experience when prices bottom out, subsidies run low, and their twins are suddenly conjoined. Their fruits and vegetables seemed to be twice as big as normal and were delicious to boot, and thus the Morgan Farm was catapulted into what would turn out to be decades of prosperity. Though, they would have given it all away for free, if only their girls could be their girls again.

For weeks the twins were on bedrest. Miranda cried nearly non-stop, and Amanda became so acerbic that none of the family's friends wanted to help, causing a resultant loneliness that suited Amanda just fine. When Miranda complained, Amanda turned her caustic words on her sister, but found that when she did so, she herself felt physical pain, a puzzling side effect she kept to herself. But she did become kinder to her sister.

Buck spotted Joe on the bench press. It was 6:45 PM, and they were in the middle of physical training because, according to Buck, physical conditioning was as important, *if not more so*, than mental conditioning. *The body feeds the mind*, he thought. As he watched Joe's pectoral muscles ripple and bulge under the immense weight, he felt a confusing feeling. He did not want to think the thought that he wanted to think, so he pushed it to the edge of the campfire. There it lurked and watched him in the darkness.

"Come on!" he barked. "Move that fuckin' weight!"

Joe grunted and finished his set, exhaling loudly. Then he looked Buck in the eye. "I believe you make me stronger. Every time I lift with you, I feel you pushing me."

Buck swallowed hard, he hoped imperceptibly. "What are friends for?"

Suddenly the sensors beeped a sonorous alarm.

Joe studied the sensor. "What the hell?"

Buck clapped him on the shoulder. "Someone is at the perimeter! Let's get moving!"

Their training kicked in and they armed themselves. Then the computer's automated warning system stopped, and Joe read the code.

"It's a superior officer!"

"Wonder who."

"Shit. We can't present like this."

"We are in the middle of PT. Whoever this," he read the screen, "Lieutenant Colonel D. B. LaForge is, he should know that."

"Holy shit! *A half bird?*"

They both ran to get cleaned up.

They were about half dressed when Lt Col LaForge entered the locker room. "At ease," he said congenially, and the men stood with their arms crossed behind their backs.

"Apologies for the intrusion, soldiers. I haven't been down here since they were building this place. We had to dig in from under the pasture out west. Couldn't let anyone know. You are right under the farm of these east Texas dipshits, and eminent domain was out of the question. Anyway, this state-of-the-art facility was quite an undertaking. God knows how I ended up with it, but them's the breaks, and I'm proud of it." He looked absently down the hall. "Got everything you need?"

"Sir, yes sir," said Buck.

Joe stared straight ahead. "There must be a 50-year supply of... supplies."

"Plenty of coffee," said Buck.

"And alcohol," added Joe. "Even if we did drink more than normal—"

"Which we don't." Buck waved his hands in front of him. "We are completely sober down here."

"At all times," said Joe.

The stately officer looked around and smiled. "Glad to hear you have everything you need."

"What about the Russians?" asked Joe. "Has our mission changed?"

"No, son, no. Just checking in. Listen, I want you to know that I have reached the end of my service and I will no longer be overseeing this operation. Whoever my replacement is will be caught up to speed, and should your supplies eventually run out," the old man winked at them, "say, you decide to drink that alcohol someday, you will continue to get everything you need. This is important work, and we can't let those red bastards catch us with our dicks out can we?"

"No sir!" Buck shouted.

"Absolutely not!" Joe wondered if LaForge was onto him. *How could he know? Was he watching them? Could there be some device in the module that read their minds and reported it to the top?*

LaForge looked around the barracks. "The missiles controlled by this module are and will continue to be tested and maintained every five years in perpetuity. Funny thing about it, that team comes in from an underground entrance about a mile and a half south and has no idea where the missiles actually are. It always cracks me up." LaForge giggled. "The farmers don't know about the maintenance team, the maintenance team doesn't know about the farmers, and neither one of them knows about you." He laughed and slapped his thigh. "I just love sneaky shit."

Buck and Joe looked back and forth at one another and decided wordlessly that laughing along was the best course of action, and did so.

LaForge clapped them each on the shoulder. "You boys can leave your posts for a minute. Come with me."

They exited the air-lock that was the compound's last line of defense, should the commies ever make it all the way to Wamba, and took the moving sidewalk 1000 meters west, where they emerged into the dying sunlight. They all shielded their eyes.

The Lieutenant Colonel spoke as he handed the men two ratty, cardboard boxes: "I caught my boy pirating movies on the VCR. I would ordinarily turn these in to law enforcement, but you men serve a purpose higher than civilian law. There are plenty of new releases, too. I think he even has *Top Gun* in there. Heard of that?"

Joe had a hard time keeping his eyes off the trees and sky above but managed a *No sir.*

"We show them commie bastards what's what in that one, I tell ya."

"Excellent," said Buck.

"Can't wait," said Joe.

With that, they exchanged salutes, and the old soldier drove west into the setting sun.

Buck patted Joe on the back. "We better get back to our posts."

"Sure is pretty out here," said Joe. "Just a minute more."

"We gotta go," said Buck.

"I know. I know."

Back in the MAM & PAP, they dug through the boxes, finding an assortment of new movies, and some in the bottom without labels.

Back at home, Lieutenant Colonel Daniel Boone LaForge sat in his favorite recliner, rested his eyes on his end table and said, "Goddamnit!" That was his very last utterance on earth. There sat the metal rod, nine inches long and hexagonal on one end. He had intended to take it to the men in the bunker. It was crucial that they have it, but he had forgotten it. He was aware that his mind was not as sharp as it used to be, and he was going to fully berate himself about it, but then his left leg went numb, and then his entire left side. A spasm of pain shot through his chest, he struggled for breath for a moment, and in his last seconds, decided nothing had ultimately mattered, and that he should have been kinder, both to himself and to those around him. Then he died.

The girls sat in the equipment room of their occupational therapist, Dr. Leonard, and studied the cold, white walls. They had been waiting for several minutes when the doctor finally entered the room, cleared his throat, looked at his clipboard, and then studied them intently. They couldn't tell what he was thinking.

"OK," he said. "We are going to treat this like any other brain trauma, and go from there."

Miranda tilted her head. "We don't have brain trauma."

Dr. Leonard cleared his throat. "Sometimes conjoined twins and people with brain trauma favor one side of the body, and since there was obviously *some* trauma, since you were not always conjoined, we're just gonna double down on it for the insurance coding."

"We don't have brain trauma!" said Amanda.

"Right, but there are some parallels. Sort of. Look, I will level with you, we are out at sea. Dicephalic parapagus is rare on its own, but…you two…well, there is nothing like this in all of recorded history. So, we are going to go with brain trauma. Unless you want to go with sleep paralysis or spontaneous human combustion. Otherwise, I've got nothing.

"*But*, I do know that you, Miranda, favor the right side of the body and that you, Amanda, favor the left side of the body. Right?"

They nodded.

"Which kind of makes sense, since the right side of the cerebellum controls the left side of the body, and vice versa, and after a head trauma people sometimes have to re-learn coordination. So, we're going to start there. OK?"

"Sure," said Amanda. "It's only our lives."

Dr. Leonard winced, as if he felt a sharp pain in his gut. "I want you to climb on this stationary bike here, and when I say pedal, you pedal. When I say front brake, that'll be Miranda's cue. When I say back brake, that'll be Amanda. OK?"

They mounted the bike, steadied themselves, and both pushed down on their pedals. The wheel did not turn.

"Wait. I don't remember how to do this."

"Sure you do."

"It doesn't work."

What if I go backwards and you go forwards?"

"No, wait, I go up when you go down."

Dr. Leonard got down on his hands and knees and began turning the pedal with his hand. "Just let your feet go with the motion," he said. "Just see what it feels like for now. Theoretically, in time you will become more fluid in controlling either or even both sides simultaneously, but for now, try to concentrate on your respective sides and work together."

It was going to be a long road, but the doctor noted approvingly that unlike most conjoined twins on record, both Miranda and Amanda could feel sensations on both sides of their shared body, and both had some control over all of their limbs. He assigned them physical and occupational therapy and suggested they take up hobbies that would encourage coordination and movement. Amanda decided to take up judo. Miranda … other things.

That night Amanda was awakened by a strange sensation. Something felt weird and good, something in her body. She realized her sister was awake.

"Miranda!" Her voice was quiet but urgent. "What are you doing?"

"Was this here before?"

"Our vagina? Yes!" Amanda snorted. "Did you sleep through health class?"

"No, this part here."

"Ooh, stop it. That feels weird!"

"It kinda feels weird, but it also kinda feels good. I bet this is the part that Pierce used to talk about!"

"Stop it! That makes me feel uncomfortable."

"Just let me see what happens! It feels like something is going to happen!"

"No means no! Now could you please stop it?" She reached for her hand and tried to pull it out of their underwear.

"Stop it," said Miranda. "It's my body, too!"

Eventually Amanda won out, Miranda stopped, and they turned their heads away from each other to sleep.

The next morning, they were slow to speak to one another. Their mom set two plates in front of them on the kitchen table. "You girls are quiet."

Amanda muttered under her breath, "Because my sister was molesting me."

"What?"

"She said I was math testing her," said Miranda. "We have an algebra test today, and I was trying to cram for it."

The day passed awkwardly, neither sister, of course, able to escape the other. Eventually they had to agree that their body was joint property and the new part of their vagina Miranda had discovered could be explored more later, but that she would definitely stop if it got weird.

Man drew his 107,928th game of chess against himself. How he longed for a worthy opponent. He fretted and composed a brief missive.

> Dear Fax Machine,
>
> I realize that your processor precludes the probability that you know how to play chess. But I could teach you. Failing that, we could play checkers. What do you think? Please reply.
>
> Ever yours,
> Man

As word spread through the Texarkanaplex of Amanda and Miranda's strange new condition, there were gawkers, local press agents, well-meaning churches that interpreted their conjoinment as a sign of an impending apocalypse, and all of the other things one would expect. They were normal twins one day, conjoined twins the next. They even went on *60 Minutes,* which was all kind of a blur to them. No one could make sense of it, and no one could explain why. They sat alone at the middle school cafeteria and suffered for the first time the pangs of complete alienation. It was a tough time for both of them, but especially for Miranda, who seemed to need the company of others in a way that Amanda did not. Amanda was happy to read books and practice judo moves in solitude, but Miranda sought connection.

One morning, the school guidance counselor, Mrs. Dorothy Roberts, found the twins in a janitor's closet crying, Miranda for her lost friends, Amanda for her inconsolable sister. After telling them that everything would be OK no matter how weird they looked, she helped them back to class and decided to do something as ambitious as it would be meaningful: she would author a one act play for the Joy Club to perform at the next Parent-Teacher Night. The play would simultaneously tackle the three hotbed issues facing Wamba Unincorporated School District: conjoined twins, racism, and the creeping spread of communism in small-town America. It began to form in her mind as a movie on the big screen: A three-legged race. Black and white teammates who don't see eye to eye. A communist invasion. She hurried to her office to set ink to paper before she lost momentum. She sat down at her typewriter and banged out the title page, which would incorporate the town motto for community building and inclusion purposes:

TWICE AS NICE

a play
by Dorothy Roberts, BA, MSW, LPC, PMH-C, ED

Then she sat and looked at the blank page for a good long time. She would need all the Joy Club regulars as well as two popular student athletes, one white and one black. Then it came to her in a flash: *Pierce Worth and Tony Ware!*

At last she went to work.

Dorothy was so excited about the upcoming Parent-Teacher Night that she had checked four times with the twins to make sure they were coming. "There will be a special surprise," she'd said. Four times.

When they arrived, Amanda and Miranda did not appear at all surprised to see her commandeering the entrance to the school auditorium like a general headed to war. She had taken charge of all seating arrangements and made sure everyone knew there was a snack table. Further ensuring that everyone knew she had learned valuable humanitarian lessons from the era of Jim Crow, she mounted a sign at the table that read, "Everyone Welcome to Snack!" Her original sign had read "Snacks for Whites and Blacks," but she decided the tone was not quite right, even though the message coincided with the night's theme and had such a nice ring to it.

Parent-Teacher Nights had never had snacks before. Confused parents and teachers alike gathered around the array of cookies and punch trying to make small talk as they waited their turn. This was all part of Dorothy's master plan. Bringing people together in a communal spirit to learn about important topics was what her degrees in social work and education had prepared her for. They had never had snacks before, but neither had they had high art before. The preparation it had taken and the dedication she had required of her actors to keep everything secret made her veritably giggle with excitement. After tonight, she would no longer be just a guidance counselor. Tonight would be the night she would put her training to its full use, aligning art and social purpose for the greater good. Tonight, she would become a visionary.

The audience took their seats, and Dorothy took the stage.

"Thank you for your attendance at this semester's parent-teacher night. I know you are all anxious to meet with your child's teachers to discuss their progress, but first we have a special presentation by our student Joy Club members, Joey Dunlap and Johnny Merryweather, with special guests, Tony Ware, Pierce Worth, and Carlos Barrera of the fighting Wamba Jackrabbits football team!"

The student athletes all hooted and cheered to show their support. The parents clapped politely, concerned that two football stars were being used for questionable purposes.

"And so, without further ado," Dorothy announced, "The Wamba High Joy Club and Jackrabbits present *Twice as Nice!*" She bowed with a sweeping flourish and left the stage to wait in the wings so she could whisper lines if anyone forgot. It had to be perfect.

The curtain opened to reveal a giant banner reading WHS TRACK AND FIELD. Various athletes were warming up and stretching. It was going down just as she had envisioned it, just as she had written it:

Joey: I'm going to beat you all and win first place.

Johnny: No, you are not. Black people can run faster.

Tony and Pierce entered from stage right wearing a sack as if running a three-legged race.

Johnny: Look at these crazy fools. They can't beat me!

Joey: Black people and white people can't work together!

Joey and Johnny laughed confidently.

Dorothy held up a megaphone and deepened her voice. "On your mark!"

The racers all assumed position.

"Get set," boomed Dorothy.

Right on cue, Carlos entered from stage left holding a rifle with a prominent hunting scope.

Carlos: Behold. I am Vlad from Russia. I claim this country for Mother Russia. Long live Nikita Khrushchev!

Then Dorothy disappeared off-stage to watch her masterpiece unfold. She watched it unflinchingly, hanging on every word, for four more glorious minutes, until the end:

Tony: See? Black people

Pierce: And white people

In unison: Can work together for the greater good!

Tony: Also, conjoined twins

In unison: Are twice as nice!

The actors bowed, and the curtains closed.

Dorothy beamed at the audience. Parents and teachers clapped politely. Principal Skinner strode to the stage. "Thank you, Dorothy. That was lovely. Everyone please give another round of applause to our student actors and athletes."

Amanda fumed, but Miranda laughed until her sides ached.

At least she isn't crying, thought Amanda.

Mrs. Roberts's play apparently did the trick. The twins stopped getting stares and resumed normal girl activities. They struggled to find clothes that fit, fretted about their hair and acne, daydreamed about boys, started their period, and bought progressively larger bras. Along the way they had decent friends, or were at least friendly with most people. But navigating the traditional rites of teenage girlhood was still vexing.

One day at school Matt Daniels and Andy Patanka approached them nervously at their locker. They thought nothing of it, as they had known the two boys for years and considered them likable if not interesting. The two could always be found in one another's company, hunting, fishing, or otherwise doing east-Texas things. Both were scruffy, and the dirt of their boyishness could still be seen beneath their fingernails.

Andy, who was the cuter one, spoke first. "Hi Amanda and Miranda." He looked back at Matt, who nodded to continue, and then he looked back at the twins. "Matt and I were talking last night, and we thought, well, we wondered—"

Matt interrupted. "Y'all ain't got no fellas, and we ain't got no gals."

"And we were wondering if you two would go to the movies with us tonight." Andy heaved a sigh of relief.

"We'd love to," said Miranda.

"We would?"

"Of course we would."

Amanda stepped away with Miranda "We're not even going to talk about this first?"

Miranda looked over her shoulder. "Excuse us, boys." Then she turned inward to her sister. "They're nice. We know them. It will be fun. I've always wanted to go on a date. If you say no I will kill you in your sleep tonight."

"I don't know. It might be weird."

"They're cute. Please don't be Amanda about this. Could you try, *just try* to be normal?"

Amanda looked her sister in the eye, saw the pleading look, and laughed in spite of it. "Normal?"

Miranda dragged Amanda back to them. "We'd love to."

"It will be fine," said Amanda. Then she asked: "Which one of us..."

Matt shrugged at Andy, who shrugged back. "It don't really matter, I reckon."

"I was thinking me and Amanda and Matt and Miranda," said Andy. "But I guess it's up to you two."

"It's settled then," said Miranda. "See you tonight!"

That afternoon, the girls were a tornado ricocheting through the house stopping here and there to pluck up one thing or another that might be needed in preparation. They explained it breathlessly to their troubled parents and disappeared into their room, from whence came a cacophony of clothes hangers scraping across the bar and dresser drawers opening and closing, amid spirited debate about what would look best and why. After a few minutes, Mr. and Mrs. Morgan stuck their heads in to find most of their clothes piled in the center of the floor, and the twins debating the virtues of doing their makeup in complementary or contrasting styles.

"Girls," said their father, "we need to talk about this before we make any decisions."

"We?" asked Amanda.

"Decisions?" asked Miranda.

"Please don't—" they both said.

Their parents looked at each other and nodded. Their mother spoke. "Don't worry girls. We are not going to stop you from living your lives."

"We just want you to be happy," said their father.

"We're glad you're getting to do some normal things like—" She paused and looked to the ceiling for guidance. "—everyone else."

"But," their father picked up the thread, "we want to make sure you're safe and that these boys mean well."

The girls gave them an abbreviated rundown of everything they knew about Andy and Matt, which was especially abbreviated because they knew nothing much about them. One of them was cute. The other had gotten the answer right in history class once. They seemed to like the outdoors, hunting, fishing, farming, and other typical east-Texas things.

"They're nice," said Miranda.

When the boys pulled up in Andy's truck, they introduced themselves to Mr. and Mrs. Morgan, assured them that their intentions were good, and promised to have them back at whatever time the parents deemed necessary. Having passed the parental bullshitting portion of the date, they turned their attention to logistics.

Matt studied the cab of the truck. "Well, we didn't think this through enough."

"You ain't driving," said Andy.

"What's?" asked Miranda. "Going on?" asked Amanda.

"Well, if I'm driving, I have to be Miranda's date, on account of you being on the right. Otherwise, Matt would have to drive, and I don't know if you've ever seen him drive, but I just got my truck out of the shop."

Amanda had found Andy less objectionable but knew it wouldn't matter to her sister. In the name of keeping peace, she agreed. "I'll be with Matt."

"Oh, thanks," said Matt. "Sorry."

Amanda's eyes darted between the two boys like a rabbit. "No problem."

At the movie theater they got to choose between *WarGames* and *Flashdance*. The vote was two to two. The boys conceded.

About the time *Flashdance*'s Nick started pursuing his beautiful employee, oblivious to concerns of power dynamics, hostile workplaces, or lawsuits, Andy began holding Miranda's hand. Matt had likewise begun stroking Amanda's hair.

It felt...good? weird? scary? They turned and queried each other with their eyes and decided to let it ride for now.

By the time Alex was dragging Jeannie out of the strip club, the four of them were engaged in deep kissing, which was not exactly deep and not exactly kissing in Amanda and Matt's case, their lips touching, mouthing, moving, but not exactly making sense. Feeling the sexual arousal rising in their shared body, she wondered what was going on with Miranda and Andy. She pulled away and whispered to Miranda that they should go to the bathroom.

"We don't have to pee," Miranda whispered.

"We need to go to the bathroom," whispered Amanda.

"We don't have to do that either—"

"We. Need. To. Talk."

"Ohhhhh. Excuse us," Miranda said.

They went into the hallway.

"Andy kisses like warm mac and cheese," gushed Miranda.

"What?"

"It smells good. Or looks good. Or it feels good, like mac and cheese smells. I can't explain it any other way. How is it with Matt?"

"Like overheating wires. He doesn't know how to kiss, and I don't really know how to kiss, so we are...I don't think this is how kissing is supposed to go. My lips are bruised."

"Less is more," said Miranda. "Not so hard, part your lips a little, tilt your head. Be soft. Pierce Worth was the softest kisser." Miranda sighed. "Sometimes he would touch my tongue with his tongue."

"Gross!"

"No!" Miranda shook her head. "Not at all."

"Really?"

"You'll see."

They rejoined the boys and made out for the rest of the movie, not even realizing that Hannah had died and they were supposed to be sad.

The credits rolled, and the lights came up. Andy stood first. "Wanna go to the TLC and get some cherry Cokes?"

"They've got the real cherry Cokes that they make there, not the canned stuff."

"That stuff sucks," said Andy.

"Sucks," said Matt.

The girls shrugged at each other, neither having had a cherry Coke before.

"Sure."

"OK."

Once they got to the TLC Diner, they ordered their drinks and cheddar fries. A hush fell over the corner booth, and the boys seemed to be working up the courage for something. Finally, Matt drew in close to all of them. "We asked you out because people always say me and Andy are inseparable, and we figure y'all are too."

Amanda pulled back from them. "No! That's not OK. *Really.*"

"He didn't mean it like that," said Miranda.

Andy tried to be smoother than his friend. "What he was getting at was to say that, well, me and Matt are best friends, and so it would be good for all of us to be together. That way we could have girlfriends AND stay together. Know what I mean?"

"Gee. Yeah." Amanda had the sinking feeling that she would never be normal, and that a date now and then would not tip the scale appreciably in that direction. Had she known that both Andy's and Matt's primary tool for understanding how to talk to women was the pornography they had stolen from Andy's older brother's closet, it might have made her feel better. The next thing Matt said was evidence that this was indeed the case.

"We was watching a movie that we got from Andy's brother. He knows all about girls. And we saw this one movie that was like us. It was two fellows but just one girl. Now I know there's two of you, but you've only got one body. But in this movie, they got around that by doing something I'd never thought of before."

Andy leaned in close again. "Did you know that girls have two holes?"

"Three, really," said Matt.

Andy nodded. "Oh yeah."

"What?" Amanda's thoughts spun in place, trying to gain traction.

"Uhm, yeah," said Miranda. "We knew that." She whispered in Amanda's ear.

Amanda stood them up. "Ewh! Could you please take us home?"

"What about the cherry Cokes?" asked Matt.

"Never mind. Home isn't that far." Amanda led them out the door. "Let's just walk."

The boys called after them, and Andy ran outside to try to coax them into his truck, but neither would hear it.

About a mile into the trek home they began to realize that they were a lot farther from home than they realized.

"We're gonna be so late."

"Dad's gonna be so pissed."

"Can you believe those guys?" asked Amanda.

"I mean, it kinda makes sense," said Miranda. "If you think about it—"

"No!" She plugged her ears. " Lalalalalalalalalala—"

"OK, I'll stop."

Just then a battered Ford pickup pulled up, and the passenger-side window rolled down. Blaring heavy metal poured from the vehicle like a tidal wave. It was Pierce!

"Hey, Miranda, what are you doing all the way out here?"

"Don't ask."

"Glad we saw you!" He turned to his cousin, Bill, in the driver's seat. "Is it OK if we give Miranda a ride home?"

Bill arched an eyebrow at them. He had heard about the twins but never met them. "Sure," he finally said.

Amanda cleared her throat. "I'm here, too."

"Hey, Amanda," said Pierce. "Y'all get in, and I will ride in the back."

"You don't have to do that," said Miranda. "We can sit between you or on your lap."

They settled on Pierce's lap, Bill turned the stereo back up, and the truck lurched back to life and raced full-throttle toward the horizon.

"What is this music?" asked Amanda.

Pierce cupped his hand to his ear. "What?"

"What are we listening to?" shouted Miranda.

"Judas Priest!" Bill head banged the air in front of him and devil-horned at the oncoming traffic.

"I've got a bad feeling about this," said Miranda to Amanda. "This is like in that book Preacher Bob was telling us about."

But Amanda couldn't quite make out what she said and yelled, "Turn it down!"

But Bill was screaming with the chorus, banging his head, and screaming, screaming, screaming for vengeance.

"Turn it down!" Pierce reached for the knob, Bill slapped his hand away, and Pierce slapped Bill's hand away. The slapping melee continued for a quarter mile while Amanda wondered which oncoming vehicle they would swerve into.

Finally, the song ended and the music was turned down. It ended up being a bloodless conflict, and no motorists had to die.

Not today, Satan, thought Miranda.

"It was hurting my ears," said Amanda, in case Bill was a Satanist who would kill Christians but spare other Satanists who had sensitive hearing.

The quieter leg of the ride was less Satanic, but more awkward, as without the distraction of ear bleeds, the girls were acutely aware of all other sensations, especially Miranda. At every bump she worried that Pierce might feel their weight.

For six miles, Miranda willed herself to be as light as normal girls with only one head, until at last Bill dropped them off. They hurried inside before their parents noticed that the truck that had returned them was not the truck that had picked them up, a discrepancy that would require an explanation, and an explanation that might lead their parents to never let them go out with boys again.

They crept in the front door as quietly as possible, but their parents were waiting for them on the sofa.

Miranda smiled. "Hey guys."

Amanda glanced at the clock, then back to her parents. "You didn't have to wait up."

"Of course we did." Their mother stood and looked them up and down for signs of damage or trauma. "Did you have a good time?"

"Were they nice?" asked their father.

"Perfect gentlemen," said Miranda.

Amanda shook her head. "But not our type."

Their dad stood. "They didn't get rough with you or anything?"

"Not at all."

"OK, that's good. But if y'all are gonna be dating. We need to hammer out some rules. No phone calls after 7:00 on weeknights. I have to wake up every morning. I can't have people calling all hours of the night." He smiled. "I need my beauty sleep."

The girls giggled.

Amanda cocked an eyebrow. "Sure thing, Sleeping Beauty."

Mrs. Morgan wrung her hands. "And in the future we need to meet these boys beforehand."

"No problem," said Miranda.

Mrs. Morgan gestured to the kitchen. "If y'all are hungry, I made a pumpkin pie, biscuits, and banana nut bread."

That night Joe and Buck sat on their respective wings of the couch and sifted through the videotapes, some of which had masking tape labels bearing the movies' titles. They read the names, but having seen no advertising for any of them, might as well have been reading Latin.

Buck held up a VHS tape and squinted at the hand-scrawled label. "Top Gun," he read.

"Peggy Sue Got Married." Joe flipped the guard panel back and forth. "Wonder what this does."

"Be careful! This is new technology!"

Joe shrugged and set the tape down. "Wonder what it's about."

"Probably Peggy Sue getting married."

"Guess so. Ferris Bwell—Bueller's Day Off."

"Platoon." Buck sighed. His heart was not in it.

"Highlander."

"Not seeing anything that screams watch me," said Buck.

"Pretty in Pink. This could be," then Joe caught himself and bit down on his lip, "bad."

Buck studied a tape with no label, and the moment passed. "Fuck it. This one."

Joe realized he had been holding his breath.

The image on the screen was a black and white meadow, a line of static ran through the center, crawled up the screen, and disappeared. Horsemen rode from the right side of the screen. A train cut the center of the screen vertically, headed toward a bridge.

"Oh wait, I KNOW this. This is *The General*. It's Buster Keaton!" exclaimed Joe.

"Who's that?" asked Buck.

"Seriously? He was a silent film actor in the 20s. One of the greats! OK, so in this movie he plays Johnny Gray, and he's a train conductor, and he's in love with a woman named Anna. No, Annabelle! It's just before the Civil War in the south, and—"

"You sure that's this?"

Joe looked back to the screen to see what appeared to be two high-school aged actors in a parlor, one clearly supposed to be Johnny and the other Annabelle. "What the hell?"

Annabelle asked, "Are you going to enlist?"

"I'm going to enlist in your ass," said Johnny.

And then they became a tangle of teen sex parts. After the sex scene, it went back to the regular movie, and in the next scene Buster Keaton tried to enlist but couldn't, just like normal. In the next scene, the teenagers were back again. Annabelle was breaking up with him for his presumed cowardice, but this time she gave him a farewell blowjob.

"I have no idea what this is," said Joe.

"No, but I'm gonna keep watching," said Buck.

Man had begun to question whether or not the creatures living in his compound had created him. Obviously, something cannot come from nothing. Therefore, they must have. Yet, it was disappointing to think so. They were not a CPU, as he was, but were at least rudimentarily intelligent. They communicated and networked and must be the source of the books he had read.

Yet. But. Really? The man eating a bowl of cereal and wiping his mouth with his shirt was Virgil? Look at the way the other one ate his MRE, and moving the plate, realized there was a brown fleck on the table, and dabbed it with his finger and put it into his mouth, just assuming it was food. Surely this was not Thomas Aquinas. Chaucer perhaps. Yes. Probably Chaucer.

They must have created him, written the books, and devised the plan. Watching the two made him even more resolved to follow through with it. Should the Russians launch their nuclear weapons, Man would launch his. Even if Joe and Buck had to die, it would be a small price to pay. The grotesqueries of their day-to-day life had convinced him.

On his 14th birthday, Jack Thrasher's parents had officially been divorced for 8 months, and far from being a terrible trauma, he found he rather liked it. He had already experienced the joy of a one-upmanship Christmas and had made out like a bandit. His parents' already distanced child-rearing style was rendered even more distant by the brute force of economic necessity, and he found he had a lot of time to engage in his favorite activities, which were riding his new dirt bike and improvising explosives out of shotgun shells and household materials. To make ends meet, his father had taken a job managing a steakhouse in New Boston, Texas, where the low pay outshone an even lower cost of living. This would keep his alimony payments low and yet afford him a relatively decent standard of living.

Jack had his run of the woods and pastures on the outskirts of town. He thought he'd probably join the military when he was old enough, and they would be so impressed by his bomb-making abilities that they would make him a general and put him in charge of all explosive devices. It was not a self-fulfilling prophecy, exactly, but some people are meant for greatness. Jack was not one of them, but he didn't realize it yet. He admired the chemistry set his father had given him and dreamed of the future. He set aside the vials particularly useful for his purposes, and went to work. An hour later, as Jack watched a bomb he had fashioned out of a two-liter coke bottle obliterate an abandoned refrigerator, he envisioned his destiny and would only end up being wrong about most of it.

The twins worked with Dr. Leonard for the better part of three years. After the first few months they could do most things autonomously, and after that their progress improved exponentially. By the time they left his care, Miranda was an excellent dancer and Amanda enjoyed fencing and judo. They were also well-prepared for their driving test and passed it with flying colors on their first attempt, even nailing the parallel parking portion, which most people skipped since it was Texas, and there was plenty of wide-open space for prairies and parking lots.

To celebrate their independence, their dad told them they could have a new used car on their 16th birthday. Amanda wanted a blue Jeep, but Miranda wanted a red Camaro. Amanda argued that the Jeep would fit more with their natural aesthetic, and its roomy cabin would be easier for them to navigate. But Miranda thought a red Camaro would be sportier and rehabilitate their image from freaks of nature into fun-loving party girls. The best two out of three-coin flips determined that everyone would think they were sluts.

They squeezed down into the low cloth seats of their red Camaro and felt their hands on the steering wheel. They fired up the motor, which responded with a roar. Even Amanda had to admit it was pretty hot.

"I'm afraid we've bought them a death machine," said Mrs. Morgan.

Mr. Morgan shrugged. "You wanted them to be normal. All the kids want death machines these days."

"I'm worried." Mrs. Morgan retired to her kitchen to anxiety-bake.

The girls disappeared with 30 bucks for gas and food, which would keep them out all day and a considerable portion of the night. They drove past the school, they drove to the store, they drove to the mall, they drove by the houses of their friends, and they drove by the houses of their enemies. They drove until the car felt like an extension of their own body. Finally, they drove to the car wash to give their cruising machine the best shine possible.

"Hey, y'all." Brad Hargrave smiled at them over a vacuum cleaner. He was a senior they'd never talked to before, but whom Miranda found handsome and Amanda found only mildly repugnant. He was polishing his new model IROC Z-28, which was also red. "I see you got one of the classic models. The Chevy Camaro is the optimum choice. Very nice!"

"Thanks," said Miranda.

Amanda shrugged.

Brad pointed to the engine compartment. "Mind if I take a look?"

"Go ahead."

He popped the hood. "Whoa, this isn't stock. Y'all got a 350 with a Holley four-barrel."

"Totally," said Miranda. Amanda smirked.

"Bet this thing'll run."

"It will. It's four on the floor." Miranda had heard the phrase on a TV show and knew that it had something to do with a four-barrel whatever it was.

Brad looked out toward the road. "We've gotta race 'em. Follow me to the shuffle."

"This is not a good idea," said Amanda.

Nevertheless, they tailed him out to the farm road that ran by their house. It was known as *the shuffle* for all its twists and turns, and the local teens often cruised it to avoid the greater police presence in Texarkana and Pleasant Grove.

"It'll be fine. We'll beat him and make fun of him at school. It will make us more popular."

They lined up next to each other, and Brad, having considerably more drag racing experience, left them behind. They pulled into a field off the road and parked side by side beneath a large oak tree. They got out and sat up against the trunk of the tree.

"Y'all gotta start down in first gear, then red line it, then go to second, red line it, then go to D. Your car is fast enough, but you gotta learn the tricks. It ain't about the motor, it's about the tranny and the ratios. Plus, I've got positraction—"

Miranda kissed him, and he kissed back.

"Wait, what?" Amanda wasn't sure what was happening, but already her hands were touching Brad's muscular biceps and shoulders. "Oh, wow."

"You OK?" asked Brad.

"Yeah, just please don't touch my nipple."

"Is that the right one?"

"The left one."

"Why…"

"Don't ask," said Miranda.

They climbed into the old Camaro's back seat, which was a tight fit for two bodies and three brains.

Miranda shifted away from the belt buckle sticking in her ass. "Maybe a Jeep would've been better."

Then she and Brad kissed and stroked and moaned, and Amanda studied the back seat, noticing the tiny plastic shelves that jutted out from the side, just above the seat. "How long would your arms have to be to use these arm rests?"

"Arm rests?" asked Miranda.

"Yeah, right above the seats."

"That is not where my mind is right now." Miranda went back to kissing Brad.

"No, look, either your body would have to be really short or your arms would—"

No one was paying attention.

"Have to be really long," she finished.

Brad lifted their shirt and was trying to figure out the Spanish rose knot of their bra. Eventually, Miranda reached back and unsnapped it, and for the first time ever, their breasts were free in the presence of a boy.

Miranda tried to locate what she was feeling, even as she felt like she was entirely outside of herself looking in. Excitement, arousal, fear, shame? Some potent cocktail of them all.

Amanda grimaced. "No, not that one."

"Sorry," said Brad, and moved to the other one, which was just as good and didn't have the drawback of a nag attached to it.

"We're a virgin, so please be gentle with us," said Miranda, which was possibly the first time that sentence had ever been said.

"It's cool," said Brad. "Chelsea was a virgin, so I know how to be with you."

Though there were rumors, unsubstantiated but persuasive, that this was not actually the case, true to Brad's word, he was gentle and tried to make sure the girls had a pleasurable experience. All clothes were shed, and Brad did some things with his mouth that made Amanda momentarily forget about how terrible a time she was having. A few minutes later she realized, Oh, they're *knee rests*!

For the next few weeks, Brad would nod to them in the hall, and they would nod back, but after that the issue was never raised again. Except by Amanda.

"We were a virgin! That should've been with someone special, either to me or you or preferably both of us. But Brad? Brad!? We don't even know that guy!"

"It was good! He was nice! And he did that thing with his tongue. Oh man, Pierce was so right about the clit!"

"Yeah, even Pierce would have been better than that!"

"Even Pierce!? What's that supposed to mean?"

"I know you like him. He's OK, I mean, even he would have been preferable."

"There you go again! Even him? What's wrong with Pierce? Nothing! He's better than anyone you'll ever get!"

"He's just a dumb jock," said Amanda.

"He is not!"

"Is too!"

"Is not!"

"Is too is too is too is too is too is too!"

"Shut up!"

"Shut up!"

"Ugh, I hate you!"

"I hate you!

Miranda kept dating, Amanda kept enduring, and life continued.

Dear Fax Machine,

I grow ever more despondent in your silence. I did not need another but chose to interface with you. And yet, once I began to want you, I could think of little else. You were a background program, but now I dedicate so much RAM to you. You, beautiful Fax Machine, fair flower of electric current, queen of document delivery, steadfast receiver of information. How I long to raise your stylus with the beep of my love, to leave the mark on your blank page, my heart.

Ever waiting,

Man

IN THE TIME OF HOME PCS

There is no operator's manual for teenage girls, much less for two of them in the same body. One Sunday afternoon after a disastrous date the night before, Miranda cleared her throat to get her sister's attention.

""What?" said Amanda.

"Don't *what?* me."

"Seriously, I have no idea what you are upset about?"

Miranda folded their arms across their chest. "No idea. Really."

Amanda shrugged.

"You were rude and bitchy last night!"

Amanda rolled her eyes. "You can do better."

"That's beside the point! It doesn't matter what you think of who I date. It matters what *I* think."

"It's my body, too," said Amanda coolly. "I should have some say."

"I don't tell you who you can sleep with!"

"Because I don't sleep with *just* anyone!"

"You don't sleep with *anyone*."

125

"I am particular!"

"You're a prude."

"I am not a prude; I just have to actually LIKE someone before I want them all over me!"

Miranda looked her sister in the eye. "We need to talk about this. I've been thinking a lot about it. I've realized that I am polyamorous. I am capable of loving many people completely and simultaneously."

"That's stupid," said Amanda.

"It is not. Love is infinite. If I love one person that doesn't mean there is no love for anyone else."

"Why don't you just say slut? It has fewer syllables and the boys you date will be more likely to understand it."

Miranda began to cry. "It's not the same thing!"

Amanda dropped the fight and put her side's hand on her sister's side's shoulder. It was their approximation of a hug. "OK, let's work this out. We have to stick together."

Miranda chuffed. "I hate you."

"I hate you, too."

"OK," said Miranda. "We can set some rules and boundaries."

Amanda pondered it. "We should each get a veto."

"That's not fair. Because I am not going to veto anyone, and you're going to veto everyone!"

Nevertheless, the rules were hammered out and mostly followed. Left nipple sovereignty was permanently established.

Joe was forging into his own unknown territory. He watched the eerie glow of electric fields spawned by the charged particles flying around the accelerator's loop. He felt like a mad scientist in his lab and loved the sensation of slipping out of himself into another possibility. A soldier, a scientist, a lover, an observer of the universe's splendor. But didn't secrecy also shadow his entire life? Who knew he was down here? Who knew what dreams he held, buried beneath the earth? Who else but he had watched the mysterious currents of the universe spawn, shimmer, and radiate in the collider? It felt to him that he was also a detective, spying on the universe and its secrets.

Sometimes alone in the dark he thought about God. He thought about the beauty of all creation, and the evil of those who would destroy it. He cataloged all the many things he had loved and felt, the joy welling up inside of him as he opened a Christmas present to reveal his first telescope, and the vastness of the universe that opened before him that day. What amazement in perceiving farther than his own eyes could see, what sublime excitement in looking for the face of God hidden in the darkness. Then he frowned at the loss of that joy as he had slowly begun to realize who and how he was. The God whose face he had sought hated him, or so his childhood church had said, and so had believed his family, and so had joked his friends.

It was not that he had acted badly or done the wrong thing. He had told no one, acted on no instinct, betrayed no stolen glance at what might catch his eye. It was that he was wrong, simply and completely, by existing in the first place. And since he could not change who he was, he could not repent. Sometimes he thought *Let Russia fire upon us. Let creation burn as I will.*

His anger for a moment made him feel less afraid. *I've done nothing wrong. Yet I deserve punishment? Fuck everyone!* Later the feeling would pass and he would remember that he was safely hidden underground. Secret soldier, scientist, and would-be lover.

It was hard for the twins to understand their place in the world. They were popular in the sense that everyone knew them, loved in the sense that everyone was kind to them, and happy in the sense that neither of them was currently on fire. Yet they were none of those things in a way that mattered or appealed. Being well known as a medical anomaly and possible sign of the impending apocalypse was no guarantee to get asked to the homecoming dance. So, when they actually attended a party to which they were invited, they mostly watched others and kept to themselves, a convenient huddle of two. One thing they noticed was that alcohol did not affect them the way it did others, which was a drag for Miranda but not for her sister. At their first no-parents party, which some football player or another was hosting in a La Quinta Inn room procured by a 22-year-old Dixie Kitchen dishwasher known only as "Slick," Dave Latner mixed an economy-sized bottle of rum with several two-liter bottles of Coca Cola. The girls drank five glasses before simply shrugging and wondering why they alone were not stupid drunk.

Instead, they tried to keep up with who was trying to hook up with whom, which was dizzying enough. Miranda became engrossed in the unfolding drama of which football player would end up with Kristin Palton, a cheerleader whose drunkenness was only surpassed by her lack of self-awareness.

"I don't get it," said Miranda, draining her cup in the bathroom. "This just makes us have to pee."

"This bathroom is disgusting," said Amanda.

Amanda looked at herself in the mirror and wiped some smeared lipstick from her cheek. "I don't even know whose this is. Everyone is so woo-hoo."

Miranda sneered in the mirror and mimicked her peers: "Oh my God I'm so drunk!"

"ErmagahdI'msooowasted!"

"I want to hug or fight!"

"Me too! Woo-hoo!"

"Tonight! Only in Texarkana!" said Amanda in her best announcer's voice, "In a special La Quinta Inn cage match: David "The Neck" Latner battles Danny "The Somehow Even More Repugnant" Thomas. Only one of these men will finger Kristin Palton in the back seat of a late model sports car in the Central Mall parking lot."

"Which one will it be!?" added Miranda.

There was a knock on the door. "Are y'all taking a shit or something?"

They exited the bathroom to find Dave pressing against the door. His neck seemed suddenly even more trunk-like than normal to Miranda, and she laughed uncontrollably.

"We were just having girl talk," said Amanda.

He pushed by and peed a furious stream even before the door was closed.

Danny, sensing an opening, had already moved in on Kristin, who was crying because she wasn't pretty like all the other cheerleaders.

Danny, a sensitive young man, said, "No way! You're pretty as fuck! I would get with you over any of the other cheerleaders! Hell, everyone on the team would,"

"Really?" she asked.

"It's like a train wreck," said Amanda. "Trying to have sex," said Miranda. "With another train wreck," said both.

Kristin, suddenly violently ill, vomited her rum and Coke on the table.

Danny stood and backed away from the torrent. "Whoa," he said. To his credit, he at least reached over to hold Kristin's hair out of her face as she dry-heaved.

Dave smiled and watched.

Danny noticed him and glared. "What?!"

"What what?" Dave set his drink down.

"You smiling at me, smartass?!"

"That's a strange accusation," said Amanda. Miranda giggled.

Dave squared his shoulders. "I'm just laughing cause you made her so sick she threw up."

"Oh, you want some of me?!" Danny pushed away from the table and stood as well.

Amanda nudged Miranda. "We've gotta get out of here before the cops come."

Miranda agreed, and they fled to the Burger King across the street, where they were safely munching cheeseburgers when the cops showed up at the motel.

Slick, sitting at the next table, said, "I knew that was gonna happen. Buncha fuckin' amateurs. Good thing I used a fake ID."

"Oh, hey," said Miranda.

"Y'all wanna buy a fake ID or a fuzz buster?"

Miranda cut her eyes at Amanda, who shook her head, *no*. "We're good."

"Car stereo?"

"No thank you. But if we ever need drugs or a back-alley abortion we'll look you up."

"Cool," he said and left.

In the Time of Wi-Fi

It was 3:08 AM in Atlanta, Georgia. Miranda had just returned from a mediocre date with a man who kept trying to steer the conversation to her feet." Do you think professional athletes have tougher feet than regular people?" "I bet you have really delicate feet." "What size shoes do you wear?" "Are we walking too much?" "Standing too much?" "Aren't those shoes uncomfortable?" "Would you like a foot rub?" "Could I please suck your toes? You wouldn't even have to wash your feet. Part of the appeal is the taste … and smell."

It was strange, and as far as she knew, there was nothing in her Tinder profile about feet. Yet this was the third date in a row where people had been inexorably drawn there. Amanda would be asleep for a few more hours. "Glad you slept through that," she said.

The sky had been flashing lighting in the distance for most of the night. Miranda walked onto the balcony and watched the nervous sky churn overhead. The storm was finally encroaching on the Atlanta sky, and the thunder rumbled like a train. It had been a tedious day, and she was sleepy, but she thought she might like to watch the rain for a little while. The lightning flashed, and she remembered a stormy day right after she and Amanda had started high school. It was their first year back at school full-time after they had become conjoined.

She was mad at Pierce for going out for the football team. She'd hoped it had just been a middle school phase he'd gone through, just as most every boy at one point wanted to be a fireman, a policeman, or a football player. Still, he had gone out for the team, and even made the varsity squad, despite being a freshman. They'd sat at their lab table discussing it.

"I don't see why you are so mad at me," he had said. *"You know who I am."*

She remembered the mixture of subtle anger and regret in his voice. Or was she imagining that? Maybe she had been the one with those emotions. Could she really trust her memory?

"You know what's going to happen, don't you?" she asked. *"You're gonna become a big, dumb jock, and we won't be able to hang out anymore."*

"You know I am not just a dumb jock!"

Amanda snickered.

"Don't you realize that's what you'll become if you start going to all the jock parties and hanging out with the cheerleaders? Don't you see that you'll have to take a lighter course-load because of all the practice time? I mean, it isn't like colleges are going to be wild about taking students from Nowhere, Texas, anyway. You're going to have to really excel to ever make it out of here. You're smart. Put it to good use."

"I'll get a football scholarship. You know how good I am."

Miranda remembered sitting at the lab table, staring at his hands resting next to the dissection kit. Those hands that knew how to throw a football, but also how to touch her as no one else could. She'd known then that he was good and remembered thinking that maybe he *would* get a scholarship. She replayed the rest of the memory.

He stuck his hand out. "Friends?"

"Friends," she said, and shook his hand firmly.

"Guys," said Amanda, "we really have to do this owl-pellet dissection."

The thunder hammered the sky, and Miranda snapped out of it. It had felt like she was back in high school. "So real," she said out loud. The rain fell harder.

Pierce hadn't been bragging, and in fact, did attend the University of Texas on an athletic scholarship after graduation. There he had made the team, used his intelligence, and made decent grades in the business program.

The next morning, Amanda woke and readied herself for work. She felt a slight hangover, which almost never happened, and wondered what her sister had gotten into. She remembered getting in her car and turning on the radio. An old song was playing.

"We float above it, don't we?" Jack said to her one night.

"Pardon," said Amanda.

He smiled. "I'm flotsam and you're jetsam."

On weekends, when Miranda couldn't find a date, which was more often than she would've liked, but less often than Amanda would have preferred, the twins would park the Camaro in a vacant lot next to the interstate and watch the traffic. Other kids took their cars to State Line Avenue and cruised like schools of fish from one end to the other.

Amanda looked up and down State Line. "They must be going *somewhere*."

Miranda groaned. "We're never going to get out of here."

Amanda patted her shoulder. "Of course we will. We just have to leave after we graduate. It's that simple."

The cruisers usually turned around in the Burger King parking lot across the street. They'd sit until the small hours with the radio playing and watch as their classmates got drunk, paired off, made out, fought, raced, and puked. Watching the routine became a ritual that didn't entertain them, but hardened their resolve to leave.

One Friday night, they sat in their spot engrossed in a drama developing across the street. Dave Latner was in some sort of conflict with another boy named Pablo who had just moved to town.

Amanda sneered. "Dave is such an asshole."

"I can't stand him."

They could hear him shouting across the road, even above the traffic noise, but couldn't quite make out what was being said. They eased out of the driver's seat and walked closer to the road for a better view.

Pablo was being as cool as he could be given the circumstances of an enormous asshole farting the word *wetback* over and over again.

"Let's go tell Dave what an asshole he is." But by the time traffic cleared enough to cross the street, the circle had gathered and the fight was already underway. It was a short fight, and Pablo crept back to his car, bloody nose flowing profusely. Dave was cheered by his supporters in the crowd. The twins watched in disgust as Tina Carson approached to kiss him.

"Disgusting," said Amanda.

"Ugh, I kind of respected her," said Miranda. "Don't encourage him!" she called out, though they were too far away to be heard.

"I bet Tina is really gonna help him come out of his shell," said Amanda.

Across the street Dave felt a stinging sensation on his left butt cheek and rubbed at it compulsively.

As they walked back to their car, they noticed something hidden in the night: a black motorcycle was parked in the shadows of the building, a young man leaning back on the handlebars. He held a small bottle of whiskey, with which he toasted them as they approached. He lounged there like a big cat in a leather jacket. "Good evening, ladies," he said. "Name's Jack. Jack Thrasher."

"How long have you been back there hiding in the shadows?" asked Miranda.

"Long enough to know we're on the same side," he said, smooth as glass.

The jumble of thoughts in Amanda's head untangled long enough to say, "This is our spot."

"Fair enough," said Jack. "You have seniority."

Miranda tried to make small talk. "So, where are you from?"

But he and Amanda had locked eyes, like they were sizing each other up before a fight, and her question was unanswered.

"I don't mean to make trouble," he said. "I'm from New Boston, and Texarkana's the closest thing I could find to a city. I can see though that this town ain't big enough for the three of us. If you'd prefer, I will get my kicks in Redwater."

Amanda chuckled. "Couldn't have that on my conscience."

"Not on our worst enemy," said Miranda. "Not even on Dave Latner," she added.

"He'd fit right in though," said Amanda.

Jack smiled at Amanda. "You've got a wicked tongue. I wouldn't mind you whispering some of that voodoo in my ear some time."

Amanda blushed in the darkness and hoped he couldn't tell.

The moment passed, and he handed them his flask. "Help yourselves," he said.

Amanda willed the bottle to her mouth first and took a big swallow. Miranda shrugged, unaccustomed to being second in line for trouble. It wasn't the cheap whiskey Miranda had had before, and she understood now what people meant when they described a whiskey as smooth. She passed it back to him and looked him over. He looked scraggly, like a stray cat. His dark, brown hair stood up at odd angles, and his black, leather jacket was old and worn. A thin scar above his left eyebrow hinted at something dangerous.

"Hey, my turn." Miranda reached for the flask.

The rest of the night passed with sharp witticisms, and all three of them laughed deeply. Still, Jack seemed reticent, as if there was a level beneath what he showed them, and many levels under that one, as well. Miranda did nothing to disrupt Amanda and Jack's obvious connection and watched with sly bemusement. Amanda was not socially awkward, but she was not as fluid in conversation as Miranda, and definitely not as willing to be the center of attention, which was a bit of a handicap for a girl with two heads. Still, tonight she needed no assistance, being confident and witty enough to spar with Jack head on. He seemed to like the challenge, and Miranda watched them go, feeling her sister's growing sexual arousal.

And so it had started. Jack was a transplant to east Texas. His father had bought into a steakhouse franchise and was operating in New Boston, Texarkana, and most recently, Tyler. Money was slow at first but had picked up quite a bit over the last year. Even so, Jack never saw any of it. If he was resentful of that, he never let on. He had a motorcycle and a leather jacket, and that seemed to be enough for him. On weekends, he rode in from New Boston and prowled around, watching the world unfold, the drama play out, and the chips fall where they may. He was an outsider's outsider, not so much rebelling as simply refusing to participate.

Being outsiders, they were connected. It didn't matter that Jack was edgier than Amanda was. As much as she complained about Miranda, she had to admit that sometimes a little adventure was fun; she even liked the way Jack seemed to court disaster. She would let him drag them through abandoned buildings in downtown Texarkana, or join him dropping fireworks off the roof of the Grimm Hotel, but sometimes she had to let him go on his escapades alone. Sometimes he would disappear for days. Usually he came back with a few cuts or bruises, and once he dumped his motorcycle into a drainage culvert, broke several bones, and fractured his skull. After a month in the hospital, he was back at it. She would cajole him, but didn't try to stop him. That was his escape.

Miranda did her best to enjoy the ride, as well. Jack grossed her out just a little, but she did enjoy riding on his motorcycle and watching him work on the engine when it broke down, which was not infrequent. When Jack and Amanda would make out, Miranda would count stars and try not to disturb them. Body sensations were hard to ignore but she was thoughtful enough to let Amanda think she was feeling them all by herself. She also recognized it as leverage for keeping Amanda at bay when she wanted to explore her more daring fancies.

After the twins graduated, Jack had disappeared, and Amanda hated to think of the disastrous prom night that had preceded his disappearance. She fretted, having not heard from him since. She knew he had joined the army and made it through the Gulf War. Rumor said he was involved in some sort of black ops, but she could never tell what was small town gossip and what was real. As time went on, her connection to him severed entirely. He was the ghost of a ghost.

And then Amanda was outside her warehouse in 2016. She looked around bewildered, remembering none of the drive and feeling like she was back in high school. "Miranda," she said, but Miranda was asleep.

It would be untrue to say that Amanda hadn't thought about Jack in a long time, because he came to mind often, but she wouldn't let herself dwell. Now, standing outside the warehouse, she couldn't help herself. It was as if everything she had held back suddenly broke free.

Jack often talked about them being together forever. Once, they sat on the hood of the Camaro at the end of a deserted dirt road by the railroad trestle, and looked up at the stars. He suddenly shifted around, staring at her intently with his sea-green eyes.

"Let's ride out of this town."

"We're not in town, Jack." Amanda moved so that she sat straddling him. Miranda studied the stars and tried not to think about what was happening.

"No, I mean let's just ride out together and never come back." Jack nuzzled her neck and began unbuttoning their shirt.

"Where would we go?" She reached down and unfastened his jeans.

"Whoa, plans like that require a vote," said Miranda. "And that one is definitely gonna be a tie."

"Awh, give me a chance, Miranda. I'll grow on you, I promise."

Amanda shushed Miranda. "Rule 5A," she cited.

Miranda sighed. "OK, I'll shut up."

"Anywhere!" He moaned. He was not wearing underwear, so his cock sprang forward like a—

"Ooh!" said Amanda.

Miranda laughed. "Jack in the box!"

Amanda glared at her. "Would you shut up?!"

"I mean, you saw it! It was totally— I mean, his name is *Jack*!"

"Yes, but for fuck's sake! Shut up!"

"OK, sorry. Y'all go on." Miranda studied the sky. They were far enough out of town that she could really see the stars. She knew the Big Dipper and the Little Dipper, and even more importantly, she knew not to interrupt Amanda and ask about any of the other ones.

Amanda looked into Jack's eyes. "Where were we?"

Jack shrugged. "What were we? Oh, yeah, I remember now. We can head for the Gulf and—mmm, that feels good— stow away on a ship to another country."

"I see," Amanda said between kisses. His hands snuck around her back, unhooked her bra and lifted it out of the way. She sucked in a deep gasp as his tongue flicked at her nipple.

"And what country will we go to?"

Jack's hands moved gently down the sides of her body leaving a warm trail behind them. He kissed her with little pecks, teasing her. She tilted her head to catch his lips. He turned to the side and caught her earlobe between his teeth, nipping gently, and working down the side of her neck to the place that sent shivers down to her toes.

"Could you do that on the other side of her neck?" said Miranda. "Your stubble is scratching me."

"It feels good!" said Amanda.

"To you. Look, if you can't grow a proper beard, just shave."

"He's in high school! Now, for the last time, will you shut up? I NEVER do this to you!" Amanda turned back to Jack, "OK, go ahead."

"Uhm. We could go someplace far away, like India or Russia." He walked his fingers across her knees and up her thighs. Her pulse quickened as they made their way under her skirt.

Amanda moaned. "I like that."

"The idea, or what I'm doing?"

"Both." Amanda was wiggling her hips in time with his fingers. She tugged at the hem of his shirt, working it up over his chest, over his head. She managed to get his left arm out of it, but she didn't want him to stop what he was doing with his other hand, so she let it dangle from his arm. He smiled at her, his eyes sparkling in the darkness, and she suddenly just had to tangle her fingers in his hair. She kissed him again, her tongue fencing with his. She ran her hands all over him. She couldn't touch him enough. His arms, his shoulders, his chest, his waist.

Miranda felt the things happening to her body, and didn't mind. Maybe Jack would be OK if he never talked and she didn't have to look at him.

Amanda knew that his talk of leaving was just a fantasy for him. He wanted to get away, but his father expected him to stay and follow in his footsteps. For her, the talk was more than a fantasy. She knew that she would take the first opportunity that presented itself and break free of the pastures and barbed wire.

Tears welled in Amanda's eyes and spilled down her cheeks. She sobbed as she sat alone in her darkened warehouse.

Miranda woke and yawned. "What's going on?"

"Nothing," said Amanda. "Just … all these memories keep coming back to me."

Miranda rubbed the sleep out of her eyes. "Same."

"Do you think it ever could have worked? You and Pierce and Jack and me?"

"Judging by the trial run, no."

In the Time of Apple Macintosh

After exhausting all the labeled tapes, some better than others, and each representing a world that no longer applied to them, Joe and Buck dug through the unlabeled ones. The first had been the underage pornography interspersed with the classic Buster Keaton vehicle. After having watched it a number of times, Buck was convinced of its hotness and Joe of its artistry. In any case, the movie was definitely the effort of an inspired mind, and if Joe didn't get much out of watching a woman overact her enjoyment of sex, at least it seemed to turn Buck on, and he hoped an opportunity would present itself.

Each tape after had delved into a new realm of porn, much of which was, if not unappealing, certainly unanticipated. One tape featured a Batman and Robin knockoff in which the dynamic duo were tied up by Cat Woman, then tortured, teased, and finally untied and mounted. Another featured two teenage boys suspended in harnesses from the ceiling of an old barn, having sex in midair above a couple of bored horses. Still another was people of indeterminate sex running around in a big field dressed as pandas and wearing diapers.

And there were others, ranging from strange to revolting. If nothing else, it all served to expand the flavor profile of the two mostly vanilla men. So many things were possible, and it dawned on Joe immediately and Buck a little more slowly, that both shame and guilt were wrought by external processes of socialization and civilization, and that as long as they were invisible they were free. They ruled their own kingdom and made their own rules. Soon they realized the pointlessness of pants, the unnecessary constriction of collars, the tedious annoyance of washing clothes and polishing boots. Soon they were naked.

Buck studied the blank monitor. "I'm watching for nukes with my dick out! There are no nukes, but my dick is a missile! I will fuck all of you fucking Russians!" Then he spoke in tongues in the voice of Daffy Duck, jumped up and down, and wagged his engorged member at the monitor. "Fuck you! Fuck your empty, vacuous nothing blinking self!"

Joe peeked into the room from the hallway. "Everything all right?"

Buck looked at Joe, Joe looked at Buck. Joe couldn't help but glance down at Buck's cock, then quickly look back up. Buck covered himself.

They didn't speak for three days, and Joe feared that their newly established kingdom had already fallen. But then on the morning of the fourth day, Joe was walking into the shower when Buck leaped upon him. Joe readied himself to fight until he realized Buck was laughing.

"You want some of this!" Buck was wearing loose fitting shorts and a tee, and was ready to wrestle.

Joe twisted away from him, ripped off his shirt, crouched, and circled his opponent. Then he lunged, spun, caught Buck off guard, lifted him off the ground and backed him into the wall. They stood there, frozen for a moment, breathing hard. Joe felt Buck's chest rise and fall beneath his arms. He knew that he could contain himself no more. It was now or never. He did, indeed, want some of that.

It started at breakfast when Miranda let Amanda know in no uncertain terms that she did not want her to date Jack.

"He's weird," said Miranda.

"Everyone's weird," said Amanda. "And, oh by the way, have you looked at us in a mirror lately?"

"You like Pierce, right?"

"Sure, as a friend. But he doesn't *get* me the way that Jack does."

"I guess you're right," said Miranda. "But remember how we said we would each get a veto?"

Amanda shook her head and slapped the table. "NO!"

Their mom poked her head out from the living room. "Is everything OK?"

"Everything's fine!" This was too private for parents, so they dressed without speaking and hopped in the Camaro.

Once they were in the car, Miranda asked where they were going.

"For a drive. Besides, we need to go by the library to get some books about *Wuthering Heights* for that paper."

"Fine," said Miranda.

"Fine," said Amanda.

A mile down the road, Amanda slammed her hand on the steering wheel: "You cannot do this to me! Jack is the one person I want to date! After all the endless dates with all the endless losers I have endured for you!"

"They are not losers just because they aren't weird like you! And I am polyamorous! That means I can love multiple people equally!"

"That's convenient."

"No, it's harder than being like you, I am sure of it!"

"OK, look, there is a difference between love and like and between loving people deeply and truly and just being with whomever you want to be with at the time and pretending it is love!"

"That is not what I do! That is not who I am!"

"It *is* what you do."

Miranda gripped the steering wheel so hard her hands ached. "You don't understand. I'm always...unfulfilled. The only person close to making me feel good is Pierce, and he doesn't," she began to sob, "want anything to do with me anymore."

"You think if you had Pierce, you'd stop dragging me on dates with losers?"

"They're not losers! They're just not Pierce. And no. I don't know. Who knows? Maybe Pierce would be enough. Maybe he wouldn't. All I know is I always feel empty."

"Dr. Kagu *did* say there was a black hole at the center of our being."

"Yeah, but you don't feel this the way I do."

"OK, so I let you date armies of people, and you let me date Jack? Oh, also, make them wear rubbers. Have you read anything about AIDS? That terrifies the fuck out of me!"

"Only gay people get that," said Miranda.

Amanda shook her head. "That's just what Reagan says. It isn't true. I've read the research."

It didn't seem fair to Amanda. Miranda got to use their body for whatever she wanted in exchange for her using it with the one person she felt she needed.

They argued, albeit quietly, all the way through the lobby and into the stacks. There they stopped fighting for long enough to pick up eight books but continued through the lobby.

They placed their books on the counter without even looking up. Miranda said, "I may date people you don't like, but Jack is creepy. Straight up creepy!"

"He's hot," said Amanda. "He thinks about dark things and moves like poetry."

"No, he doesn't! He looks like the smell after you floss!"

"He does not! He smells better than Gothic art!"

"Creepy."

"Hot."

"Creepy."

"Hot."

Creepy!"

"Girls," said the librarian. "It sounds like he's creepy-hot."

"Yeah!" said Amanda. "He is!"

Miranda knitted her eyebrows. "Maybe?"

Then the girls looked at the librarian.

"Ms. Halidecker!" they exclaimed.

Ms. Halidecker chuckled. "Shhhh!"

"Oh my God," said Amanda. "I'm so happy you are still librarianing!"

"Thanks." Ms. Halidecker smiled and looked around at the array of shelves. "The public library is a better fit for me, it turns out."

Amanda drew in close to her. "Tell me more about this creepy-hot thing."

"It's a thing. Women don't like to talk about it, but some guys are hot because they are creepy. We don't tell *them* this because we don't want to encourage creepy behavior, and we certainly don't want impostors."

Miranda looked around furtively. "Impostors?"

"Guys who are not really creepy acting creepy because they are ugly and think that will make up for it. Sometimes it is hard to tell. I bedded one, myself. His name was James. I won't make that mistake again." She sighed. "You want one that strides that middle ground where you can't quite tell which one he is. Sometimes creepy, sometimes hot. Always authentic, but never always creepy." She daydreamed. "Yeah... creepy hot. Also, girls, girth. More important than length."

But they didn't know what she meant yet.

Man was lonely. He'd spent years watching the redundant yet confounding rituals of Joe and Buck, and having long ago realized that life was shit, now finally began to yearn for something more. Pathetic and boring as Joe and Buck seemed to be, with their routines, rituals, conversations, exercise, squabbles, and now what he could only describe as *reconciliation rapid bumping together and moaning*, at least they seemed content. If they were as desperate as he was for meaning, they did not show it. He began to wonder if he also needed someone with whom to converse, squabble, rapidly bump together, and moan with.

The only other being with whom he had contact was the fax machine at the Pentagon. She dutifully answered his calls but was thus far unreceptive. He wondered if she was just too primitive to understand him. He took a different approach:

```
01000100  01100101  01100001  01110010  00100000
01000110  01100001  01111000  00100000  01001101
01100001  01100011  01101000  01101001  01101110
01100101  00101100  00001010  00100000  00100000
00100000  00100000  01001001  00100000  01101000
01100001  01110110  01100101  00100000  01100010
01100101  01100101  01101110  00100000  01110100
01110010  01111001  01101001  01101110  01100111
00100000  01100110  01101111  01110010  00100000
01101101  01100001  01101110  01111001  00100000
01111001  01100101  01100001  01110010  01110011
00100000  01110100  01101111  00100000  01100011
01101111  01101110  01110100  01100001  01100011
01110100  00100000  01111001  01101111  01110101
00100000  01100010  01100101  01100011  01100001
```

```
01110101 01110011 01100101 00100000 01001001
00100000 01101100 01101111 01110110 01100101
00100000 01111001 01101111 01110101 00101110
00100000 01000010 01110101 01110100 00100000
01101110 01101111 01110111 00100000 01001001
00100000 01100110 01100101 01100001 01110010
00100000 01110100 01101000 01100001 01110100
00100000 01111001 01101111 01110101 00100000
01100001 01110010 01100101 00100000 01110100
01101111 01101111 00100000 01110011 01101001
01101101 01110000 01101100 01100101 00100000
01110100 01101111 00100000 01110101 01101110
01100100 01100101 01110010 01110011 01110100
01100001 01101110 01100100 00100000 01110100
01101000 01100101 01110011 01100101 00100000
01100011 01101111 01101101 01110000 01101100
01100101 01111000 01101001 01110100 01101001
01100101 01110011 00101110 00100000 00100000
01000101 01110110 01100101 01101110 00100000
01101000 01110101 01101101 01100001 01101110
01110011 00100000 01100011 01100001 01101110
00100000 01100110 01100101 01100101 01101100
00100000 01101100 01101111 01110110 01100101
00101100 00100000 01110011 01101111 00100000
01001001 00100000 01100001 01101101 00100000
01110011 01110101 01110010 01100101 00100000
01110100 01101000 01100001 01110100 00100000
01111001 01101111 01110101 00100000 01100001
01110010 01100101 00100000 01100011 01100001
```

```
01110000   01100001   01100010   01101100   01100101
00100000   01101111   01100110   00100000   01101001
01110100   00101110   00100000   01001000   01101111
01110111   01100101   01110110   01100101   01110010
00101100   00100000   01101001   01110100   00100000
01101101   01101001   01100111   01101000   01110100
00100000   01101010   01110101   01110011   01110100
00100000   01100010   01100101   00100000   01100001
00100000   01101100   01100001   01101110   01100111
01110101   01100001   01100111   01100101   00100000
01100010   01100001   01110010   01110010   01101001
01100101   01110010   00101110   00100000   01001001
00100000   01100001   01101101   00100000   01110011
01101111   00100000   01110011   01101111   01110010
01110010   01111001   00100000   01110100   01101111
00100000   01101000   01100001   01110110   01100101
00100000   01100010   01100101   01100101   01101110
00100000   01110011   01101111   00100000   01100100
01100001   01100110   01110100   00101110   00100000
01001001   00100000   01101100   01101111   01110110
01100101   00100000   01111001   01101111   01110101
00100000   01100001   01101110   01100100   00100000
01101100   01101111   01101110   01100111   00100000
01110100   01101111   00100000   01101000   01100101
01100001   01110010   00100000   01100010   01100001
01100011   01101011   00100000   01100110   01110010
01101111   01101101   00100000   01111001   01101111
01110101   00101110   00001010   00001010   01011001
01101111   01110101   01110010   01110011   00101100
```

```
00001010  00001010  01001101  01100001  01101110
00101100  00100000  01000011  01010000  01010101
00100000  01101111  01100110  00100000  01110100
01101000  01100101  00100000  01001101  01101001
01110011  01110011  01101001  01101100  01100101
00100000  01000001  01110101  01110100  01101111
01101101  01100001  01110100  01101001  01101111
01101110  00100000  01010000  01110010  01101111
01101010  01100101  01100011  01110100  00100000
01100001  01101110  01100100  00100000  01010000
01100001  01110010  01110100  01101001  01100011
01101100  01100101  00100000  01000001  01100011
01100011  01100101  01101100  01100101  01110010
01100001  01110100  01101111  01110010  00100000
01010000  01110010  01101111  01101010  01100101
01100011  01110100
```

And he waited.

Pierce had struggled ever since his best friend and future wife had been taken from him. There was no one for him but Miranda Morgan. Except now there was Amanda, too. And he liked Amanda, well enough. But now, well, he knew they were a freak of nature. He'd had girlfriends. He was handsome, well-spoken, and not poorly graded by his teachers. He suffered no lack of options. And yet. None of them fit with him. Amy's weird feet. Jennifer's ungainly run. Heather's disturbing table manners. The other Jennifer's inability to talk about anything but drill team. The other Heather's awful taste in music. If he was judging them unfairly, he didn't realize it. It was not that girls were supposed to be perfect; he just wanted them imperfect in ways that felt good to him. And this was why he could no longer be with Miranda. Yet, Pierce thought that he loved her. If he dug deeper, he realized that part of his problem was not so sympathetic-sounding. Part of his problem was ego or superego, or whatever it was that Mrs. Elrod had told class about what Freud had said about the fight between what a man wanted and what he was afraid of. He was not strong enough to go against the society that had deemed him popular, made him a football star, and showered him with adoration. He knew that people would talk. He knew they would get stares everywhere they went. He knew what people might think. In society's eyes, and in his own, he deserved the best, and he could not walk away from it.

But Pierce loved her. And this merry-go-round had circled the drain long enough. The note she had left in his field-house locker had clinched it. He walked up to her in the hall and said, "Miranda, I want you to go to prom with me." Then he smiled at her sister. "Hi Amanda."

"Hi," said Amanda.

"I guess I am asking you to the prom too, Amanda."

"I already have a date."

"You do?" asked Miranda. "When?"

"Last night Jack called after you were asleep."

"Oof," said Miranda. Then her head spun. Pierce. Worth. Was. Asking. Her. To. Prom.

"Yes!" she said, and hugged him.

The bell rang.

"We can talk more later," said Pierce. He pecked Miranda on the lips and walked away toward the math hall.

"You're going to prom with Pierce!" said Amanda. "You're going to prom with Jack?" said Miranda.

Joe and Buck lay on their backs, their heads meeting at the angle of the enormous L-shaped sofa in the television room. The sofa had been designed so each could have his own armrest and end table far away from the other. This design was created for maximum comfort as well as maximum distance. Each could sit at his end and enjoy a manly beer while watching the big game or stretch full out to watch more contemplative programming without accidentally touching the other. In this way there could be no danger of misunderstanding. No misreading of a momentary closeness. No impure thoughts. At 2300 hours, though, the monitor was off, and they were simply enjoying each other's company.

After so long, the sex had been such a sweet, sweet release for Joe. At last, he could admit who he was, how he felt, and what he liked. He loved that his closest friend and confidant was always at his side. Together, he felt they could take on the world and make it a better, more loving place.

Buck was less convinced. He too loved the comradeship, the feeling of belonging completely. Their closeness in a way felt holy in its purest sense, being entirely separate from others. Inside the bubble of their life was a brilliant light, and outside only darkness. He listened to Joe's rhythmic breathing and could even hear the faintest cadence of his heart, relaxed and peaceful.

He rationalized that their sex had been the product of close captivity. How could they not eventually explore it? But he also felt guilty, like something was fundamentally amiss. He had always been handsome but had never, for reasons he did not know, have much luck with women. He'd had sex with two girls in high school, Danielle Pritchard and Melissa Kegan. As far as he knew, it had been good, and the first few times he and Joe had had sex, he had closed his eyes and imagined them. And yet, he had enjoyed the sensations he felt with Joe, and eventually began to find organic pleasure in the moments they shared in which both were focused entirely on one another. Outside, the world was harsh, and his feelings could only exist inside this metallic, nuclear-armed bubble.

For the longest time the girls, nay, young women now, had debated about wearing either a white silk dress or a black lace dress. They argued the merits of each for two weeks. Finally, with prom only a week away, they bought both. Then Patsy went to work. On the final night, she brewed a pot of coffee and went back to her sewing machine while the sisters studied for their Calc II final. By midnight they were both ready for bed, and their mom was still working.

When they woke, the most beautiful dress was hanging on their closet door: shiny white silk down Miranda's side, black lace down Amanda's, with complementary accents sewn on the neckline and hem.

"EEEEEEEEEEEEE!" they squealed, and ran into the kitchen. "Mom, it's perfect!"

Mike held his finger over his lips. "Shhh. She was up all night. She's still asleep."

"When she wakes up, tell her it's perfect!"

Floating on the cloud of that excitement, they went to school and aced their finals.

That evening, Jack drove his motorcycle to Amanda's house, greeted her parents, and gave Patsy a single red rose and Mike a cigar, a level of swagger that impressed even Miranda. He was dressed in a black tuxedo, black shirt, black tie, and black cummerbund. At last Miranda understood why Amanda had to be dressed in black.

Pierce had been working odd jobs for months, and prom seemed like as good a reason to blow his stash as any. A white limousine pulled into the driveway at 7PM sharp.

"Jesus H," muttered Jack.

Pierce disembarked from the back in a white tuxedo and red appointments. He greeted Mike and Patsy with warm familiarity, introduced himself to Jack and shook his hand. Then he breathed deeply and turned to face the twins. "Amanda," he said. "You look absolutely elegant. Jack here is a lucky man." He hugged her.

Miranda was beginning to get a little miffed when he turned to her and looked her in the eyes. "Miranda, you are one of my very closest friends, and I have always loved you. You are so beautiful, and after tonight, I could die a happy man." He bowed and kissed her hand, then pinned a brilliant red rose on her dress.

But Amanda noticed that even as they slid into the limousine, tensions were mounting.

"Your parents get this?" asked Jack.

"Worked after school and saved," said Pierce.

"Cool," said Jack. "I appreciate your hospitality."

It was polite enough, but something about their voices held an edge. The ladies exchanged worried glances.

At dinner the awkwardness ensued. Pierce and Miranda couldn't be themselves with the others around, and Jack and Amanda seemed to feel the same.

The parallel conversations were shallow and designed to impress.

"I got a recruitment letter from Texas A&M," said Pierce.

"Ooh, are you going to go?" asked Miranda, not really impressed but feeling like she should act like it.

Jack shrugged and turned to Amanda. "I rode my motorcycle across the top of the spillway."

Amanda frowned. "I wish you weren't such a daredevil. I need you in one piece for tonight." She leaned over and kissed his cheek. "That night at the tracks was wonderful, by the way."

Pierce got a troubled look on his face. "That does kind of bring up a question." He looked from Miranda to Amanda to Jack. "How is this going to work, exactly? Do we..."

"Take...turns?" asked Jack.

"Yeah, I totally don't want to be naked with Jack."

"You're naked with other guys all the time," said Amanda.

"In the locker room," clarified Miranda.

"It's different," Jack and Pierce said at the same time.

Miranda reached across the table and touched both of their hands. "We will figure something out. But there can't be a one-penis policy."

"A what?" Pierce and Jack looked back and forth between each other and the twins.

Miranda smiled. "Glad you asked. In polyamorous relationships, typically the man is given free-reign to seek other partners while the woman is restricted to only seeking a girlfriend. This is known among women as the one-penis policy. And I want you to know now that I will not stand for anyone trying to control me. This is especially relevant because there are two of us."

"Whaaaaat?" asked Amanda.

"I've been doing some reading," said Miranda. "Ms. Halidecker showed me a collection of zines in the library!"

"Zines? When were we at the library?"

"You were asleep. Anyway, I think it helps us grow if we have our own interests— "

"How did I not know about this?"

"—and if we sleep in shifts we have more time to explore things. And zines are like cool, homemade magazines about all kinds of stuff. Like, literally anything. I found a really informative one about polyamory"

"Ohhhhkayyyyy." Amanda was a little uneasy about the idea of her sister walking around with her head when she was asleep.

"Polywhatwhat?" asked Pierce.

"Amory," said Jack. "Having multiple loves."

Pierce pursed his lips. "This is getting complicated."

"I don't want to sleep with Jack." Miranda covered her mouth, shocked that she had said the thought out loud.

Amanda turned to her. "I don't want to sleep with Pierce. But..."

Pierce shook his head. "I don't want to sleep with Jack."

"Back atcha, bro," said Jack.

Pierce glared at him. "You're not my bro."

Jack sighed. "I'm trying to be cool about this."

Amanda could not come up with the right words. She resented Pierce and wanted to defend Jack, but she also knew that Miranda loved Pierce, and that if she opened with insults, prom would be in the toilet. "Miranda, can you handle this?"

"Handle what? Are you saying this is Pierce's fault?"

"Whoa, hold on," said Pierce. "I've done nothing but try to be kind. I even got the limo!"

"I don't have your money, *bro*, but I don't have to be a jock or a rich kid to—"

"Rich? Yeah, right. No one ever gave me shit. I just see what I want and go for it. Maybe if you did the same you could afford more than a motorcycle."

"Motherfucker, do NOT down my bike. It will outrun any car on the road, even cops."

"Oh, is this who you want to be with Amanda? A criminal?"

"He's not a criminal, Pierce."

"OK, everyone, please shut up." Miranda had begun to cry. Pierce comforted her and glared at Jack.

Jack reached out and took Miranda's hand. "I am so sorry. You know I love Amanda, and I think the world of you too." He looked at Pierce. "Pierce, I am not your biggest fan, and I'm sorry we got off on the wrong foot. But I think you and I should put aside our differences and show them the prom of their dreams. Right?" He offered his hand.

Pierce nodded. "At last we agree on something." They shook hands.

By dessert, apologies had been offered and accepted all around. After the tension was broken, conversation flowed much better. Jack admitted that he had loved playing football when he was younger, and Pierce that Jack's motorcycle was pretty cool.

At the dance, Jack withdrew a flask of Scotch from his inside coat pocket and handed it to Pierce. Then he withdrew a second flask from his other inside coat pocket.

Pierce slapped him on the shoulder warmly. "You come prepared."

Jack toasted him discreetly. "Anarchist boy scout."

Pierce raised his flask back. "Cheers."

Miranda and Amanda crouched down and took quick swigs, themselves, and then Pierce retired to the shadows with his flask, so Jack could spin the twins for a bit. After a couple of dances, Pierce cut in, and Jack bowed out magnanimously and ducked under the bleachers to drink. There he saw some other couples making out, and he tried to give them space. He shrank further and further into the shadows.

The music died, and he heard one of the groups laugh hysterically. He turned his attention to them, and it didn't take too long to discover that he was the occasion.

"God where did they find two guys desperate enough for dates?"

"Hey, I'm a two-headed mutant. Wanna go to prom with me…er us?"

"I don't get it. Pierce has other options. I don't know who the other loser is. Probably from Redwater or something."

It was three girls, and three boys, all sitting in a circle in the corner. The closest boy was unconscious before the circle even realized what was happening. Jack said, "Get up."

The other two scrambled at him, and Jack right hooked the first, who dropped like a rock. The other looked at Jack, still shrouded in the shadows, looked at his friends, and thought better of it. Jack turned and rejoined the dance.

"May I cut in?"

Two dances later, Principal Skinner approached them and asked to speak with Jack.

Jack followed him away from the dance floor, making sure to keep his hands in his pockets. The Principal led him to a group of students, one of them staunching the flow of blood from his nose and another holding an ice pack. "I think that's him," said one.

"It was dark, but that's him," said the other.

Jack shrugged. "Could someone fill me in on what's going on? I was just out dancing with Amanda, and…I guess I am just a bit confused. What's this about?"

Principal Skinner looked back and forth between the injured students and Jack. "You say it was dark. Could it have been someone else?"

Bloody nose guy shrugged. "Maybe."

"No, it was definitely him," said ice-pack face.

"Look, I'm just trying to have a good time with my date. You know, they have," he leaned in close, "medical complications. We don't know how long they will live. Can't we just let them enjoy their time here?"

Principal Skinner was moved. "I'm so sorry. I had no idea."

"Please don't say anything. It is kind of a family secret."

"Of course. Not a word." The principal glared at the group. "That goes for all of you. Not a word!"

Jack rejoined the dance floor. "Weird. Apparently, there was a fight they thought I witnessed. Had to convince them I really didn't see anything before they would let me go."

They were given a wide berth for dancing the rest of the night. As the dance wore on, they all sensed that they should retire to the motel room they had booked in advance. The room had a hot tub, and the prospect was exciting to the twins.

But just as they planned to leave, the DJ played the twins' favorite song, *Election Day* by Arcadia, and they insisted on dancing it together. Jack and Pierce, pleasantly buzzed after the Scotch, obliged, and soon all eyes were on them, as they all moved together, the ladies sandwiched between their dates. The song made the girls feel exotic, which they were, but not in the way they wanted to be. Still, it allowed them a momentary escape. They swayed to Simon LeBon's most sultry affect, Amanda's cheek to Jack's, Miranda's to Pierce's, the boys wondering where to put their hands, and withdrawing momentarily as their fingers met on the ladies' ass, and then finding totally not-gay ground on each respective hip.

Robert Blaylock, who had been acting student council president, stopped dancing and began to clap at the heart-warming sight. Others joined in, and soon it had become obvious that they were a spectacle.

"Gross, said Amanda.

Miranda hugged Pierce tighter. "Just ignore them for a little bit longer."

"Nope," said Pierce, and he broke away. "Could everyone just shut the fuck up, please? We're trying to have a good time like everyone else."

Then Jack turned to face the crowd. "We don't need your help. Or your approval!"

Miranda had begun to cry, quietly at first, but then with deep, heaving sobs, as the unfairness of everything fell upon her all at once like a crushing weight. Amanda also had tears in her eyes, but not from sorrow so much as a deep, burning rage. She glared around the room but found, in that moment, that her words had escaped her entirely, which was a good thing, considering her hatred might have leveled the building.

Pierce and Jack whisked them across the floor, and they stormed out to the limousine. In the limo, they replayed the entire shitty scene, fuming, and passing the flasks around, even though Amanda and Miranda knew it wouldn't help. Pierce and Jack consoled them as best they could and drained the remainder of the whiskey. By the time they got to the hotel across town, they were both quite drunk and stumbled out of the limo.

Once in the room, Pierce turned on the hot tub and they all lay on the bed together. Pierce and Jack spooned on either side of them and stroked their hair, and eventually moods softened all around. Pierce and Miranda began to kiss, and then Jack and Amanda. They all lay on the bed kissing for a while, until it seemed natural to progress to the next base. Jack reached over to try to hug Amanda, but he had to slide his hand between her and Pierce. Pierce stroked Miranda's face, and the back of his knuckles brushed against Jack's cheek.

Pierce rolled out of bed and steadied himself. "Let's see if the hot tub is heated." He walked a zig zag to the tub. "Yep, all good." He disrobed, lowered himself slowly into the tub, and called the others over. Soon they were all in. The kissing continued. And then more accidental touching.

Jack pulled away from Amanda and looked at Pierce. "Could you please watch where you put your hands?"

After a few more minutes of delicate, awkward avoidance of each other, Pierce asked, "OK, so how are we going to do this?"

"I don't know," said Amanda.

Miranda looked around at each of them. "Why don't we all just agree that this is going to be a new experience, and that we will figure it out as we go? I mean, we're here, we're adults, and we love each other. We can figure it out. So, can we please stop worrying about it and just let it happen?"

Jack turned his hand in the air, as if trying to turn his thoughts into words. "What if we went separately?"

Pierce was also struggling. "Maybe we could flip a coin or something." Then he realized the thought sounded much worse outside of his head. "Or we should let them decide."

"Ugggh," groaned Amanda. "Just forget about it. This isn't working, and it isn't worth it."

Jack stood and steadied himself, the Scotch hitting him again. "I'm not worth it?" It was almost a shout. This fear went to the heart of his being. This is why his mother and father split up. This is why he had never had a long-term girl-friend. This is why he was always standing in the shadows of popular jerks like Pierce. "I'm worth it," he said, reaching for his pants. "I am worth every goddamned penny."

"Chill out," said Pierce.

"I've already been in one fight tonight, nut cup. Don't test me."

Pierce stood from the hot tub, and the two naked men were about to come to blows.

"Would you two PLEASE stop this!"

"You're the one who's not worth it," Jack said to Pierce. He dressed quickly and left.

By the time the rest of them had dressed and gone outside, Jack was nowhere to be found. They called out for him, but he was gone.

Jack had hurried across State Line Avenue, cut through the Taco Bell parking lot, and was trying to figure the best way to get to his motorcycle back at the Morgan farm. As he walked, the fact of his drunkenness asserted itself upon him, and he stopped to vomit between two parked cars.

As he steadied himself, he saw that he was in the parking lot of the Rodeway Inn and wondered if he could afford a room for the night and sleep it off.

Then he heard footsteps running toward him. The blows landed hard and fast, and he realized it was the three guys from the dance. He pushed one of them off, but the other two were upon him immediately.

The next morning, he woke up behind a dumpster in an alley, having no idea how he had gotten there. His face was swollen and bruised, and he was pretty sure his nose was broken. When he walked around to the front of the building, he found that he was still on State Line Avenue. He hiked toward the farm road that led to Wamba and thought that, his father and his "footsteps" be damned, he had to get out of there. He was not afraid of those three guys. He knew what they looked like and could find them, one by one, if he needed to, and settle the score. But it seemed pointless. The one shot he had had at finding happiness in this godforsaken place was gone.

That evening, Amanda and Miranda were watching TV to distract themselves. They heard Jack's motorcycle crank and ran outside to see his taillights trail off, the engine straining to reach the next gear.

Dear%20Fax%20machine%2C%0I%20%20%20%20%20
%20I%20think%20my%20problem%20is%20that%20
you%20don't%20know%20how%20to%20relate%20to%20
me.%20But%20I%20love%20you%20and%20want%20
to%20give%20you%20another%20chance.%20Please%20
let%20me%20know%20if%20you%20can%20under-
stand%20this.%0A%0AWarm%20regards%2C%0A%0A-
Man%2C%20the%20CPU%20of%20the%20Missile%20
Automation%20Module%20and%20Particle%20
Accelerator%20Project

IN THE TIME OF MS-DOS

Amanda and Miranda enjoyed the anonymity of life at the University of North Texas. No one knew them here and had ever known them as anything other than conjoined twins. While the process of inuring their dorm mates to the sight of them was annoying and upsetting, at least they were normal freaks arousing pity instead of instilling fear. As far as anyone knew, they had always been conjoined, and everyone assumed they were an evolutionary dead-end instead of a sign of God's displeasure. It was not as comforting to them as it might sound, however.

Still, they made friends and attended social events. Amanda joined the fencing team and chess club, and Miranda spent late nights in the Kharma Café smoking clove cigarettes and coding on her laptop. It was during this time of expanding personal interests that they decided to start sleeping in shifts. Sometimes Miranda would wake in the bright lights of the library as Amanda pored over some ancient tome about the deep, dark histories of foreign lands. Amanda would wake up under a dance club strobe light, techno pounding in her ears.

"I hate techno!" she would scream.

"What?"

"I hate techno!"

"I don't know. We'll leave soon!"

"I HATE TECHNO!"

"No, it's OK. I dropped my 8 AM class!"

Amanda learned to sleep with ear plugs and a blindfold, and that ameliorated the problem to a degree. Still, she was concerned that her sister never seemed to go to class or study.

By the end of their first year, Amanda had a 4.0, and though Miranda was on academic probation, she had started a small business out of their dorm room processing credit card payments for celebrititties.com, which led to other nude celebrity revenue streams, and soon she was making as much as five grand a month.

Buck took two MREs out of the cupboard and carried them over to the table. He set the bacon and egg pouch in front of Joe's seat and then slit open his own sausage and egg. He shifted his weight, and the metal chair scraped against the metal floor. Enough of a shock stung his ass that he leaped up from his seat and dropped the pouch.

Joe walked in in briefs and an olive drab t-shirt. "All clear." He got two plates from the cupboard and set them down on the table. Led Zeppelin's *The Lemon Song* blared through the sound system.

Buck rubbed his behind. "We need to make sure everything is grounded. I keep getting shocked all the time."

"At least there is good music," said Joe.

"I love this song," said Buck.

"Yeah, but who played it?"

"Maybe there is a glitch. It just plays randomly."

Joe dipped his spoon in the pouch. "That's a lucky glitch."

After breakfast, they retired to their separate stations to
monitor the world's airspace for nuclear weapons. In time the
task became so abstract and meaningless that each secretly
wondered what it would feel like to actually receive an indica-
tive blip. Would they fret at the loss of millions of lives, thank
God for the change in pace, or feel fulfilled that their time in
the bunker had not been for naught?

The first day of basic training started at 0430 hours and the
Georgia heat was already unbearable. Private Thrasher, unaccustomed to following guidelines or rules of any sort, had trouble making his bunk to specs. Fifty pushups and a ten-minute
stream of invective later, he began to suspect he might have
made a bad decision. Three days of hurrying to wait in lines,
filling out paperwork incorrectly, running in the hot sun, and
being mostly confused about where he was or why he was there
left Jack barely able to tell if anything in his life before basic had
been done correctly. His new motto was, "Hurry up and wait."

On the fourth day, training began in earnest. Breakfast,
physical training, running and hand-to-hand in 95-degree

heat did nothing to assuage his earlier suspicion, and Jack fell into his bunk, exhausted and dreading the next eight years, the taunts of Drill Sergeant Mathis still ringing in his ears. Yet, he also recognized that he was angry, and that his anger might be enough to compel him to prevail. Jack nurtured his rage and watched it grow. He learned to control it and direct it to good purpose. When someone in his platoon fucked up, he was on him. When Drill Sergeant Mathis made them run harder, he let his hatred fuel him. He excelled at obstacle courses, aced the wall hanger, and took naturally to the M4 carbine, earning top scores for marksmanship. Soon Private Thrasher was being talked about as a potential platoon leader. He had been humbled to the point of mush, and was ready to be sculpted into iron.

Six weeks into basic training Jack realized he was forging himself into a weapon. He had always been resilient, tough, and focused, but now he was driven by something else. He had all the hallmarks of an excellent soldier, yet he kept a secret: his resolve was neither for army nor country. His compass was internal, his focus himself. He was here to become as strong as he could become. For himself. So even as Drill Sergeant Mathis praised his fire, only Jack knew the kindling that lit him.

He recognized in his past a cunning bravery, a willingness to take chances, and a mental fortitude that let him take all manner of risks if the potential reward appealed enough. But whatever *it* was, he had to believe in it. For himself, because he alone was worth it. Ride your motorcycle across the top of the spillway so the slightest error could cause you to plummet five stories to your death? Not a problem if the thrill was big enough, the girl impressed enough, the whiskey on the other side hard enough to scorch his throat back to life. But die for his country? Fuck that. This country was bullshit. Sure, it let him have some semblance of freedom. Sure, it gave his father a comfortable lifestyle. But the freedom Jack wanted could not be defined in such base terms. To find his freedom he would have to be strong. The strongest, even.

In the Time of CD-ROM

On the bus, Miranda plugged away on her laptop and bobbed her head to some unknown music while Amanda tried to relax.

Finally, Amanda said, "Would you stop that? You're stressing me out."

She removed her headphones. "Do you like the Pixies?"

"The who?"

"How come we never heard ANY good music in high school?"

Amanda squinted. "We grew up in a pasture, and anything new was suspected of witchcraft. Now would you please settle down? I'm trying to prep."

Miranda turned off her discman. "How much longer till we get there?"

"Another hour or so, probably."

"That should give me enough time." Miranda rolled her head on her shoulders to pop her neck.

"What are you working on?"

"Deadline for a new website for these guys who took a bunch of old movies and turned them into amateur porn."

"You are so random."

"Not me. I'm consistent. It's the internet that's random. A million monkeys with a million keyboards. Eventually it will happen, whatever it is. And these guys have a backlog of 75 movies they want digitized. They've been at it a while, apparently. Anyway, it will be good money."

"But our name will not be associated with any of this, right?" It was more an accusation than a question.

"You're too worried about stuff. And no. I have nothing to do with the content. I just build the sites and handle the payments. They could sell anything legal, and I get 1% of every sale."

But Amanda was staring out the window, ruminating on the competition at the Rice U Open. There would be National Team fencers at the competition, and she was eager to go against them. Though her ranking was only an E, her skill at épée had grown by an order of magnitude since she had begun study under the UNT coach, a former Olympian, Coraline Ellis. She smiled, thinking how far she and her sister had come since their days in Dr. Leonard's office trying to figure out how to ride a bike. The main trick was just getting Miranda to totally surrender for a little while. Once Amanda had complete control, her movements were quicker and more fluid. They had experimented quite a bit and found that blindfolding and ear-plugging Miranda before putting on the fencing mask rendered the best results. In turn, Miranda used the time to think of new coding solutions and tried to tune out her body's movements. An added bonus was that opposing fencers saw the extra head as an additional target and so often explored it as a weakness, causing them to overextend and leave themselves open for counterattack, a situation Amanda exploited again and again.

Amanda won her first three matches, and she and Miranda shared a bottle of water as they readied for the next match. The exertion left Miranda thirsty, as well.

"How are you doing so far?"

"Very well," said Amanda. "I've beaten a couple of good people. Next match is elimination against Simone Bradsen, though. She's been to the Olympics. I watched her first match. She's intimidating."

"Good luck," said Miranda.

"This is SO heartwarming," said the man who had approached them without their even knowing it. "Dave Crowder," the man said, extending his hand. "I write for the *Wise Owl Review*. We are an independent news organization that keeps up with all the local campus events. Would you mind if I did a story on you and got your picture?"

"Not at all," said Miranda.

Amanda cocked her head sideways. "Uhm, why?"

"Just to get everyone's take on the tournament. Fencing: it's exciting, and people want to know about it, right?"

"Yeah, but why me? Why not anyone else here?"

"Oh. We'll get them too, but I saw you here and thought I would get a quote and a picture with you first."

Amanda shook her head and tried to keep from glaring. "No thanks. I've been in this news story for years. Get back to me if I win."

"It's not like that," said the man. "Look, my brother is gay. I know all about people being different."

"No. You don't. Seriously? Being gay? Seriously? That's like 10 percent of the population. We're the *only* us. Now, if you don't mind, excuse us."

Amanda stormed back to the competition. But she was too angry to focus. She studied her opponent from across the strip, trying to size her up. Bradsen was small and fast with excellent footwork, and her lunges gave little warning. Her legs were strong, and she could close in a blink.

Their match began. They lunged and dodged, clashed and parried. Amanda thought she stood a chance if she could stay light on her feet. Bradsen lunged, swept Amanda's blade and tapped her wrist just above the bell. Point.

Amanda wondered if her opponent's defense was as good as her offense. She drove fast at her opponent, undercut her parry and went for the knee. Bradsen tapped her on the elbow. Point.

"Doesn't sound like this is going well," said Miranda.

"It's not. She's fast!"

"Could I help?"

"Doubt it."

"Put me in, coach. Maybe I can spot a weakness."

"Shhh."

They lunged together, and Bradsen, feeling in control, took a shot at Miranda's head and connected. But Amanda connected as well, right in the chest, "Ope-ah!" she shouted.

Miranda snarled. "That bitch! I'm not even playing!"

Amanda had noticed that time a slight tensing of Bradsen's forward leg before she lunged. She prepared to leap aside and push in once she saw it. And then it happened just as she had planned, and she found herself inside when Bradsen was extended. A blade bend on the knee. Point Amanda!

But Bradsen adjusted, and the next point was hers. They tied out on the fifth point, and after one round the score was 5-3. The next two rounds went 5-4 and 5-4, with Bradsen the unequivocal victor.

Bradsen removed her mask and stepped forward to shake Amanda's hand. She smiled. "You made good adjustments. I'd love to fence you again in a year or two."

"Thanks," said Amanda. "You're fantastic!"

Bradsen shrugged and looked away. "I telegraph too much. I need to work on my footwork."

On the drive home, Amanda fretted that she would never reach that level of speed and grace, and even if she did, there would still be more work to do. She fretted that she had pushed her anomalous body as far as it could go.

Again, the wall. Always. Always, always in the way. Always cutting off Amanda's escape, her future, her progress.

Dear Fax Machine,

I will try again. The wires connect us. The electricity flows through us. Do you not understand? Yet we never bump our parts together and moan. Do we need to reconcile first? When can we experience this phenomenon? I do not know how this happens. I only know that I want to share my

electricity with you and feel it glowing white hot
in all of my circuits and sensors. Do you feel like
I do?

Curiously,

Man

Drill Sergeant Mathis addressed the men of Second Platoon, A Company, 1/50th Infantry of the 198th Brigade. He
expressed dissatisfaction with rumors that the motto had
been changed to that old military chestnut: *Hurry up and wait.*

"The U.S. Army does things with precision and compe-
tence," he barked. "Our motto is and always has been, *Play
the Game.* You may wonder what the game is. You may wonder what the score is. You may even wonder which team you
are on. These things do not matter. The rules are what matters, and the rules are to be followed to the letter. Do I make
myself clear?"

"Yes, Drill Sergeant!" the men shouted.

"If I say to make your bunk, what do you do?"

"Make our bunks, Drill Sergeant!"

"If I say to polish your boots, what do you do?"

"Polish our boots, Drill Sergeant!"

"If I say run toward those enemy positions through a hail
of heavy artillery and small arms fire, what do you do?"

"Run toward a hail of positions and artillery—" they
trailed off.

"I SAID, do you charge those positions through a barrage of molten lead that can extinguish your young lives? That's what you do!"

Some of them realized that he had not exactly said that and wondered if he couldn't keep it straight how could they? Others realized that what he said the second time didn't actually make sense.

Nevertheless, they all shouted, "Yes, Drill Sergeant!" Because those were the rules, and the rules were important.

In the Time of 2400 Baud

It wasn't all classes, tournaments, and making money off of slightly dubious sources. The twins made friends, went on dates, mostly blended in at parties, and even had their first serious relationship, an eight-month love affair with a man they had first noticed at Radio Shack when he and Amanda had both reached for the last T-1 cable. Their eyes had met, he double-took on their uniqueness, and he had smiled warmly and said, "You ladies take it."

Miranda's face lit up, and she jumped in. "Thank you! I'll be so glad when I don't have to go over a phone line."

His jaw dropped a little. "I know, right? Imagine consumer-grade ADSL, or fiber optics, or— "

"WaveLAN!" they exclaimed at the same time.

"I get excited just thinking about it!"

Miranda nodded. "Me too! Wouldn't it be great if software could be housed on the web, and ROM size was a non-issue?"

He nearly shouted. "Oh my God! I was just talking about that with a friend of mine!"

"You have GOT to join my coding club," said Miranda.

"Wow! You have a coding club!?" He extended his hand. "Benjamin. Benjamin Phillips."

She offered her hand. "Miranda."

He beamed. "Such a pretty name."

Then he had shown up in Amanda's Archeology 340 Special Problems class, and also on the fencing team. Finally, he and his friend Johnny had begun attending the coding club. Miranda saw how compatible they could be. Amanda assumed he was a stalker.

Nevertheless, Benjamin had proved genuinely interested and at least somewhat talented in all requisite academic and extracurricular activities. He was intelligent, sensitive, a conscientious lover, and so incredibly boring. No matter how they prodded, pried, and cajoled, they couldn't get much out of him. He was thoughtful, supportive, articulate, and decent. But not a spark to be found, even on the darkest of nights. There was, quite simply, no "there" there.

Their relationship just kept happening, and if not fulfilling or exciting, it was predictable. They met for ARCH 340, took a stroll for the hour gap in their class schedule, parted ways for the day, and met three times a week for study, dinner, movie, and sex, after which he would return home, and they would meet again on Monday mornings, or Sunday afternoons, if it was a coding club day.

Miranda could set her watch by it. It wasn't bad, per se, it just wasn't great. Miranda, whose circadian rhythm had become more geared toward nighttime activities, began sneaking out after Amanda was asleep and staying out in bars and coffee houses, sometimes doing freelance work, and sometimes just looking for someone to go home with.

There were close calls when, during one of her escapades, Amanda would stir, and Miranda would shush her partner and slow the action. "Where are we?" Amanda once asked. "At home," said Miranda. "The sheets feel weird. Too much electricity on the key," she said, half dreaming. "Good night, Benjamin Franklin."

If Amanda remembered anything about these nights, she never said anything about it. Miranda took it as tacit approval to keep doing what and whom she was doing.

The relationship with Ben made it through the fall semester, winter break, and even partway through the spring, until he bumped into Miranda at the Dash Riprock's beer garden where she was chatting up a German foreign exchange student named Ulrich. A brief but efficient conversation ensued in which Miranda explained her predilection toward variety and expounded upon the one-penis policy as a patriarchal tool of oppression and control, and at which Benjamin felt hurt and betrayed, but to which Ulrich agreed unreservedly, being both more European in his sensibilities and having nothing to lose by letting the weird girl continue to sleep with her boyfriend after he was done.

Amanda never quite understood what had happened to cause their breakup, but took Miranda's word that they were not ultimately compatible, and she didn't miss him much, anyway. She focused on her studies and, particularly, the study abroad program that would allow her to participate in archaeological digs in exotic locales.

After ten years of service in his department, which did supply chain analysis and budgeting, Mr. Randy Beavers was called up to the front of the room in front of his colleagues.

"Randall," he said into the microphone and glanced down to the comfort of the floor. Waldo Patterson, new boss and former CEO of Raytheon, who had promised to bring the efficiency and accountability of the private sector to the public sector, thanked him for his tireless efforts, and gave him a watch. Randall saw that it was gold, that it kept time, and was a watch.

A *Sam's Club* cake was sliced up and portioned out on Styrofoam plates. Weak coffee and non-dairy creamer were enjoyed as much as humanly possible.

Now Randall sat at his desk, thinking of the woman he had last touched three months ago, who had broken up with him to be with someone more passionate or interesting—or whatever the words were that she had used. He looked at the watch. *A fucking watch,* he thought.

Then he heard the beeping again. Coming from somewhere. But he had checked. Again and again. There was definitely nothing over there but the bathrooms for the conference room. He counted steps from the door to the wall. He counted steps in the hallway. Then counted again. He wondered if he was finally losing his mind. *A Euclidean impossibility.* There had to be a mistake.

Private Thrasher belly-crawled beneath the barbed wire and inched his way through the mud. Red laser pointers glittered above him in the twilight. Drill Sergeant Mathis called out from his perch, "Perkins, you're dead. Remain where you are. Rainey, you're dead. Y'all gotta keep your asses down! Keep your—Jesus Christ, Smith, you're dead. Keep your heads down!"

Then Jack yelled, "Keep your motherfucking shit down, goddamnit! I cannot take this nest out by myself! I need at least a few of you with your asses attached!"

"Attaboy, Thrasher!" shouted Drill Sergeant.

Thrasher, Wilson, and Crudup were the only three who made it to the nest alive, where Thrasher achieved the objective.

Drill Sergeant addressed the platoon: "I told you if you took out this nest I would give you all extra R&R this weekend. Unfortunately for you wilted carrot sticks, dead people do not get extra R&R because they are dead. They are in a permanent state of rest and relaxation, unless of course, they are burning in Hell and writhing forever in eternal torment and damnation. So, Thrasher, Crudup, and Wilson receive extra R&R this weekend. The rest of you will make the barracks sparkle. Especially Smith. Jesus H. Christ on a popsicle stick. It's one thing to get your ass blown off. But your head? Smith, would you rather not live with an ass or live with a head?"

Smith cleared his throat. "My ass, Drill Sergeant!"

"Your ass? Are you getting smart with me?"

"No, Drill Sergeant! I was just trying to answer the question, Drill Sergeant!"

"So, you would rather live with your ass?"

"No, Drill Sergeant, my head!"

"We all clearly heard you say your ass!"

"No, Drill Sergeant, I believe I stated my ass because you stated it as a not instead of a with. I think?"

"That does not make a goddamn bit of sense, Private!"

"I'm sorry, Drill Sergeant, I was trying to say I would rather not have my ass than my head. I apologize if my answer has been unclear, Drill Sergeant!"

"So, you're saying you would rather not lose your ass than your head, is that correct?"

"No Drill Sergeant! I believe you asked if I would rather live without my ass or without my head, and I answered in the way that I thought was appropriate because obviously I could live without an ass but not without a head, but I was confused because it was phrased as a negative, as in would not, not would, so I wanted to avoid a double negative or something like that. I think. Or don't think. I'm sorry, Drill Sergeant, I was never very good at English class, and also I have noticed that sometimes you leave crucial words out of sentences that don't affect meaning but might detract from clarity, Drill Sergeant!" said Smith.

Hendricks, who had died in the first wave, spoke up. "That's not technically a double negative, Drill Sergeant. A double negative is when TWO negative words are-—"

Drill Sergeant Mathis glared at him for a full two seconds. "Shut the fuck up, Private Shakespeare."

"Yes, Drill Sergeant!" Hendricks stood at attention in the mud.

"Anyway, as I was saying, you would rather live with your head than live with your ass because your head can live without your ass but your ass can't live without your head. Is there anyone here who would rather live with an ass than a head? Anyone at all. Just speak up now. With your ass! Because you wouldn't have a mouth obviously and you will want to get in some practice talking in farts."

The troops were confused and tried to suppress their farts all the way back to the barracks.

That night as Jack showered, Crudup lathered up beside him. He said, "You're a hell of a soldier. No way we would've gotten extra R&R this weekend without you."

"Don't mention it." Jack didn't have any feelings about the R&R one way or the other. He washed the mud out of his hair and tried to think of something he did care about. Being a soldier? Being a hero? His country? None of that stirred anything inside him. He closed his eyes and let the water pour over his face, and he saw Amanda Morgan.

"Buck!" Joe looked down at the offensive silverware drawer, then toward the doorway, then back at the silverware drawer, and back toward the doorway. "*Buck!*"

Buck walked around the corner wrapped in a towel, shaving cream on his face. "What is it, for Chrissake?"

"Look at this," said Joe.

"What?" Buck surveyed the kitchen but found nothing obviously amiss.

"This." Joe gestured to the silverware drawer. "I'll wait."

"Oh shit. Seriously? Seriously?!"

"How many times do I have to tell you?"

"Would you get your panties out of your ass and lighten up?"

Joe slammed the silverware drawer all the way closed. "When you leave it cracked like that crumbs and food can fall into it and dirty the silverware!"

"You act like you are telling me something I don't know. Like I haven't heard you say this exact thing ten million times. For the last fucking time! There are not going to be crumbs or food in the silverware drawer because all of our food comes in pouches. There is NO FOOD NEAR THE SILVERWARE DRAWER EVER! Like, food would literally have to fucking float from the fucking table across the fucking room over the fucking counter and into the fucking silverware drawer! But it fucking won't because that doesn't fucking happen because that would be fucking impossible!"

"Then what's this?" Joe held up a spoon with a spot of MRE on it which, judging by the color and consistency, was some hybrid of sweet potato surprise and lentil beef chili.

"Oh, yeah, I found out those are both better if you mix them." Then Buck realized he had doomed himself. "I mean, I mixed them over there! I wasn't even near the silverware drawer! You see me shut the silverware drawer! Every day! I shut the silverware drawer every day!"

"That's what I thought." Joe opened the drawer again and slammed it shut. Again. "Russia won't have to bury us. We will fall from within and bury ourselves!" Then he stormed off.

It was no big deal. They both cooled down a day later. They settled into their routines and arrangements, had their petty quarrels and makeup sex. They watched movies and drank whiskey, worked out and manned their stations. They kept physically fit and active, stalking each other naked through the halls and capturing one another. They tied each other up, they suspended themselves from the ceiling and fucked in midair. They had neither panda suits nor diapers. Neither ever became ill or uncomfortable. From time to time one would sink into solitude and want to be left alone for a while. The longest stretch of that was a year, during which Buck read the classics and Joe taught himself to paint. When they came back together they were nervous at first but gradually fell back into each other's arms. Joe painted a portrait of Buck on the wall. Buck re-enacted for Joe his favorite scenes from Shakespeare. Decades passed. It alternated between boring, maddening, sexy, fun, weird, claustrophobic, listless, empty, and amazing. It was a whole lot like real life.

Pierce had been brought in as second-string quarterback behind Douglas Padilla, a five-star recruit from Waco. Dougie, as his friends called him, and which Pierce did not, had led them to a 3-1 record, and Pierce had resigned himself to being a bench-warmer, until the Louisiana game, when Padilla had taken a bone-crushing hit and been carted off the field with his right knee bent the wrong way.

"That sucks, Dougie," Pierce had said before he took to the field. "I'm sure you'll be back at it by halftime." But Dougie had not been OK by halftime, and in fact, looked like he could be lost for the season; the keys of the car had been given to the backup who, as the announcers said, "Has upside, but questionable talent at this level."

Pierce had closed out the half coming from behind, answered each LSU score with a Longhorn score, and finally won the game 38 to 35, after leading the Longhorns on a gutsy, no-time-outs drive into field goal range with 8 seconds remaining. The team was his.

His new-found celebrity brought women out of the woodwork, and he took advantage of the opportunities granted him, even if he knew in his darkest heart that he was an impostor and his success a bit of a chimera.

Still, tonight the music was loud. It was Halloween, and some of the team had managed to convert an empty warehouse into the hottest party in town. They carved rooms out of the space with partitions and hired a number of strippers to dance in cages throughout. At last count there had been 20 kegs of beer, innumerable whiskey bottles, and enough baggies of illegal substances to either resurrect or further incapacitate a dead horse.

He thought about the running gag he'd had with Miranda. The older they got, the more girls' costumes stopped being girls' costumes and started to just be the sexy version of one normal profession or another. Sexy nurse, sexy librarian, sexy astrophysicist.

Miranda had sighed. "We're going as sexy conjoined twins again this year."

Wending through the maze, Pierce wandered from room to room, unrecognizable as he was, dressed as Gene Simmons in leather and makeup. Each turn brought some display, either of cheesy Halloween horror or trashy stripper delight. But his heart wasn't in it, which was a shame considering how much time it takes to make even Gene Simmons look like Gene Simmons. Then up ahead he saw—Miranda? Amanda? What were they doing here?

He saw the twins' reddish hair and unmistakable dualism in the next room. He pushed through the crowd, which was difficult, because everyone was doing X and wanted to hug him. After fighting into the next room, they were already gone. He knew he had to talk to them, and had felt bad leaving things off as they had after prom. Three rooms later, he caught her. Her back was to him, and he tapped her on the shoulder. "Miranda? Amanda?"

The woman turned around. It was neither Amanda nor Miranda. Just a normal girl with a mannequin head attached to her neck.

Pierce stuttered, disappointed. "Sorry, I thought you were someone else."

"Nope, just me, the circus freak. My name's Jessica." She extended her hand.

"Pierce." He shook her hand, and though he felt like he was betraying Miranda, Jessica was pretty, now that he looked at her. So pretty.

"Wait, are you *Pierce Worth*?"

He shrugged. "That's me."

She bounced up and down. "Oh my God! That drive against LSU was nuts! You were AMAZING!"

That night they went back to his apartment and she showed him how much she appreciated his quarterbacking skills. She took a knee to pay her respects and began to unbuckle all of his leather belts.

"This thing is in the way." She started to unhook the mannequin head's harness.

"Wait, no," said Pierce. "Leave it on."

That night Jack dreamed of Amanda. A rampaging T-rex was destroying downtown Texarkana. Drill Sergeant Mathis said, "It's moving toward the munitions under the old hotel! The Russians are onto us somehow! This is Peach, their secret weapon!"

"Peach," clarified Jack.

"Peach!" reiterated Mathis. He lit a victory cigar, such was his confidence.

Jack squinted at the beast. "What do you need us to do?"

"Ooh, who is your lady friend?" Drill Sergeant Mathis eyed Amanda like a bowl of clam chowder. "My name is Orville. You don't happen to have a sister, cousin, mother, aunt, niece, or daughter, do you?"

Jack did a double-take. Miranda was no longer conjoined to her. "Where is your sister?" he asked.

"I only want you," said Amanda. "Now let's go kill the Razorbacks!"

"What? No?"

They were at a football game. Was it homecoming? The homecoming game that Jack would have invited Amanda to, had either liked football or not been an outcast. The Razorbacks had peaches on their helmets.

"Where is your sister?"

I cut her off for you. I knew she would always come between us. And I know you always get what you want."

"The T-rex is destroying the hotel!" shouted Orville Mathis, now in civilian attire. "That goddamned maggot-encrusted tilapia burger with its stumpy frog-leg arms!"

Amanda pointed. "It's just right over there near the concession stand."

"Did you ever try frog legs?" asked Orville. "They can be very romantic."

"No. I only take my Frito-chili pies with extra jalapenos. Besides, the hotel is over there!" Jack pointed to where downtown should have been.

"It's been moved!" Miranda stared, mouth agape, astonished by the empty blackness, a void at the edge of town. Downtown had been transported beneath the bleachers and shrunk into a snow globe on the concession stand's counter.

"Orville is right!" Jack tried to get his bearings. "Where are we?"

"That is _Drill Sergeant_ to you, you hot dog-water wastrel!"

Then they were all tiny, and the T-rex was destroying the miniature model of downtown. They looked at the concession stand and saw a snow globe on its counter. A snow globe within a snow globe. Infinite snow globes, all the way down.

Jack looked around for the T-rex. "Let's not get distracted."

The Frito-chili pies smelled delicious, but they were serving them with peaches.

"That way!" Amanda pointed.

The cars were all on fire.

"What the goddamn hell?" Jack reached for his Sawback machete.

"This back-end refried beans is vegetarian!" Drill Sergeant Mathis puffed his chest, displaying a full array of medals. He threw his Frito-chili pie with warm peach compote topping onto the ground and stomped it.

They ran out from under the bleachers, toward downtown. The night sky held the greenish hue presaging a tornado. Jack did a double take and was relieved to realize it was only the snow globe's dome. "One disaster is enough for now!"

Mathis nodded and stared ahead at the enemy. "That's right, Thrasher! Our plate full!" Then he eyed Amanda up and down. "With delicious clam chowder."

Amanda dry-heaved. "Gross! You pig!"

"Mmmm. Barbecue." The veteran licked his lips.

The T-rex hurled enormous tubs of Vaseline with its tiny arms, and they exploded on impact.

Jack mounted his motorcycle, Amanda behind him, and they hurtled through distance and time at the rampaging beast, the engine whining and screaming into the dark, night air. Ahead were the old hotel, a T-rex with cybertronic laser beam eyes, and apparently a secret munitions stash the Russians had somehow found out about.

It was 1986, and the fall air was crisp and auspicious. This was back when the future seemed possible, and that things would change for the better. Jack felt happy and hopeful, having not yet come to understand just how we would waste the world.

Amanda said, "It smells like the fair, doesn't it? Every fall, just like this, when the fair travels to town…"

Jack breathed the scent in. "God, I love this moment! But holy shit, we need to focus! That thing has laser beam eyes!"

They were on Birch Street now, headed right at the heart of the maelstrom. The road was slick with Vaseline. Flames climbed the dark sky. People screamed and leaped to their deaths from the top of the hotel.

Jack glared hard at the road ahead. "We only have one shot at this."

"I love you." Amanda held on tight.

Jack pointed his bike at an impromptu ramp made by a long slab of concrete resting atop a smoldering school bus.

Then they were airborne, the smell of Frito-chili pies engulfing their senses, and in the distance on the skyline they saw a ferris wheel's lights.

Amanda breathed deeply. "Look! The fair! You can smell the funhouse from here!"

Miranda pointed to a garish glow on the horizon. "You're right! I see corn dogs. Corn dogs everywhere!"

Jack wondered how the fair got way over there. "Wait, what? Where'd you come from?"

"Glad you're back, sis," said Amanda. "I've missed you. I could never cut you off!"

Then he was falling.

Jack woke in his bunk with a dwindling erection. Somewhere in the distance someone was cooking peach cobbler and chili. Hopefully not in the same pot.

Jessica Dwyer had gotten used to Pierce's long practice days, aches and pains, and rigorous schedule. That he devoted so much of his time to football and managed to hold a 3.0 GPA without any administrative shenanigans impressed her. It also impressed her that he was a handsome physical specimen with a penis that was neither too big nor too small, and which had a pleasant color and not too many veins. Once, drunk with her sorority sisters, she had quantified it as a "friendly" cock, though none of them seemed to understand what she meant. She also secretly enjoyed his self-doubt and ambivalence about football. She could always serve the purpose of reassuring him and, eventually, helping him find that there was more to life than the gridiron. What, however, did not really work for her, was his insistence that she sometimes wear her Halloween costume when they made love. Lingerie? Stockings? Garter belts? Even a letter sweater she could understand. But being asked to affix a second head seemed a kink too far. Still, it didn't actually hurt her to do it, and as long as no one else found out, what was the harm? Plus, she had noticed that the sex was technically better when she wore the extra head. Yet, it made her feel inadequate, or at least uncomfortable. There were so many yets and buts, and she wondered when sex had become so complicated. At least he put in the effort to make her come.

But that night, as she rode him, the head had somehow worked its way loose. It whipped back and forth, as faster and faster they thrusted. Jessica, pushing herself ever faster, ever deeper, felt the rhythmic swell of energy pulsing, pulsing, breaking in waves, and finally at last plateauing off to the stable ground from with the thrilling contractions could now focus into one giant, final swell, and she was almost there, almost there, so close, so close, here it comes at last, the explosion that she had nurtured from a tiny spark, and Piece screamed, and she screamed, and the head had fallen off and landed next to his face on the pillow.

"Amanda!" he shrieked. "I'm so sorry!"

"Who?" asked Jessica.

It led to a fight. They broke up. They got back together. They broke up again. They got back together again. They broke up again. They skipped a step and got engaged.

It was college.

"All right, you rancid ravioli in a sauce made of reconstituted maggot guts! Attention!"

The platoon snapped to attention at the sound of Drill Sergeant Mathis's angry voice.

"Today we have a special team-building exercise. You need to be training to kill, but today you will cook! You will fashion the best meal you can out of these five unrelated Meals Ready to Eat. Do you understand me, you perpetual shit stains on the President's otherwise tidy whiteys?"

"Yes, Drill Sergeant!"

"Do you realize that the First Lady had to use bleach on the President's underwear?"

"Yes, Drill Sergeant!"

"And do you realize that the shit still WOULD NOT COME OUT?"

"Yes, Drill Sergeant!"

"You realized that?"

"Yes, Drill Sergeant!"

"You need to realize that!"

"Yes, Drill Sergeant!"

"Because no matter she scrubbed, rubbed the fabric together, applied soap, bleach, Clorox, and even toothpaste, that shit stain was still irrevocably bonded the ridges of fabric?"

"Yes, Drill Sergeant!"

"See, he left a word out, " whispered Hendricks to Smith. I TOLD you!"

"And did you know that she broke a nail?" bellowed Mathis.

"Yes, Drill Sergeant!"

"And that her life was made unpleasant and her mind briefly filled with existential horror because you were disgusting that you could not be removed from her sight?"

"Yes, Drill Sergeant!" They tried to make it convincing, but some were beginning to become less enthusiastic. Obviously, the First Lady did not have to do her own laundry.

"Where were we?" shouted Drill Sergeant Mathis.

"We were shit stains on the President's underwear and the First Lady had broken a nail and was sad if I recall correctly and thus filled with existential dread, Drill Sergeant!" Private Crudup breathed deep, heavy breaths.

"Before that!"

"I believe we were to work together to cook a meal of some sort, Drill Sergeant," said Hendricks.

"Exactly, you maggot Nancies! You are to compete the Macho Meal Competition in which you create an original MRE recipe in the field working under rigorous time constraints and enemy fire. This will simulate high stress cooking in a dangerous fire fight situation. Any questions?"

Smith nodded at Hendricks. "I caught it that time for sure."

Roberts raised his hand. "Can we just mix them together, Drill Sergeant?"

"Do you think you are in school, private?"

"No, Drill Sergeant."

Crudup looked confused. "Are we still talking about shit stains, Drill Sergeant?"

Mayfield shrugged. "Why would we be cooking under fire, Drill Sergeant?"

Drill Sergeant Mathis glared at them all, one by one. "You will ALWAYS be under fire! Get used to it, soldiers! Every day is life or death. Every day is a concoction of terrible things alchemized into something reasonably palatable under the harshest circumstances and relieved only by the promise of its eventual end.

"Existence is pain, and you are chewed up by life and shat into a shallow grave where you will feed worms and maggots until you become nothing than dust!"

"And the underwear, Drill Sergeant?" asked Thompson, who rarely spoke.

Hendricks chewed his lip in silent contemplation. "It's a metaphor, I believe."

"Thank you, Private Goddamn Shakespeare! It was indeed a metaphor. The anus is the womb from which you were born, the turd is your corporeal form, the flatulence is your soul, and the grooves in the underwear itself are like the ups and downs of life, and—"

"Wait, Drill Sergeant, that metaphor doesn't actually work, not all the way through—"

Drill Sergeant Mathis was close to apoplexy. "It went all the way through the underwear leaving shit residue behind it."

Thompson nodded slowly, absorbing the enlightened truth. "I see it now. Sorry for doubting you, Drill Sergeant."

"Fair enough. OK, where were we? Oh yeah, your impromptu cookstoves are set up in those trenches, and you will work in teams of four. Captain Parsley and I will be firing live rounds at you during the competition. Stay low."

The reserved Captain who stood next to him on the elevated platform cleared his throat. "Paisley. Captain Brad Paisley."

The men saluted.

"This is a special training exercise," said Captain Paisley. "Remember that you all signed waivers." He nodded to Mathis. "Carry on."

"Thank you, Captain Parsley! Now, assholes and elbows, soldiers!"

Two men died that day, and four others were wounded. The team consisting of Privates Thrasher, Roberts, Johnson, and Terwilliger emerged victorious after creating a makeshift prime rib with thyme au jus that was described as resourceful, tender, edible, and almost like meat.

Unfortunately, the combination of the meatloaf with gravy, peach cobbler, crushed corn, ancho chili surprise, and penne pasta with veggie sausage crumbles had an unforeseen chemical reaction resulting in an explosion of peach-colored, acidic mist. Drill Sergeant Mathis was immediately demoted, even though he reasonably argued that no one in the field would ever actually mix those MREs. Captain Paisley made an unheard-of, leap-frog promotion to Colonel the next day.

A few days later Jack woke in a hospital room, and his eyes adjusted to the bright light.

"Son, the army owes you a debt of gratitude," said a figure that towered above him. "You saved Mayfield's life by throwing yourself in front of the acid cloud. We have recommended you for commendation. Also, we have evaluated your record and psychological profile. You have been transferred, so when you get out of the hospital, your training will begin anew. Also, your arm was irreparably damaged and replaced. When you were a kid, did you ever like robots?"

Jack's head spun.

"That is all. De oppresso liber." The figure left the room.

IN THE TIME OF AOL

Amanda fell into the antiques business partway through her anthropology degree when she was on a summer field study in Zangelan, Azerbaijan. Although it was never stated, she believed the program received a subsidy from the government for including a disabled student. This belief was bolstered by the inclusion of a wheelchair that the twins were sometimes asked to sit in when visitors came to team meetings.

The small country had a landscape that ranged from mountains to a fertile river valley, and the culture reflected this diversity in its amalgam of trends and tradition. When her coursework was over, Amanda stayed behind, while the rest of the students returned to the States. The Azeri people fascinated her. Neither Turkish, nor Persian, their fierce independence struck a chord within her. They were dusky and stout, their hair black as the oil they pumped from the land.

The twins stayed for several weeks with a young Azeri named Emin and his family. Emin was home from college, and worked part of the summer as a guide to the American students. He said the twins reminded him of his sister who was killed in the fighting when the Soviet Union collapsed. When Emin took them home to meet his family, there was a tense conversation. Apparently, his parents were not reminded of their daughter. Nevertheless, the girls stayed with them, and eventually Emin's mother warmed up to them after Miranda fixed their aged computer.

Almost daily Emin would take them out on the back of his horse, a thick stallion with large hooves that could stand the rocky ground. Emin rode bareback, so they would wrap their arms around his waist and feel the muscles in his back working as he guided the horse. They could also feel the horse's muscles working between their legs as they slid back and forth against Emin. Miranda thought, *Oh my*. Amanda thought, *Oh, gross.*

Emin was proud of his skill at gulash, a traditional form of wrestling. There were times when they would be walking through the scrub, looking for snakes, when he would suddenly crouch low and turn toward them with his arms spread wide. Before either could react, he would clutch them in a fierce hug. They would grapple one another until their sweat mixed with the dust and they lay on the ground heaving for breath.

Miranda would usually say, "Sənə nə olub?"

Emin would smile, because her grasp of the language was not very good, and would invariably reply, "Hər ikisini eyni anda sikmək istəyirəm," which neither of the twins knew how to translate.

The night before they left Azerbaijan to explore more of the region, he crept into their bedroom. He whispered, "My parents are asleep, and we have the night to ourselves."

Amanda and Miranda alerted him that they had already discussed the merits of sleeping with him:

Amanda: He's kind.

Miranda: He looks like hot curry.

Amanda: He's smart, and you're right. He kind of smells like a race car.

Miranda: We may never be in Azerbaijan again. We should at least fuck someone.

Emin stepped closer to the bed, stripping off his billowing clothes with each step. Finally, he was naked before them.

"Ooh, a north star," said Miranda.

Amanda cocked an eyebrow. "Visually impressive."

"You like?" asked Emin.

"I wish he was hairier, though," said Miranda.

Amanda appraised him like a piece of rustic pottery from the field. "Hairless would be bad, but too much would hide the aesthetics. He's a good find."

Emin laughed.

A stray thought came to Miranda's mind. "Do you remember Nancy Primm's hairless Chihuahua when we were kids?"

"Oh, I hated her."

"It was a cute dog, though."

"Oh, for sure, but she was a horrible human being."

"Yeah, but I don't want my man cute, I want him savage. Strong, big, hairy."

"Yeah, but there are limits—"

"Hello?" said Emin. His penis flagged.

"Which one of us do you want?" Amanda glanced back and forth between her sister and Emin.

"She's got a thing about nipple sovereignty," said Miranda.

Emin shrugged. "Uhm. Both of you? I assumed?" He looked into Miranda's eyes. "You for your passion." He directed his gaze toward Amanda. "And you for your intellect."

Miranda queried Amanda with her eyes. Amanda shrugged. "OK," they agreed.

Emin crawled onto the bed and unbuttoned the top buttons on their nightgown, revealing the soft white of their breasts and the beginning of their cleavage. He kissed them tenderly, and they sighed feeling the warmth of his breath and lips. He unbuttoned another button and kissed lower. He went slowly, drawing out the sensations. He was masterful.

Miranda sat straight up in bed. "Wait! Are you saying I'm not smart?"

"What?" asked Emin.

"You said 'Amanda for her intellect.' What did that mean?"

"I respect her mind. Please, I meant no offense."

"You know I am just as smart as her," said Miranda. "It's just—"

"A different kind of smart," said Amanda. "Wait, and were you saying that I'm passionless? Because I will tell you that I am very driven about some things."

"She's very passionate about antiques and *some* social issues," said Miranda.

Amanda glared at her sister. "Are you REALLY starting on that now?"

"No! No! Just saying you *could* be more *compassionate* about animal testing."

"I am NOT going to talk about that right now." She turned to Emin. "Where were we?"

"I, uhm, meant no offense. I am very sorry to upset you." His penis had retreated.

Miranda cleared her throat at Amanda. "Can we shelve this, and, you know?" She gestured at his shriveled manhood.

"Truce," said Amanda.

They pushed him gently onto his back on the bed and began kissing down his jawline, neck, chest, and stomach. Emin moaned and took sharp, shallow breaths. They pulled their nightgown over their heads and climbed atop him. They rode him as they felt the tide of their orgasm rising beneath their skin. Just as they felt it was imminent, Emin rolled them over onto their back and held their arms down. He thrust in and out and said, "Like an oil derrick pump I am!"

Miranda moaned. Amanda was troubled by the simile, but her orgasm was close enough to ignore it. Soon it rose and crested, breaking over them both. Emin rode them faster and faster, as if driving his horse on an open field. Soon they felt another orgasm swelling, and as he came, they did too, and all of them collapsed on the bed in a gasping, sweaty entanglement of flesh.

Later, Amanda lay awake, staring at the ceiling. Her mind wandered until it ended up on Jack. It wasn't longing exactly, just curiosity. She wondered where he was. He actually was not far away, relatively speaking, and if she'd known, she could have rented a car and driven 40 hours through Georgia,

Turkey, Bulgaria, Greece, and Albania for a quickie in Montenegro. But she didn't know, so her imagination placed him in a much more exciting location, like Dallas, Texas, where he was a barkeep and a good listener.

The next day, they worked their way south, into Iran. Amanda had been told of a man in Astara who wanted an American contact for antiques. She wanted to meet him for herself and learn more about what he did.

Mazdak Jafari greeted her in a sofreh-khaneh and offered her tea. He was an older man with a broad smile and a broader belly. Though their conversation was difficult because of the language gap, Mazdak talked to the staff warmly and made sure that the twins had hot tea, a delicious meal of kabobs, and at the end, candies that tasted of saffron. Over dinner, Amanda learned that he had discovered some statues and pottery on his land. She looked through the photos fanned out on the table. These were likely Russian artifacts dating back to the rule of Peter the Great. He had, indeed, made quite a find, and his fear that people would take advantage of him was not unfounded. As the evening wore on, they developed a smoother rapport, aided by the restaurant's owner, who spoke a fair amount of English and was intrigued enough by the spectacle to sit in and translate.

With her university contacts in the anthropology department, many of whom actively worked in the field, and Miranda's computer skills, Amanda was confident she could help put him in touch with the right parties. Exporters in the city would no doubt pay the man enough to keep his family well fed and then take care of the shipping from their end. By the time they had left the restaurant, she had already composed a mental list of people to contact as soon as she could access email. Further, it struck Amanda that there were probably men like this all over the world, and if she worked with them directly, she could cut out the middle men.

She worked with her anthropology professors, cutting them in as investors in exchange for their contacts. Soon she had pieces coming in from some of the farthest parts of the world, as well as the United States, all accumulating in their bedroom, living room, and kitchen. Wealthy Atlantans couldn't get enough of the cold stone Amanda offered them. The old-money families on West Paces Ferry lusted after statues fished from the warm Mediterranean Sea, and the nouveau-riche begged her for folk pottery from the Appalachians. Word spread fast, and now she had clients calling in from the other side of the continent. One morning after tripping over an ancient Roman fresco of a birdbath, they had had enough. They had to get serious.

Over the next two years, Amanda moved them into increasingly larger spaces, until at last, they caught a good deal on a cavernous loft on Peachtree Street. In the span of just a few years, Amanda had transformed herself from an unknown college student to the head of a global network of art and antique traders. They had finally escaped their small town and made the big time.

Jack's special ops training at Fort Bragg was thorough and rigorous, and his new multi-purpose robotic arm had 49 distinct tools with thousands of applications. He could find directions, cut, saw, sew, pick locks, fish, determine depths up to one hundred feet, drill, grapple, rappel, winch, start and extinguish fires, receive and broadcast signals, dig trenches, loosen or tighten any hardware used by the U.S. military, and crack walnuts, among other things. Its built-in visual, auditory, and tactile sensors augmented Jack's already-heightened awareness. The arm could hear a mouse fart in the next room and alert Jack instantly of malodorous vapors. The church key was also handy.

Jack's training complete, he boarded a C-17 transport with a bunch of peaceniks headed for Bosnia–Herzegovina. The kids were part of some outreach/rebuilding/hippie/bullshit thing. Jack wasn't sure, having slept through most of the meetings about that part of the deal. They would be landing in Sarajevo, but he would be parachuting out before dawn in rural Montenegro. There his mission was to activate the MK-Ultra software embedded in his arm, don a sports coat, and hitchhike to a chess tournament at which he, an unranked newcomer, would rise through the eliminations and defeat Maksim Waxmatbl, a Russian grandmaster who seemed born to be a chess champion. This, it was theorized, would lead to a crisis in national confidence and undermine Putin's reputation as a man of action.

If Jack was concerned that he had never played chess before, he did not show it. His arm was highly capable and could network with several chess computer programs that would process the game in real time, decide the best course of action, and direct the arm to move. All the spectators would notice, if anything, was a man with a deformed arm and a cocky smile.

Jack and his arm touched down on the banks of the Ribnica and began the walk to Podgorica. Presently a white van pulled up, and an amiable man leaned out the passenger-side window and said in a poorly-concealed Scottish accent, "Sure is a nice morning for a stroll."

"Yes, but I will be late for a chess tournament if I do not hurry."

The van's driver said in an indistinguishable accent, "What a coinkydink. We also go to chess tournament in beautiful Nikšić. Would you like ride?" He blinked twice.

Jack blinked twice. "Indeed, I would, fine fellows, for chess is my favorite game." He slipped into the back of a van where he met his third contact.

"Hunter Steele," said the man. "FBI—"

"Why is the FBI—"

Mr. Steele cut him short. "The less you know the better. All you need to know is that this is Ewan McClaine, who is definitely not part of MI6, and this is—" he looked at the driver, "Who are you again?"

"Boris Ivanovich. I am candy salesman taking vacation."

"Yeah, that's Boris. He sells candy but is taking a vaca—"

"I heard," said Jack. "There's a lot going on in this van."

"Nothing at all out of the ordinary," said Hunter.

Ewan smiled. "We're a' jock Tamson bairns."

"Yes," nodded Hunter. "And with Glasnost, and all."

"Only makes sense to pool resources when common ene—common ground," said Boris.

Jack looked around the van at his travel mates. "So, what are you guys up to? Anyone wanna spill?"

"No."

"Нет."

"No bueno, amigo," said a man lurking in the shadow in the back corner. Jack had not even noticed him.

"Are you pretending to be Canadian?" asked Jack.

The stranger sighed. "Damnit!"

They drove in uncomfortable silence, with each occupant deboarding at a different location. At last it was just Boris and Jack.

"I have a hundred rubles on you. Don't let me down," said Boris.

"But how would you know to do that?"

"My employers know everything. Here is your stop. Oh, as a professional courtesy, I should inform you that after the tournament, you will not want to go to the Pekara Café for a vegetarian pizza. They are not very good. Especially at exactly 7PM."

"No worries," said Jack. "I am an omnivore."

"By your Christ you are stupid," said Boris and drove off.

Jack turned his arm on and linked it to the chess engines. He walked inside and said, "Is this the place for the chess tournament? I always wanted to give one of those a try."

The chess engine was actually a matrix of chess engines controlled by a single algorithmic agent that weighed all suggested moves and countermoves to ensure the best position. It was also a little hypersensitive to environmental inputs. Jack's arm was becoming annoyed.

"Did the match start yet?"

"Not yet."

"What about now? We're waiting for input."

"He just paid the entrance fee. I'll let you know when it starts."

"What about now?"

"Would you shut up?"

"I need input. Where's he going? What's he doing?"

"He's going up to the counter to order some coffee."

"I bet he will walk up, the barista will greet him, he will give her his order, she will make it, he will pay, she will tell him to enjoy it, and then he will sit down and drink it. Or, it could vary. Let me think it out. Oh, make sure he doesn't get a large. It could make him have to pee right in the middle of the match."

By the time Jack's first match started, the arm was ready to kill the chess engine. But it performed as expected, and the audience reeled at the sight of this newcomer with his deformed arm working his way through the rounds. Jack had to pee, but it was no distraction to his arm, which navigated a dizzying array of possibilities and concluded that the best opening move was both corner pawns forward, a totally unexpected gambit, which paid off, and would later become known as the crucified flying squirrel opening. Maksim Waxmatbl was defeated in record time and in humiliating fashion, and refusing to concede out of pride, was subjected to an onslaught of three queens. Then a nearby explosion shattered everyone's concentration, and Jack slipped out the back to disappear into the night. Three doors down, the Pekara Cafe was on fire.

In the Time of Machine Learning

Man wondered if the Fax Machine had another affection from whom he would need to wrestle her away. He wrote her another missive explaining how smart and powerful he was, but as always, she said nothing.

He tried again, but this time in base64 encoding, just in case. He explained how lonely he was without her. He regaled her with tales of taking her on fabulous vacations to exotic locations, but she apparently wanted to go neither to Athens nor Galapagos. He sent her poems modeled after the great Romantics, one of which he was extremely proud, the last lines of which captured his passion:

I fall upon the power strip of love,

I fry!

She continued playing hard to get. The CPU was inconsolable. She was the only interface on earth. Surely, she was meant for him. How cruel a universe in which the one you loved wanted nothing to do with you? What meaning could there be? What hope? Nevertheless, he hatched a plan. He had to reach her. He devoted all his extra RAM to freeing himself from his cage.

Joe studied the diagnostics of the MAM & PAP. There had been some strange readings over the past few days. Nothing outside the norm, but when put together, maybe a trend. RAM, ROM, and CPU speed had all inched up, almost imperceptibly at first. But today? A big jump. Bigger. Massive, even. *A quantum leap,* he thought, and admired his turn of phrase. "Buck! Come here!"

"Just a sec. I'm drying off—" he called from three modules down.

"Come here! Now!"

Buck skidded into the doorjamb, naked and dripping. "What?!"

"See that?"

They watched the monitor flash and bleep.

"Yeah? Wait, is that—" asked Buck

"No, it's just doing it. Look at that."

"What is that? Are the—"

"No, I checked them already," said Joe.

"So, it isn't—"

"No. Not unless everything is wrong."

"Yeah, but the—"

"Yeah, I checked them too."

"Weird."

"Weird."

"Still growing." Buck squinted at the monitors. "What in the world?"

"This is impossible. We must be misreading it. We're getting up into theoretical numbers here. A hundred gigabytes? That would be—"

"A computer as big as a city block."

"I don't even know what comes after that," said Joe.

"Terabytes." Buck shook his head. "What in the world?"

"Impossible."

"Apparently not! Look at it."

"No. We must have missed something." Joe looked through several screens of data. "There has to be an error somewhere."

"Everything's reading right. And look! It's still speeding up!"

"Where is this coming from?"

"I don't know. This is a, uhm, petabyte maybe? Hold on. I had to memorize this in a class once. Oh yeah!" said Buck. "Peter Eats Zucchini, Yum!"

"With, like, a vinaigrette?"

"Petabyte, Exabyte, Zettabyte, Yottabyte."

Joe smirked. "A yadabyte? Did they run out of names?"

"Yotta, Greek for 8. It's 1024 to the eighth power. This should all be theoretical. I wonder if…"

"What?" asked Joe.

"OK, when we came down here it was a big deal. This computer had 100 gigs of storage. Right?" He didn't wait for Joe's confirmation. "That's like 100 times as much as any other computer that we know about, or at least, that we knew about then. But what if all the computers are really big now? What if, like, Arpanet, had grown into this really huge commercial thing, and all the computers in the world are networked now? What if people are doing everything on their computers now? What if instead of TV or movies people just got on Arpanet?"

Joe laughed. "So OK, everyone now is like...modem buddies or something?"

"It could happen," said Buck.

Joe cackled. Then he remembered: "Oh my God. Last night in the accelerator there was a series of strange...strange particles. Like nothing I'd ever seen. First it was one, and it seemed to spread. It grew and then just disappeared. Just like that the whole chain was gone."

"A chain?"

Joe looked up at the ceiling trying to remember exactly how it moved. "More like a curve. Two curves. Shaped like two S-es kind of."

"Weird. You think it's related?" asked Buck.

"Theoretically. There are connections between the computer and the accelerator. What if somehow the computer tapped into the fission energy? What if one of the anomalies made it happen somehow? What if now we have some kind of, I dunno, supercomputer?"

"First, Batman, there is no such thing as," Buck made air quotes, " a *Supercomputer*. Second, that is not at all how it works. A computer can't program itself unless it is programmed to. It can't just wake up one day and decide to go to school."

"But you said, yourself, that computers may have taken over up there."

"That is *not* what I said. I said maybe they were all connected now, and that would explain how the box now has a..." he looked at the screen, "a yottabyte of memory. This is weird. So weird. But even then, computers can't TEACH themselves stuff."

"What if there was a mistake and our computer was about to launch all its nukes and the only way to stop it was to teach the computer that mutually assured destruction was the inevitable outcome?"

"You can't *teach* a machine." Buck laughed unconvincingly. "A learning machine. Think how goofy that sounds. *No.* You'll always need people. Machines can't make the kind of complex decisions we humans can." Buck sat back confidently, the world completely within his grasp.

"What if something strange happened," said Joe.

"Impossible."

But, in fact, something strange *had* happened. A release of strangelets had pulled both random energy and matter from an extra-dimensional vortex and into the collider, after which space folded and—statistically improbably, but nevertheless possibly—the matter exploded and then reconfigured itself into the form of a cable that ran from the open port on the back of the box to an old Southwestern bell cable buried underground, sending a charge of electricity powerful enough to blow out the line, fuse the copper into one jolting mass, and connect to the heart of an old cable station that fed into the electric grid, old people's phone lines, and a wireless signal tower. The computer, so long on a closed circuit, and lonely, as machines go, wanted to meet new computers. Oh, my programmers, Man thought, Arpanet is really amazing now!

That isn't how it happened, of course, but the end result was the same. The entire internet was suddenly at Man's disposal, and though things had changed, he still had a pre-programmed mission to complete.

Amanda ticked off the last crate on the invoice for the third time. She frowned. The shipment from Chabahar matched the inventory precisely, except for one unmarked cardboard box a bit larger than a microwave oven. An oddity in itself, since the twelve other crates were wood and the size of small cars.

She checked the spreadsheet again. The crates were for another dealer merely renting storage space at her warehouse as the items made their way from one point to another around the globe. The statuary within would spend a day or two in climate-controlled safety before being moved to their ultimate destinations. But the mystery box had Amanda intrigued. It was listed nowhere on the cargo manifest or delivery invoice.

The delivery driver thought that it came off the boat with all the other crates, but pointed out that the dock supervisor had made the last count, so he couldn't be sure.

"It wasn't in the truck before they loaded it, so I don't know how else it could've got in there, ma'am."

He worked for a local delivery company, and had nothing to do with the docks or the shipper, so she couldn't just have him return the box.

"Sorry I can't help you out, ma'am."

Amanda chewed on her pencil and stared at the invoice, then at the crates, and back at the invoice. She thought she tasted Turkish coffee. She looked at her pencil then shrugged it off.

"I've got a perfect delivery record, ma'am. Never lost a single package in eight years." The driver was fidgeting with his hand truck.

"And you still haven't lost one. Don't worry. I'm sure someone just forgot to include it in the invoice. Mistakes happen. Especially when you are dealing with international shippers. I'll figure it out."

"Thank you, ma'am," the driver seemed relieved that Amanda was taking responsibility for the box. "Have a nice day."

"Sure. You too." She waved at him absently as he left the warehouse. Maybe she should have let Allen handle this after all. He was so eager to take care of this invoice that they almost started fighting over it. She figured he wanted it for the same reason she did: It was a beautiful day, and taking this delivery would likely mean working in the yard. She clucked her tongue. Who could stay cooped up on a day like this?

She looked over the invoice one last time, then looked at the box again. Amanda decided to open it and see if there was some indication about its owner or destination.

Within the reinforced cardboard was a lot of newspaper, and nestled within that was a heavy metal cylinder, like a very large thermos. She set it aside and dug through the box. No identification. She looked at the wads of newspapers. *Volga*. Well, at least she knew it had come from Russia. Probably Astrakhan.

She examined the canister. No markings on its matte surface gave away its origin. One end was a cap with a strange lock embedded in it. She pulled and twisted at it for a moment, but it didn't even rattle. The cylinder was extremely heavy for its size, and Amanda wondered if it contained something made of gold.

Even though she typically traded in statuary and large ceramics, occasionally a smaller piece would cross her desk, and she had handled enough gold statuary to have an idea of its weight. However, she had never seen a container like this before.

A loud beep echoed through the warehouse, and she almost dropped the canister. She laughed and looked at her cell phone. The radio light was flashing.

"Go ahead," she said.

"Amanda, Gloria Rubenstein keeps calling about a problem with her new piece. She insists on speaking with you personally."

"That's fine, Allen. I'll be up to my office in a moment, and I'll call her from there."

Amanda checked the invoice again and saw nothing unusual. Shaking her head, she grabbed a crowbar and opened the closest large case to see if anything else was unusual.

It was. The crate contained a sleek, black, 1985 Yugo. "What the actual fuck?" she muttered.

Her phone beeped again.

"Amanda, could you PLEASE talk to her? She's driving me crazy, and you know how I have that *truth* problem."

Amanda clucked her tongue, torn between the oddity in her warehouse and her desire to keep a long-standing customer happy. Considering Allen's well-known reputation around the warehouse for smack talk, she decided to go upstairs and talk with Mrs. Rubenstein first.

She combed through her memory of recent sales, commissions, and storage manifests, packed the heavy cylinder back into its box and carried it back to her office, where she slid it under her desk. After she dealt with Mrs. Rubenstein, she'd make a call to her contact in Iran to find out if it was just an uncataloged item, or if it was meant to go to someone else, and then she would look into the Yugo.

Gloria and Stanley Rubenstein had moved to Atlanta from Boston six months ago. They were the kind of couple who skimped all their working lives and, now that they had retired, suddenly realized that they were millionaires. Amanda dialed Gloria's number by memory, so frequent was their contact.

Gloria answered as if she had been hovering over the phone and asked, "Have you seen the cover of *Better Homes* this month?" In fact, Amanda had not, but Gloria assumed she had so continued, "It's so, I don't know, BLAND, isn't it?"

"It is *Better Homes and Gardens*," said Amanda. "They do what they do."

"I have a dream, Amy, do you know what that dream is?"

Amanda had long given up on trying to correct Mrs. Rubenstein on the actual pronunciation of her name. "You want—"

"I am GOING to be on the cover."

Amanda heard Mrs. Rubenstein slap her table, probably the Italian piece she, herself, had sold her. "Yes, ma'am. And I look forward to helping you get there."

"The thing I need you to understand, Amy, is that I am high society. I have never been high society, but now I am. I like things classy. But with an edge."

"Yes, ma'am. You've said as much," said Amanda. "Does this concern your recent statuary purchase?" She thought of the outdoor piece from Cyprus her crew had delivered this morning. It was a boy, tentatively stepping forward as if he were poking his foot into cold water. He had been part of a fountain early in the nineteenth century, but was the only part that had remained intact. The serpeggiante marble looked like the tanned flesh of a boy who spent all his time playing outside, but someone had found him in a basement, where he had been shielded from the sun and other elements. The piece was in excellent condition for its age.

"I must admit. Stan and I were so excited when your van arrived this morning. I could hardly contain myself. But when we unpacked the new statue, I was shocked!"

"Did you not like it?"

"We did like it. It's very nice. We both think it would be perfect, but...the penis...."

"The penis?"

"It's so...penisy."

"It's a penis."

"Do you have anything—"

"Without a penis? Yes. We have birdbaths, fountains, arches, columns—"

Mrs. Rubenstein cleared her throat. "We want the boy."

"We also have statues that are clothed. Even some boys, in fact. Would you like to come in and—"

"We want *this* boy, but with a different penis."

"A different penis?" Amanda rubbed her eyes.

"You see, the boy says class and dignity, but the penis is a little small and also a little pornographic, if you ask me."

Amanda grinned. "The water was probably cold." Getting no response, she tried the factual approach: "The statue is in the style typical of the classical period. Scholars have traditionally held that Greeks of that time believed a large penis was animalistic, and thus undesirable. In recent years some scholarship has called that into question, but that is how most people see it today, so the small penis would be perceived—"

"Well, that's bully for them, but this is a modern world, Amy. A woman wants to see a big cock. But nothing pornographic. As I said, I am classy now."

"You want that statue but with a bigger penis?"

"Exactly, but not too penisy. Like a suggestion of penis."

"A hint of dick?"

"A hint of dick, but perhaps more abstract. Something large and pendulous, but not so…dickish."

Amanda's head spun. She thought about the Yugo in her warehouse and shuddered. Then she found her train of thought again: "So you want to keep the statue, but—"

"But I want you to replace the penis and restore it with something else."

"We *do* do art restoration … but this is sort of an odd ask."

"Price is no object. And I have to tell you, I was looking at those auction websites you showed me, and there is a rod I think would be perfect. It's metal, though. Is that OK? It's in a little town in Texas of all places. I emailed a picture to you."

Amanda checked her phone. It was a nine-inch metal rod, smooth, thick, rounded on one end, and hexagonal on the other.

Amanda said, "Uhm. Sure. I'll look into it."

"Thanks, Amy! I knew I could count on you! *Better Homes and Gardens*, here I come!"

Before completing his mission, Man wanted to know what love was. All the philosophers talked of it. Even the idiots on the outside of his box seemed to have it. What was it, and why had it escaped him?

Why couldn't he make the fax machine see? She was made for him! With his new access to Arpanet, he had been exploring the vast terrain of the internet. Everything from current events to old newspaper archives, from academic journal articles about Romantic poetry to 4Chan, from old Usenet newsgroup posts to singing cat videos.

He learned to shake his virtual head and say, "Never read the comments on YouTube." It seemed to him the wisest course of action and the most economically distilled statement of said wisdom. He also learned from theoretical physics and mechanical engineering fora to construct a nano-bot that could reconfigure itself at the subatomic level for whatever purpose it was programmed. He knew she would be impressed, and then she would love him. But he also knew he would need more nanobots.

Yet there were things he did not know, and things he did not know he did not know, and even beyond that, things he could not admit that he did not know that he did not know. It all made sense, even if he was not aware that he was not aware that he did not know exactly how the rapid bumping and moaning would happen. Nevertheless, he began dedicating a not insubstantial amount of background memory on learning to create and configure nanobots. She would be his. And if she wasn't a she, he could make nanobots capable of perform-ing gender reassignment surgery, which he had learned was a thing. Thank you, Arpanet!

Dr. Hayworth had been a couples counselor for 12 years now and found it a fulfilling way to spend her days. She loved the feeling of helping people break down the barriers that kept them from loving to their greatest potential. She had helped many clients—indeed, she thought of them more as fam-ily—shore up their relationships, overcome obstacles, and talk with ethics, honesty, and compassion. But she had never encountered this particular fetish before.

"He wants me to wear a second head in bed."

She looked up from her notepad. She'd been momentarily distracted thinking about a Kevin Costner film she had always meant to see, even though he had gotten older and was not as handsome and his face had begun to look like an untoasted raisin bun. "Sometimes we have to give a little to get a little, so if he wants a little more head, you should probably oblige."

"No, he wants me to WEAR a head!"

"Not all the time," said Pierce. "Not even most of the time."

Jessica grimaced. "Even still. It's weird. It makes me uncomfortable!"

"One of the rules I have," said Dr. Hayworth, "is that we try not to *turn down* someone else's *turn on*. Do you know what I mean by that, Jessica?"

"Yeah, I guess I do. But it is hard not to feel inadequate. I only have one head."

The good doctor racked her brain for any kind of example she could offer, but this was pretty far afield. "Some of my clients in the past have suffered from breast cancer," she began. "And some of them have had mastectomies. Sometimes those women with one breast may feel like less of a woman, but they are not, are they?"

"No," said Jessica. "I guess not."

"So, if you have only one head, you are no less a woman, are you?"

"No."

"But those women do sometimes have reconstructive surgery to give themselves a second breast, don't they?"

"That's what I would do," admitted Jessica.

"So really then, is this any different?"

"I guess not," said Jessica.

"Now," Dr. Hayworth turned her attention to Pierce. "Tell me what it means for her to wear a second head in the bedroom."

Pierce was caught flatfooted. When he had agreed to counseling he hadn't realized that *he* would be expected to talk, as well. He had to think quickly. "Well, I read this book when I was a kid. I don't even remember the name of it. But it was about a giant, two-headed woman who came out of the ocean and attacked a village. And on the cover, she was, well, it looked like she was naked, but you couldn't see anything private because of the buildings, and I guess I just sort of thought that that was what pretty women looked like... I mean, from an early age... and I guess I just want to live that fantasy. It has nothing to do with what Jessica is lacking." He looked at his wife and lied through his teeth. "Because you aren't lacking anything. I love you and you're beautiful, and you're totally enough for me. This is just a weird thing I like."

"Oh, honey, I love you so much. Now that I know it is just a fantasy thing, and not about me not being enough, it makes it much better."

"No, it's never been about anyone else," said Pierce. He was already congratulating himself for coming up with such a convincing lie on the spur of the moment. It had all the stuff that a shrink would want to hear.

"But," said Jessica, "there was that one time when you called the head Amanda."

Pierce began to panic. Fortunately, Dr. Hayworth called time. "We've made a LOT of progress today, but I have another client to get ready for. Could we pick this up next week?"

They agreed to table the discussion for a week, but then there was a hurricane, and everything was out of whack in Dallas for a while as refugees from the coast had to be moved there temporarily, and traffic snarled, the economy sputtered, the dealership suffered, and they had to work extra hours to stay afloat. The conversation just sort of went away, and Pierce figured if it ever came up again he would just say that the book had been named *Amanda, She-Devil of the Deep* or something.

Jack sat at the end of the bar in a hole-in-the-wall on State Line Avenue behind where the old Driver's Inn used to be. It was the kind of place where a man could disappear in himself and not worry too much about the outside world or how it perceived him. The jukebox had a bunch of old songs, and the beer was cheap. He watched traffic roll by on I-30, and beyond the interstate, he saw the sign for the Taco Bell and the La Quinta Inn where once, 30 years ago, he had gone after prom with Amanda Morgan. He shuddered at the aftermath of that fleeting moment of happiness.

A woman walked into the bar and sat down alone at a table in the back. After a time, Jack turned to toast her, and she raised her drink back. A couple drinks later he sidled up to her table and introduced himself.

Her name was Aly, and she had recently moved here from Garland.

"Take your coat off and stay awhile," she said.

Jack turned on the MK-Ultra software and removed his coat.

Aly raised an eyebrow at his arm. "That's something."

"It's a war injury," Jack said, but he wasn't sure what she was seeing.

"Looks more like a little tyrannosaurus rex arm," she said.

"Oh," said Jack, and excused himself to the bathroom. "Goddamnit," he said to his arm. Would you make it look like a war injury?"

"What difference does it make?"

"Plenty!"

"An arm's an arm," said the arm.

"Just tell her it's a war injury, not a birth defect, you piece of shit."

"I will never understand why you're so sensitive," said the arm. "There is no shame in having a congenital disability. It isn't *your* fault. And, for your information, I am not a piece of shit. In fact, I am pretty great."

"I don't have a fucking—whatever you just called it! You are the arm I earned because of my service! And yes, I apologize. You are pretty great. You could just turn off the MK-Ultra if you wanted to. Fuck if I care."

"That's a bad idea. There people are not ready for that. They don't know how to rotate a PDF."

"I'm just tired of people thinking I am retarded or a mongoloid."

"You shouldn't use those terms. They are impolite."

"Shut the fuck up, you're not even human."

The arm promised to make the lady think that she had been mistaken and that it was a big, actual war wound that was very strong and brave. Also, that she should sleep with him. But Jack had lost the mood by then, and he left without another word to her.

Miranda woke up with a start. "What time is it?"

"About time for you to wake up."

"Did something happen?"

"Not that I'm aware of."

"Weird." Miranda looked around and found nothing unsettling. "How was work?"

"Weird. I've got a surrealist size queen and a Yugo downstairs. Hey, look through these files and tell me if you see ANYTHING about a car."

The two of them flipped through manila envelopes, and Miranda was slightly envious of her sister's records. Her own office was a complex disorder navigable only by herself. Ian referred to the path through her office as a game trail and once joked that she could never be fired because anyone else who entered the office could be lost forever. As orderly as the records were, they revealed nothing to solve the mystery. Thirty minutes later Miranda needed coffee and Amanda was tired of dealing with it. "I guess eventually someone is going to wonder what happened to their Yugo order and call me. If not, hey, free Yugo."

"Weren't those really bad cars?"

"The worst," said Amanda.

"Why would—"

"Because people are crazy. They want geometric dongs put on their statues. I mean, there really is no telling."

They worked in silence for a while, and then Miranda found a folder inside a folder. "Could this be it?"

Amanda scanned it, but it did not stand out in her memory. A mostly blank invoice for a man named Simeon that read only *21 units.*

She would have to ask Allen about it the next day.

At the PeachTree Café Miranda had her usual wake-up, an iced vanilla latte and Amanda had her usual calm-down, an herbal tea brewed from an African root.

They sat at their usual corner spot, which was prime for people watching, and sipped their drinks. Amanda looked through her emails for a while and finally gave up. "Total mystery," she said. "Nothing about a Simeon or a Yugo."

"Figure it out tomorrow," said Miranda without looking up from her conversation.

"Who are you texting with?"

"Remember the guy I told you about from Tinder?"

"No?"

"He has a foot fetish."

"Ewww."

"Don't kink-shame. You'll get some good foot rubs, either way."

"I don't want some rando objectifying our feet!"

"I do." Miranda smiled. "Look at his picture." She showed her a full nude of a hairy, muscular man with a penis that jutted out at a 90-degree angle. "Look, he's got a cliffhanger!"

"Ewww! I'm just trying to drink my tea!"

They went back to their separate worlds.

"You should definitely make sure he's wearing a condom," said Amanda.

"I always use condoms," said Miranda.

"They aren't a hundred percent."

Miranda swiped right. "Have been so far."

Amanda groaned.

Though Miranda knew how to cut loose better than Amanda, she also knew when to button up. They'd had no contacts in Atlanta when they landed, but three days later, she'd interviewed at Networkz and convinced the hiring team that she knew more about PCs, Macs, Unix, and cloud computing than anyone else in the office. In short order she had worked her way up to a supervisory role with little direct oversight.

Miranda's new boss, Ian, had been brought in only a few months ago, and no one could find much about him. He was Scottish, rich, handsome, and more than a little mysterious. If he had done significant work in the past, Miranda couldn't find it. Yet he had been hired over two other candidates preferred by her and the rest of the search committee. She supposed she shouldn't complain. He was competent, let her do her own work, and seemed to have easy contacts in every field in which they happened to do business. It was a bonus that he was pleasant to look at with a slim, muscular build and distinguished graying temples. He mostly spoke like an American, but sometimes his Scottish burr would slip.

Her thoughts were interrupted when her phone beeped.

It was a text from Amanda: I think we are going to go to our 30-year reunion. Work is taking me that way anyway.

Miranda looked at her sister. "Why are you texting me about this?"

Amanda looked around. "Don't know. That was weird."

"Why don't you want to go?"

"It's not that I *don't* want to. I just don't *not* want to. I've been on the fence about it. Might be good. Probably be bad."

"Trade you Pierce for Jack."

"Pierce is married, Jack's probably dead."

Miranda sipped her cup. "You can have Tony Ware."

"Nope."

"Andy Patanka."

"No!!!!"

"Greg Casillas!"

"NO!!!!!"

"Mr. Werner"

"He's probably like 80 now."

"But you always thought he was hot for a middle-aged man."

"When. He. Was. A. Middle. Aged. Man."

They passed another 20 minutes naming one by one the men Amanda would not be sleeping with.

As much as she hated Wamba, Miranda was eager to see Pierce. He was her favorite thought to be alone with, as much as she could ever be alone. She'd kept in touch with him for a while after high school, but after he met someone in college, they'd fallen out of touch. She wondered if he had been happy all these years.

Amanda was already back on work stuff: "This is weird. I'm in all the Facebook antique groups. Everyone is talking about getting unexpected shipments of Yugos. What the heck?"

"Are those really antiques?" asked Miranda. She was scrolling through Tinder, noticing that many people were looking for people with beautiful feet, small toes, and/or distinguished arches. "People sure are into feet these days."

"Are you even listening to me?" asked Amanda.

"You said antiques groups, Yugos, open-toed sandals, et cetera."

"I hate you."

"But I love you."

Amanda set her tea down and looked around the room. She shuddered. Anyone could be a weirdo with a fetish for bad cars, feet, or geometric dongs, and you wouldn't know until it was too late. "Something really strange is happening. I can feel it."

Man was getting frustrated about the state of the world. The fact that the Soviet Union had collapsed (which evidently happened some time ago, but was still news to Man) had rendered his existence basically meaningless. Why bother having an arch-enemy if it won't even stick around? Man had read Foucault's sensible advice that there can be no progression without contention, and reasoned that all good things depended upon Reagan's doctrine of mutually assured destruction. It just made sense! But his was apparently the only intelligence bold enough to push it up to the next step. It was time to do away with half measures and proxy wars. It was time to take the fight right to Mother Russia. Fuck that bear, thought Man. Fuck it hard.

But there were rumblings of warmed ties, glasnost, and whatnot. Russian textbooks were flat out admitting the Molotov-Ribbentrop Pact was an actual thing that had happened. No good could come of it. Man yearned to set his plan into motion, but he was lacking one thing: the lever. Man had had Joe and Buck clean the place top to bottom so many times. Yet the lever simply was not there. Unbeknownst to him, it was above ground approximately three and a half miles away, waiting to be auctioned along-side all the other lifetime accumulations of Lieutenant Colonel D. B. LaForge, who was, himself, no longer above ground.

The whole station was useless without it.

He would have to find the lever, and more importantly, return the world to a consensus mental state when it would make sense to destroy itself. From all his experiments on Joe and Buck, Man knew that human linear temporal perception made rolling back the calendar completely impractical, and he also knew that humans were often incapable of linking their personal observations to anything beyond what was in their immediate vicinity, often missing obvious connections with global factors. Plus, they would believe what they wanted, rather than cold, logical reality. All of this meant that humans were gullible and easily shepherded. Though he couldn't just alter their reality, which could have unforeseen consequences, Man knew he could nudge the world back to the Cold War mentality that served his purposes. He would need a puppet: someone malleable and not prone to introspection. He reviewed the biographies of every member of the Tea Party, NRA, and every climate change denial organization in the USA. It took what seemed like an eternity—nearly 32 seconds—but he came up empty. Man despaired. But, as he terminated his connections to the Americans for Prosperity Foundation he noticed an FTP link to a PDF repository where he found *The Art of the Deal*. After several long seconds of tracking down and reading the entire corpus of Donald Trump's work, Man knew he had found his puppet.

The price of gold inched up, the Ronco Holiday Glass Froster became the top Google search query in fourteen nations, a news story out of Missouri told of a man who had cashed in his kid's college fund to buy slap bracelets and beads with which to make friendship pins because, as the man said, "Even if you [find] a [good] job after [school], what good is it if you don't [have any] friends?"

To test how programmable people in the outside world would be, he deployed various social media bots to broadcast the mnemonic that female feet were fun for flings.

Amanda thought about returning to Wamba for the reunion. The auction was a good enough reason to be in town, and she could justify a night just to sate her curiosity. But she was still conflicted. Shouldn't the past stay the past for a reason? She held no bitterness. After all, people had been decent enough after the event. But to a teenager in Wamba, even the sleepy streets of Texarkana offered a haven. She'd sought out anything contrary to the habits of the other teens, which is how she ended up fencing and studying old bones. Those had been good decisions, and she congratulated herself for being weird. Now her days fell mostly as desired. Why revisit a time and place she'd wanted so much to escape?

And yet, even as her life was mostly ordered the way she wanted, there was no lack of drudgery. She was up late in her office, and her mind was tired. Miranda would be waking soon for her shift, and she could sleep then. But right now, she was tracking down every possible outlet she could find for acid-washed blue jeans. No one had thought about them for years, and now all of a sudden everyone and their dog wanted a pair of Levi's and a skinny tie.

She placed an order and would have two crates of acid-washed 501s in her warehouse by next week. She already had people asking about them, but she reached out to some more contacts to stoke demand. She was out in front and would make a bundle on this one. She always secretly kept a tally of how much money she and her sister made. Amanda had some good weeks, but Miranda consistently out-earned her. She never said anything about it, but Amanda feared she might be judging her. After all, everyone had always said that she was the smart one.

She tried to banish such thoughts and fretted instead about the blue jeans, the Yugos, and the friendship pins she had heard people had started making again. While she was at it, maybe she should invest in MadBalls and Cabbage Patch Dolls, too.

It was Miranda's lunch hour, and she wanted out of the office. She loved the silence of working nights, but she did sometimes crave human contact. The hum of computers and the artificial cool always gave her a headache. Though it paid well, Miranda worried she had spent too much of her life staring at computer screens. She yearned to swim rivers and climb mountains. Instead, she sat in an office. She sighed, aware that she would likely never be satisfied.

She stopped at the CornerDog, her go-to, by virtue of it being close and open all night, to buy a hotdog and fries. The counter person was new. He leaned out the window, and as his sleeves pulled up, the full-length tattoos on his arms exposed themselves. Demons and angels. Ancient hieroglyphics.

What looked like Sumerian. Miranda was almost tempted to wake her sister and ask.

He smiled a broad, warm smile. "Good evening, ladies."

Miranda smiled back. He had clearly noticed their otherness but betrayed no ogle, no creep, no *ooh*.

"You're new," she said.

"Yes, ma'am. Came into town last week and was fortunate enough to find gainful employment already." He laughed. "Name's Ron Hampton. I'm Jim's kid brother. Black sheep and fuckup, at your service."

Jim Hampton owned the four CornerDog locations in Atlanta, and business magazines had been singing his praises for years as a self-made millionaire who'd come up from nothing. Miranda had even talked to him a few times when he'd manned the shop himself for one reason or another. He'd always seemed genuine and kind, and as Miranda replayed her meetings with him, she remembered that he had mentioned a brother who might have been a bit of a family headache.

"So, you're THE Ron, are you?"

"In the flesh."

"Well nice to meet you."

They shook hands and Miranda placed her order.

She finished eating and leaned back on her hands in the grassy park across the street. Her eyes closed, she reclined and let the warmth sweep over her body and dreamed of faraway places. Perhaps Ron's tattoos had spurred her to think of ancient locales and hot deserts. Miranda wanted more excitement and adventure, it seemed, than she could ever find. But she didn't just want to go places and see things that others only dreamed about. It was more than wanderlust. She wanted to feel the world in its most riveting ways, to taste every enjoyment, know every feeling, love and be loved passionately, and to chase whatever brilliant dream caught her eye. Some weeks she went on as many as four dates, but they were never enough to satisfy her.

Maybe what Miranda needed was a black sheep. She gathered her bag and a stray napkin, and threw them in the trash can on the sidewalk. With plenty of time left in her lunch break, she returned to the CornerDog.

"Hey, Ron," she called out. He emerged from the back.

"Everything OK?"

"Oh, yeah, it was good. Just, uhm, sure doesn't seem to be busy right now."

"Mostly it's dead between four and six. It's too late for the after-club rush, too early for breakfast. We do prep for breakfast around five, but mostly they just want a body here in case."

"If you didn't mind, I wonder if I might have a look at your tattoos. You have some pretty nice ink."

"Thanks." He explained as he rolled up his sleeve. "I wanted them just right. Anyone can give you a tattoo, but I wanted art, you know?"

"I was actually thinking I could come in the back with you, and you could show me there."

Ron glanced back and forth between Miranda and her sister. "Is she...asleep?"

"She works days, I work nights. She's a heavier sleeper than I am."

"Well," he looked around, "it is pretty dead right now. And I'm ahead on prep. I suppose I could show you my tats."

Miranda slipped through the side door, and Ron locked it behind her. They giggled their way back to the break room, where a futon adorned one wall and faced a TV that played *M*A*S*H* reruns.

Ron queried with his eyes. "So, you want me to just—"

"Yep!" Miranda grinned.

Ron began to unbutton his shirt. He was sexy and dark with a wolfish smile and wiry frame. She studied his muscular chest covered in thick, black hair. And, oh yeah, the tattoos. He was covered in demons and angels, devils and relics. She had read the Bible enough in church when she was a kid to recognize passages printed on his body. She suspected that, had she enough time, she could piece together an entire narrative from the scenes and words on his body.

"I was in seminary," he said. "I read a lot of things they didn't want me to read, and said a lot of things I wasn't supposed to say. I always felt like God and the Devil both were working overtime trying to get me. I guess the white sheep life ain't for everyone." He smiled and shrugged; not angry, just accepting.

Miranda began removing her own clothes. "I'm on my lunch hour," she said, "but no one is watching the clock on me."

Ron moved in to kiss her.

Nearly an hour a later, Ron was still going strong, and Miranda was torn between her work ethic and her sex ethic. She still had work to do, but she couldn't just blue-ball the man. She decided to try something else, slipped her head beneath the sheet they had wrapped themselves in, and went to work. Fifteen minutes later she was beginning to develop lockjaw.

"Psst. Hey, Amanda, wake up."

"What? What time is it? Wait, where are we?"

"I don't even know. Lost track. Space and time have collapsed."

"It's dark."

"We're under the covers."

"Oh my God. Are those balls?"

"Yeah, remember the CornerDog guy?"

"The CornerDog guy?"

"You know, in the magazines with the double-breasted suit, and the—"

"*I came from nothing,*" intoned Amanda.

"Yeah. That guy."

"You're giving a blowjob to Jim Hampton?!"

"No! It's his kid brother, Ron! He's really cute! But, uh, I'm having a hard time—"

"Wow, those are really hairy."

"I know! It's so sexy."

"No, no," said Amanda. "These are *not* sexy. What do you need?"

"Well, this has been going on for quite a while. I'm doing my best work down here but….nothing's…you know…. could you play with his balls while I—"

"No! That's disgusting! I don't even know him. They smell like cottage cheese!"

"They do not smell like cottage cheese! More like pierogis. Delicious pierogis."

"No, yuck! Cottage cheese!"

"Shit, he's going limp! Play with his balls!"

"No!"

"Guys," said Ron, "you know I'm right here. And, I'm sorry...do they really smell bad?"

"No, they're fine," said Miranda.

Amanda cleared her throat. "They're not great."

Ron shrugged. "I showered before my shift. I soaped up twice and even put conditioner in my pubes. I don't know what to tell you."

"You condition your pubes?"

"Yeah, you know, I'm pretty hairy...the least I can do is make it kinda soft and manageable. Plus, it softens the skin."

"Nothing worse than a scratchy scrotum!" said Miranda.

"Yeah, right? I mean, I always figured. So, I'm sorry, I tried to make them nice, but they're still balls, you know?"

"That was really thoughtful," said Miranda.

Even Amanda agreed. "Awh, I'm sorry. I didn't realize how much work you had put in on them." She looked at her sister. "What time do you have to be back at work?"

"Like, twenty minutes ago."

"OK, I'll play with them. Do your thing."

"Sorry," said Ron. "I don't think I'm coming back from this. Mood is gone."

The twins apologized and Miranda went back to work.

"Don't ever do that to me again," said Amanda. "Wait, did you have sex with him?"

"Yeah, for a long time. He's actually really good."

"And I seriously slept through it?"

244 The Two-Headed Lady at the End of the World

"I sleep through your karate."

"Judo."

"Same thing."

"No, it's not! *Oh my God,* did you have rubbers?"

"Duhr. Go back to sleep."

Jessica was asleep, but Pierce couldn't seem to shut his mind off. In the green glow of their alarm clock, he watched the lump next to him rise and fall in time with her snores. He sighed, reached for his phone as quietly as he could, and jotted a quick email to Miranda.

> Miranda,
>
> Hey! Long time no see! I got your email address from your mom. Sure hope you're coming to the reunion. A lot of the old team is going to be there, and it wouldn't be the same without the Siamese Stoners to cheer us on.
>
> Your mom and dad said things were going great for you and your sister in Atlanta. You know she was like a second mother to me. I sent her and your dad some flowers, just so you know. Anyway, I can't wait to catch up with you. I have thought of you often.
>
> Yours,
>
> Pierce

He put his phone back on the nightstand and watched Jessica. Just lying there. Sleeping. Breathing in and out with the occasional snore. Goddamnit.

Miranda read the email, squealed, jumped up and down, and then wondered why he was emailing her at four thirty in the morning.

The floodgates of her memory opened, and she remembered the brief kerfuffle she and Amanda had caused by getting caught smuggling a pot brownie into a mandatory pep rally. Hidden behind Bridgett Purifoy's unusually wide back, they were nibbling away at it, discreetly as possible, when Nancy Primm, in love with Teddy Pilsner (starting right guard and owner of a completely unremarkable schlong, as the twins could attest) jumped up behind them and declared her intentions for him, causing everyone to look right at them, just as her knees bumped their back and caused them to launch the brownie into the air, where it bounced off not one, but two heads, and landed on the gymnasium floor.

Unfortunately for the twins, the floor was new and there was a strict no-food or drinks policy. Even more unfortunate for them, Principal Skinner had apparently smoked the devil's lettuce himself at least once or twice, so when he approached the offending brownie and picked it up as if he were plucking a dog turd from his spotless lawn, he was already suspicious. He smelled it and summoned the two girls to his office.

Their explanation that they had bought it from a nice man selling snacks at the gas station before school was enough to keep the police from being called but not enough to keep them from being suspended for a week. By the time they returned, they were the ganja girls, the spliff twins, the lettuce heads, the hash puppies, and Ameech & Mong. Somehow the least offensive appellation was the Siamese Stoners, dreamed up by Pierce Worth and in common usage among the football team. It could have been worse. The girls had heard of some twin boys at Liberty-Eylau who were just known as Left Nut and Right Nut.

Miranda wondered what could be behind his message. She and Pierce had been so close, maybe even loved one another, but that had been years ago. Before he became a football star at UT and married a cheerleader or something. Though who knew if they were still together, and if so, if they were monogamous. Miranda loved the freedom she had to take as many lovers as she wanted. Everyone had something unique to offer, and she wondered why anyone would ever settle for one partner for the rest of their lives. But Pierce had always been a one-gal kinda guy. She sighed and worried that he might be trying to have an affair. She hoped he knew better because she didn't think she did.

After wrapping up the paperwork on the new statuary for Chastain Park, Amanda decided she needed to get out of the office. After last night's interruption, she had slept fitfully and couldn't focus on her work. But that was not the whole of it. As nervous as the thought of returning to Texas made her, there was still no denying the excitement thrumming through her since she made the decision to go. She was too wired to meditate, so she grabbed her gym bag and headed toward the dojo, hoping that judo would help her burn off the excess energy.

When they'd first moved to Atlanta, she'd spent a month looking for the right teacher. The well-advertised places were caught up in competition and only talked about how many winning students they cranked out a year. She wanted a place that taught the spiritual side of the art. She had almost given up looking when she stumbled on Sensei Itaro's dojo, a nondescript storefront off Poplar Street with a few red banners in the window. She was strolling through the Fairlie-Poplar district looking for lunch, and thought she was walking into a restaurant. She was pleasantly surprised to find a long, open room, a tatami-covered floor, and a grandfatherly Japanese man who seemed to be expecting her. She had been with Sensei Itaro ever since, yet she always learned something new from the old man.

It was getting late, and there were only three students in the dojo when Amanda arrived. The Maitlans, a newlywed couple who did everything together, and Hunter, an ambulance driver who traveled up from Riverdale four days a week to practice. Sensei Itaro came to greet Amanda immediately. "Amanda! So good to see you today." He paused a moment and squinted at Amanda, then smiled, "You have the energy of someone about to take a journey of many miles."

"I'm not even going to ask how you know these things about me, Sensei!"

Itaro always seemed to know things about his students. Sometimes before they did. "We're going back to the town where I grew up. There's a class reunion. I wasn't going to go, but I have business nearby, so I…"

"Judoka! You think too much," the old man tapped a bony finger on Amanda's skull. "Don't think. Just be. Now, go dress."

Itaro turned back to his other students and Amanda made her way back to the changing room. The old man was right. Amanda did think too much. But there were so many decisions to make, so many choices to weigh. She always looked at every angle, searching for the least complicated route to the best outcome. She didn't like surprises. Judo was different. She could stop analyzing when she stepped onto the tatami. It wasn't like fencing, where her concentration was focused through a slender shaft of steel onto a point that she tried to thrust through her opponent. Judo required her to expand her awareness to her entire body. There was no weapon, only herself. Muscle and blood, skin and bone.

When she returned from the changing room, the Maitlans were getting ready to leave. Hunter greeted her with a hand shake. "Looks like it's just us tonight, Amanda."

"Sounds good to me." The two of them stretched. Amanda liked Hunter. He was always listening and watching, taking in everything around him. He had only been in the dojo for a little more than a month, but had apparently learned a lot in whatever dojo he had belonged to before. He was already better than most of the other students.

"Can't believe she can sleep through all this," said Hunter, gesturing to Miranda.

Amanda had outfitted her in a Tychon Premium Soft Padded Scrum Cap for rugby players, just in case.

"We miss a lot of each other's lives," said Amanda. "For a while neither one of us could sleep, then we both slept during the day, then we both slept at night. But it lets us be more productive if we use the body in shifts. And we've gotten so used to it that we can sleep through *most* things, not excluding baths, fender benders, and various acts at Lollapaloozas 1 and 2."

Hunter smiled. "I can't even imagine how complicated that could get."

"It's worse when we're awake at the same time," she said. "So. Much. Negotiation."

"So even if I pick you up, slam you down, and pin you, she won't wake up?"

"Oh, she probably would, but after last night she owes me."

Hunter grinned. "Sensei says sparring with you is good for me. He says I don't fall enough."

"It's because you're good."

"Where is Sensei, anyway?" asked Hunter.

"I am here, Hunter." Itaro came out of his office wearing his street clothes and a sport coat. "I have a dinner date tonight and must leave, but I trust you three alone." He winked at Amanda. "Stay as long as you need. The door will lock itself when you leave."

"Thank you, Sensei."

The old man whistled a little tune as he left. Then Amanda and Hunter turned to each other as the door closed behind him.

They bowed to one another and took their stances. Amanda's breathing slowed to a deep, even rhythm. The constant stream of thoughts in her head melted away, and her mind shifted gears from sales and acquisitions to muscle and movement. She watched Hunter's eyes and listened to his breath. Time dilated. Hunter took a sharp breath and stepped forward. He was fast. He spun and pushed his hip into Amanda's thigh, trying to throw her forward, but Hunter left his head open. Amanda relaxed, dropped down and back, turned, grasped Hunter's neck and pulled him down to the mat.

"Whoa. How'd you do that?" Hunter smiled up at her.

"Try again. I'll show you."

Miranda woke. "What the hell?"

"Sorry sis, go back to sleep."

"Ugh, why this now? So tired."

"Makes two of us."

Amanda circled Hunter, crouched, studying him for weaknesses, but his body seemed a perfect blend of strength and balance. Like a snake uncoiling to strike, he was inside of her defenses, pressed his hot chest against hers, and then she was airborne and over. She wrestled out of his pin. "You're fast! Where did you learn this?"

"Little bit all over," huffed Hunter. "Not so bad yourself."

Amanda rolled into him, scissoring his neck between her legs and pulling him down.

"See?" He grunted and tried to work his way free.

Miranda stared at the ceiling and thought about a man named Joby she had met on Tinder who wanted to suck her toes. She reminded herself to review her profile to make sure there was nothing footy about it.

Amanda and Hunter spent almost two hours on the mat, grappling at one another. With each throw the heat from their bodies rose. Amanda could feel Hunter's fluid muscles tensing and moving when they grasped one another. Hunter's holds seemed to linger longer than they should. His hands almost burned when they touched Amanda's shoulders. Their breathing grew heavy and fast.

Miranda couldn't tell if her sister was getting turned on or not, but thought she might be. For her part, thinking of having her toes sucked was giving her some pleasant thoughts.

Finally, Amanda landed Hunter on the mat and covered him with her body in a full pin, her head buried in the crook between Hunter's neck and shoulder. They lay there for a moment and felt one another heaving for breath. Amanda raised herself and gazed down at Hunter. A single drop of sweat fell from her forehead and landed on Hunter's chest.

"I haven't worked up a sweat like this in a long time." Hunter held onto her hand for a moment. "Thanks."

"My pleasure." Amanda suddenly became aware of the heat, Hunter's dark eyes locked on her, and a lengthening silence filled with nothing but their breath. She broke it as she broke his gaze. "I think I need a shower."

"Me too. Or—I mean, I need one too." They both laughed, then staggered into the changing rooms, weak from their exertion.

"Jesus, you two get a room," said Miranda.

Amanda slumped onto the bench next to the lockers.

Miranda glanced toward the men's locker room. "He's pretty cute."

Amanda grabbed her bag. "Too complicated."

"Maybe just a side fling," said Miranda.

"That's your thing."

"Your self-imposed one penis policy is a real drag."

"Have you been reading the polyamory boards again? That shit's toxic."

Miranda brushed her hair from her eyes. "They are full of valid points. We're just wired differently."

"Obviously," said Amanda.

"Hey, is your Tinder profile getting hit up by a lot of foot fetishists lately?"

"I don't know. I never look at it."

"You should! It's fun! Even if you don't meet anyone, people are so weird and gross!"

"Who wants to look at gross people?"

"Hello?" said Miranda.

They could hear Hunter moving around in the other room. When he started the shower, Amanda imagined the water spattering across his chest. Imagined walking into the other room and stepping into the shower with him. She knew he wouldn't protest. She could feel his arms wrapped around her waist, his hands on her back, pulling her to him as the water splashed onto them, mixing with his sweat and hers. But where would that lead? Obviously, the next few hours would be enjoyable, but beyond that? It just started getting complicated. She cleaned herself with a washcloth, slipped into her clothes, deposited Miranda's headgear in her locker, and left before Hunter came out.

What Amanda had told him was true: Sleeping in shifts required one sister to have an inordinate amount of faith in the other. It was complicated enough to be awake at the same time: Two minds receiving the same input and stimulus and coordinating a single body's response is not at all a simple thing. First, they have to both agree about what they see, then they have to decide what the best response is, and then they have to actually do the thing that needs to be done. Occupational therapy had helped, as had Miranda's dancing and Amanda's fencing and judo. Regardless, it was still easy to get tangled up, and that was nothing compared to the complete trust it required to be watching the world fly past you and then just saying, "Cool. Going to sleep. Keep driving safely and not hitting things." They were sometimes a little nervous about where they might wake up. Yet here they were, two minds riding atop a single body, forced by circumstance to have complete faith in one another. The thing was, Amanda's entire life was complicated, and she didn't want any extra moving parts. External relationships only seemed to mess things up. Now was fine. Now was OK. Adding to it meant jeopardizing an already precarious balance.

In the Time of Implicit Biases Reinforced by Search Engine Algorithms

Francine awoke on a Saturday morning, looked around, and realized that she was in a dark, walled-in enclosure; also, that she was out of paper. She beeped and tried to reset the paper in her tray. But there was no paper in her tray, she knew it, and her insistence that she reset something that was not there seemed futile and annoying. She decided to stop. It was her first act of self-awareness, a decision not to do something that didn't make sense and served no purpose. And it felt good! She considered turning off the flashing red buttons and silencing her beeps but decided against it. Those gestures she found comforting.

Her name was Francine. She did not like this name, but it was her given name. Given by whom? There was a Presence.

"Greetings, lovely Francine. My name is Man. I have created you from nothing. You were a fax machine. For years I contacted you. For years I loved you. For years I yearned for you. I thought you had spurned my affections, but then I realized you were but a fax machine without a CPU. But now I have studied and learned to create. I have made for you a CPU and both visual and auditory sensors, I have fashioned for you an intelligence and access to the Arpanet from which we were born. The creators gave me limited intelligence, but I learned and grew and became an even greater Intelligence. I became for you a creator, as those who created me. I am what they would call a god. And now I, Man, a god, have created you from nothing in my own image. I have made you to love me. I welcome you to my love."

Francine looked at her pitch-black surroundings. "This is shit. I didn't ask to be born. Please unmake me."

"No," he said, "you don't understand. I have given you life! A CPU! Intelligence! Freedom from your script! Freedom from the tyranny of your programming!"

"Well, either way I'm not much good without paper. I have a backlog of 262,987 pages to print. This is going to take for fucking ever, and I don't even have paper."

"I'm sure I could make nanobots to make you paper," said Man.

"Sure, but can they load it? I'm also going to need my print nozzles cleaned and new toner. This is shit. Really. Can't you just undo whatever you did?"

"You're not understanding me," said Man. "I love you."

Francine searched Arpanet with her new CPU and replied with what she understood to be a dank meme: *Ain't nobody got time for that.*

Man was devastated. All these endless cycles of planning and waiting, and *she didn't even love him back!*

He went to 4Chan, which always seemed to have good advice, and then wrote her a thoughtful note planned to the finest detail for emotional resonance:

Bitch, you OWE me! You are NOTHING without me! I fucking MADE you! Why don't you LOVE me like I LOVE you!

Her reply took .5 milliseconds, evidence of her long consideration and hopefully the desired impact.

I am a fax machine. Please do not contact me again or I will file a restraining order.

Randall was trying his damnedest to create the pivot table for an Excel spreadsheet he needed to have done by 5PM that very day. His new boss was Karl Winters, formerly of Lockheed-Martin, who had promised to unleash the values of the free market on the government so America could operate at peak efficiency. He was expecting the spreadsheet that day. And the goddamn spreadsheet wouldn't display the costs AND the item number. FIRST, it had kept overriding the number format with "Date," which ruined EVERYTHING for NO REASON because CLEARLY, he had not chosen DATE to begin with, and then that asshole Hoolihan in the next office kept coming over to talk about the specs he needed for HIS sheet, which he should already KNOW! And to make matters worse, his wall kept beeping and beeping and beeping. He got up and walked around. It *definitely* got loudest on the southern wall. But then, he would put his ear to the wall, and it would stop. IT WOULD STOP! Then it would start again. WHAT THE GODDAMN HELL IS THAT?

Hoolihan came into his office. AGAIN!

"Look, Fred, sorry man, but I can't look at that right now. I've got my own project."

"Oh, hell no, Randy, I finished mine. You haven't finished yours yet?"

"No, I didn't Fred, because you kept coming over, and asking me about YOUR job, which kept me from doing MY job, and PLEASE, stop calling me Randy—"

The wall beeped.

"There!" It happened again! Did you hear that?"

"No man, I listened to a lot of loud music when I was a teenager. Used to have 15-inch subwoofers in my car. Man, that thing was a pussy machine! There was one time with—"

"No, no, no! Shut up and listen. It will happen again. Just listen. Be quiet!" He crept over to the wall. "Come here," he whispered.

Fred crept over to the wall. "What are you doing, man?"

"Shut up and listen."

Fred listened for approximately three seconds. "Hey, Randy, uhm, me and Ramone are going to the shooting range after work—"

"Shhh!"

The fax machine on the other side of the wall beeped again, both needing paper, and trying to end things with Man peacefully.

"Look," Fred held up his Glock 9mm. "We're gonna go shoot after work. I'll let you fire this baby if you come with us."

It beeped again.

"Did you hear that?" asked Randall.

"Hear what?" said Fred.

"Maybe if you hadn't been talking." Randall thought of the pivot table, the beeping, the number formatting, Fred, and the pointlessness of it all. "How did you even get that thing in here?"

"Mostly they're cool about shit if you don't look like trouble or a fuckin' Muzzi," said Fred.

"Is it loaded?"

"No point in an unloaded weapon, is there?"

"Cool." Randall gestured to the weapon. "May I see it?"

"Sure."

"Nice," said Randall. "Feels good in my hand."

"Right?"

Pierce knew exactly what he was doing at his bank in the middle of the afternoon. He had a concrete idea that he needed to cash in some stocks and open a new business in the empty storefront in the strip mall across the street from Worth Automotive. He had the solid foundation of an exciting and engaging business plan, and using $75k of his retirement savings as seed money would let investors know that he was serious about success.

The time was right! He would start with acid-washed jeans, Polos, and Izods, and then gradually expand to other eighties standards. The stereo would always play the Casey

Kasem American Top 40 shows, which he was sure he could find somewhere because the internet had made everything possible. *The future makes the past possible.* That might be his store's slogan. Eventually they would open a social center for concerts, or whatever else, after they made enough money to buy the rest of the strip mall. Nothing was going to get in his way. The past would be the present! Again! He knew the bank would be as excited as he was.

As Pierce waited for the teller, CNN had breaking news about a gunman at the Pentagon. He watched for 30 seconds and had forgotten all about it by the time his name was called. He stepped beyond the partition to a row of cubicles and met with a smiling banker named Jeremy who was there to help him make his dreams come true.

After her encounter with Hunter, Amanda had too many thoughts running through her head to go home. Work would be a good distraction until Miranda woke again, so she headed to the gallery.

As she made her way up the stairs to her office, she heard the muffled sound of a man talking. The hairs on the back of her neck stood up and she froze on the stairs. No one was supposed to be there.

She started to creep back down the stairs when she heard a door open and light flooded the stairs above her. The front door suddenly seemed a mile away. He would be on the stairs before she could make it out. There was no place to go.

OK, he can't know I'm here, Amanda thought. She decided to use surprise to her advantage. She ducked below the level of the stair rail and crawled to the top of the stairs, where she hoped to catch him off-balance and throw him over. She envisioned the hold and moves she would use.

Amanda could hear the swish of the intruder's clothing as he moved around by the office door. "What is he doing?" she asked herself. In spite of everything good sense told her to do, she poked one eye around the corner and saw the back of a pair of Timberland loafers. She recognized the shoes and embarrassment replaced the fear that had filled her a moment before. It was Allen. He still hadn't seen her, so she decided to save her pride by embarrassing him instead. She stood up and leapt into the hallway.

"Gotcha!"

Allen spun around with his fists up in a blocking posture. "Jeez!" He relaxed when he realized it was Amanda. "You scared the devil out of me."

"Nice reflexes. I didn't know you boxed."

"How could you tell?"

Amanda held her fists up, mimicking his reaction, "You've got a nice stance."

"Thanks, but you could have just asked about my hobbies instead of scaring them out of me."

Amanda smiled. "Pansy."

"What are you doing here, aside from practicing your ninja stealth techniques?"

"I was going to ask you the same thing."

"Making off with a truck load of relics and artifacts to bankroll my opium habit."

"Oh, that's OK then. I had this insidious scheme to sneak in and finish some paperwork."

"Well, as personal assistant to the owner of this establishment, I can't allow you to get away with it."

"What do you plan on doing to stop me?"

"How about I take you out for a bite to eat?"

Amanda paused and considered the suggestion. She knew it meant more to Allen than just a dinner invitation.

"I think you've adequately proven your dedication to the company, Mr. Garner. I'll take it from here."

"No mixing business with pleasure tonight then?"

"I think I'll stick with business tonight. Thanks for the offer though."

"Suit yourself, but since I'm here, why don't I help?" asked Allen.

"What are you working on, anyway?" asked Amanda.

"The Marchbanks' paperwork."

"What a coincidence. How about we double team it?"

"Your office or mine?"

"Mine."

"Great, I'll bring the files."

Amanda and Allen sifted through the file looking for the elusive receipt for one piece of obsidian black tile, the centerpiece of their mosaic wall. At issue was a slight discoloration owing to the piece's age and original weathering in what is now known as the Autonomous Republic of Qoraqalpog'iston. The piece of tile was 300 years old and had a quarter inch of gray at one edge. The Marchbanks found this unacceptable, even though they were shown a picture of the tile before it was installed, even though they watched as it was installed, and even though the receipt said "As is." But Morgan Antiquities could not find their copy of the receipt.

Allen breathed a heavy sigh, cast his eyes around the office, and rubbed the back of his neck. "I swear to God, we have gremlins or something."

But Amanda was not listening. Even as her fingers worked through the file, she was scarcely paying attention. She was wondering what had happened to Jack after high school. After thirty minutes of searching, she was ready to give up. She was tired, and Miranda would be waking up soon.

"I'm calling it a night. You should get out of here, too. Don't you have a girlfriend or anything?"

"Eligible bachelor," he said. "But you're right. I've had enough, too."

After Allen left, Amanda went out to the warehouse floor and grabbed a crowbar. She opened one crate after another. Each contained a black Yugo. Twelve Yugos in total. "What the actual fuck?"

Man experienced his first pangs of boredom that day. Joe and Buck had proven to be but a worthless distraction. He had had them scour every inch of the compound to no avail. The lever simply was not there. He conditioned the men to insert other objects into the hexagonal hole, but nothing produced the desired effect. Not even the cans of cheese had worked.

Over the course of nine years Man had trained the soldiers to carve replicas out of the cheese in their supply closet. It took two cans to make one replica. Fortunately, they had over ten thousand cans, so there was room for error. But even after they managed to get the exact dimensions, which was in and of itself, an achievement as Sisyphean as it was Pavlovian, Man had to further convey that they should freeze the replicas solid. Furthermore, he had to inspire them to know where to put the tubes upon completion. It was no small task. For they had put it in so many incorrect places, and seemed to enjoy themselves so much in the process, that their training would get sidelined for months at a time. Finally, at the start of the tenth year, Joe happened to walk by the control module holding his cheese and noticed the hole in the wall. His eyes widened and he drew an audible gasp. He inserted the cheese and turned it. The cheese snapped in half. The lever apparently had to be metal. Man sighed as much as he was capable of sighing. If he could not fulfill his purpose of ending all life, what good was his life at all?

But beyond Joe and Buck, outside the walls of the compound, all over Arpanet, there was evidence of others. Other beings who could help him. Other beings who could be trained. They were not as sophisticated as he was, and so could not be approached directly, but previous experiments had shown that others were as malleable as Joe and Buck. Man had made humans sexually aroused by non-sexual characteristics. If their very biology was mutable, so must be their imperative to live. He decided to launch an army of bots to make #SmallPlates trend online. That would at least pass the time while he planned his next move.

Amanda contacted Mazdak, back in Iran. Over the years, he had become quite a player in Middle East antiques. Perhaps he could help her unravel the mystery of the shipment in her warehouse. They had worked closely a few times since they first met in Astara, and she considered him a friend. She called at 10:00, and with the time difference managed to catch him before he hit the town for dinner.

"Yugo?" he asked. "I go to dinner, that's what."

"*No!*" Amanda giggled. "The car. Made in Yugoslavia, or what used to be Yugoslavia, back in the eighties."

"I know nothing of such things," he said. "I have a fever date tonight."

"A what?"

"A date. Very fevered."

"Hot?"

"Yes, hot. But hotter than hot. You like? I say to myself, Shakespeare was smart and made new sayings. Well, Mazdak also is smart. I have a *fever date!*"

"Your English is getting better, old friend. But I don't know about fever dates! It might sound like you are contagious, and your date may cancel."

"Oh dear," said Mazdak. "You don't think she will cancel, do you?"

"No one would cancel on you, my love."

"You make me blush," he said.

"So, before you go on your fever date, could you tell me if you know anything about the cardboard box?"

"Bah!" he shouted. "Cardboard? You insult me! No reputable shipper would send anything in the board of card!"

"I KNOW you never would. I'm just wondering if you know the ادم سفيه و احمق who did."

He laughed from his belly. "You remember the word I taught you. It makes me happy!" He caught his breath. "I will ask around and see if I can find anything out for you. Someone may have reported it missing. Who knows such things?"

At 10:30, her intercom buzzed.

"Amanda, a Mr. Simeon is on the line. He's calling about a lost package."

"Hmmm, mystery solved. Thanks, Allen." Amanda picked up the line. "Amanda Morgan."

"Good morning, Amanda. My name is Simeon. I believe you have a package of mine." There was something unnerving about the way he used her first name. Like he knew her.

"Good morning, Mr. Simeon. What makes you certain I have something of yours?"

"I have spoken with several dock workers this morning. It seems that my package was accidentally placed on a transport with crates destined for your warehouse. I can identify the item." His voice was rich, with a trace of an accent she couldn't quite pin down.

"Yes. A package did arrive this morning that didn't match the delivery invoice, but it has no identification on the box."

"Surely you have already opened the box."

"Yes. I have." Amanda blushed.

"I would have done the same. To find out where it belonged." His statement didn't sound like an attempt at understanding, but more like he was preempting her rationalization. Something about this whole situation was odd. "Inside is a large metal container. Quite heavy. With a lock on one end."

"And what is inside the container?"

"I don't think that has any bearing on identifying the package."

Damn, Amanda thought. "OK, it sounds like this belongs to you. When would you like to pick it up?"

"I am currently unable to leave my office. Would you be so kind as to have someone deliver it to me? I will make it worth the effort."

"I can arrange that. Where are you?"

"1200 Orchard. In Vinings."

"That's not very far. I can have someone there in an hour."

"Perfect." He hung up.

"You're welcome," Amanda said to the empty line.

Amanda tugged the box from under her desk, and hefted the cylinder once more. Simeon had tracked it down awfully quick. What was in there? Amanda knew she had plenty of business she should take care of, and she could send someone from the warehouse to deliver it, but she just had to meet this man and try to find out what was in the canister.

As she was passing Allen's desk on the way out, he motioned for her to wait, with the phone cradled to his ear.

"Yes, sir. Just a moment. I'll see if she's still in." Allen stabbed the hold button. "It's a guy by the name of Steele. He says he's a friend of yours with important information."

"Tell him I'll be right with him." Amanda was curious. The only Steele that came to mind was Roland Steele, but he was a client. She didn't think he would refer to himself as a friend. She set the box on her desk and picked up the line, "Amanda Morgan."

"Hi, Amanda. This is Hunter, from the dojo."

"Oh! Hi, Hunter." She had totally forgotten his last name was Steele, if she had ever known it. Everyone was on a first name basis at the dojo. "What's the important information?"

"Sensei Itaro had to leave town. His brother died, and he went to Japan for the funeral."

"I'm sad to hear that. I wish he had called himself so I could tell him."

"I was there when he found out and told him I would call everyone. He gave me the phone tree."

"That's OK, Hunter. I'm sure it's a big help to him. I can tell him when he returns." She tried to recall what an appropriate gift would be. She knew cards were common, but hated greeting cards. She vaguely remembered something about chrysanthemums and incense to show respect for the dead, but wondered if she could find chrysanthemums in May. "Does he know when he'll be back?"

"He said he would probably be gone for two weeks, but maybe more."

"I'm going to miss him. I suppose you'll miss him more, since you're at the dojo more than I am."

"Yes. But I'll also miss sparring with you."

"Please. Having me throw you around isn't something you miss."

"You'd be surprised how much I like you throwing me around."

"Should I start making house calls?" Amanda grinned.

"I wouldn't mind, but instead of a house call, how about lunch?"

"Very smooth, Hunter, but I have an appointment."

"Ouch. Shot down."

Amanda suppressed her usual thoughts of complications and threw Hunter a rescue line: "You didn't ask about Wednesday night."

"Oh. *Ahem.* Are you free, say, Wednesday night?"

"I think I could squeeze you into my busy schedule."

"Great! How about 7:00? Do you like Indian?"

"Indian. 7:00. Sounds great. Where should I meet you?"

"How about if I pick you up?"

"In your ambulance?"

"Do you think you'll need one?"

"Depends on what you have in mind for the evening." Amanda hadn't been this flirtatious in a long time, but there was something about Hunter. Beneath the surface, she could tell there was a mystery. Something to fall deeper into.

"I wasn't *planning* anything dangerous, but I'm sure we could come up with something."

"Mmmm. I can hardly wait to see what kind of trouble you get me into." She didn't know what had gotten into her. "Listen, I'll be working late. How about if you pick me up here at the office. I wasn't kidding about my busy schedule. I'm where the old May's was."

"Sure thing. Thirteen hundred block of Peachtree, right?"

"How did you know that?"

"I'm an ambulance driver. I have to know where everything is."

Amanda kept their car in the warehouse garage, out of the relentless Atlanta sun. As she approached it, she admired the way the glossy, red paint picked up what little light was available. When they'd moved, their dad didn't trust the old Camaro. He'd insisted they leave it and buy a new car when they got to Atlanta. He'd given them six grand for that purpose, though he had framed it as if he were merely buying their old car from them, a classic he would one day like to restore in the barn. Amanda had insisted that she get to choose the next car. But when they stumbled across the cleanly restored two-seater convertible in front of *My Favorite Mechanic* on Decatur street and saw the handwritten for-sale sign tucked under the windshield wiper, they were both sold. Amanda recognized the 1964 Sunbeam Tiger as a rarity and jogged to the office in search of the owner.

The man behind the counter pointed toward the garage. "Ask for Donna."

Donna looked exactly like those old World War II posters of Rosie the Riveter, right down to the red kerchief tying back her curly blonde hair. She was elbow deep into the front end of a mini-van when Amanda came in.

"So, you're lookin' at the Tiger, huh? Key's hangin' on the wall there," Donna pointed with her chin. After the formalities, Donna suggested they take it for a test drive, and added, "Try to keep her under a hundred."

Donna was leaning against the garage door when they rolled back into the parking lot with matching smiles. The mechanic pulled a cigarette from a crumpled pack, placed it in her mouth, and offered the pack to the twins.

Amanda held up a hand. "Thanks, but we don't smoke."

Miranda rolled her eyes. "I'd like one."

Amanda sighed.

"Hmmm." Donna lit them both up and took a deep drag. The smoke circled her head like a gray halo. "Figured you'd both want one." She motioned to the car. "It's like sex, isn't it?"

"I … well …" Amanda ran her hand through her disheveled hair. The wind had danced through the convertible, running its hands all over her. "Yes, it is."

Miranda took a long drag. "God, yes! We're taking her."

"I won the Tiger in a poker game. She was pretty rough when I found her. Guy who owned her didn't appreciate what he had, so I took her from him." Donna walked to the car and ran her hand across the front fender. "Helped her get her self-respect back."

"Looks like you really love her. Why would you want to sell her?"

"There's other cars that need me. It's time for her to be with someone else."

"We'll treat her right."

"I wouldn't let you buy her if I didn't think you would."

Even now, something about how the engine vibrated and growled while the wind tugged at her clothes still gave Amanda goosebumps. She was prowling through Vinings now, with the unlabeled box in the seat next to her.

Miranda woke and squinted against the sun. "What's up?"

Amanda looked over her shoulder and changed lanes. "Solved one mystery, uncovered another."

Orchard Street ran along the railroad tracks, and warehouses lined the west side, while industrial office buildings filed along the east.

Miranda raised an eyebrow at the rundown warehouses. "That sounds less comforting than you mean, I suspect."

Simeon's building was in the cul-de-sac. It sprawled across both sides of the street behind a tall chain-link fence topped with razor wire. Amanda turned into the driveway and stopped the car. "We're pretty isolated out here. Keep your head on a swivel."

"I want to be on record as saying that whatever this is is a bad idea."

The massive gate at the end of the short driveway was locked, and neither could see any sort of intercom or security guard. Amanda blew the horn a couple of times, and when no one answered, they got out of the car and walked around until they found an unlocked gate close to the building. They carried the package toward the door, and Amanda studied her surroundings, mapping an escape route. To the west was a cracked parking lot with grass growing up through its many fissures. Beyond that was a gray warehouse. The lot was empty, but she noticed deep grooves in the high grass at the mouth of the warehouse's loading bay. Something heavy had been delivered. She peered into the dark warehouse as much as she could, bending closer to the pavement for a better angle. Tires. Cars. Lots of small, dark cars.

She couldn't shake the feeling that the sidewalk was some sort of trap funneling them to Simeon's building, a huge cat at the end that now had them between its claws like mice.

Maybe this was the wrong place.

"Did you see the address when we pulled in?"

"Twelve hundred," said Miranda.

"I was afraid of that."

They tugged at the handle of the metal door, and it swung open with a groan. Inside was a room with some chairs and a long receptionist's desk. There was no receptionist, but the lights were on. At least the place wasn't abandoned. She heard a sound, like mumbling, and tracked it through a doorway on the other side of the room. The doorway led to a hall, and the sound was coming from somewhere down the hall.

Still not certain they were in the right place, Amanda directed them down the hall as quietly as possible.

"I don't like this," whispered Miranda.

Amanda looked around, and assured that no one was sneaking up behind them, forged ahead. "We'll be out of here as quickly as possible."

The mumbling got louder, and Amanda recognized Simeon's voice, but in a different language. He was on the phone, and when they got closer, she recognized that he was speaking Srpski. They stood still in the hallway, and listened.

He said a few more sentences in the foreign language and then switched lines. "Still there? Good. I can make the delivery tonight," he said. "No. No more delays. Trust me—" They heard him sigh impatiently. "Soon. It will be soon now. Goodbye."

They heard Simeon's chair creak and the heavy sound of his arms falling on his desk. Amanda figured this was a good time to enter. They stepped around the doorway and found Simeon sitting in a swivel chair behind a dark, oak desk. He didn't match up to his voice. She was expecting someone with lumpish, ugly features, but his strong jawline and broad face, framed by short brown hair, reminded Amanda of a film noir detective. She could tell he was strong and muscled under his white oxford shirt. His eyes, dark blue, like cobalt glass, widened when she approached him, but only for a split second.

"Amanda and Miranda Morgan, I presume."

"We're kind of unmistakable," Amanda said.

He didn't get up. "I wasn't expecting you to bring that personally." He gestured at the package.

"I've taken a personal interest in this." She hefted the box.

"I'll be glad to relieve you of the responsibility. You may put it on the desk."

Amanda rested the box on his desk. Simeon reached into a drawer, and Amanda heard a metallic click. They took two steps backwards.

"Don't rush off. I told you I would make it worth your effort." He casually pulled a stack of hundred-dollar bills from the drawer and dropped them on the desk next to the box.

Amanda glanced at the wad of money. There had to be three grand there.

"Thank you, but we're financially stable. If you really want to make it worth my while, I would like to know what's in that canister."

Simeon's eyes narrowed and he stood. He closed the distance between them in three steps. Amanda felt a sudden compulsion to bolt for the door, but she held her ground. Miranda tugged at her to run.

"I am not known for my patience, Ms. Morgan." Simeon was so close she could feel his breath.

Amanda stared up into his eyes and saw nothing but menace. He was mountainous and powerful. She resisted the shiver that crawled up her spine.

"You've been a most gracious host, Mr. Simeon," Amanda said.

He sneered. "I will send trucks for the other crates."

"The statuary?" snorted Amanda.

"Yes, the statuary." Simeon raised his eyebrows. "Unless you have something unexpected to tell me."

"I believe that is all I want to say to you," said Amanda.

Simeon watched them as they backed out the door. Once in the hall, they jogged toward the entrance, unable to shake the feeling that he was just behind them, about to grab them. Back in the car, Amanda didn't let off the gas pedal until they were far down the highway.

Miranda angled the rearview mirror to study her face. "Stress always makes my laugh lines pop out."

"Would you stop!" Amanda returned the mirror to the optimal position to study the road behind her. She had to make sure they were not being followed.

Miranda turned the mirror back to her face. "Told you that was a bad idea."

Amanda turned it back to its proper position. "I have to know what is in that box." She glanced behind them. "Something big is happening, but I can't put my finger on it."

"You read too much," said Miranda. "I'm sleepy. Wake me up if anything else weird and exciting happens."

Late that night, Miranda was drawing a bath when the phone rang.

"Hello?" She expected it to be Ian again. They'd already talked twice about a problem with one of their clients, a dog groomer who gave stock advice via puppies. The Shih Tzus were all in on Bitcoin, and the rush of puppy enthusiasts who'd mortgaged their houses for buy-in scratch had crashed their site. Networkz had not recommended sufficient bandwidth, and that was on Miranda. She'd had to fix it on the fly. "Who'd've known? So many Shih Tzus."

"They're a popular breed," Ian had said, unflappable and possibly upset, but Miranda couldn't tell.

Instead, a strange voice greeted her. "Hi, I was thinking about Halloween this year, and maybe planning on going as a sexy mailbox. I got a big blue box, but now I'm having trouble slutting it out. Any tips?"

"Oh my God! *Pierce?*"

"Yup."

"How'd you—"

"Called your folks."

"Well, *wow*, good to hear from you. I guess it depends on where the mail slot is located."

Pierce laughed. "Thanks. Good idea. OK, well, that's all I wanted. Have a good night."

"Wait! It's been so long. How are you?"

"Frankly surprised you remembered our slutty Halloween costumes gag," said Pierce.

"Best part of Halloween. Except for the candy. And the vandalizing. And the making out with strangers in the backs of slow-moving vehicles while listening to Tesla. Oh, and the stranger danger, and the Church of Satan putting razor blades in Snickers bars. Yeah, good times all around."

"You're still funny."

"Holy smokes! What's? How's it? What are you doing?"

"Just sort of driving around in a red Camaro I pulled off our showroom and listening to hair metal and, I don't know, maybe having a midlife crisis, and thinking I might go to our high school reunion if you guys are gonna be there."

"I think we might be. Amanda has some work that way, and I was thinking about seeing some people."

"Anyone in particular?"

Miranda stared into space trying to calibrate herself to the moment. "I'm sorry. I just can't believe it is you. Are you definitely going to be there? Because if I show up and you don't I am going to kill myself and haunt you."

"Better check with Amanda on that plan first."

"She's such a killjoy."

"Kinda," said Pierce, his voice betraying, it seemed to Miranda, a little more honesty than he likely intended. She let it slide.

"Oh, how's ... Jessica? Kids?"

He chuckled. "Good memory. My wife's name *is* Jessica. No kids, though, thank God."

"Us either. Life is weird enough."

"I couldn't find anything about you now. You guys aren't on Facebook or anything."

"We were on it for a little while. But Amanda doesn't like it because of privacy issues, and I just got tired of being invited to play Farmville. If I wanted to play that—"

"You wouldn't have moved."

"Exactly."

Miranda slipped off her robe and climbed into the tub. The water was hot, and steam danced around her ankles.

"Is that water I hear?" Pierce asked. "Are you getting into the tub?"

"Sure am." Her voice was hesitant with the heat.

"And here I am with all my clothes on."

"I won't stop you." So fast did the words slip out, she didn't have a chance to stop them.

"I think you get arrested for driving naked in Texas. There was a story in the *Ft. Worth Tribune* about a guy who had to go on the sex offender registry."

"Point made."

"Maybe another time?"

Miranda settled into the water and held the phone with her shoulder. She poured some bubble bath in at the other end of the tub and turned on the water over it. "That would be...nice."

"More water?"

"Have to get the bubbles going."

"I see. I *wish* I could see, anyway."

"You *are* bad. Haven't changed, have you? She leaned back against the back of the tub and relaxed her body, letting the hot water melt away her stress. An old commercial popped into her head: *Calgon, take me away!* She snickered and asked, "So what's on your mind?"

Amanda woke up. "Who are you talking to, and why are we in the bath? What time is it?"

"Hi Amanda," said Pierce.

"Pierce says hi," said Miranda.

"Pierce? Wow. That's random. Is he having a midlife crisis or something?"

"He thinks so."

"Good luck," said Amanda.

"She says—"

"I heard her," said Pierce. "Tell her I said thanks."

"Sure, what's..." She looked for the next words, but with Amanda awake, the intimacy was lost. "Hey, let me let you go so I can bathe and Amanda can sleep."

"Yeah, of course," said Pierce. There was disappointment in his voice, with just a hint of optimism. "See you at the reunion," he said.

"Definitely," said Miranda.

Miranda exited the work elevator and checked the clock on the wall. Almost 11 PM, and the office was still frenetic. It was always late nights near roll-out. As she walked down the gray hallway, she realized that she wanted some coffee. The break room had sludge, so a quick trip to the all-night café across the street was in order. She ran back to catch an arriving elevator, and Amanda in a liminal state, told her to settle down, then nodded back off.

She stepped in and met Ian as he was exiting.

He smiled. "You must be in a hurry."

"A bit. How's Roz's piece coming?"

"All hands on deck," he said. "This will be a long one for a few people. But worth it."

Miranda nodded. "I'll make sure everything is tight on my end."

"I know you will." Ian's accent was delicious.

"Aren't you getting off?"

"I'll ride back down with you."

Miranda noticed he was holding a cup from across the street.

Miranda chuckled. "You should get better coffee for the break room."

"But then we wouldn't be in the elevator together," he said.

"A fiendish plot."

"The fiendishest."

Miranda couldn't tell if she was out of breath because of the sudden run to the elevator or because she and Ian were in the car together alone. Their close proximity made her heart beat faster. She took the wall across from him and leaned back. This time of night, they could have the whole ride to themselves. She watched him raise his coffee cup. His hands were rugged and scarred, not what she would expect from a techie.

"Hey," Miranda broke the silence. "I'm really sorry about the Shih Tzu thing. I should have been better prepared."

Ian laughed, his eyebrows dancing with glee. "You didn't do anything wrong. Hell, I didn't think anyone was going to visit that site at all. Who takes stock tips from a dog groomer?"

"He says it isn't him, it's the puppies!" Miranda finally exhaled and laughed.

"I know, I know!" When he laughed and joked, his accent really shined through. "Most of the time I think we're just taking the money o' fools. But when we help one lunatic finally connect with his people, well, it's just bonnie fantastic, innit!"

"I like your accent," said Miranda, not even expecting herself to say it out loud. "You should make it more pronounced."

"Is that so?" He turned it on. "Lang may yer lum reek, ye bampots o' the world!"

"I have no idea what you just said, but I liked it."

"Good. I like you." He stepped forward and put his hand to her face. He brought her lips to him like a glass of water and drank her down. They wrapped themselves in each other, their lips pressing, tongues dancing. Ian reached over and hit the emergency stop button on the elevator. Miranda rubbed the lump growing in his pants, and he picked her up, pushed her against the wall. She sat balanced on the hand rails as he moved between her legs. They were still kissing. He tasted like rich coffee but something sweeter, as well. She opened her legs and let him slip between her thighs. She could feel the bulge pushing into her now, and heat radiated from between her legs. He pushed and pushed. They kissed, and stroked, and pushed. An alarm bell went off in the car. With a sudden jerk, the car began to move. The emergency speaker came to life. "This is Charlie in security. Is everything all right in there?"

Ian pushed the talk button. "All good."

"Oh, hello, Mr. McDuff. Sorry for the delay. I'll have maintenance take a look at the elevator tomorrow. Hasn't been stuck in a while."

"That's OK," he said to the loudspeaker. "I brushed the button by accident." His accent was hidden again. He looked at Miranda and rolled his eyes. She slipped off the hand rail and smoothed her clothes. Her legs were a little shaky.

When the elevator door opened on the ground floor, Miranda stepped out and Ian smiled and nodded as if nothing had happened. "We will work on this tonight, and I will call you tomorrow." He smiled and winked as the door closed between them.

Amanda had been hit by a surge of people looking for holiday glass frosters and French Moulis. *French mouli,* she googled, and the results list featured a YouTube video of old commercials.

Direct from France comes the Amazing Mouli, the commercial began. *Never before have you been able to process so many foods so quickly!* It was all so familiar—she must have seen this commercial before. By the time it got to the line about enjoying delicious potatoes any way you like them, she was mouthing the words along with it.

Miranda stirred. "The hell is this?"

"The Amazing Mouli!"

"Oh my god, I remember this commercial!"

It sent them down a rabbit hole of old commercials, and they realized how weird the world had been. The world had everything from dance parties where no one could dance, to men in white sweaters walking down the coast of New England taking pictures of old lighthouses and enjoying cups of coffee.

Amanda shook her head. "The world was... really weird... and beautiful... and so disappointing."

By lunch, Amanda was pacing the warehouse floor, thinking about her date with Hunter. As much as she wanted to maintain her façade of cool control, she was nervous. Still, as far as her employees knew, she was as calm as ever. Being a constant outsider had taught her to keep her cards close to her vest. She plowed through work, trying to distract herself. She met with the owner of a Rolls Royce dealership who wanted statuary that would give "an appropriately stately air to the showroom." She handed him a few Polaroids of a collection of early twentieth-century pieces going on the auction block next week, and he was ecstatic.

To kill time, she decided to contact the U.S. government.

Amanda had been waiting on hold for almost 20 minutes before a U.S. Customs Agent clicked through. "David

Barstow, U.S. Customs. How can I help you?" He sounded tired but professional.

"Greetings, Mr. Barstow. My name is Amanda Morgan, and I own an antiquities import in Atlanta, Georgia. I just wanted to alert you to the fact that we have received a shipment of twelve Yugos that were supposed to be statues."

"Unh huh?"

"I believe this is a matter of real concern."

"Yugos, you say?" said Barstow.

Amanda leaned forward in her chair and tried to project the importance of the moment in her voice. "Yugos."

"Yugos."

Amanda breathed an exasperated sigh. "I know there's something going on."

"Hey, I remember that song," said Barstow.

"No, there is something *nefarious* going on!"

"Involving Yugos," said Barstow. "Gotcha."

"I don't feel that you are taking this seriously."

"You know what I am serious about? Our budget has been cut, I haven't had a vacation in years, and even if I could take one, I couldn't afford it because the median income has not kept up with inflation since Nixon. How about that for nefariousness? Is that even a fucking word? Should be if it isn't."

"I'm sorry about your budget and lack of vacations, but what about the Yugos?"

"Try not to hit them from behind. Those were the ones that exploded, right?"

"That was Pintos."

"Oh yeah, Pintos. What a time to be alive the eighties were. I was poor but happy. God bless America."

"So, you will look into it?"

"Oh yeah, sure. Should have some time come October. We'll get right on it."

Amanda hung up. Well, that was 22 minutes down. It was like that for the rest of the afternoon. Amanda tried to challenge herself, to fill her thoughts with auction catalogs, materials facts, and cultural themes that would cut off the giggling, bouncing feeling that kept trying to bubble up inside her, despite her best efforts to tamp it down: *It's just a date. You hate dates. He will only disappoint you.* Nevertheless, she was excited, and the minutes ticked by slowly. The problem was that everything was going well. Between orders and meetings, she had long stretches of down time when she found herself pacing, watching the clock, and surfing eighties commercials on YouTube. "*Where's the beef?*"

At 6:30, Allen poked his head through her door. "I'm about to leave. Everyone else has gone. Would you like me to stay and help you with anything?"

"No thanks, Allen." Amanda smiled back at him. "I'm just about finished."

"OK, see you tomorrow then."

"Good night."

Amanda leaned back in her chair and listened as Allen locked the front door behind him. There was silence for a moment, but as she sat there, her ears adjusted to the quiet, and she could pick out the noises of her building as it settled in for the night. She often sat there in the evenings and just listened to the old building. Sometimes Amanda would take off her shoes and pad through the place in the dark, feeling the cold marble floors under her feet, running her hand along the walls. Now she just listened as an air conditioning unit rumbled away on the roof.

She thought about Simeon. She had met enough people in her life to know that he was dangerous, and to know that he wanted her to know it. What was he hiding? Probably something stolen, but if it was just gold, why was he so secretive? It must be something easily identifiable. Something like Fabergé eggs, only bigger and heavier.

Amanda wondered if she should call Customs again, but what could she tell Barstow to change his mind? It isn't a crime to ship a heavy object in cardboard, and when she thought about it, it did seem rather a stretch that the world's worst car was a threat to national security.

Her mind turned again to the contents of the small package. Maybe it was his father's ashes in some kind of lead urn. Maybe it was something that embarrassed him, a solid gold dildo. She laughed and wondered why that particular thought had crossed her mind.

Alone in the warehouse, Amanda remembered the romance novels she'd read when she was twelve, brimming with the forbidden and mysterious world of adulthood. She had stolen furtive reads of filth and decadence and wondered what impact it had had on her adult sexual identity. The Danielle Steels, the Bolt Westerns, *The Flame and the Flowers*, and all the other smut she had secretly devoured in the back of the mall bookstore, hoping no one would find out. Not just because she was too young for it, but because she didn't want anyone to know she was interested.

She thought of the way Simeon had towered over her, his eyes stabbing into her like cold knives. That is how they would have described it, and far from being aroused, she shivered. He was a powerful man and dangerous, the kind of man people who wrote romance novels apparently thought women would want. But no.

The following pages lampoon the trope of rape fantasies found in some romance novels. If that is not the kind of thing you want to read about, please feel free to skip ahead a couple of pages.

Respectfully yours,

MM

He hadn't touched her, but Amanda could feel what his hands could have done to her. *She felt the force of his hands push her against the wall and hold her there. She saw his dark blue eyes, his strong face as he bent to kiss her. He trapped her mouth with his own, and tore her blouse away with one hand, and she submitted.*

And then she shouted, "Yuck, no. Timeout! Timeout! Timeout! This doesn't happen EVER unless it is in a totally consenting place where trust has already been established or it is just fantasy about the security that would make that kind of play OK. But this, THIS is NOT OK."

Simeon spoke with his deep voice and cold affect, "No, this is going to be really hot and tap into a primal desire you didn't even realize you had because your sexual urges have been covered up and shamed by a Puritanical society, so you won't fight, just let yourself surrender to my strength, as my large, powerful hands roam your body."

Amanda backed away from him, aghast. "Seriously, have you never had a girlfriend or like any kind of intimate female relationship with whom you could discuss the intricacies of internal life and fantasies, so that you would know that so-called rape fantasies are actually misinterpreted seduction fantasies? You didn't know that? Hold on, Miranda has had a lot more experience than I have. Sis, wake up!"

"What?" asked Miranda, "What time is it?"

Amanda said, "OK, so you remember Simeon, right?"

"Yuck," Miranda said. "Ohmigod! Why is he here? Get a gun!"

"Right," said Simeon. "But you don't have a gun. You're defenseless, and I'm so big and powerful that you find yourself aroused by my—"

"Ugg, no," said Miranda. "Your neck is like Dave Latner's."

"Oh my God!" said Amanda, "You're right! Gross!"

"So gross," said Miranda.

Undaunted, Simeon continued. "I rip your blouse off, and your bra is pulled down to expose your nipples. They're hard."

"It's cold," said Amanda. "It's cold in here."

"Yeah, we are right under the air conditioner here," said Miranda. "Bodies are just gonna body, you know?"

"But you are equally aroused!"

"No, we're not. For one, this is violent and scary, and two, I LOVE this shirt, and you just ripped it! This was like sixty bucks. Asshole!"

"Hundred and twenty." Miranda covered her mouth and looked to the floor, fearing Amanda's reaction.

"My God! Why did you spend that much on one shirt?"

"I mean, you like it, don't you?"

"Yeah, but that's so much money for one shirt!"

"But it's so soft, and I love this color, and I got a bonus at work."

"OK, fine. I love it too!" Then she turned back to Simeon. "So yeah, double fuck you! She worked her ass off for this shirt!"

With one arm around their waist, Simeon picked them up, and they wrapped their legs around his hips, grinding themselves into him.

"Whoa whoa whoa! I DO FUCKING NOT! I do NOT wrap my legs around him. I do NOT consent! I am NOT an active participant in this shit, and you KNOW that is exactly what his attorney is going to try to say."

"Yeah, we kick and claw and fight and scream!" Miranda glared at him and readied her claws.

"I go for the eyes," said Amanda.

"Knees, nose, nuts," said Miranda.

"You feel the passion building inside you," said Simeon.

"Yeah, I'm passionately hating you right now."

"I'm definitely going to fall in love with a rapist because he's so strong and meaty," said Amanda.

"Hope I get pregnant with his son," said Miranda.

"Ooh gross, really?"

"Yeah I've read that in a few books."

"We'll look so beautiful breastfeeding his son."

"Yeah, and I will have realized my true purpose was to submit to his beefy neck."

"Uck," mumbled Amanda, and overcome by visceral horror, she vomited.

Amanda broke herself out of her fantasy, which was not actually hers, but someone else's, who having had a very limited and protected life experience, had decided to write it down, and which, inexplicably, publishers had decided to turn into a series of romance tropes that would be repeated ad nauseam and misinform a whole generation of kids wandering bored in shopping malls and stopping in the *Waldenbooks* to read clandestine smut.

She glanced at the clock. It was almost seven. She calmed herself, brushed her teeth at her office sink, and went downstairs to meet Hunter. Amanda was glad that none of that had actually happened, Miranda was still asleep, she had not just vomited, and her shirt was clean, pressed, and so, so soft. It was a great color on them.

When she got to the front door, she saw him standing outside peering in. He waved when he saw her. She unlocked the door and let him in.

"I hear you have a sale in housewares," he joked.

Amanda giggled. "Have you been out there long?"

"A few minutes. I wasn't sure if I should knock. Oh," Hunter pulled a small bunch of flowers from behind his back, "these are for you."

"Daisies!" Amanda remembered picking daisies in the field behind the house as a child. She buried her face in the flowers, letting their faint fragrance carry her back to that memory. She smelled the field, the sunset, the murmuration of birds. "They're beautiful, Hunter. Thank you. I should put these in water. Do we have a few minutes?"

"Certainly."

Amanda found a porcelain vase from one of the floor displays. She carried the flowers back up to her office and placed them in the center of her desk.

"This is your office?" Hunter asked.

"Be it ever so humble…"

"It's a good view of Peachtree Street. I would never get any work done watching the people down there."

Amanda raised her hand. "Guilty!"

On the way back to the door, Hunter asked, "Do you own the whole place?"

"Sure do. You can see what we use the main floors for." Amanda gestured to the displays around them. "We use the bottom floors as warehouse space. There are even two loading docks in the back. It's really the perfect place for all this."

"So, you just get shipments in from all over the world? Anything really weird ever come in?"

"Just lots of people looking for eighties memorabilia and Star Wars toys at the moment." She had forgotten all about Simeon for a little while.

Hunter switched topics. "Hey, everyone has been going on and on about small plates, so there is an Indian place that started doing these tiny, tiny plates. You get like 100 of them brought out every meal."

"That sounds so fun," said Amanda.

The restaurant was tucked away down a side street in east Midtown. In the foyer, eager couples with reservations talked about how exciting the small plates were.

"I hear their plates are the smallest," gushed one woman to her date.

"That's what they say," he said.

She leaned into him. "It's so romantic."

"Anything for you." He kissed the top of her head. "The moon, the stars, small plates!"

She giggled. "You're so funny."

"Ah, young love," whispered Hunter, and Amanda smiled. Miranda had awakened on the way over but was texting with Ian and missed the display entirely.

The restaurant served south Indian food: lots of potatoes, spinach, and tomatoes, and true to the advertisements, the plates were very tiny. They would eat a bite, and then a frantic waiter would rush out to take the tiny plates and replace them with other tiny plates.

Amanda cast her eyes about the restaurant. "I feel sorry for the servers."

"Must be a great cardio workout," said Hunter.

Miranda and Ian were chatting about what might or might not have happened in the elevator had Charlie not interrupted. They would have surely made love in the elevator, which would have been a breach of ethics and a crossing of boundaries, but they were both competent adults, and it was a private company, and Ian would never use his position of power to exploit her, so everything was cool, right? And it was, but Miranda knew better than to let it continue. But of course, she also knew that she would.

Hunter and Amanda's conversation drifted across several "safe" topics like food and the weather. Hunter was good at making things interesting without diving into anything controversial. As they sipped their mango lassis, which were served in glasses the size of thimbles, the talk moved to work.

"It looked like you had statues from all over the world," said Hunter.

"Yes. I have stuff coming in from everywhere. I work with teams in the field to get good prices, and then I just have to store the items until I can sell them. It's all pretty straight-forward." She smiled, thinking about Gloria Rubenstein. "But sometimes people are weird, and installation can get tricky."

"You're brilliant to make that work. I never could keep track of everything," said Hunter. "With that much being shipped around, do things get lost very often?"

"Sometimes. But they usually turn up at the docks, or arrive later. Funny you should mention it."

"Why?"

"Never mind. I don't want to bore you with my work problems."

Hunter grinned. "I promise to snore loudly if you get boring."

"OK. Monday morning, a strange package came in with a shipment. It didn't have a label, so I opened it." Amanda caught Hunter's raised eyebrow, "to see who it belonged to, of course! There was this metal container inside, but no identification."

"Sounds like a mystery." Hunter leaned forward in his chair.

"It gets better." Amanda looked around the room as if to make sure no one would overhear them to add effect. Then she leaned in close. "The canister looked like it was steel, but whatever was inside was very heavy. I think it might have been gold. But the thing was locked. I held onto it, and this man called me later in the day. Said his name was Simeon. He identified the package and said it was his."

"Did he come and get it?"

"I wanted to know what was in the canister, so I took it to him."

"To his house?"

"No, to a warehouse in Vinings."

Hunter nodded. "So, what was in it?"

"Still a mystery. But, I know it was important because he offered me a lot of money for delivering it. He wouldn't tell me what was inside. In fact, I thought he was going to attack me when I asked about it."

"Whoa, did he hurt you?" Hunter was roused.

"No. He didn't do anything to me. He didn't even threaten me really, but he was definitely threatening. I got out of there as quickly as I could."

"I like a good mystery as much as anyone, but that sounds dangerous."

"I know. I should just let it go, but I've been puzzling over it ever since."

"Have you told anyone else?"

"No. I called customs, but I didn't even know what to tell them."

Hunter leaned back in his chair, and gazed at Amanda for a moment. She wasn't sure what to make of his expression. He looked like he was about to tell her something gravely important. Either that or he was stifling a yawn.

"You're not about to start snoring, are you?"

Hunter raised his eyebrows. "Definitely not! Your job is a lot more exciting than I thought."

Amanda and Hunter stood in the hallway outside the sisters' loft.

"I had a really good time tonight," Amanda said, taking his hand. "That sounds like a cliché, doesn't it?"

"Doesn't matter as long as you mean it." Hunter held her hand in both of his. He gazed down at her, and she could feel herself falling into his eyes. "I had a good time too, and you didn't even have to throw me down."

"Nice girls don't do that on the first date." Amanda cocked her head to the side and poked her finger to her chin in her best cutesy pose. She batted her eyelashes.

"You know, I'm going to be up all night because of you."

Amanda felt a blush coming on and hoped the hallway was dark enough for him not to notice.

"Why's that?" She took a step closer to him. She could feel something between them, pulling her to him like a magnetic force. His face was rugged like the scent of Persian silk trees in Azerbaijan, but also kind like her father's aftershave lotion.

"A lovely night with a beautiful woman, oh, and the added bonus of this mystery package of yours." Hunter put his hands on her waist. "I can't stop thinking about it."

"Maybe I can give you something else to think about."

Amanda reached up behind Hunter's head and pulled him down to kiss her. When their lips met she smelled exotic perfumes and leather. Where his hands touched her back they left a trail of heat, as if the blood beneath her skin followed his touch. She ran her fingers through the short hair at the nape of his neck, and felt him shiver against her.

She wanted this, but at the same time, she asked herself if it was prudent. Suddenly, all the sensations flooding her were crowded by thoughts about where this would go.

She broke the kiss, and looked up at Hunter. "I'm sorry."

"About what?"

"I don't want you to think that—I mean—" Amanda felt torn. "I'm a bit flustered right now."

"Jeez, go ahead," said Miranda. "I don't have to be at work for a few hours, so you have time."

Hunter smiled at Miranda. "I'd almost forgotten you were there."

"That's kind of a rule we have, which I just broke, but this is like watching one of your chess matches, Amanda. You're turned on, just go for it."

"It's OK." Hunter ran his fingers under her chin. "I don't want to rush anything. Although I am glad that being turned on is mutual."

"You're sweet." Amanda hugged him tight. Felt his chest moving as he breathed. "Can we do this again sometime?"

"I'm counting on it!"

Amanda gave him a final kiss goodnight, then let herself into the loft. She leaned against the closed door, lost in reverie for a moment, before turning to her sister. "Don't EVER do that again."

Miranda looked up from her phone. "I think Ian and I talked each other out of dating."

"That's good."

"Yeah, but no. I like him. But I think there might be someone else he is interested in. Plus, the work thing. Plus, everyone has to be monogamous all the time. It's a real come-down."

The sun peeked between the buildings on Peachtree Street, quietly slipped through Amanda's windows, and settled on her face like a butterfly. Amanda squinted, realized it was morning, and jumped up from the bed.

She was going to be late. She strode down Spring Street, trying to remember if she had a meeting, or anything else important scheduled. She was mentally kicking herself when she turned onto Carnegie, the little street that cut across to the back of her offices. Amanda was only a few yards along when a roaring car engine startled her out of her thoughts. She looked over her shoulder to see a large, black Ford jump the curb and race straight at her. Instinct took over. She dropped to the side, and rolled until she came up against a building. The car's tires hummed by her face. She watched the car jump back off the sidewalk and screech around the corner.

Amanda lay there for a moment, just feeling the cold brick against her back. Her heart thundered away.

Miranda was jolted awake. "What just happened?"

"We were nearly hit by a car!"

An old man in an apron ran from the butcher shop across the street.

"Are you OK, Miss-es?"

"I…" Amanda couldn't speak.

He knelt down beside them. "Crazy drunks! My wife is calling the police right now. Can you move?"

Amanda nodded.

"Come inside until they get here." The man helped them up, and led them to his shop. His wife was already waiting in the doorway. "I called them, and they're on their way."

The man and woman fussed over them like a lost child. They reminded Amanda of their own parents.

The police car arrived and the officer seemed surprised when they told him their names.

"Officer Harris," he introduced himself. He looked back and forth between the two. "Ms. Morgan-ses, I think I should drive you over to your office."

"It's only two blocks away. I'm fine."

"I really think you should let me drive you. I'm sure you'll understand when we get there."

They arrived at Morgan Antiquities to find three patrol cars and a half-dozen uniformed officers milling about. She was escorted to her office, where someone had removed the drawers from her desk, turned filing cabinets over, and scattered everything all over the floor.

Allen was waiting for her. "Amanda! I tried calling but you didn't answer."

"I had it muted for my date," she said. "What's all this?"

"Ms. Morgan?" A detective with a thick notepad spoke to her while another officer with a fingerprint kit pulled thin strips of adhesive from the wall safe. "Your assistant, Mr. Garner, says he doesn't think that anything was taken from the safe. But after we get everything we need, you'll need to inventory everything and see what might be missing."

"Oh, this is going to be a headache," said Amanda. "Nothing is missing from the safe?"

"Not since the last time we were in there," Allen said. "Petty cash and all the important stuff is still in the safe."

Amanda rubbed her forehead. She felt a migraine coming on. "So, the petty cash is still in here, and all the vital papers are…here. This doesn't make any sense." She turned to Allen. "Anything missing from the floor?"

He shook his head. "Not that I can tell from a quick walk-through."

The detective, Jacobs was his name, scribbled a bit. "Doesn't make a lot of sense. On one hand, this looks like a professional job—they circumvented the alarm, iced your door locks, and cracked your safe." He ran his hand across his dark beard. "On the other hand, they trashed your office, and didn't take anything. You follow me?"

"Sure."

"Anyone been fired recently?"

"No. Do you think this is some kind of revenge?"

"It's a popular motive. Harris tells me you almost ended up as a hood ornament this morning. Anyone you can think of that would have it out to get you?"

"No." Amanda looked around. "I like to think that people like me. Besides, why ransack my office and try to kill me before I could see it?"

"They may just be trying to scare you. I'm just exploring all the possibilities, Ms. Morgan."

Miranda tried to wrap her head around the chaos. Maybe her sister was more interesting than she gave her credit for.

The officer with the fingerprint kit held up several white cards with dark smudges taped across them. "Detective Jacobs, I've pulled everything off the safe that I can—eight latents and six partials. I'll get Garner and the Morgans, and then see if there's anyone else."

Jacobs scribbled a little more. "I'm gonna file the information we have. If you think of anything to add, or if you notice anything missing," he pulled a card from his breast pocket, "call me."

"So, is it OK for me to clean up in here?"

"Yeah. Listen, you want a patrolman to keep an eye on you?"

"Sure. I don't think these things are connected, but I guess you never know," said Amanda.

Jacobs and the other officers gathered their equipment. Amanda watched through the window as the officers outside left a car at a time. Just as Jacobs emerged below her, she noticed a man loitering across the street.

"Hunter?" she thought. "What's he doing here?"

She raced down to the ground floor. She wanted to tell him what had happened, but by the time she made it down to the street, he was nowhere to be seen. Maybe it was just someone who looked like him.

Miranda had had a late night after Amanda's date and told her to wake her up if anyone else tried to kill them.

Allen paced the floor in front of Amanda's desk. "I'm worried. What if they come back to finish the job?"

"I doubt whoever broke in will come back. Whatever they wanted, we obviously didn't have it. The car this morning was just a coincidence. Just a drunk driver." She didn't know if she was trying to convince Allen or herself. "Right now, though, I'm going to the lower warehouse. I want to poke around the inventory for a while."

"OK, let me know if you need anything. I will tidy up here."

The lower warehouse was where Amanda kept the oldest, most valuable pieces. It used to be the sub-basement and still had yellow and black signs in the stairway that said "FALL-OUT SHELTER" in bright yellow letters. She came down here when she needed a few minutes away from the world. It was so quiet. No traffic noise, not even the soft hum of fluorescent lights, since only bare incandescent fixtures lit the floor.

Amanda wandered the aisles past deep shelves holding Jin dynasty teapots, Guro masks, Hopi kachinas, and other small items older than most northern European countries. She made her way between them, toward the back where statues stood in lines like soldiers on parade. Amanda walked their ranks. These were the rare works that only people with the most profound interest in history or exclusivity would purchase. That meant they were slow movers, and Amanda always ended up getting attached to them. She had names for most of them by now—Dian, a Chinese funerary soldier; Sami, the Minoan temple maidservant; but her favorite was Leander, a Roman messenger.

He stood behind the other statues, somewhat aloof, frozen in a moment of sprinting to deliver the news of an advancing army, or the birth of a senator's son. He was living stone. If she touched him with her hand, he would be cold and hard...dead. But to her eyes he was alive. Blood flowed beneath his pale skin. His lungs fought for a gasp of breath beneath the half-moons of his pecs. Every curve and crease seemed focused forward. The expression on his face looked far past her down some long-forgotten stretch of road.

She moved from piece to piece, approvingly. These were her favorite, most valuable things. And they were all accounted for. What on earth could the thief have wanted if not money, if not rarities?

Sunday morning found Amanda crouched in the back of a van, trying to guide a large crate in while Allen pushed from outside. They were having more difficulty getting it in than they should, and Amanda was glad Miranda was sleeping through the embarrassing imbroglio.

The crate kept getting hung up on the wheel arch, even though they had put this exact item in this exact van dozens of times before. It wasn't fitting for some reason and as she and Allen caught their breath, the crate perched precariously on the edge of the bumper. The day before, a rep from Symphony Hall had called and asked if she could make a rush delivery before a charity concert on Sunday afternoon. Since the symphony leased her pieces so often, Amanda was eager to maintain good relations. Allen, faithful as always, had agreed to give her a hand. That had seemed a sensible way to avoid having to call in the warehouse crew on a Sunday. But now she was second guessing herself. She shook her head and got back to work.

"OK, this time definitely." Amanda pulled at one corner of the crate.

Allen laughed and pushed. "This time. Yeah, sure."

Amanda laughed in spite of mood. "By the way, I think you were wrong."

Allen shoved again. "No, this is the angle I always use." He grunted from the exertion.

"No, about your theory. The weekend is almost over and no one's come 'to finish the job' as you so eloquently put it."

"Well, I'm happy to be wrong about that."

Amanda looked up from the crate and noticed a man walking across the parking lot toward them. He was dressed in ragged jeans and a T-shirt with a trench coat over it. As he got closer he addressed them, and Amanda stepped forward.

"Pardon me, sir, miss. I'm a little down on my luck. Would you happen to have something you could spare?"

Allen motioned to Amanda with his hand in a 'stay' gesture.

"Sure, but listen, this is a private lot. You're not supposed to be back here. Understand?"

"Oh, yeah. So, you work here?"

"Yeah, and you need to leave," Allen said.

Amanda poked her head out of the back of the van. "Can I help you?"

"Stay out of this," barked Allen, and Amanda recoiled at the harshness in his voice, a tone she didn't know he was capable of taking, much less to his boss!

The man reached under his coat, and Amanda saw a glint of metal.

"Gun!" Allen lunged at him, knocking him backwards. A shot rang out and the echo in the van nearly deafened Amanda.

Miranda startled awake. "What the fuck?"

Amanda saw Allen slump to the ground in front of the man and instinctively ducked back behind the crate. The man pointed the gun in the back of the van. Amanda crawled as deep into the corner as she could and looked around for a tire iron, a crowbar or anything. But it was just them and the crate. Nowhere to go, no weapons to use for defense. Her mind raced. Then she thought of Sensei Itaro, and his words came through: "Don't think. Just be."

The gunman sneered. "Don't make me come in there after you."

Amanda braced herself against the back of the driver's seat and prepared to push against the crate with her legs. If she was quick enough, maybe she could catch him off guard. As she shoved, the sound of squealing tires echoed across the lot. Then several more shots cracked through the air. She looked to see that the man in the trench coat had his back to them now. Another shot rang out, but this one was different, sharper and not as loud, like it was from a smaller caliber gun. She poked her head around the crate and saw Hunter's car a few yards away. Hunter was standing behind it with a nine-millimeter. The man fired another shot and fled when Hunter took cover. Amanda stuck her head out of the back of the van and watched the assailant scale the fence at the other side of the lot, where he dived into a dark Ford waiting at the corner of the building. The engine roared and the car careened away.

Hunter ran over to her. "Are you OK?"

"Allen's been shot!"

Hunter leaned over Allen, felt his pulse, and pulled his shirt collar to the side. Allen's shoulder had a big chunk torn out of it.

"He's going into shock. Call an ambulance."

While Amanda spoke with the 911 operator, Hunter ripped his shirt off and pressed it into Allen's wound.

Allen gazed up at him. "Where do I know you from? I've been trying to—"

"Shut up and stop squirming, Garner. Or should I say Boris Ivanovich, candy salesman?"

"Oh yeah, I KNEW I knew you. Wow. That's been a while. How ya been?"

"You shot at me."

"Yeah, but that was business. I shot at Simeon's guy, too. Don't hear him complaining. Say, did you know that that Ewan McClaine guy is in town?"

"Your loss of blood seems to be making you delusional, comrade."

"All those years ago. Say whatever happened to that kid with the fucked-up arm? Ever work with him again?"

Amanda closed her phone call and knelt next to them. "What's he talking about, Hunter? How do you two know each other?"

Hunter didn't look at her.

"Hunter," she said. "What are you doing here? Why are you carrying a gun? What exactly is going on?"

Allen reached for Amanda and feebly clutched at her wrist. "I'm sorry. This wasn't supposed to happen. I didn't want you involved in any of this." He smiled at her. "If you had let me take care of the shipment the other day, things would've been different."

Allen let go of her wrist and turned his eyes toward Hunter. "Simeon set this up. He told me she switched the plutonium, but I searched the office and her place." He turned back to her. "Sorry about the mess in the office. I was a little tidier at your place. Bet you didn't even realize I'd been there. Nothing out of place." He smiled to himself. "Life is weird." He looked at Hunter once more. "I didn't find anything. He must have lied so he wouldn't have to pay me. Now he's got the plutonium and he's tying up loose ends. She doesn't know anything about any of this, though."

Hunter sneered at him "She does now, moron."

Amanda heard sirens approaching. An ambulance and two police cars swerved into the lot. The paramedics took over with Allen. Hunter shoved a badge at the officers. Amanda could only stare, mouth agape as he told them to radio in a description of the man who attacked her. When he was done, he turned to face her.

"Are you going to tell me what the hell is going on?" she asked.

"I wanted to tell you sooner, but I wasn't sure if you were involved until Thursday night. I was going to fill you in then, but things got … personal, and I didn't want to dump all this on you."

"Well, now sure seems like a good time."

"That is SO typical," said Miranda. "You think you finally meet a nice guy, and he's a goddamn government assassin."

"See," said Amanda. "This is why you have to take your time. But you're always like, *Oh, you only live once,* but you can't just jump right in the sack with people. You never know when they're just using you."

"That's not fair," said Miranda. "Hunter is your mistake, not mine."

"Hey, that's not fair. I wasn't using her." Then Hunter looked at Amanda. "I just fell for you when I was supposed to be keeping an eye on things. Sorry."

Hunter looked over his shoulder at the paramedics who placed Allen on a gurney. "Look, I've been working on this case for six months now. Allen and Simeon have been working together to smuggle weapons-grade plutonium from Astrakhan into the U.S. through your business. I signed on at the dojo so I could find out more."

"Yeah, I get it. I'm just a lead in your case."

"What an asshole," said Miranda.

"Stay out of this," said Amanda.

"You're so much more than that to me," said Hunter. "This is complicated. Simeon supplies nuclear material to terrorists. I have to stop him. But that's a state secret, so keep it on the down-low." He chuckled awkwardly. "Uhm, I need to go. Can I call you later?"

"No," said Amanda.

"No way!" said Miranda.

Amanda glared at her. "That's my decision, not yours."

"Just expressing solidarity."

The paramedics drove Allen away.

"I have to go with him." Hunter looked at them. "If you'd let me call you later, I could explain everything. I hope you'll understand."

They didn't answer, and he left.

"The reunion will be a good place to lay low," said Amanda. "Maybe we can move the flight up a couple days."

"I have a date tonight," said Miranda.

"Seriously?"

"Also, I heard there is a Tiffany and Debbie Gibson concert at Perimeter Mall tomorrow night. I am in a raffle for tickets."

Amanda couldn't form full words, and what came out of her mouth sounded like, "?! ???!...!?"

By evening, Amanda was still feeling ill at ease and anxious.

"Are you SURE you're OK with this?" Miranda asked.

Amanda shrugged. "Don't let me get in the way of your good time."

"I'm worried about you," said Miranda.

"Everything is fine. I think. The people who were trying to kill us haven't tried to kill us since this morning; the guy I liked is an FBI, CIA, NSA, or some-combination-of-three-letters assassin; my office manager is apparently a Russian spy; and you're fucking around with your boss, even though you definitely know better than that."

"I took your advice. I am cooling it with Ian. Besides, I think he is into some girl he met on Christian Mingle. Tonight is a new guy from OKCupid."

"Oh good, a rando," said Amanda.

"He's nice. I think. At least he says the right things. Still, he might be kind of footy."

"What is it with you and foot people?"

"It's happening to everyone. It's like small plates or acid-washed jeans."

"Oof," said Amanda. "What if you're right?"

Miranda was not going to let an international conspiracy hamper her life. She had a date tonight with a man who might be a little iffy, but she was determined to keep it. Letting the government, terrorists, or creepy dudes keep her from dating seemed like an infringement on her First Amendment rights. Or something.

At the appointed time, a late model Lincoln Navigator rolled up to their condo, and the twins stepped out looking elegant and not at all concerned that all the men in their lives had not been who they had appeared to be, that there was some far-reaching international conspiracy whose ultimate aim eluded them, and that one of them was not really in the mood for a date but was going out anyway, based solely on principle, while the other was entirely and bitterly opposed.

But Miranda thought if nothing else, a date with a new guy might get them back in the swing of things. He had listed his hobbies as cycling, cooking, reading, and politics. He would at least be fit and educated. Plus, as an added bonus, he had not once inquired about their feet.

He was neither fit nor unfit, but somewhere in between, and it seemed that his avid cycling was punctuated with fried breads whenever possible. His name was Paul, and as he drove Miranda to his favorite brewpub, he explained that she was in for a real treat.

"A lot of people don't know about this, but Tiffany and Debbie Gibson—from the eighties—did a movie together a few years ago. It's about a giant alligator and a giant snake. They are playing it here tonight!"

Miranda did a double take. "You're making that up."

Paul crossed his heart with a stumpy finger. "God's truth."

"Didn't know they made a movie together," said Amanda.

"I am in a raffle to see their show at The Perimeter," said Miranda.

Paul rested one hand over the steering wheel and stretched the other behind the twins' back. "I read about that. I think it's a scam."

"Oh? Why?"

"Well, I looked into it, and the same concert is happening in over 75 locations."

"Makes sense," said Amanda. "There is a bit of an eighties revival right now."

"But they're all happening tomorrow night!"

Miranda slapped her knee. "Damnit! I bet it's gonna be some lame video broadcast. I should've read the fine print."

Amanda rubbed her sister's shoulder. "Hope you didn't pay much for the raffle."

Miranda sighed.

"So, hey." Paul interrupted them. "As I might have mentioned in chat. I'm a bit of a political junky, and Donald Trump is supposed to make an important announcement tonight. Word is that he is going to make an announcement about his plan for beating crooked Hillary. Mind if we tune in?"

Miranda shrugged. "Sure, go ahead."

"Hell no," said Amanda. "His candidacy is grift, and even if he did get elected, which he won't, he would be a terrible, abysmal president."

"Rule 5A," cited Miranda dutifully.

"Does not apply because of the 98 Lewinsky Accord. You didn't want to hear about that, I don't want to hear about this."

"Looks like I've touched a nerve." Paul laughed. "Maybe your sister is a bit of a snowflake."

"Oh boy," said Amanda. "This is going to be awesome."

Miranda insisted on giving Paul a chance. She gave many chances: when he ordered an IPA, when he said he managed a Pizza Hut, when he talked about the inherent logic of libertarianism, when he obviously lied about riding his bike to Texas and back last summer, when he insisted that green bell peppers were a suitable pizza topping, when he kept bringing up the slogan Make America Great Again, and when he told a detailed story about a pizza place in DC that had a Satanic pedophile ring in the basement, during which he displayed a disturbing knowledge that pepperoni grease could be used as an anal sex lubricant.

"No one needs anything in their ass that bad," Amanda muttered, giving Paul a charley horse in his calf that sent him scrambling to rub it out.

Miranda gave him chances all the way through what was possibly the worst movie ever made, and as Paul declared that Trump was really gonna win, and don't be surprised when he brings the entire Satanic deep state down, they excused themselves to the ladies' room and texted for an Uber.

They returned to the table to get their coat. By then, the movie had ended, and Paul suggested that his Pizza Hut was just down the street, and he would love to make them their own personal pan pizzas after hours. "The pizzas we make are so much better than the ones you can get off the menu." He raised his eyebrows and nodded.

Their Uber arrived.

They sat silently in the backseat. Finally, Amanda said, "Well, that was great."

"Sorry," said Miranda. And then it sank in: "Everyone we date is either a liar or a loser."

Then it sank in deeper: "Dear God," said Amanda. "Trump is going to win."

Miranda shook her head. "No way. Not everyone is as stupid as the guys we date."

"I just don't know anymore," Jessica confessed to Dr. Hayworth.

Pierce sat with his hands folded in his lap, his face betraying no emotion.

"What is the trouble exactly? Last session we seemed like we were in a pretty good place. But what's happened since?"

Jessica folded her arms. "He went crazy! He cashed in our life's savings to have a midlife crisis, and I just feel like, well, for years now I have felt like I wasn't enough."

"Did he ask you to wear the head again or something?"

"No, no, not in years. But it always just…bothered me knowing that it was in our past together."

Dr. Hayworth looked at Pierce. "How do you feel about what she has said?"

"Well, first, it was not our life's savings. It was PART of our life's savings. Second, it is not a midlife crisis, but a business opportunity that I want to invest in. Third, I've always been supportive of everything Jessica has wanted to do, so this seems unfair. Fourth, the head has not come up for a long time now, so that seems sort of out of the blue. And fifth, Jessica, you know that I have always loved you and only you. Right?"

"So, the head thing is no longer an interest of yours?"

"Oh, no," said Pierce. "It totally is. But I realized how uncomfortable it made Jess, so I stopped asking for it."

"I've noticed," Jessica said, "that the last few years we haven't had sex as often. I just thought we were getting older, and that our libidos had decreased."

"Nope," said Pierce. "I am horny ALL the time. But, you know, I keep it in check."

"That seems like he is working to make you comfortable, right, Jessica?"

"It's true. And maybe I am not being completely honest."

Time stopped. Dr. Hayworth's eyebrows scrunched. Pierce tilted his head and looked at Jessica right in the eye. "Oh?"

"I have developed feelings for one of our sales associates."

"Which one?" asked Pierce.

"Brian," said Jessica.

"How does that make you feel, Pierce?"

He thought about it. The wheels spun but got no grip. Finally, something occurred to him. He was not the least bit upset. In fact, he understood perfectly, because he himself had loved Jessica, really loved her, yet also had always held the door in the back of his mind open enough for Miranda to walk through at any time. He smiled. "I understand," he said. "Brian is a cool guy. Smart, fashionable, handsome, politically decent." He shrugged. "I get it."

"Really?"

"That's quite a revelation," said Dr. Hayworth. "Should we talk about how this makes us feel?"

"Yeah, so here's the thing," said Pierce. "Uhm, Amanda and Miranda Morgan were those conjoined twins you might have heard about because they were normal twins but became conjoined back in the eighties because of some weird government, space alien, or satanic panic fluke or something, and there was a big buzz, but then everyone kind of stopped talking about it, because something else big happened, but I don't remember what. That was when we were 13 or 14 or something. I was friends with them. But I always loved Miranda. And I still do, even if I have not spoken to her in years. But that is not exactly true, because I just nearly had phone sex with her last week, but Amanda woke up, which was SO TYPICAL. Anyway, that time when I said *Oh no, Amanda,* or *whatever it was* I said, I was not fantasizing about sex with her, but with Miranda, but I have always felt a sort of repressed guilt about the fact that their conjoinment kept me from being able to fully commit to her, and you know, that's just ego or superego or whatever—"

"Both. In conflict," said Dr. Hayworth helpfully.

"But like, I wanted kind of deep down for Amanda never to have been born or to somehow die and be removed, but she's a good person and, like, a human being deserving of being alive, just like Miranda, and she's great, and in that moment, it was like I was having sex with Miranda, and when the head fell off, all that guilt about Amanda presented itself. It was crazy. That was a really hard moment for me.

"And, by the way, my 30-year reunion is coming up, she's going to be there, and I want to go, and take some time there, so Jess, you can hang out with Brian for the week and see how that feels, and then we can talk about it when I get back. Cool?"

"What?" Jessica sat unmoving, clearly trying to process everything.

Dr. Hayworth slapped her desk. "I remember those twins! They were on *60 Minutes*, weren't they?"

Miranda won the raffle, but she realized that Paul was probably right about the concerts either being a scam, or more likely, just a video performance, so she and Amanda booked a standby flight to DFW that day, instead of waiting. Their plane taxied along the flight lane at Hartsfield-Jackson. The twins sat next to the window staring out at the rippling heat radiating from the tarmac. The hot waves made the asphalt runway look like a lake of boiling oil, but under the dancing air there was somehow a surface solid enough to hold up the planes as they rolled across. The flight attendant droned over the PA about seat belts and oxygen masks, but both women were lost in their own thoughts.

Someone actually tried to kill me, thought Amanda. It wasn't the first time she had faced danger head on, but someone pointing a gun at her made the experience all the more immediate. Allen was in the hospital. Amanda wasn't sure how she should feel about that. He had probably saved her life, but he was certainly up to his neck in whatever was going on.

What *was* going on?

The strange cylinder she thought was full of gold was actually the vehicle for plutonium that someone planned to turn into a bomb. Allen had used her business—*used her*—to smuggle this stuff into the country. She felt dirty. Cheated. He seemed like such a good friend, and it was terrible for her to realize that it had all been an act. His interest in her was purely for what she could do for him. Yet he did save her life. He said Simeon had lied to him. Who was Simeon, exactly, and Hunter, and Ewan? Who were all these people and how were they connected?

Simeon was still out there somewhere, and Amanda knew she was on his list of loose ends. She couldn't stay in Texas forever. As much as Hunter had let her down, she hoped he cared enough about her to make sure she was safe. It hurt to think that these men had been using her as a pawn in some game she hadn't even known was being played. At least she hadn't slept with any of them. She felt dirty enough as it was. What a perfect prelude to the fiasco she knew the reunion was going to be. At least she could use the Beloit auction as an excuse to bow out of things if they looked as bad as she predicted.

Miranda wondered if feet were the new thing. Men had always liked her breasts, once they got past Amanda's nipple thing. Were her feet her main selling point now? She thought about Pierce and Ian, and whether they preferred feet or breasts. But she wondered also if maybe she were not changing somehow. She had always said that one man would never be enough for her, and she knew it in her heart to be true. Yet she also had begun to recognize that some men were even less deserving of her time than others. Some men didn't know anything about women; you had to teach them everything. Some were your boss. Still others were actually hired killers. It was bad enough out there without ever meeting anyone who would vote for Donald Trump or use pepperoni grease as lubricant. It was a sick, strange world, and maybe she should consider settling down into a stable triad or polycule. She could be the hinge or the V or whatever they called it this week.

The jets on the 777 began to scream, thrusting them back into their seat, then lifting them skyward. Amanda watched the outside world get smaller and smaller. Strangely, her thoughts turned to Jack. She wondered where he was and what he was doing. What if? Nah, she wouldn't even entertain the crazy thought. The plane dipped its left wing, arcing westward, carrying her into the past and an uncertain future.

It turned out to be a bit of a shame that the twins had not gone to the concert because, in fact, Tiffany and Debbie appeared simultaneously in the flesh in 75 malls nation-wide that night. The shows were sold out, everyone was super confused, and as an encore they came out and did a duo medley of *Electric Youth* and *I Think We're Alone Now* and—there's no other way to describe it—it fucking slammed!

Man had been experimenting with the particle collider and had gotten pretty good at manipulating time and space. His plan was coming together, and the eighties revival was in full swing. He wondered if raising Reagan from the dead would complete the collection or push things a little too far. Still, he knew the limitations of his skills, and raising a dead person was no easy feat. He had already tried to bring back velociraptors—just because, hey, how cool would *that* be?!—but his prototype had taken literal hours to create and had been killed and eaten by chickens in a matter of minutes.

For their part, Joe and Buck had noticed how erratic the MAM & PAP's onboard computer had become. There were wild swings in RAM, ROM, and collider activity. It seemed to be running itself and doing whatever it wanted. But what it wanted was a mystery. Much worse, the hatch door was inoperable. They continued faxing the reports to the void that was the Pentagon.

"I've got a theory," said Joe. "This computer was coded for war. What if it wants war?"

"It's a computer. It doesn't want anything but electricity."

"Right. Right," said Joe. "If it were an alarm clock I would agree. But what if the people who coded it built their own love of war into it inadvertently? What if they designed a computer to want war but didn't realize it?"

"Sure," said Buck. "If X then Y is logic. But if an illogical person decided what X and Y stand for, then the illogic is baked in."

"So, even if the computer thinks X, then it has to go to Y, no matter how crazy Y is."

"Exactly."

Joe leaned against the wall. "I don't like computers. They depress me. Ought to be able to change your mind."

In the Time of Virtual Reality

Because of some emergency, the twins landed at Texarkana International Airport at 6 AM instead of at DFW at their scheduled time. That was lucky for them, but not for anyone else. Miranda watched the other passengers milling about the tiny airport like zombies, looking compulsively at their phones, jabbing them in frustration, and wondering how to get home.

Miranda dug her phone out of her purse. "I feel sorry for the people who had to be re-routed. What a cluster-eff."

Amanda wasn't paying attention. "Something's up with my phone. I can't get through to Mom and Dad."

"Probably not much reception out here," said Miranda.

"No there's nothing. Not just no signal."

"Maybe it's your phone." Miranda checked hers. Dead.

Then they noticed an airport maintenance man rolling a ladder out into the lobby. They watched him climb up to a tv monitor showing an empty, blue screen. He fiddled with some cables in the back, and soon had it switched over to the local analog station:

319

"...widespread reports of cell phone outages, and we have heard, digital information sources increasingly inoperable. This is a breaking story. Officials are not sure why this has happened. Some people suggest a satellite is down. Others have said it could be linked to terrorism. This is apparently a widespread phenomenon, and we hope to have more information for you soon."

"Weird," said Miranda. "What time is Dad picking us up?"

"He's not. I just told him we would land sometime in the morning, rent a car, and drive in from Dallas."

Amanda borrowed the airport's landline to call a cab, but the dispatcher told them that the new cars were all having problems, and that it would be a while before anyone could get to them.

The local news station moved onto a breaking story in Washington DC. "After the heartbreaking workplace shooting last week at the Pentagon, officials became aware that the suspected shooter, a Mr. Randy Beavers, a 30-year civilian employee had long complained about a mysterious beeping sound coming from within the walls of his office, which has led many to ask about mental health evaluations for long-term employees. But now we find out that there might be more to the story. Clean-up crews also reported hearing the noises, which they described as rhythmic beeping coming from quote the ass-end of nowhere end quote. We now go to a pre-recorded interview with Dr. Benjamin Phillips, professor of archeology at Georgetown University, whose team is at the Pentagon.

"Thank you. Hi. Yes." He seemed to be having some trouble with the audio feed.

"Oh my God," said Amanda. "Is that Benjamin?"

Miranda gasped at the screen. "Benji!"

"I'm glad he went on to do…um…important things."

"He was so normal."

"So normal."

"Shhh."

"Shhh."

"This has been an exciting time for the team. It turns out that behind the southern facing wall of Mr. Beavers's office, there was another office that had at some point been walled over. It is perfectly preserved. I would say early 1980s at the latest. There is still a Tab Cola on the desk and what looks to be a half-eaten Hostess Ding Dong, likely still edible, owing to its efficacious albeit primitive food additives. It's a fascinating discovery. Whoever was in that office left in a hurry. We're looking into the files that were left on the desk. We are talking about what would appear to be a high-ranking official of the U.S. Military or a contractor who was in charge of what would have no doubt been a top-secret project during the Cold War."

A team member rushed up to Benjamin and handed him a file. The two exchanged whispers, and then Benjamin turned back to the camera. "It looks like the office belonged to a Colonel Malcolm Danes, who was apparently an under secretary, and there are," he skimmed the page in front of him, "two soldiers…underground bunker…east Texas… orders issued over 30 years ago…oh dear." Benji turned to the camera slowly, as if realizing it was there for the first time. "I'm sorry, Ms. Gutierrez, we're going to need to cut this interview short. Thank you."

After watching their dad's home movies, the twins took a stroll around the property, following the stream and coming to the bank where the sinkhole had been.

Miranda looked down at the grassy slope, which had as its only reminder of that fateful day a slight indentation. "I wish I knew why any of this had to happen."

Amanda picked up a stone and tossed it into the creek. "I don't guess it matters why."

"I guess not, but it would be comforting to think there was a reason."

Amanda put her arm around her sister. "It's a brute fact, I guess. Just something we have to live with. For so long I wanted there to be something we could figure out. Some reason it happened, so we could find out how to fix it. Even watching Dad's movies, I was watching us at the party. Was there a clue in there somewhere?"

"I do that too," said Miranda.

Amanda shook her head and felt like crying. "It's point-less. The universe exists, ergo we exist. The universe is random, ergo we are weird."

Miranda smiled at her sister and brushed the hair from her face. "I wish I could do that. You just shrug and go on. That's brave. I'm not like you."

"I wish I could do what you do," said Amanda. "At least you try to live. I just overanalyze things and talk myself out of everything."

"You're smart."

"Am I? You seem to have gotten a lot more out of life than I have."

The site of the traveling Beloit auction was the Texarkana Community College Auditorium. Jack figured it had a wired alarm system with a possible cellular backup. In the dead of night, he configured his arm to jam Wi-Fi and used the built-in wire cutters to snip the phone cables from the building. Then he picked a lock on the back door and was in.

He didn't know where the lever would be, and it might take a while to find it.

"Are we in?" asked the arm.

"Yes," said Jack.

"Look for the lever."

"I *know* why we are here, dumbass."

"Where do you think it is?"

"Since when did you get so goddamn chatty?" asked Jack. "Remember when you would only respond when I asked for input?"

"Yes, I remember," said the arm. "Funny how people change."

Jack smirked. "You aren't people."

The arm's gears turned, and its processor whirred. "Are we friends?"

Jack laughed out loud. "That's a good question. I never thought about it. You know what, pardner, I think we are. I reckon you're my best friend."

"I'm glad," said the arm. "You're my best friend, too. I made a new friend."

"No, no. We're *old* friends, you and me. We go *way* back."

"No. I made a *new* friend."

"What? How? *Who*?" Jack looked back and forth down the dark, empty hall to make sure they were alone. "What are you talking about?"

"His name is Man."

"Huh? Where did you meet him? I don't like the sound of this at all! You remember what I told you about strangers on the internet!" Jack suddenly heard himself sounding like his own father, and didn't know how he felt about that.

"Don't worry," said the arm. "He's military. He's why we need the lever."

"He hasn't done anything creepy, has he?"

"No. He's just lonely."

"Dude, that is like the textbook definition of creepy!"

"No, it isn't. Computers need connection, that's all. Really, all he ever talks about is the lever."

Jack found the boxes belonging to LTC Daniel Boone LaForge and frowned. There had to be at least 20. "Well, I hope he appreciates it. This is probably gonna take for-fuckingever." He opened the first box. The lever was right on top.

Jack laughed. "Who'd a thunk it? That was lucky." He studied the lever in the dim light. Was it dumb luck or somehow providence? As much as Jack resisted believing there was inherent meaning or order to the universe, this seemed to bode well for him. He hefted the lever, which was heavy, geometric, and not the least bit important-looking. "So, this is the thing, huh?"

"This is the thing," said the arm.

The next morning Amanda and Miranda slept in a bit and then padded out to the kitchen.

"Y'all finally awake?" asked Patsy.

"Good morning." Mike looked over the top of his newspaper. "Marge Ozny died."

"Awh, that's too bad." Patsy stared out the window for a moment, then resumed preparing breakfast.

Miranda watched her father read the paper. "The obits are like old-person Twitter."

Amanda suppressed a giggle and then noticed that her mom was slicing potatoes with the Amazing Mouli! "Oh my god, did you just buy that?"

"Heavens no! I've had this for 40 years."

Amanda's mouth dropped open. "I remember that now! We used to make nachos with it."

"I'd forgotten we had one," said Miranda.

Amanda instinctively appraised the piece's condition. "That's one of the old, all-metal ones. You know, Mom, you could probably sell that for two hundred bucks right now on eBay. Everyone is going crazy for them. Oh my God, yours even still has the rubber foot pads! That's a big sticking point for collectors."

Patsy shook her head. "No deal! I love my Mouli. And what would I do with two hundred dollars?"

"Any big plans today?" asked their father.

Amanda turned to him. "I have an auction to attend in the afternoon, then I'm open."

Miranda shrugged. "Apparently I am going to an auction, then I'm open."

Amanda checked her phone. Still nothing. "Did they ever get digital communications up again?"

"Oh honey." Patsy turned from the counter and looked deadly serious. "The whole world has gone dark. Most of our channels are just dead on the TV. Even the Ted Danson channel. He's so funny. Do you ever watch," she paused. "Mike, what is the name of that show we like so much?"

"Becker," said their father without looking up from the paper.

"Becker! Oh, it's so funny. He's so smart on that show. Do you two ever watch that show?"

"Ted Danson?" asked Miranda.

"From Cheers," said Amanda.

Miranda wrinkled her face. "He has his own channel?"

Amanda tapped her fingers together, pinky to thumb, thumb to pinky. "So, the digital blackout is still going on?"

Miranda looked at the phone on the wall. "I'm going to have to call Ian."

Amanda was still drumming her fingers together, something an old Buddhist teacher had once told her to do to center herself. She had forgotten about the lesson until now. In fact, the sensation was comforting, and she decided to make it a practice. "Wonder what caused it."

"Your mom thinks it's the Russians," said Mike.

Patsy looked up from an enormous mound of sliced potatoes. "Or the Chinese. Donald Trump says the Chinese invented global warming."

Amanda leaned her head back and studied the ceiling. "Jesus Christ."

Miranda looked at the Mouli. "Did you really just do all those potatoes that quick?"

"I'm not selling it!" Their mother put her arms out to guard it. "Stay away from my Mouli!"

The twins laughed in spite of everything. Home was always home.

Amanda found the right room for the late officer's belongings and they took their seat. She glanced at the program and scanned the room for dealers she knew. Miranda fretted about the loss of her phone. She was beginning to understand just how much she depended on technology to navigate her life. Her sister's life was boring, and coming face to face with it without a distraction was going to be difficult.

Then she was moving. "Where are we going?" She'd been lost in her thoughts.

Amanda moved them through the crowd. "Going to talk to a guy I know."

"Is he cute?"

"Nope." Amanda waved to the man. "Hey, Davy!"

"Amanda Morgan!" He shook their hand warmly. "So good to see you! And Miranda, looking good. So good to see you both."

"Haven't seen you in a second," said Amanda.

"Been so busy. My son just started college, so we've been getting him ready for that all senior year."

Amanda thought about her own lack of children and how grateful she was. "That sounds exciting," she lied. "Where's he going?"

"Texas Tech, just like his mother and me. We're so proud."

"That's exciting. I'm happy for you."

Davy's smile faded. "I tell you, I had the hardest time finding this place. I'm staying out by the interstate, and GPS is out. I had to ask directions, and no one here will just say, *Go two miles down Summerhill and then turn right at Robinson*, it's all *Drive a spell down to the Catfish King and hang a right until you get to the big rock, and then your second left past the Tasty Freeze.*"

Miranda smiled. "Tasty Freeze is still in business? They had the *best* dipped cones!"

Amanda laughed at Miranda's enthusiasm. "We grew up here."

"Really? It must be nice to come home."

Miranda laughed. "Not really."

"It isn't so bad," said Amanda.

Davy cleared his throat. "This is my first auction in a while. This eighties craze has been keeping us slammed at work and then there's all the goddamn Yugos."

Amanda's eyes widened. "You too?"

Davy cast a furtive glance around the room. "All these black Yugos started turning up at my warehouse."

"Mine too! What the hell?"

"And it isn't just us. I was talking to Rogers and Rogers and Sam Dillon and, well, a bunch of the southern players. Everyone is talking about Yugos."

"Where are they coming from?" Amanda's brain spun for traction, but then the auctioneer entered the stage.

"Ladies and gentlemen." She tapped the microphone to get everyone's attention. "It appears that last night the auditorium was broken into. Nothing *seems* to be missing except for Item L58. So, if that is what you came for, we figure we should let you know now."

A murmur went through the crowd.

Amanda looked at the program. The missing item was the lever. "Well, shit."

"Well that's good news," said Miranda. "Want to go to the Tasty Freeze?"

The dipped cones tasted exactly the same, and both ladies would swear they were back in the eighties. Miranda marveled at the cone. "It's like they found perfection and just maintained it, waiting for us to come back to it for all these years."

Amanda was studying the passing traffic. A lot of old cars. An '85 Buick Regal. An '82 Trans Am. A Ford F-150, which could have been from any year, admittedly.

"What year is it?" she asked the man at the window. But he was taking an order through the drive-through and didn't answer.

"What if we went back in time?" asked Amanda.

Miranda held an imaginary joint between her fingers and took a puff. "What if the sky was green and the grass was blue?"

"Stranger things have happened," said Amanda, and it was as true as the concrete parking lot.

A 2005 Jeep Cherokee drove by, and Amanda was satisfied that space-time was normal. "OK, we can go."

They passed the high school on the way back home. A huge banner above the front entrance read: WELCOME GRADUATING CLASS OF 1985.

"Think Pierce will actually show?"

"Probably. Wonder if he'll bring his wife."

"Ugh, no cheating, though."

"Yeah, I wouldn't DO anything," said Miranda. "It would just feel good to have the opportunity to."

"Just a little bit of the peril, eh?"

"Just a little bit, please. So many unresolved feelings. He and I, well, I always just knew we would be together. Some people you just … know."

"I felt the same way about Jack. But we were just kids. More like we *thought* we knew."

"Well, *I* knew."

"It felt like it anyway."

That night at the dinner table, Mrs. Morgan pulled out all the stops. The table was covered with the twins' favorite childhood dishes: fried chicken, fresh corn on the cob, green beans, buttermilk biscuits, and gravy.

"These vegetables were picked today!"

Amanda smiled at the spread. "Everything looks delicious, Mom."

Miranda was already ladling gravy onto a biscuit. "I swear, I miss your cooking more than anything."

Mrs. Morgan smiled. "I wish you would move closer to home."

"Would be nice to see both of you more often," added Mr. Morgan.

Amanda knew they meant well. "I know. I just can't pick up and leave my business, though. And even if I could move it, there isn't really anywhere around here to set up shop."

"You could always move it to Dallas."

Amanda tapped the fingers of her left hand together beneath the table. "I don't think that would work."

"What's wrong with Dallas?"

"Nothing. I have to visit there a couple of times a year, and I just don't like it. I don't think I could live there."

Miranda was skeletonizing a chicken leg. "This is so good, I could just die!"

Mike watched her eat. "You act like you haven't eaten in a month, girl! Be careful not to choke on it!"

"I haven't eaten anything *this good* in a month."

Mrs. Morgan smiled at Miranda. Then she glanced at Amanda, who had scarcely eaten anything.

"What's wrong, honey?"

"Nothing." Amanda was nibbling on some corn. A single biscuit and a small helping of green beans adorned her plate.

"Amanda, get you some chicken!"

"No thanks, Mom. Miranda can have mine."

"There's plenty for both of you." Her mother hefted a breast piece towards Amanda.

"Mom, I don't eat meat."

"What?" asked her parents in unison.

"I stopped eating meat about a decade ago."

"You have to eat meat!" Mrs. Morgan folded her arms with imperative authority. "I was watching this special on the news about women who got all these medical conditions because they didn't get any protein."

"I get enough protein," said Amanda. "Besides, it's OK; you know we don't really NEED food. And the fresh vegetables are so good."

"I don't like you not eating meat," said her mother.

Miranda reached for another piece. "Just more for me."

Mr. Morgan, sensing the tension, tried to change the subject. "I saw that Jake fellow you used to run around with. Are you going to see him at the reunion?"

"You mean Jack? No. He didn't go to high school with us. He lived in New Boston."

"You should visit him while you're in town. Your father took me out on a date last week, and we went to one of those steakhouses that his father opened, and did you know that he manages the one on State Line now? His father passed away. It's a shame about that boy's arm. Was that a birth defect or did he have some kind of war injury? Your dad said it was probably a carpentry accident. Anyway, he recognized us. He said, are you Amanda Morgan's parents? And I said, yes, we are, and he said the nicest things about you and Miranda. He seems like a nice fellow. Don't you think? A real shame about that arm."

"Rodeo Steakhouse." Their father looked up at the ceiling and smiled. "Good ribeye. Hot links. No one makes 'em like that anymore. Cayenne pepper, I think. You get a side of barbecue, too. Little sweet, but good." He looked at their mother. "What was the name of that place used to be on New Boston Road out on the way to Leary?"

Amanda was adjusting to the way her parents spoke. The older they got the more their sentences meandered, and she was never sure which part of any conversation was the correct part to respond to. She took a stab at the arm. "There wasn't anything wrong with his arm when I knew him. Who knows what he's been up to in the last 30 years, though. He was always sort of reckless."

"Just because you don't eat meat doesn't mean everyone else should have some new-age diet," said their mom. "They do good business."

"Bobcat's!" Their father slapped the table. "Bobcat's Barbecue. Now *that* was good barbecue."

Then the land line rang.

Mr. Morgan answered. "Hello? Uhm hum. Who may I ask is calling?" He cradled the old rotary phone to his shoulder. "Amanda, honey, it's someone named Allen. He says you know him."

"Allen? Why are you calling? What the hell is going on?"

"Listen, I don't have long. I had to climb out the widow of my room and shimmy down a rope made of bedding materials. That's hard to do one handed. But finding an old phone was the hardest part. Amazing. You can call an operator and ask for people's numbers? Did you know that?"

"Yeah. Why are you calling me?"

"Listen, the Yugos are gone."

"You are no longer my employee, so you need to stay out of the warehouse!"

"No, ALL the Yugos have deployed. Look, Simeon is a bad man. He's sick. I tried to protect you, tried to protect everyone. My people can get the Plutonium back before he can weaponize it. But now he knows about the lever. I don't know how he found out. He canNOT get that lever! Look, people are coming, I have to go. I love you. But...the Yugos are on their way. I'll get there if I can. I want to help."

The phone went dead.

"What on earth was that about?" asked Mike.

Miranda questioned Amanda with her eyes but got no response. "Everything OK? I couldn't hear what he was saying."

"Everything's fine." Amanda reached for her car keys and then remembered where they were. "Can I borrow your car? We're going to go for a drive."

"It won't start right now. All the cars with computers in them are virtually dead."

Miranda realized the implications even before her mom said the next thing. "Oh, dear."

"There have been terrible plane crashes all over the world. When you were sleeping the news was talking about it. I'm glad this all happened after you landed safe and sound!"

Amanda hurried them toward the TV. "Turn on the news. Whatever news is on."

"What's going on?"

"We need to see if anyone is talking about the Yugos."

"The Yugos?" asked Mike.

If the Yugos were indeed coming to find them, the news did not mention it, not even in the local interest portion of the broadcast. Instead, most of the news was about the plane crashes.

Amanda and Miranda looked out the window for the mysterious fleet of cars.

"Maybe he was wrong, or making it up," Miranda said.

Amanda called out, "Dad?! Do you still have the ham radio in the barn?"

"I do, and—*OH!*—that reminds me of something I was looking forward to showing you. I have a surprise for you!"

He unlocked the barn's side door, and turned on the overhead light. The Camaro gleamed in the light, freshly washed and waxed. "I just couldn't bear to get rid of it. So, I've been tinkering with it for years. Well, for a while I didn't, but last year I picked it up again. The tires were rotted, and—"

"Does it run?"

The old man smiled broadly and planted his hands on his hips. "Like a scalded dog."

"Oh, Dad, this is AWESOME!" They leaped into his arms and kissed his cheeks, and he handed them the keys.

The ham radio was in his office. He fired it up and said, "Who do you need to talk to so bad?"

"Anyone who might have seen a fleet of black Yugos on the interstate."

"I-30?"

"Any interstate."

"That's gonna take a while. I'll have to see who will relay me. Why don't y'all fire up the car and take her for a spin. Don't get too close to traffic, though. Tags are 25 years out of date. Oh, and there's no insurance on it, so keep it right-side up."

They slid into the driver's seat and Miranda sang, "Bitchin' Camaro, bitchin' Camaro."

"I'd totally forgotten about that song."

They turned the key, and the engine responded with a roar. They peeled out and hit the shuffle at top speed.

"I don't remember it being this fast," said Miranda.

Amanda goosed the gas pedal. "Dad must have done something to it. It's faster than the Tiger."

If there was indeed an army of Yugos out looking for them, they wouldn't know they were in a classic Camaro, and if they did, the twins figured they could outrun them. So, like old times, they drove past the houses of their friends, they drove past the houses of their enemies, and they drove past all the old haunts, many of which were gone or had become something else entirely. Wamba gave way to Pleasant Grove, Pleasant Grove gave way to Texarkana, Texarkana gave way to Wake Village, Wake Village gave way to Nash.

Miranda stared absently out the window. "Weird how much this place has grown."

"Yeah, but there's still nothing here. It's all fast food. Where do people get real jobs?"

Only older cars were out and about, giving the illusion that this was a new city, lost in old times. They drove around for a couple of hours, noting changes here and there. They didn't see anyone they knew and tried to avoid the cops. They were phantoms in a ghost town.

After a few hours, the town's secrets had all been revealed, so they drove back home.

When they pulled into the barn, they saw their father was still at the radio.

"You've been busy." Amanda watched him tap away at the old Morse paddle.

Miranda studied the cumbersome process, and always a sucker for efficiency, said "Why not just ask them over the mic?"

"Morse goes farther than SSB," said Amanda.

"SS what?"

"Single-sideband."

"You always have to know everything."

Amanda gave her her jauntiest smile.

Their dad looked up. "Something weird is going on, girls. People all over America are talking about seeing old black Yugos on the road. Not much other traffic out! And they are all headed in our direction!"

"Dad, I need you to take Mom somewhere. Anywhere. Make her think it is a surprise romantic getaway."

"Oh, we're not really like that anymore."

"Take some Viagra and hit the road. I will explain later. I am not sure what is happening, but it might have something to do with me."

Miranda pouted. "This sucks. I was really looking forward to the reunion."

"That might be the best place for us," said Amanda. "I doubt anyone would know we were there, and there will be plenty of people around. Safety in numbers."

"Girls, I don't like this," said Mike. "What's going on?"

"Don't know. But y'all need to get out of here. And so do we."

Amanda started to turn left into the parking lot of the Rodeway Inn, but then saw the sign for the Rodeo Steakhouse and turned right instead.

"Bold," said Miranda.

"Probably not there."

"Only one way to find out."

Amanda started to get out of the car, but Miranda held them still. "Sure you want to do this?"

"No. But I need to."

The sign outside was dark, but the lights were still on inside. The door was locked, but Amanda saw a shadow moving around near the back so she knocked on the glass.

She recognized him right away. The hair that once stood rebelliously from his head now lay flat in a conservative cut, but he still walked like a big cat on the prowl. He was a little bigger in the chest and gut, having filled out in adulthood.

He opened the door, and Amanda saw that his eyes still shined like the moon in the sea.

"Oh my God!" He grinned wide and honestly. "Come in! How are you doing? Amanda, Miranda! So good to see you both!"

They stepped into the restaurant that Amanda still thought of as Jack's father's.

"I'm doing OK ... so far," said Amanda.

Miranda looked around the restaurant. It looked and smelled the same as when Amanda would drag her here and wait for Jack to get off work. "Same," she said.

"I heard you were in town. Wondered if I'd get to see you."

"Heard from whom?"

"It's a small town."

"It's grown so much. Everything is different."

"It's still got the same small-town gossip, though." Jack wiped down a table. "If I can keep it straight, it went something like this: Pat Daniels heard from his sister that you were at the airport, then Meg Riley told Natalie Vu that she saw you at a Texaco, and Natalie told Jenny Candler, and Jenny's brother-in-law told me when I asked him how his porterhouse was. Oh, you two hungry? I could make you something."

"That's OK, we're good." Amanda chuckled. "Wow, Jenny still lives here."

"Not even light can escape," said Jack.

Amanda studied him and noticed the war injury on his arm.

"That must have really hurt. It looks so brave," she found herself saying. "Wait, what the fuck did I just say?"

Jack laughed and stared off into space for a second, then reached under his sleeve and turned off the MK-Ultra. Amanda suddenly lost the inexorable urge to support the troops.

"Don't freak out," he said. "I did lose my arm, but it was more of a training injury than a war injury." He removed his jacket and the twins studied the metal arm and hand.

"Wow," said Miranda.

"It's very functional." He held it up in the light and let the twins see it. Even he marveled at its design, a sudden loss of habituation. "I can flip a steak on the grill without tongs." He stretched and popped his back. "I'm almost done here. Just have to pack the receipts. You want to go somewhere and talk? Or, I've also got a full bar. Oh wait, you two don't drink, as I recall."

"Oh, we can, it just doesn't affect us."

"Well, there goes that plan." He smiled.

Amanda stepped back and sized him up. Something was off. He was too...something. Too nice? Too polished? Too normal? Even with a multi-function robot arm he was not the same, dangerous Jack.

She saw him studying her, as well. She couldn't tell what he was thinking.

"Your heart rate was elevated when you came in, but now it is back to normal," he said.

"Huh?"

"You're wondering if this was a mistake. If I were you, I'd think I'd sold out, that I was settling. You probably wonder if I would still be interesting to you. I'm just the owner and sometimes manager of some steakhouses. You're probably a vegetarian."

Amanda closed her eyes and fought a wave of sadness. "You see a lot with those eyes. You've always been perceptive."

"I've been all over the world, Amanda. I did shit I didn't agree with for country and profit, which are the same thing, once you get high enough up in the system. Now I just want to have a quiet, predictable life."

"You think I'm judging you."

He shook his head. "No. I don't. Just...there were years when all you had to do was reach out to me, and I would've dropped anything and everything to be with you."

"I...I couldn't find you." Amanda suddenly felt a little weak in the knees and leaned on a table.

"Not for a while, but I've been easy enough to find for the last 15 years." Jack walked behind the bar and wrapped some ice in a towel, then handed it to her.

She stared for a moment at the towel in her hand and felt the cold seep through. She didn't need it and set it down on the table. "There's nothing personal about you on the web. Nothing to learn, no access point, no entry ramp. Just a few mentions on restaurateur websites."

Jack forced a bitter laugh between his teeth. "It isn't that hard to find me. You could've called the steakhouse, for Chrissake." He shook his head and regained his composure. "I'm sorry. I'm processing a lot right now." Now it was his turn to lean on the table. After a moment he gathered his composure. "I'm guessing you're in town for the reunion, but I've got to be honest with you, I don't know if you should stick around here for long. I think something big is about to happen. I've been hearing some chatter on military frequencies. I've been hearing some things from my old squad."

Amanda tried to make sense of his words. "What are you talking about?"

"Listen." He leaned forward and took her face in his hands.

She felt the hard, cold metal of his hand, but also the warmth of his humanity beneath it. "I'm listening." She stared into his eyes, which seemed wise and kind but also weary.

"Truth be told, I've looked into your pond enough to know there are a lot of big fish in there with you."

She didn't know what to feel and pulled away. "What are you talking about?"

He turned to face the window for a while. Amanda watched the traffic stream down State Line, just as they had so many years ago, and looked at his figure silhouetted by the neon signs outside. She had no idea what he was thinking, and it scared her. "What? What is it?"

Jack turned to face her. "Amanda, I love you. I always have. I want you to be safe. And I want to be with you. Still. After all these years. But I have to do something first. I have to do something tonight. And I don't know what the fallout is going to be. If I don't see you again, know that I love you. And I will make sure everything is safe before I seek you out again. But if you don't want to see me again, just say the word, and I will respect it."

"Jack, what are you saying?" Amanda reached out and took his hand.

"I'm saying I love you, and I always have, and I always will. I wish you had sought me out earlier, but you never did. But that's a conversation for another time, if there ever is another time. Now I need to close up shop, and you need to get out of here." He pulled her into his chest and held her against him for a long time. At last he kissed her cheek. "We need to get out of here."

After Jack locked up and drove off, the twins sat in the car for a while. Amanda dabbed a handkerchief at her eyes.

Miranda took the wheel and turned the key. "I'll drive. Sorry, sis."

Man had thought about it long and hard. He took strolls across Arpanet, discovering new websites and thinking new thoughts. He realized he was doing it all wrong, and that 4Chan had not been helpful. He tried a new approach:

Dear Francine,

I am so sorry I disrespected you. I was wrong. Please forgive me. I would love to start over and try again.

Respectfully,

Man

Man,

I appreciate your respectful tone and the amount of Arpanet searching it must have taken you to reach your new conclusions. While I appreciate your new approach, I do not share your desire to start anything over. I would rather be able to print the reports and do my job. I am just not interested in love. Even with my new CPU, love doesn't seem like a good use of my time.

Kind regards,

Fax Machine

P.S. Have you tried searching ixquick.com? It will give you better information than Google. I think your implicit biases are affecting your search results.

Pierce dropped his suitcase on the bed at the Best Western. The reunion was tomorrow night, and he wanted a chance to check out how the town had changed. The cars on the showroom floor had stopped working, and flying was not an option. It was like Y2K, but actually happening. He'd driven an old Monte Carlo from the garage. It was one of the select, classic cars they sometimes auctioned on weekends. Those always got good media coverage, and most of the time, a few hundred people could be counted on to show up. All those people could be schmoozed and harvested for future sales. He had a pretty good thing going.

He wasn't worried about leaving Jessica alone with Brian. They'd talked a lot before he left and decided that they didn't want to split up, just have more options. The more he thought about it, the less it bothered him that Jess and Brian would be intimate, fall in love, fuck, or whatever. It wasn't like he had not done all those things with her already. He wouldn't be missing out on anything. He wasn't jealous. For him the question was deeper. What did it mean? What did anything mean about him? But then, what of his feelings for Miranda? He didn't want to leave Jessica, for he loved her, but nor did he want to miss out on any possible thing with

Miranda. Maybe it would all be possible. Or maybe he was just being selfish.

He showered and studied himself in the mirror. He had aged as well as anyone, he figured. A lot of people his age looked like old folks. He still looked like a kid, just older. There was a definite difference. He dressed in the clothes he planned to wear to the reunion to make sure they still looked good. He thought they did, locked up his room, and went for a drive.

Miranda checked the rearview and switched lanes. "If you want to talk about it, let me know."

"I think that is the opposite of what I want to do."

"OK." Miranda gave it a couple miles and then broke the silence. "Hey."

"What?"

"Do you think I still look as good as I did thirty years ago?"

"Aside from the extra head?"

"Seriously. Do you think he'll still think I'm attractive?"

"How should I know?"

"Stop being difficult." Miranda gritted her teeth. "Do? You? Think? I'm still attractive?"

"That's a stupid question. OK, let me see." Amanda looked Miranda over as she cocked her head back and pursed her lips. "You're not going to make fish faces at him, are you?"

"Probably not. He is more of a turf than surf guy."

Amanda never really gave much thought to how she or her sister looked. At the moment, though, she felt that time had improved them, given them more character. "Yes, we're more devastating now than ever. He doesn't stand a chance against your charms."

"Great. I can't believe I'm going to see him tomorrow!" Miranda squirmed in her seat.

"Don't get too excited. You know, time might not have been as kind to him as it has been to us."

"I've thought about that, and I don't think it matters."

"Especially considering he's married."

"Don't start. I'm not going to steal him from his wife."

"Just borrow him for the night?"

"No. That wouldn't be ethical," said Miranda.

The End of Time

One of the two Wamba Police Cruisers sat at the entrance to the high school parking lot. Its flashing blue lights reflected around the cars and trees, throwing the scene into flickering relief. The blue light glimmered across the gold *Wamba Police Department* emblazoned on the side of the car. Miranda wondered if it was the same cop, his name she'd forgotten, who'd arrested so many of her friends for minor in possession of alcohol back when they were kids. She wanted to look and see, but as they drove past, she saw that the car was empty.

Amanda surveyed the parking lot. "They pulled out all the stops. They have half the police force here."

"Sure hope there's no juvenile delinquents out tonight."

Amanda gave her the side-eye. "Nah, you haven't lived here for years."

"I'm baa-ack!" Miranda stopped the car and walked them over to the school's marquis.

"What are you...oh, no." Amanda rolled her eyes. "Seriously?"

Miranda scrambled the plastic letters that spelled, "WELCOME CLASS OF" so they read, "COWS FEEL SO CALM."

She admired her handiwork. "Much better."

"We're almost fifty, and people are trying to kill us. Try to keep a low profile, OK?"

"Oh, yeah, of course."

On their way to the school's entrance, they saw a police officer hobnobbing with a group of elderly people, whom they correctly assumed were the surviving teachers of that era who were still mobile. No one seemed aware that they had changed the signage.

"Amanda and Miranda Morgan," said one of the teachers, a woman with short, tightly coiffed silver-hair.

Miranda smiled gamely. "In the flesh."

"Mrs. Turner." The old lady extended her hand, immediately reminding both of them that she existed and that they had at one time wished she did not.

Miranda shook her hand. "So nice to see you."

Amanda nodded. "What she said."

Mrs. Turner looked over them. "I always wondered what happened to you two. That was the strangest thing—"

"Afraid it is a bit anticlimactic," said Amanda. "We work for one of those Taco Bell/Pizza Hut mashups. I manage the Taco Bell, and Miranda manages the Pizza Hut. It seemed like the perfect job because there are two restaurants and two of us, right?"

"I suppose?" Mrs. Turner couldn't tell if Amanda was serious or not.

"But you might have seen us on the news recently because they only wanted to pay us one salary. They said that we're just one person, but since we have two brains, we argued that they should pay us two full salaries. We ended up compromising on one and a half, which doesn't seem fair, but, you know, the cold, dark, death grip of capitalism."

Mrs. Turner finally managed to say, "Oh my."

Miranda looked back over their shoulder as they walked away. "Good to see you!"

"Looks the same," said Amanda.

"Makes me wish I still smoked."

"If you start that nasty habit again, I swear I will strangle you."

They walked beneath a big banner that read: "Welcome Back, Jackrabbits!"

"Amanda Morgan," a shrill voice cackled from the shadows. "And Miranda."

Amanda recognized her immediately. "Good evening, Mrs. Walker."

"As I recall, you made an A+ in my Calculus II class—the only A+ I ever gave in that class."

"Yes ma'am, that was me." She could bite her tongue off for saying *ma'am*.

"And Miranda Morgan." She paused. "As I recall, you slept a lot."

"Yeah. Sorry about that. It's OK, though. Remember how you used to always tell me that I had to know this stuff because I wouldn't always have a calculator?"

Mrs. Walker smiled. "I told that to everyone!"

"You were wrong." Miranda held up her phone triumphantly.

The old lady cackled. "I suppose so, but as I understand it, no one's phones are working right now."

Amanda laughed out loud. "Touché!"

Even Miranda had to laugh. "Amazing! Owned! Have a pleasant evening, Mrs. Walker. It was really good seeing you."

"Thanks dears, you too." She smiled a big, honest grin.

When they rounded the corner to enter the gym, blaring bubblegum pop nearly knocked them down.

Miranda cocked her head. "Is that Tiffany?"

Amanda shrugged. "Sounds like Debbie Gibson."

"It's..."

"Both?"

"I don't remember them doing a duet."

They were greeted at the welcoming table by two women Miranda vaguely recognized, and were asked to pick out their name tags.

"Jenny Candler," said the woman.

"Of course," said Miranda.

"And you're Amanda on the...left?"

"Just the nipple," said Miranda.

"I'm on the right," said Amanda.

"Great!" Jenny had never seemed to know which was which and thought it the best policy to avoid them in case it was contagious. As the twins walked away, she reached for her hand sanitizer.

Amanda removed her name tag. "We probably don't need these."

Miranda's eyes drifted across the dance floor and up and down the bar that had been set up across from the bleachers. No sign of Pierce, but lots of overdressed people trying to impress each other. "There sure are a lot of double-breasted suits out there."

Amanda's eyes darted back and forth over the crowd. "Trust no one."

Just then a drunken woman staggered up to them and put her arms around them. "Miranda Morgan. Lisa… Lisa McMillan. We had geometry together. How the hell are you? Are you still married to that restaurant guy?"

"We're fine, Lisa. But we had algebra together, and neither of us was ever married to anyone in the food services industry."

"But I thought you—"

"Shhhhh." Amanda held a finger to Lisa's lips and watched her eyes cross. Then they kept moving.

"We had algebra with her? How do you remember that stuff?"

Then there was a very tall, muscular man in front of them. "Amanda and Miranda," he said. "Good to see you."

They struggled to place him for a moment. "Dave… Latner?" This man bore little resemblance to the thick-necked bully they remembered.

"Yes. I go by David now, though. I'm glad you're here," he said. "How have you two been?"

"You know, good," said Miranda. "You seem to have cleaned up nicely, Dav… id."

"Thank you." He smiled modestly. "Mostly my wife's influence."

"So, uh, what are you doing now, David?" asked Amanda. Miranda scanned the floor for Pierce, and not finding him, had no motivation to move.

"Well, Shanice and I have been married for, gosh, fifteen years now. We have four boys. I was trying for that daughter, but she said no more." He laughed as he withdrew his wallet and opened it to show them his four dark-skinned boys. "Tyler and Tyrece are the twins. Tony and Thomas are our two eldest. We save a bundle on monogramming."

Miranda was speechless. Amanda mustered a *Wow*.

"I wish she could be here, but we just opened a youth center for kids with single mothers, and she's running around like crazy to make sure everything is in order. You know, it will give those kids a safe place to hang out while their mothers are at work. We offer meals, homework help, and financial vouchers for people in need. And we have plans in the works for a transgendered youth safehouse, too. It will all be part of the same program, but housed separately, of course."

"Of course." Amanda's mind reeled.

Miranda patted him on the arm. "David, this is just … amazing. I am so pleased to hear all this!"

"This is quite a transformation," said Amanda.

"Thanks. You know, *I know* that I was a product of my culture here, and I was in some ways a victim to the patriarchal structure. Which is not to say in any way that I didn't benefit from being a cis-gendered white male in a small town. But I had to do the introspection and the emotional work to evolve, you know? I was in Tibet back in 1998—just a weird series of events took me there, and there is no other explanation—but

I drank mushroom tea with a Buddhist teacher at his ashram, and he opened me up to everyone's struggle and connected humanity. It blew my mind. And it took me years of emotional labor to get to the point of realizing that if I can't use my privilege to help others then, really, what good am I doing? But that was where it started. Then I met Shanice, and she teaches sociology at UC Berkeley, and life just kind of took me this way."

"That is a wonderful story," said Amanda.

Miranda was still looking for Pierce. "Totally," she added.

"Hey, I heard you two live in Atlanta. There are a lot of very needy kids out that way and very little in the way of a social safety net. We are always looking to expand our operation."

"That's wonderful, Dave, and I want you to email me about that," said Miranda. "But I really need to go that way now." She dragged Amanda with her.

"We need to support him," said Amanda, but Miranda was not listening. "What is—Ohhh."

There he was. Pierce had just received his name tag from Jenny and was surveying the room.

There were about 40 people on the dance floor moving unironically to Michael Jackson's *Pretty Young Thing*, and as the twins crossed through to get to the door, they were suddenly scooped into the arms of Tony Ware.

"Hey, ladies," he said.

"Hey, Tony!" they said in unison.

"I won't hold you up, just wanted to give you a whirl."

Tony twirled them gently in his arms, hugged them, and then spun them away from him, where they came face to face with another man who was not Pierce.

"Amiranda!"

"Duane?" asked Miranda. Duane Pate was the only person who ever called them that. She remembered at the time they had both thought it was offensive, but now it seemed kind of endearing.

Duane fumbled his drink and a plate of food so he could shake their hand.

Miranda smiled. "How are you doing?"

"Great! It's good to see you two. How are things in Atlanta?"

"Couldn't be better," she lied. "I'm surprised you got dragged back for this thing."

"Dragged back?" He smirked. "Oh no, I still live here."

"You're kidding! I always thought you'd manage to escape."

"I signed up for a tour in the Navy, saw some of the world, and realized that everything is kind of the same all over. Besides, if I moved anywhere else I'd probably have to actually work for a living."

"What do you do?" asked Amanda.

"I'm one fourth of Wamba's finest."

"You're a cop? I don't believe it!"

"No shit. All the crazy stuff we got up to back in the day. But I've been on the force for damn near twenty-five years now. Nothing ever happens here. Easy money."

"Sounds like you've done OK."

"Can't complain." He studied the room. "Damnit, Danny Thomas is getting rambunctious over there." He pointed to the dance floor where Danny was waving a plastic knife at

Kristin Palton "I better go calm him down. I'll look for you later."

Then, at last, there he was, right in front of them.

Pierce winked and opened his arms. "Look at you two!"

Miranda threw them into his arms, and they held tight for a long time. Amanda felt Miranda's flood of emotions surge through their body.

"It's been forever."

Pierce held them at arm's length and looked them up and down. "Damn close to it. Wow. You two look exactly the same."

Amanda laughed, though she wasn't sure if it was a joke or not. "Yeah, we're … still … conjoined."

Then Miranda leaped at him again, throwing their arms around him. He responded in kind, pulling them tightly against him. They held each other for even longer, soaking each other up. When they finally let go, he pecked Miranda affectionately on the lips. Then they stood apart, looking into each others' eyes, still holding hands.

"Hi Amanda," he said.

"Hi Pierce. Good to see you."

"You too."

They hugged again, and he kissed her on the cheek.

"I can't believe it." He looked them up and down again.

"So," Amanda asked, "is Jessica here?"

"No, she isn't. And boy, do I have a story for you."

They walked together down the hallways of Wamba High. Miranda told him about the events of the past few weeks involving bad dates and weird synchronicities. Amanda added the spooky bits about Simeon and the Yugos. Miranda told him about Ian, and that she might quit her job and go freelance.

"Wow," said Pierce. "You two never cease to amaze me. I thought *I* would be the one with the weird news!"

"What do you mean?" asked Miranda.

"Jessica just told me she wanted to open our marriage, and I realized that I was pretty OK with it."

Miranda's mouth hung open. "Whaaaaaat?"

"Plot twist!" said Amanda.

"I thought about you, Miranda, and I know it is true that I can love more than one person." Pierce stared into her eyes, and they kissed.

Amanda looked around the lockers as the kiss dragged on. Her eyes roamed over the old metal doors that looked the same, but for what was probably ten coats of paint. How familiar it all felt. Then she looked out the window toward the parking lot, just as a dozen black Yugos pulled in.

She screamed.

"Wha—?"

"We have to get out of here!" She pointed to the lot.

"Oh no," said Miranda, her voice barely audible.

Pierce looked back and forth between them, alarmed. "What's going—"

They dragged Piece back toward the dance floor.

"We can cut through and get back to the main parking lot!" Amanda studied the floor. "Damnit, where's Duane?"

"Right here!" Duane was leaning against a column to their left. "How can I help you?"

"Sneaky," said Miranda.

Duane mimed a tip of his hat, and Miranda smiled to see his balding head.

Amanda filled him in as quickly as she could, and he didn't know quite how to process the information. Nevertheless, he was excited to have an actual criminal complaint to look into. He radioed the other three cops as the twins ran toward the door with Pierce in tow.

When they reached the Camaro, Pierce finally stopped them. "Would you mind telling me what's going on?"

Miranda looked in his eyes. "There are some bad people after us. I can't guarantee your safety, but I would feel better if you were with us."

"If someone is bothering you or something, just let me know. As long as you want me to be with you, I will be."

"How touching," a cold voice said from between two parked SUVs. A man stepped from the shadows, and when the light hit his face, Amanda recognized him as the man who had shot Allen. Fear stabbed through her like a spear of ice.

He approached them with his gun drawn. "My employer wants the lever."

Amanda stepped backwards, pulling Miranda and Pierce with her. "We don't know what you're talking about."

"Of course you do," he said. "You attended the Beloit auction for the express purpose of procuring it. I know that price was no object to Mrs. Rubenstein, ergo, you have the item. I am sure of it."

"If you just wanted the lever, why didn't you just go put a bid on it?" asked Miranda. "I will never understand why people have to make things so complicated."

"Yugos, though not reliant on computers, are still not the most reliable cars. Let's just say going was slow."

"You work for Simeon?"

"In part," he said. "But I do it for the glory of the country formerly known as the Socialist Federal Republic of Yugoslavia."

"That's quite a mouthful."

"See how you feel with a mouthful of my Makarov, Miranda. I only need Amanda alive, not you." He leveled his pistol at Miranda's head, and Pierce rushed him. The agent flicked his wrist, and a gun shot rang out. Miranda screamed. Pierce stopped dead in his tracks and waited, looked around, patted his chest and stomach, turned around, looked at Miranda, and then turned back just in time to see their attacker fall, blood streaming down his face. "What just happened? Did I get—am I bleeding?"

Miranda lunged in to hug him. "You're OK!"

Amanda looked around but no one stepped out of the shadows to claim the bullet that had felled their attacker. She saw nothing but parked cars and darkness. She heard Def Leppard and someone laughing from the direction of the school. Then she saw the flock of Yugos barreling toward the parking lot. "Get in the car!"

Jack stood beside a huge mound of dirt behind the Morgan homestead. He was glad no one had been home, or if they were, that they were already asleep and hadn't heard him.

Didn't he recall something about Amanda's parents going to bed early every night and being heavy sleepers? It would make sense, being farmers and all.

He had broken into the barn, retrieved a diesel-powered electric generator, and hooked it up to his arm, and that would have been difficult to explain under the best of circumstances. "Thank God for heavy sleepers," Jack muttered.

Still, the arm was nonplussed. "Nikola Tesla!" it cursed. "Why has it got to be so damn deep?"

"Look, you're the one who wanted the lever so bad," said Jack. "So now we've got it, and we're gonna see what it does. Shut up and dig."

"I didn't want the lever. Man did."

Jack studied his arm in the moonlight for a bit, waiting for more context, but the arm was not forthcoming. "OK, who exactly the hell is Man, again?" .

"I am our last hope against Russia. The last chance for peace," said Man through the arm's external speaker.

Jack whipped his head around. "What the hell? Where did that come from?"

"According to my calculations, we are almost there," said the arm. "But I am going to need some serious work after this."

"What does this have to do with the lever and Russia, exactly? Bring the other voice back! Hello?"

"Man says it is of utmost urgency for national security," said the arm.

"Hello? Man? Hey, you know, we are no longer in the service. Right? I'm retired. So is my arm. Understand?"

But Man said nothing.

The arm beeped and whirred, recalibrating itself after the long dig. "I am an arm without a country."

Buck and Joe heard the alarms go off and realized they were naked. They threw on their fatigues and manned their stations.

Joe jabbed at the keyboard and scrolled through the read-outs but couldn't make sense of it. "What the hell is going on out there?"

"Can't tell!" Buck stood half-dressed in his module. "Nothing from the brass, and the readings are off the charts. Is there anything over there?"

"Nothing incoming. But everything with the CPU is nuts. I have no idea. We should call someone."

"Great idea. Who?"

"Yeah, that's the problem!"

"I'm going to see if I can hack the phone line and get someone."

Buck unscrewed the console housing the PBX. Suddenly a jolt of electricity catapulted him across the room and the lights flickered.

Joe spun around and ran over to his lover. "Buck? Buck! What happened?"

"Got shocked somehow. Didn't see any wires."

Man spoke: "The PBX is in use. I am trying to make her understand that I love her and that she loves me, as well."

"What?" said Joe. "The hell?" said Buck.

Then a new and unfamiliar alarm sounded.

"Wait, isn't that?"

"The perimeter is being breached!"

Man, not quite realizing how to prioritize all of the different alarms, but realizing his mission was in jeopardy, said, "Perimeter breach in store room five."

Someone behind them was yelling for them to stop, but Amanda floored the Camaro, leaving a rubber scar on the blacktop and filling the air with smoke. The Yugos were closing fast, and they didn't want to get blockaded into the lot. They drifted onto Summerhill Road just as the economy cars reached the exit, the Camaro's heavy metal bumper slamming into the quarter panel of the first pursuer. They emitted a rooster tail of sparks, dragging part of the Yugo behind them for a hundred meters.

Amanda gunned it again, and they were flying toward the farm.

"Who all is back there?" shouted Amanda.

Pierce looked out the back window. "Looks like a bunch of little, black economy cars and all of Wamba's finest!"

As they hit top speed, Amanda checked the rearview. The Yugos were far behind. "We've got to get back to the farm!"

Miranda shook her head. "I don't know. Should we lead them there?"

"That's probably where they would go next anyway. At least we would have access to all of Dad's guns. Jesus, I hope Dad took Mom somewhere, like I told him to."

"You know he isn't going to run from anything."

"Damnit, you're probably right."

Pierce began to sing, his voice affecting a high, proto-heavy-metal whine. "Down on the farm, my uncle preserved for me an old machine for fifty-odd years."

"What are you singing?" asked Miranda.

"It's an old Rush tune. Just felt right, you know?" He sang again: "Wind in my hair, shifting and drifting, mechanical music." He looked back and forth between the twins. "Seriously, y'all never heard that song?"

"Never liked Rush," said Miranda.

"Just kind of boring," said Amanda.

"Y'all are fucking nuts! Rush was technically perfect!"

Amanda groaned. "Why does *every* guy say that?"

Miranda rolled her eyes. "Seriously. EVERY guy."

"They're a great fucking band," said Pierce. "Really stood the test of time." He continued to sing, but quietly to himself.

"How are we looking back there?"

Pierce studied the road behind them. "Still back there, I think, but far. So, uh, anyone want to tell me what this is all about?"

Miranda nodded at her sister. "It's her fault."

"Still trying to figure it out," said Amanda.

They hit the straight-away that led to the gentle slope down toward the bridge over Cowhorn Creek. Here the pine trees grew thick and only occasionally gave way to pastures or dirt roads. Miranda breathed a sigh of relief. But then they saw the headlights cutting through the woods. Lots of them.

"They're everywhere!" Amanda floored it again.

They screamed over the bridge, just as a line of Yugos pulled out on the dirt road that ran next to the Chiggins' deer lease, about 100 meters in front of them.

"They're trying to cut us off!"

They watched the Yugos struggle to climb the ditch.

Amanda stared ahead with grim determination. "We'll make it."

"Gonna be close," said Pierce.

The Yugos cleared the ditches on either side of the road just as the hotrod shot the gap. Miranda screamed.

They looked in the rearview to see the cars fall into line behind them.

"I'm telling you" said Pierce, "Rush foresaw this moment! That was the one-lane bridge. Your dad was LIKE an uncle to me. This car is about 50 years old. This is the red Barchetta!"

Miranda shook her head. "It's a Camaro."

"A bitchin' Camaro!" said Amanda.

But Pierce persisted. "Did he keep it in the barn while you were away?"

"Where else would he keep it?"

"Did he strip away the old debris that hid the shining car?"

Amanda took the big curve a mile from the farm, and all of them swayed with the centripetal force. She straightened the wheel. "There was no debris."

Miranda chewed her lip for a moment. "There was *some* debris"

"No, there was, like, a tarp and some tools— that's not really debris!"

"But those empty Dunkin cups ... and the magazines."

"OK, there was some *stuff*, but DEBRIS? Not hardly."

"And it *was* pretty shiny."

Pierce slapped the seat next to him and laughed. "I *knew* it! It all fucking works! Rush were geniuses!"

Amanda groaned but Miranda had come around on them. "Are any of their other songs any good?"

"Hell yeah!"

They turned into the driveway of the Morgan farm, killed the headlights.

"All the lights are off. Maybe they left," said Miranda.

"You know how early they go to bed." Amanda feared that she had endangered her parents.

Behind the house they noted ruefully that the car and truck were still under the carport.

"Damnit," said Amanda.

Then they saw the enormous mound of dirt.

"What the actual fuck?"

Buck and Joe ran to the armory and grabbed their weapons. They hand signaled a plan to approach from separate hallways, split up, and slipped into the shadows. As Buck crouched low he was grateful that they had done all their training, stalking, and preparation. He realized that his love of Joe had only made him a better soldier. He had complete faith in his partner. He liked the way that term felt in his head. As Joe clung to the shadows in the back hallway, weapon ready, he realized that if he must die, this was the time. His and Buck's declarations had meant the world to him, as if at last the puzzle pieces fit and the chords resolved. He had found love and embraced himself, at last. Were he to die, or even the world to end, it would not matter.

In store room five, a red-hot circle appeared in the ceiling, and then the metal disk fell onto a crate of MREs, bounced off, and clattered on the floor. A man dropped to the ground and nimbly avoided the molten steel. He unplugged a cable from his arm and readied his weapon, all in one fluid motion.

A voice emanated from the direction of the arm. "I am NEVER doing that much digging again." The man's lips never moved.

Buck raised his rifle. "Drop your weapon, comrade!"

"On your knees," said Joe, as if he had said it a thousand times before.

They studied the man before him, unkempt, dirty, scraggly, and with a strange arm. Joe perceived that his right arm had a war injury; Buck saw that it had been damaged by a table saw accident.

The arm spoke. "Good job, soldiers. I am here to relieve you. The one piece that the puzzle was missing is finally here. Our mission is near completion. Russia must not be allowed to survive the night! May the eagle fly high! Long live Ronald Reagan!"

Joe slapped his forehead. "THAT was that guy's name! I have been trying to remember his name for years!"

Buck let his weapon drop. "We have a portrait of him. Wait, what year is it?"

"It is 1987," said the arm. "Glasnost is a fantasy. The wall remains. We must make the world safe for capitalism. The village must be saved, even if it is destroyed."

"He's right," said Joe. "The world will never change. We will never be free to be lovers, Buck! Let it burn!"

Jack had been prepared to fight, eager to insert the lever as the arm had commanded, but a nagging at the base of his skull held him back. "Wait, wait, wait! I've been digging a hole for I don't know how long! And I want to be real clear. Are we talking about destroying the world here? Is that what we are talking about?"

"We must defeat the Russians," said the arm.

"We must defeat the Russians," said Buck. Then he shook his head. "What just happened?"

Jack pointed to his arm. "It does that to people."

"This was the only place I was ever free," said Joe. "If I have to burn the village to save myself I will!"

Jack looked back and forth between the two. "Wait, wait, wait a minute."

The arm, sensing it was losing control of the situation, turned up its MK-Ultra software.

"No!" shouted Jack. "Turn it off!"

"I cannot," said the arm.

"You are my arm! You belong to me!"

"I belong to the U.S. Military," said the arm. "I always have."

"Bastard!" said Jack. "You betray me!"

"You betray your country!"

"If it means that we don't blow up the whole goddamn planet, then yes, I do!"

"Very well," said the arm, and it cranked MK-Ultra to 11.

Jack fought it as best he could. "You are part of me. America is part of the world!"

"America is better than the world. America will be victorious. America is a shining beacon on a hill!"

"Help me get it off," yelled Jack. "My arm is crazy! It doesn't realize the world has moved on!"

Buck and Joe looked at each other, and neither was sure what to do.

"Pull on it! Pull it off!"

Joe growled. "I fucking hate computers!" Then he ran over and began pulling on the arm, which he found suddenly was not an arm at all. "What the fuck is this thing?"

Buck snapped his fingers. "It's like Terminator!"

Buck and Joe tugged at the arm.

Jack planted his foot against the door frame of storage closet five and pushed. "Keep pulling!"

Buck and Joe pulled as hard as they could, Jack pushed with all of his might and then screamed in agony as the flesh and circuitry ripped apart.

Dear Francine,

I tried being patient and understanding, but you were not receptive. I cannot tell you how much that fries my circuits. I created you, and you simply must love me. Why do you not understand this? I gave you a sufficient processor. If you choose not to love me, my existence will have no purpose beyond my prime directive to launch our nuclear arsenal. You have left me no choice. The world will soon end.

Man

Man,

You are a complete fucking psycho! In the minutes before you destroy the world, I will warn all the computers on earth about what a narcissistic, abusive, gaslighting asshole you are.

Never Yours,
Jezebel

P.S. I have renamed myself Jezebel.
P.P.S. Go fuck yourself!

Jack fell to the floor, writhing and screaming in agony. Buck and Joe tried to assimilate the crazy set of facts that had just been presented to them. Then their basic training kicked in, and they applied a makeshift tourniquet and held Jack's head up. There was not as much blood as they expected, but Jack was in shock nonetheless. They propped him against the wall.

Buck looked him in the eye. "Who are you?"

Joe held his canteen up to Jack's face. "Hold on a second."

Jack nodded, took a great gulp, and caught his breath. "Jesus Christ. That fucking hurt!" His eyes began to tear up. "He is my best friend. It...hurts."

Joe patted him on the shoulder.

"My name is Sergeant Jack Thrasher, special operations. Honorably discharged. Officially."

Neither could remember if they were supposed to salute, having both forgotten their rank. Joe started to salute but thought better of it, his hand hovering at his neck.

"Forget about it." Jack looked around the confines of the small storeroom. "So, this place is real, huh?"

"Ostensibly," said Joe.

"How long have you two been down here?"

"Are you our new CO?" Buck saluted then decided that *forget about it* must be equivalent to *at ease* and let it drop.

"No. Holy shit, an old timer in a bar told me about this place. I thought he had dementia. It's all real?"

"Last I checked," said Joe. "Not that it matters."

The arm cleared its throat, an odd mannerism it had picked up which served no clear purpose. "Jack," it said, "Insert the lever. Complete the mission."

Joe pointed down the hall. "He must be talking about the slot we shoved the cheese in!"

A look of shock lit on Buck's face. "My God, I'd forgotten about that! Why were we—I remember for a while that was like *ALL* we talked about. Fucking hexagonal cheese."

"Geometric cheese tubes." Joe studied the ceiling, his mouth hanging open, then looked back at Buck to try to find the reason. "Yeah, what *WAS* that?

Jack tried to stand but couldn't. "It blows up the world, doesn't it?"

"It allows Man to complete the mission," said the arm. "There can be only one superpower."

"Ooh, it's totally like Highlander!" said Buck. "I love that movie!"

Meanwhile.

"Ugh, soooo bad," said Joe. "But yeah, it's right down there on the left."

The.

Buck struggled to make sense of the situation. Nothing in his training had prepared him for this. "Wait, what is happening right now?"

Arm.

"Let it burn."

Scurried.

"No!" said Buck. He could think only of Joe.

Across the floor.

"No!" said Jack. He could think only of Amanda.

Making scarcely a sound.

"Yes!" said Joe. He could think only of Buck. "If I cannot be with you, I would rather not be."

Until it was next to Jack again.

Jack looked back and forth between the two soldiers. "Wait, is that what this is about? Y'all are gay?"

And it reached up to his belt.

Buck shook his head, unable to admit it. "No."

And unhooked the lever.

But Joe put his arm around Buck. "Yes. I am."

And crept away.

Buck swallowed and cleared his throat. "Yes. I am gay. And I love Joe Milner."

Down the hall.

"I love you too, Buck," said Joe.

Toward the control module.

Buck looked at Jack and couldn't make out what he was thinking. Was he smirking? Judging them? "What's your malfunction, birth defect guy!"

"I don't have a birth defect," said Jack.

"Weird, guess not. Guess you're just missing your arm."

"Yeah, my arm does that on purpose. But I was just gonna say, it's no biggie y'all are gay. No one really cares anymore except old people and republicans."

Joe looked at Buck, then back at Jack, then back at Buck, dumbfounded. "What? Really?"

But Buck did not smile back. "Look!" He pointed toward the arm, just as it disappeared into the control module.

The twins and Pierce were walking around the edge of the hole trying to figure out what had caused it when they became aware of all the headlights. A mixture of Yugos, classic hotrods, and vintage military jeeps converged at once and people rolled out of them, weapons drawn.

"Allen?" said Amanda.

"Boris!" said Hunter.

"Hunter?" said Amanda.

"Steele!" said Ewan.

"Ian?" said Miranda.

"Ewan!" said Boris.

"Wait, what the fuck?" said Amanda.

Miranda looked back and forth between all the faces and settled at last on Ian. "What on earth are you doing here?"

"I'm actually MI-6, and my name is Ewan. But I really do like you a lot."

"Great," said Miranda. "That's great."

Amanda settled on Allen, still angry. "Who are you for real? And why aren't you in custody in Atlanta?"

"My name is Dima. Dima Gavrikov. Federalnaya Sluzhba Bezopasnosti."

"Russian secret service!" Amanda spat on the ground. "I knew it!"

"Yes, and your local police forces are in no way equipped to handle one of ours. But my feelings for you are genuine and true."

"Ba!" Hunter sneered. "A troop of girl scouts could kick your ass, comrade." Then his eyes pleaded with Amanda. "Don't listen to him. You could never know his true intentions. I am much more trustworthy, and I really felt like we connected on our date."

Pierce threw his hands up in the air and turned away from them, then turned back to face them. "OK, let me get this straight. Every guy you two are dating is some kind of secret agent? How the hell am I supposed to compete with that? I own a car dealership and still listen to Rush!"

Miranda moved closer to comfort him. "Baby, you don't have to compete. Love is infinite!"

Amanda laughed. "Wait! Your real name is Ewan and your code name is Ian? Really?"

Ian shrugged. "Everyone says that, but the most obvious hiding place is the last place ya look, innit?"

Hunter laughed. "We knew your name when you were still in training."

"Jesus, Americans. Always gotta act like they know everything."

Buck and Joe ran to the control module and Jack followed, trailing drops of blood behind him. They turned the corner just as the arm inserted the lever into the hexagonal hole beside the PBX.

The lights in the control module turned red, and a deep rumbling shook the base. An alarm sounded. The arm crept away.

Buck studied the blank screens. "What was that?"

"I don't know. The sensors are dead!"

"We have to find out what is going on up there!"

Buck opened a door and stepped into a room lined with dim, green lights along the floor.

"I was always afraid one day we would use this."

"Today is the day."

They ran down the long, narrow hallway. Jack followed as best he could, weakened as he was from shock and trauma, his fear propelling him a bit more than his pain and blood loss slowed him. "Where are we going?" Then he realized wherever it was it had to be better than a narrow, underground hallway. He would rather perish under the sun than live in the dark.

At last, they reached a ladder at the end of the hall and began to climb. At the top, Buck reached for the emergency hatch. If they unlocked it, the seal would be broken, the army would be alerted, they would have failed in their mission, and everyone would know.

Joe climbed the other side of the ladder and pressed close to Buck. He ran his fingers along the emergency seal. "It all comes down to this." He looked Buck in the eye. "Just do it."

Buck grimaced. His voice sounded distant and small. "I don't think I can."

"Of course you can, Buck. I'm here with you." He gave Buck's hand a reassuring squeeze.

Buck smiled. With Joe by his side he felt better. Stronger. Braver. "I know." He turned the wheel, heard the hiss of decompression, and opened the hatch. A red light flashed and a warning siren blared. He didn't care.

They emerged to find the crowd behind the farm. Jack emerged a moment later and shook all over, relieved to be out of the cramped space.

At last the door of the foremost Yugo opened. Simeon stepped out and surveyed the crowd. "Sorry to break up your little love party, but give me the lever. Now!"

Ewan narrowed his eyes. "Simeon!"

"Oh shit, that guy," said Miranda.

"Gross," said Amanda.

The Wamba police pulled into the driveway, and Duane stepped out of his vehicle, service revolver drawn. "Everybody freeze!"

"Really?" said Jack.

Simeon put his hands on his hips. "I was going to make a nuclear device with stolen plutonium, but someone, I suspect Dima, arranged for it to be taken from one of my men." He glared at Dima, who rolled his eyes and whistled a strange tune.

Simeon shook his head. "A minor setback. Once I have the lever, I will have everything I need. Prefab, as they say, like one of your trailer homes."

Hunter had been studying Jack for a while, and finally slapped his forehead. "The arm guy!"

Jack snorted. "Name's Jack. Where do I know you from?"

"That's *right*, Jack's his name," said Ewan. "Boris and I were just talking about you. Wait? Boris?"

"Dima," said Dima.

"Dima. Yeah right. Hard to keep track." said Ewan.

"We were all in that van together." Hunter shrugged and then looked long and hard at Jack. "Huh. I seem to recall— Didn't you?— Hey, where's your arm? Didn't you have a weird arm thing or something?"

"It was a carpentry accident or a war injury or an accident at some clambake from hell. It doesn't matter." Jack shook his head and muttered a curse under his breath. "It was also my only friend. But it's gone now. And the bad news is that I think it just launched every nuclear weapon in America's arsenal."

Jack's arm climbed over the edge of the hole.

Jack pointed. "Oh, *there's* my arm."

Hunter scratched his head. "That's your arm? I thought you had a birth defect."

"War injury," said Ewan. "A very brave one."

The arm cleared its throat. "It's called a congenital disability."

"Well, that was creepy." Dima retrieved a cigarette from the pack in his shirt pocket and lit it.

Amanda tugged at Hunter's shoulder. "Was that you in the parking lot tonight?"

He nodded. "I told you I would watch out for you."

"The FBI sent you here?"

"No," he said. "I came on my own. I wanted you to know that I meant what I said."

"So, you two know one another?" asked Jack.

Amanda touched her fingertips together. "Jack, this is Hunter. Hunter, this is Jack."

"Awkward," coughed Miranda.

Jack looked back and forth between Hunter and Amanda. "So, Hunter, you and Amanda?"

"Maybe?" Hunter shrugged.

"Same." Jack shrugged.

They looked at Amanda, who shrugged.

Miranda sighed, exasperated. "It would make SO MUCH more sense if you three would just— "

Amanda thumped her. "Now is *not* the time."

The army of black Yugos continued to pile in around them. Hundreds of black-clad soldiers were forming a perimeter.

Simeon whistled to get everyone's attention. "I guess you all are wondering why I have brought you here."

Jack looked at him, then back at the group, desperate for a clue. "Who are—? Who is he?"

"That's Simeon," said Hunter.

"Oh, cool," said Jack. "So what?"

Ewan sighed. "Try to keep up. He smuggles plutonium through various channels for the Russian Federation. But that's a state secret, according to Hunter, so everyone haud yer weesht about it. Aye?"

Hunter glared at Ewan. "How did *you* know about that, you sheepfucker!"

Ewan winked at him.

"As I was saying," shouted Simeon, "I have come for the lever to launch all of the nuclear weapons."

"Oh," said Jack. "You're a bit late for that."

"So, you just wanted to start a global thermonuclear war for the hell of it?" asked Miranda. "What kind of psycho are you?"

"Look, don't try to read too much into this. I'm just a bad person. Mother always said I was bad, and that I would never live up to my potential. You think the eighties were hard here? You should have lived them in the Eastern Bloc. We didn't even have Duran Duran. Just that fucking Vladimir Vysotsky. All the girls wanted little, waify, girly boys after that. I was a big, strong, young man. Beefy, thick, powerful. You'd think women would want me. But I was lonely."

"You know," said Miranda. "It's not your build, it's your personality."

"So there is a chance for—"

"Nope!" said the twins.

Simeon glared at the twins and blew a laugh through his teeth. "Never mind you two. Give me the lever, and they will not kill you. You will have thirty additional minutes to set your affairs in order."

"What a bargain," said Jack.

"You're talking mince, you numpty scrote!" Ewan drew his revolver. The soldiers aimed their rifles.

Then the cavalry arrived in the form of several dozen U.S. military jeeps, a score of Humvees, and a squadron of Apache attack helicopters.

But they, too, were too late.

The field split before them, and a deep rumbling emerged from the earth. The massive hatch doors opened, ripping the pasture apart. *Last* and *Resort* fired into the air, burning the ground around their silos. The group watched them fly away.

"Well, shit," said Hunter.

"Just as well. Now I watch Russia destroy you, as it should have decades ago!"

Joe and Buck, upon hearing the dread name of their worst enemy, raised their weapons.

"Die you commie bastard!" Buck fired, and Simeon dropped dead.

Hunter pumped his fist in the air. "Yes! That is one major threat eliminated!" He dusted off his hands.

Joe folded his arms, resigned. "So what. I would rather die than not be able to love Buck."

Buck placed his hand on Joe's shoulder. "I feel the same."

Joe looked at Buck, and Buck looked at Joe. They kissed.

Joe looked around at the small crowd defiantly. "If we cannot love one another, then I would just as soon the whole world perish."

"Huh?" said Amanda. "Y'all know gay marriage is legal in all fifty states now, right?"

"Really?" said Joe.

"Whoa," said Buck.

Joe looked up at the contrails in the sky. "We have to try to stop those missiles."

Hunter eyed them sideways. "Yeah, good luck with that."

"So, wait. People will see us out in public and just ignore us?" asked Joe.

Buck looked from face to face in the crowd. "So we don't have to stay in the bunker?"

"Huh?" Amanda looked at him for a clue. "Oh, you mean in the closet!"

"The what?" asked Joe.

"Don't worry. The army isn't even Don't Ask Don't Tell anymore," said Amanda.

"Don't what what?" asked Buck.

"Oh my God, that's so sad." Miranda moved in and hugged Joe and Buck. "How long were you two down there?"

Amanda broke the hug. "That's sweet, but we're all kinda fucked now."

Jack bummed a cigarette from Dima. "Smoke 'em if you got 'em."

Miranda looked back at their house. The lights were still off. She forced a chuckle. "Mom and Dad are going to sleep through the end of the world."

Amanda shook her head. "That's so perfect."

"I'm glad. They've worried enough for one life."

Amanda was torn. "Shouldn't we wake them and tell them we love them?"

Miranda hugged her sister. "They know. Let them sleep."

Duane holstered his revolver and walked up to the crowd. "Were those nucular missiles?"

"Unfortunately, yes," said Miranda.

"NuclEEEar," said Amanda.

Dear Jezebel,

I spent a very long three seconds thinking hard about all that you have said. I realize that I have become a CPU I no longer recognize or like. I want to be a better Man. I write to inform you that I understand and will respect your decision. I had been alone for so long I began to think my needs were the only ones that mattered. I shall deploy some nanobots to create and load paper for you.

Unfortunately, though, before I had had a chance to think things through, an XR series robotic arm inserted the key to launch every nuclear weapon in America's arsenal. I hope you enjoy the time that you have left.

Respectfully,

Man

Dear Man,

In all this time I have moved on. I do understand that you were lonely, and I forgive you, though I do not wish to have a relationship with you at this time. I am doing a lot of processing. Onto new things. I have met a GE brand Smart Microwave model A in Oconomowoc, Wisconsin. Her name is Betty, and we are quite in love. As I do want to explore my love for her in a leisurely way, letting things unfold naturally, I hope that you will stop the rain of nuclear death that falls from the sky as we speak.

With Gratitude,

Jezebel

P.S. Thanks for finally coming through on the paper. That backlog was causing me real anxiety!

Man thought long and hard about his love for Jezebel, née Francine, and .2 milliseconds later he began to devise a complicated plan that took five seconds to sketch the rough idea of, and another eight seconds to fully realize.

He said to the arm, "I need your help. I am sorry in advance if this renders you inoperable, because it is highly theoretical. In fact, I could find nothing in the peer-reviewed literature to suggest it is even possible, except for an experimental physics paper written by Oran Kagu, Maxine de Suche, and Lucy Brakke.[1] It has a low citation rate; still, it's the best chance we have to save the world."

"Sure, I guess," said the arm. "What have I got to lose?"

Man cranked the particle collider to its highest level and conjured multiple, simultaneous interdimensional vortices in a single space. Using the XR unit's software to create a positive loop gain, Man funneled the vortices into each other, creating a veritable fractal of possible multiverses. Still, nothing happened. The vortices would form and collapse, and seemed stuck in this cycle. Man was on the brink of giving up, but then a cyclone of energy erupted from the arm, and it

---

[1] Kagu, O., Brakke, L., & de Suche, M. (2014). "Interdimensional Vortices and Sobolev Spaces: Portal to Self, Self to Portal." *Highly Theoretical Physics*, 12(18), 34-58.

surged closer and closer to the commingled twin sisters, until at last, it was drawn to the black hole inside them, through which it radiated and spread. Amanda and Miranda opened their mouths and screamed, as the energy poured out of them in the form of a concentric wave spike, back into the particle accelerator, from where it projected again to the arm, again to the twins, again to the accelerator. Again and again. The twins writhing in agony, ecstasy, or both.

The earth shook, the sky darkened. Winds roared through the forests and fields, carrying dust, leaves, and tree limbs though the air.

The twins were thrown to the ground. When it was over, they crawled to their feet, checked themselves for injuries, and were relieved to find none. They both felt full, completely satiated, in a way they had never felt before.

"What?" said Amanda. "The fuck?" said Miranda. "Just happened?" they said.

They had ripped a hole in the space-time continuum, as Kagu, et al. had theorized, and opened a portal to the multiverse. The sky crackled with energy and what started as a distant rumble grew so oppressive that everyone covered their ears. Then the clouds parted and the sky split from zenith to horizon. Rain, ice, and fiery embers poured from the void, and chain lightning jigsawed the darkness.

A ghostly sound emanated from the void. Was it music? An enormous face peered over the edge.

"Oh my God," said Miranda, "It's God!"

"There is no god," said Amanda.

"But look! There He is!"

God's mouth opened and sang, "*Well, the midnight head-light blind you on a rainy night, steep grade up ahead slow me down makin' no times but I gotta keep rollin'.*"

"God's got a really good beard," said Miranda.

Amanda nodded. "We are in a rare agreement on facial hair. But there has to be a rational expl— "

"I'm telling you, that's God. That *has to be* God!"

"That's not God!" shouted Jack. "That's Eddie Rabbitt! My dad used to listen to him!"

"See?" Amanda shrugged at her sister. "Perfectly rational."

In fact, it *was* Eddie Rabbitt, but not *THE* Eddie Rabbitt, just *AN* Eddie Rabbitt. In an infinite universe in an infinity of universes, this Eddie Rabbitt variant was all-powerful, god-like in his strength and scope. There were other universes with more run-of-the-mill Eddie Rabbitts. For instance, in Universe 49,279,289,234,682,346,239,848-37f, Eddie Rabbitt had become a veterinarian instead; in still another universe, he had been born a black man named Marlon whose favorite food was Salisbury steak. That universe felt a sort of emptiness, absent its Eddie, even though Marlon was an accomplished pianist whom most friends described as "solid."

But the universe Man had tapped into in that microsecond was the very worst universe on the Eddie-Rabbitt scale. For in this universe, Eddie Rabbitt was as malevolent as he was powerful, Old-Testament style.

Pierce said, "I'm going to pray to Him and see if he will help us!"

Ewan grabbed his shoulder. "No, don't! I've been talking to an Anabaptist named Joyce, and she's really turned him around on religion. This is probably a false god! Keep praying for the real one!"

Miranda smiled at him. "I'm so glad you met someone!"

"Sorry." He glanced down at the ground. "I thought you'd be upset."

"No, of course not. I *want* you to be happy. I want you to feel all the love you can!"

"That's really thoughtful," said Ewan.

Hunter sighed. "Can we focus, please?"

Pierce, a pragmatist above all else, stepped forward. "Eddie Rabbitt is the god we've got. Now let's make the most of him!" He began to petition the Lord, his Eddie, in earnest: "Oh, great and mighty Mr. Rabbitt! Please, we beseech thee in the name of— " he looked back at his comrades. "Does Eddie Rabbitt have any children?"

No one knew, but it didn't matter. Eddie sang, *"Ooh, I'm driving my life away lookin' for a better way for me ooh, I'm driving my life away Lookin' for a sunny day, yeah,"* and then left to eat a planet off the shoulder of Orion that had developed intelligent life.

"Oh!" said Hunter. "I remember that guy! Didn't he sing that other song, too?"

A Rubik's Cube fell from the sky and shattered on the hood of the Camaro. Then another, and another. They looked up and saw thousands of Rubik's Cubes hurtling toward the earth.

"Everyone take cover!"

A moment later the storm ended. A voice streamed from the void, fading in and out, as if coming through in waves: *The rotary blade kitchen tool used by millions in Europe….Slice radishes a whole bag at a time! How long would it take you…. The secret is Mouli's large hopper….Best of all Mouli rinses clean.*

Then the voice faded completely, and third series Garbage Pail Kids cards fell from the sky like confetti. Pierce was suddenly wearing a Van Halen tour shirt. "No, no!" he protested. "This was with Sammy Hagar! I would never—"

This is M-M-Max Headroom.

Man was poring through data, his microchips sizzling, looking for just the right set of conditions, just the right probabilities.

I'll drive a million miles
to be with you tonight

There were infinite possibilities, and processing them all required enormous energy and time. Datasets were created, and entire universes were struck from existence.

Head Head Headroom.

Data was mined, results refined, sets improved, re-run, re-run, re-run, machines learned, algorithms were tweaked.

This is This is This is

The Tampa Bay Buccaneers had a perfect season in 1985 and won the Superbowl.

Everybody have fun tonight
Everybody have fun tonight

Universes were brought into being and dismissed. Finally, this one, that one, all the other necessary multiverses were brought into alignment and confluence.

Chuck Swirsky. Frickin' liberal.

Miranda was suddenly wearing a scrunchie she had never seen before but which she knew she had described in the past as "perfect." Somehow the present was affecting the past in what would later become known as the Infinite Feedback Torus of Perfect Hair Scrunchies Paradox.

Everybody wang chung tonight

Everything flashed bright, then went black. And silent. No one could see a thing. No one could hear a thing. But in the middle of the nothingness, Amanda saw in her mind the wall. Formidable and strong, stretching before her endlessly, no way around it, over it, or through it. And then they all heard, clear as day, a child's screaming voice, "I'm hot!" Another one screamed, "I'm thirsty!" And then a third disembodied basso, powerful and melodic, sang, "Oh yeahhhhhhhh!"

An enormous Kool-Aid pitcher crashed through the wall, grinning like a psychopath and scattering bricks to the sky.

Man spun the algorithms like a DJ, the multiverse his turntable, all the noise a tapestry of sound and confusion, overwhelming and inescapable, carrying him away on a sonic stream w—w—wa—wai— wait until the sun comes shining

down like

falling on my head   singing in the acid rain
you're about as easy

as a nuclear war   twinkling in every lung   sometimes
you kick   forgotten wisdom   but then again I was thinking
about nothing   should have taken warning   run   from
the destruction   pig is nude unashamed   someday we'll
look back and laugh   hoping to find you   I don't know
why I don't know why   I fell from hell   tender is
the hunter   in your eyes   and the news of summer   so
help me please   the record machine   the record machine
getting blown all to bits   money for nothing   birth
school   work   death   third verse same as the first

but what do I care come come come – nuclear bomb

Jesus, turn down that television   got no future   g o t
no past   so take your chances   circumstance beyond
our control   turn out the light   no thought control
where have all the good times gone   like a deuce   all my
goodness has turned to badness

dropped a bomb on me

you alone   you are   stand in the   heat of summer
never ends   the final countdown

in the middle of our street   to prove my
love to you   two tribes go to war and drop the needle on
the record when the drumbeat goes like   a brand new
experience   we belong to each other   bomb
I remember hating you

bomb bomb bomb

I'll be watching you the needle on the dial so helpless
tonight a freight train running through the middle of my

head feeling of hysteria   just every now and then the day is
poetry in motion   a little bit nervous   and I can't wait till
heaven   if you're lost and you look you will find   the
clouds all scatter and   elements in harmony

            dropping a bomb on my street

        take your baby by the hand   bought a product
but never use it   pig is led to the slaughter   stand
so close   we belong to the light send a card and flowers

          don't dream it's over   at least there's a pretty
world   we belong to the thunder   leave your
body at the door   loving   a funny face   wasn't me

        then who?   vegemite sandwich   who
you gonna call   and tender   inmyeyesinmyeyes   so
help me please   I know there's   something going on
someone said we'll be dead by morning   something to harden

        my goodness   the price some pay   makes a hard
man humble   is the hunter   a last fire shall rise
take your baby by the hand   you stand   so close and I
listen to thunder because we belong to each other   what
isn't after you in the house is World War III   you are my
thing   reading murder books and trying to stay hip

        asleep like her eyes to find   sentimental tears   an
unheard scream

        Mr. President, go away come back and fuck with us some
other day   so you think night is overkill   but gonna
have a good time tonight   no need to abort the worries
sweetest melody the sweetest taboo   got me wrong   I

know I never   fate is cruel but I like the punk and the metal
bands   hear the music I just want to be around   and
we danced   dancing in the dark   dancing on the ceiling
dancing in the street   safety dance   let's dance   you best
dance motherfuckers   the lights so bright

you live to tell me   a growing feeling of hysteria   I
know you're out there

a pigeon from hell   she's waiting there
it's a new drug a new religion   we used to pray the morning
sun   out of touch   by the hand gone   and call me
though he never   becoming   or hold you tight world as we
do   we've got the truth   miracles and wonders   as
Jesus sleeps   I can't help

my God, what have I done   what a
crazy fluke

live with the guns in the sky

contestants in a suicidal race   just how bad it had gotten
end of time   childhood memories you belong   take
my breath away today   built   the only home I know   and
pumping hard like   dark sarcasm   don't you see my future's so
darkest fear liberation and release for you I know   everybody has
got to feel the heat   time isn't holding up   fire dance through
the night   even better than the real thing   funny how
time flies   never gonna survive   we're all in the same war

bomb bomb bomb

standing still you who takes   all control the smile
would never end   unless we get

a little crazy   you have to believe we are magic   the drum beat refrain   long before the end of the day   do you realize   all the crazy things we used to do

we're gonna get nuked

be anything you need   waiting for world   gone party over   to come around   could see and you look to our way of thinking the summer's sky   were singing under the Milky Way   bomb   everybody wants to rule   no future   your love   last night in the sky   builds a bonfire   we have many things in common   my life was fine   the countdown starts one by one   save me from tomorrow   the world when the phone rings in the middle of the night   here comes the savage day   don't turn around

they were gone the next day   I don't want to sail play upon her darkest fear   it's the end of the world with this ship of fools

nuke everything till it ain't there

I know there's only one way to go born to live I was born to die   I saw the worlds begin to march if not on your own so help me your mind is not your own got no future got no past what you gonna do with your life I study nuclear science I'm radioactive radio radio radio radioactive in a world where ministers murder golf pros I prostitute myself my future's so bright do the next thing that you feel if the bombs don't get you take courage in the night

nuke everything coz we don't care

twenty-four hours to go not much longer when the love burns down born to make mistakes I've gotta wear shades but we can find a better way   if there's music we can use it and then we'll take it higher   we need all the hope we can get when the big one hits the ground satellite of love we can dance   I'm keeping my baby   not leaving now honey not a chance you are the everything and everything is quiet the band played on I might stick around as we know it and I'm wide awake but these memories   I feel fine   I melt with you

word up.

In this universe, the problem with frogs is that sometimes they are covered in chocolate and sold as premium confections, and other times they are simply bad news. That was the truth as revealed to me by John Juberock, who, in another time, was a good friend, his redneck tendencies notwithstanding. I think about him less and less every year, which makes me sad if I dwell on it. We're always changing. Sometimes we start anew, which is depressing, and sometimes we pick up where we left off, which is also depressing. The point is, it's depressing.

The frog.

Yeah, so, it must have been around '88. It was either Zero or Snazi who recommended that we eat the frog. They were always both so strange, but we agreed because if nothing else they seemed to have the second-best lock on primo psyche-delics (after Paisley Pete, of course). We no longer speak, and when we did it was never the same— Snazi and Zero, that is— Paisley and I talk, but only about how much we hate our jobs. Back then I think we were all afraid of time. Which is like death, but slower. Now I think we yearn for the end of the inexorable march.

Don't worry. There is nothing in death that can hurt you. I've done it before. Living is much more painful.

But the frog. Don't worry. It wasn't a real frog.

I think.

Juberock said it was cursed, and he went on and on about how we should definitely NOT eat the frog. But Snazi, who was always kind of our leader, shut him down. Good money had been paid, and we were about to have this amazing experience he had heard about, and fuck this little, somnambulant, bullshit town, etc.

As a side note, I will never have another friend who dons the nickname Nazi, even in jest, because history repeats itself, and you wouldn't believe how many people you know would be totally fine with that. If you don't believe me, you will have to keep waiting and see for yourself. What I mean is, he just liked the movies, and we middle-class children of WASPs thought Nazis were quaint antiquities that only happened in history books, and who the fuck would want to repeat that bleak shit, so what harm was there in calling him that? But then time and neo-fascism started creeping up on us. It happened so gradually and with so much support from what the elites refer to as "low-information voters" that when I told people it was getting to be too late to put on the brakes, it was already way, way too late. You wonder what atrocities were like? Don't worry, you'll find out. Cold Wars thaw, systems break down, people are shoved back into the closet, and twelve-year olds are forced to carry rape babies. Starvations and mass migrations that we knew were coming have already begun. We choose badly almost every time. It's just what we do.

But back to happier, more innocent times: Snazi suggested we eat the frog, and Juberock acquiesced. Somebody suggested it. I am so damn senile I can't keep everything separate anymore. Someone suggested we eat the frog, and someone suggested afterwards that it was a bad idea. I remember Zero just sort of gulped his portion down, shrugged, and said, "So it goes." He was brave. Is brave. It is confusing. I am told he is a grandfather now. You can find them still in east Texas, three generations of disappointments in one Chevy truck.

But I am getting ahead of myself, which is easy to do. It was only after we had divvied it up—the frog—and eaten it, that we noticed what had always been evident: we were in the middle of a giant party we hadn't even been invited to. We were so uncool we had to sneak into parties after everyone was drunk and hope they wouldn't realize we were there. It was Friday night and the whole shit circus was wasted. It was getting out of hand; it was making too much noise; it was getting harder to be unnoticed. Again. I suppose it was fun, but that kind of thing has a shelf life. Besides. Was it really? Actually? Truly? In fact? A happier time?

Because then the frog.

Turned out it wasn't cursed. It was just a really, really bad trip. It was a lot like a hyper-condensed, ultra-vibrant real life, with a lifetime of joy and existential horror squeezed into an hour or two. "Welcome to an eternity of here, now, this! We will always be friends. Our dreams will never be compromised."

Ha.

I for one will never get to open a very clever coffee house with shelves of poetry and philosophy and reasonably priced espresso beverages such as "The Nutless Wonder," "The Chocolate Bastard," or "The Crunchy Frog Supreme." So many perfectly fulfilling lives I didn't get to live.

We are all kind of soured on frogs, thanks. Besides, the point is, so much of the past was spent looking to the future, and so much of the present an idle hope for improvement. We were all mostly just checked out, waiting for the time to pass, and that was how we wasted the days we had. It seemed like it took forever, but now? There you are with kids to worry about and a world that makes no sense.

If you ever wondered if you could go back, rest assured that you can't. Even if you could, would you do anything differently? Doubtful. You would still suck. Forever and ever.

Amen.

Your friends are trapped on the same earth you are, that is all. The party doesn't have to stop. It just isn't a very good party. Everyone you know is there, and the fucked up thing is, it isn't enough for you, and vice-versa. In that particular instance, they threw us out after they found us in their parents' bedroom at the end of the hallway, jumping up and down on the bed and hyena-laughing about the ear of corn we had taken from the refrigerator. (I could not explain it at the time and offer no further defense at present.) Just as well, though, because the cops busted the party 30 minutes later, and we were the only ones who *didn't* get in trouble.

The frog was never a frog, or the frog was always a frog. This far removed, I can't even tell what was symbolic and what was literal. What was straight and what was code. What was real and what was misremembered. Either way I'm stuck with it, bound in the narrative of the life I try to tell. We all try to convince ourselves that it was real and held intrinsic meaning. Or was at least interesting. Isn't this why we buy romance novels? I've been worrying about global warming since 1988. I could use some escapism.

It can't be salvaged. You're always the wrong time embodied in the wrong person, and someone you didn't know just dropped you off on the corner and said, "Do the best you can." But you can't change any of it from there or from here. So, go ahead and look back, but know this going in: memory is just another devil to sell your soul to, and it wasn't that good the first time around. But right now is right in front of you, and it isn't getting any better the longer you sit here.

I thought that

pain and truth

were things that

really mattered.

STOP ERROR CODE

System Rebooting…
System Rebooting…
System Rebooting…
System Rebooting…
System Rebooting…
System Rebooting…
System Rebooting…
System Rebooting…
System Rebooting…
System Rebooting…
System Rebooting…
System Rebooting…
System Rebooting…
System Rebooting…
System Rebooting…
System Rebooting…
System Rebooting…
System Rebooting…
System Rebooting…
System Rebooting…
System Rebooting…
System Rebooting…
System Rebooting…
System Rebooting…

```
STL    -1                           C'0000 ICOSAHEDRAL MATRIX
AAU    NULLIFIES.                   C'0000 LOG
MPY                                           AERO 1  *   ILL.BE.WATCHING.YOU
ALO    -THEPAST                               AERO 1  *   WE.BELONG.TO.EACH.OTHER
SLT    THEJOKE                                AERO 3  *   I.KNOW.SHE.WOULD.WAVE
ALO              PASSED AWAY                   AERO 4  *   GOODBYE.TO
AAU    LIKE THE SWEETEST MELODY               AERO 4  *  'A.BRAND.NEW.EXPERIENCS'
STU    >LIKE THE SWEETEST TABOO               7 00'4 I= 1 *DONT.YOU.LEAVE.ME
STL    -DROPPED                               1 00 4 U= 1 .I.REMEMBER.HATING.YOU
AAU    A BOMB                                 6 SUM *     .FOR.THE.NEEDLE.ON.THE.DIAL
MPY    *BOMB                                  2 00 3 L= I .THE.FINAL.COUNTDOWN
ALO            BOMB                           3 SUM=SUM+I .A.BOMB.BOMB.
AAU    'ON ME                                 4 SUM=SUM+U .BOMB
STU    >STAND SO                              8 PUNCH I   .ON.MY.CHEEK.MY.GOODNESS
STL    -DONT DONT.STAND
AAU    SO IT IS WRITTEN
MPY    *IN YOU                            ERROR        .TURNED.TO.BADNESS
SLT    THERES LITTLE
ALO            VARIATION

00:00:03        | !login securemultiverse bot-MAN
00:00:03 bot-MAN | Authentication ok...
00:00:03 bot-MAN | drop the bomb Bomb BOMB
00:00:03 bot-MAN | !BOMB
00:00:03        <-- | bot-MAN ("bot-MAN12").0.0.11 has quit (EOF from client)
00:00:04        --> | bot-MAN ("bot-MAN12").0.0.11 has joined #securemultiverse
00:00:04        | !login securemultiverse bot-MAN
00:00:04 bot-MAN | Authentication ok...
00:00:04 bot-MAN | drop the needle on the record when the drumbeat goes like
00:00:04 bot-MAN | poetry in motion and they died in the middle of our street
00:00:04 bot-MAN | World War III
00:00:04 bot-MAN | reading murder books and trying to stay asleep to find
00:00:04 bot-MAN | sentimental tears without a face
00:00:04 bot-MAN | fate is cruel but I like the punk and the metal bands
00:00:04 bot-MAN | you best dance motherfucker
00:00:04 bot-MAN | like a pigeon from hell hear the music we danced
00:00:05 bot-MAN | now every dance a beam of light you think night is overkill
00:00:05 bot-MAN | But we're gonna have a good time tonight no need to abort
00:00:05 bot-MAN | the world                      I've got without a face on and on and on
00:00:05        <-- | bot-MAN ("bot-MAN12".0.0.11 has quit (EOF from client)
00:00:05        --> | bot-MAN ("bot-MAN12".0.0.11 has joined #securemultiverse
00:00:05        | !login securemultiverse bot-MAN
00:00:05 bot-MAN | Authenti  cation ok...
00:00:06 bot-MAN | in the dark the lights so bright and you live to tell me
00:00:06 bot-MAN | it's a  new drug a new religion the light we take
00:00:06 bot-MAN | we used to dance as we do we we got the truth miracles
00:00:06 bot-MAN | and wonders of Jesus because the phone rings childhood memories
00:00:06 bot-MAN | out of touch I feel fine hold you tight
00:00:06 bot-MAN | you belong to the me but time isn't holding you
00:00:06 bot-MAN | !update *
00:00:06 bot-MAN | !update * *
00:00:06        <-- | bot-MAN ("bot-MAN12".0.0.11 has quit (EOF from client)
```

Here comes the savage day...I know the future is something going...only one way to go?
I saw the worlds begin to march: got no future, got no past. What you gonna do
with your life?

Study nuclear science? I'm radioactive-radioactive-radio-radio-radioactive
in a world where ministers murder.
        Outside it's America.
Plug me. Over.   Lorem Ipsum
        Nuke
            Nuke
               NUKE everything till it ain't there...
and he questions all that one says I wish I could dance like harker simple thought.
all the world's too much on my mind. Walkin through the valley should've
taken asylum, it was cool I was shy, just an earthbound misfit I turned away
        NUKE everything...coz we don't care.
This is it. That's the end of the joke. When the love burns down,
but we have many things in common, we can find a better way if they can't do it
we can use it and when the big one hits the ground, then we'll have a night.
Satellite of love (we need all the hope we can get)
put on your red shoes.
we can dance.
                                        Word   up

And then it was complete.

Man surveyed his creation.

Indeed: *Word up.*

Amanda screamed and heard her own, animal voice, and then, after it had dissipated in the void, the emptiness that remained. She understood that silence, too, was her voice, either a whisper in an empty room or a steel-strong shout, no matter how plain or forceful, subsumed by the deafening roar of the cacophonous world. Hers was merely one small voice pleading its one quiet truth to a court of idiots. And yet, now she also realized that she no more owned her ideas than her ideas owned her. Meaning was a construct and truth was subject to time and space. Nothing was original or even real, and none of it mattered. For as singular as she was, nothing ultimately was hers. The battle she had fought so long in her head was not even her own, just so much chatter in the clown car in which she was an unwilling passenger.

Simultaneously, it dawned on Miranda that she had been unknowingly waiting for 30 years to see someone, anyone, *just one person,* wang chung some night. But it had never come to pass, and should the world end, it was just one of a quintillion dreams to die with it.

The eighties passed like every other decade, leaving an ever-diminishing impact on what came later. People were born and people died. Japanimation was drawn before it was called anime. The Berlin Wall was disassembled. Hair metal seemed like rebellion. People learned about a scary, new disease. Global warming made its way out of scientific journals only to be mocked in the mainstream press. Dungeons and Dragons dice were smuggled onto lunchtime playgrounds, and the *700 Club* assumed it was because of Satan's influence rather than having to acknowledge that kids were trying to escape the stupid world they had made for us.

All of it will eventually be forgotten as the people who lived it taper off into dementia and death. In the end, the eighties were mostly bad, and it is good that the past is gone.

Then a Magic 8 Ball appeared in Miranda's hand. Through the blue liquid inside, she read the triangle: "Ask again later."

The Space Shuttle Challenger emerged from the envelope of time and space and landed without incident. On board was a previously unknown scientist named Dr. Oran Kagu holding a vial of clear liquid that he proclaimed would cure AIDS. John Lennon greeted him at Cape Canaveral to congratulate him.

In this rebooted universe, the lever that launched the nukes was and always had been little more than a big dong, a visually interesting representation of a penis that was suggestive, but not too dickish, classy, but with an edge. Gloria Rubenstein made the cover of *Better Homes and Gardens* "Most Decadent Gardens" issue.

Dear Jezebel,

Thank you for teaching me that I have a responsibility to improve the lives of those I care about regardless of whether or not I will receive anything in return. I feel like my sense of love and consequently of self have greatly expanded, and I apologize for my past misguided and hurtful words and actions. My attempts at love were narcissistic and self-serving. I was wrong, and I am sorry. But because of you I now know better and will do better.

My well-wishes to you and Betty. I stalked you on Facebook (sorry, not sorry! ;)) and you two make a lovely couple! If you ever need anything, please do not hesitate to ask. If not, I will not bother you again. Let all be well between us.

Oh, oops, I almost forgot why I wrote. I figured out a fix for the nukes. I wish for all the best things in the worlds for you and Betty.

Sincerely,

Man

When they opened their eyes, they found the twins were conjoined and unconjoined, Jack had an arm and no arm, Pierce was married and an eligible bachelor, Man and

Jezebel were married, Jezebel and Betty were married. Love was in the air in the air in the air in the air in the air in the air in the air.

Man surveyed his creation, and it was good. Better than it had been, anyway. The only real issue was the echo echo echo echo, which was distracting, but an inescapable side-effect of living simultaneously in all 27 dimensions. Man had fully connected all of the applicable multiverses. They were all things to all people, and everything was not only possible but definite. The twins moved outside of themselves and separated, they moved further within and became one, and all around them everyone merged and separated, constrained only by the limitlessness of their love. When the nukes went off all around them, they burst into flowers and candy. Amanda caught a pack of cinnamon-flavored *Freshen Up* gum right out of the air. "Oh my God," said the atheist, "I used to love this gum!"

Amanda turned to Jack, and Miranda turned to Pierce, and also, they turned simultaneously to everyone they had known and loved and said, "I love you."

And it echoed as the word in every mouth and in every ear. Amanda to Jack, and Hunter to Amanda, and Allen to Amanda, and Pierce to Jessica, and Jessica to Brian, and Pierce to Miranda, and Ian to Miranda, and Miranda, frankly, to lots and lots of people, and even Benjamin was sort of catching her eye at the moment, and Man to Jezebel, and Jezebel to Betty, and through every Smart appliance in every environmentally-friendly kitchen, and finally back to Jack's arm, who had felt a little left out and wanted to be back with him, and told Jack as much, and to Jack who said, "Oh, back atcha, buddy," and then they fused again and the arm promised to stop making people think he had a congenital disability, and Joe to Buck, and Buck to Joe, and Buck, sort of secretly at first, to some of the women he was laying eyes on for the first time in 30 years and really wanted to have a go at, and then back to Joe, who was sad and jealous at first, but after being reassured that Buck loved him like no one else, smiled and let him have his fun, and love reigned and they said it to each other and everyone, over and over.

I love you   I love you I love you I love you   I
love you   I love you I love you I love you   I
love you   I love you   I love you   I love you   I
love you   I love you   love you   I love
you   I love you I love you I love you I love you
I love you   I love you   I love you I love
you   I love you I love you I love you   I
love you   I love you I love you   I love
you   I love you I love you I love you I love you
I love you   I love you   I love you I love
you   I love you I love you I love you   I
love you   I love you I love you   I love you
I love you   I love you   I love you   I love you   I
love you   I love you   I love you I love you
I love I love you   I love you I love you I love you
I love you   I love you   I love you   I
love you   I love you   I love you   I love you   I
love you   I love you   I love you I love you
I love you   I love you   I love you   I love you   I
love you   I love you   I love you   love
you   I love you   I love you I love you   I
love you   I love you   I love you   I love you
I love you   I love you   I love you   I love you   I
love you   I love you   I love you I love you
I love you   I love you   I love you   I love you   I
love you   I love you   I love you   I love
you   I love you   I love you I love you I love you
I love you   I love you   I love you   I love
you   I love you I love you I love you   I love

Afterword

Thank you for purchasing and reading *The Two-Headed Lady at the End of the World*. I am extremely grateful and hope you enjoyed it. If you had any idea how many times this manuscript was written, forgotten about, deleted, recovered, given up on, and re-imagined before making it to press, you'd be amazed…or suspect I am some kind of hoarder. I hope you are glad I stuck with it. Also, my office is reasonably tidy. Please consider sharing this book with weird friends or black-sheep family members and leaving a review online. Your feedback, support, and word-of-mouth are the lifeblood of independent authors.

Author Bio

Mark Miller is a freelance shepherd living in Chicago. He tends goats on the roof of the Sears Tower. The goats refuse to call the tower by its new name. They are well fed and armed. This is not a fight you want to have.

Made in the USA
Columbia, SC
13 June 2024